PRAISE FOR M. L. BUCHMAN

The first...of (a) stellar, long-running romantic suspense series.

— BOOKLIST, THE 20 BEST ROMANTIC SUSPENSE
NOVELS: MODERN MASTERPIECES. *THE NIGHT IS
MINE*

Top 10 Romance of 2012, 2015, and 2016.

— BOOKLIST: THE NIGHT IS MINE, HOT POINT, HEART
STRIKE

One of our favorite authors.

— RT BOOK REVIEWS

Buchman has catapulted his way to the top tier of my favorite authors.

— FRESH FICTION

A favorite author of mine. I'll read anything that carries his name, no questions asked. Meet your new favorite author!

— THE SASSY BOOKSTER, FLASH OF FIRE

M.L. Buchman is guaranteed to get me lost in a good story.

— THE READING CAFE, WAY OF THE WARRIOR: NSDQ

I love Buchman's writing. His vivid descriptions bring everything to life in an unforgettable way.

— PURE JONEL, HOT POINT

TWELVE TALES OF CHRISTMAS

A SHORT STORY COLLECTION

M. L. BUCHMAN

Buchman Bookworks

SIGN UP FOR M. L. BUCHMAN'S NEWSLETTER TODAY

and receive:
Release News
Free Short Stories
a Free book

Get your free book today. Do it now.
free-book.mlbuchman.com

Other works by M. L. Buchman:

The Night Stalkers

MAIN FLIGHT
The Night Is Mine
I Own the Dawn
Wait Until Dark
Take Over at Midnight
Light Up the Night
Bring On the Dusk
By Break of Day

WHITE HOUSE HOLIDAY
Daniel's Christmas
Frank's Independence Day
Peter's Christmas
Zachary's Christmas
Roy's Independence Day
Damien's Christmas

AND THE NAVY
Christmas at Steel Beach
Christmas at Peleliu Cove

5E
Target of the Heart
Target Lock on Love
Target of Mine

Firehawks

MAIN FLIGHT
Pure Heat
Full Blaze
Hot Point
Flash of Fire
Wild Fire

SMOKEJUMPERS
Wildfire at Dawn
Wildfire at Larch Creek
Wildfire on the Skagit

Delta Force
Target Engaged
Heart Strike
Wild Justice

White House Protection Force
Off the Leash
On Your Mark
In the Weeds

Where Dreams
Where Dreams are Born
Where Dreams Reside
Where Dreams Are of Christmas
Where Dreams Unfold
Where Dreams Are Written

Eagle Cove
Return to Eagle Cove
Recipe for Eagle Cove
Longing for Eagle Cove
Keepsake for Eagle Cove

Henderson's Ranch
Nathan's Big Sky
Big Sky, Loyal Heart

Love Abroad
Heart of the Cotswolds: England
Path of Love: Cinque Terre, Italy

Dead Chef Thrillers
Swap Out!
One Chef!
Two Chef!

Deities Anonymous
Cookbook from Hell: Reheated
Saviors 101

SF/F Titles
The Nara Reaction
Monk's Maze
the Me and Elsie Chronicles

Strategies for Success (NF)
Managing Your Inner Artist/Writer
Estate Planning for Authors

CONTENTS

Christmas and I have a complex relationship—a real after-and-before kind of thing. The after-part has been awesome! The before-part, not so much.

During my early years, Christmas was a major trial in our household. My dad wasn't particularly Jewish; he just thought things like Christmas, birthdays, and holidays in general were ridiculous follies and was always willing to give voice to that sentiment. Mom, despite also being Jewish, embraced the tree and lights for all she was worth. Despite her efforts, the charm didn't survive much past my turning five years old.

Then came the transition night, the first Christmas I spent with my wife and step-kid.

The tree was almost the least of the event (in some years we were so broke that the best that can be said for the tree was "pitiful"). What my wife taught me was that Christmas was all about family and joy. It was about giving from the heart, not the big gift, but the thoughtful one.

There were a hundred little Christmas traditions, some as simple as the ringing of hundred-year-old Nova Scotian sleigh bells that had come from the family's farm sleigh. Others included hot chocolate and scones on Christmas morning. Personalized knit stockings with nuts in the shell and an orange slipped into the toe (because back when they still used the sleigh, the father had given a rare and precious winter orange to each kid on Christmas morning).

We also made traditions of our own. For an entire decade, we baked a dozen, dozen, dozen cookies (that's 1,728 in case you're counting) and mailed them to friends and family scattered across the country.

Even in the hard years, and there were some, we kept all of the little traditions that made Christmas so much bigger than my parents' tall trees, boxes of ornaments, and piles of gifts.

That first Christmas Eve I sat for hours watching that tree with my new family. I was never a Grinch, but I know how his heart felt when it grew to three times its former size. Even after my family slept, I could only watch that tree. I cried for all those lost years, all those years of *not* understanding what was possible.

We don't restrict our joy to the celebration of Christmas, we spread it through the year. But for me, each Christmas is a reminder of that conscious choice we make to embrace the good. To wallow in the joy. One year my wife immortalized it for me with a license plate ring for my car: *My Default Position Is Happiness.* This may sound weird, but I enjoy trying to live up to my license plate ring.

I am Jewish by birth. My beliefs (as you'll see in these stories) are rooted, not in any particular religion, but rather in the good hearts of people. And it is my joy to have written a dozen stories of Christmas and to contemplate what tales will appear in the next dozen.

There are tales here of romance, adventure, growth, and even atonement. They've all been inspired by my embracing the Christmas spirit as surely as if I had been Ebenezer and was reborn in a single night.

For indeed I was, as I wept for joy before a simple Christmas tree.

M.L. BUCHMAN

Ghost of WILLOW'S PAST

A NIGHT STALKERS ROMANCE STORY

THE GHOST OF WILLOW'S PAST

*M*aster Sergeant Dusty James *returns to Portland, Oregon on his one week's Christmas leave. A visit to his parents' favorite rose bush may change the course of his life.*

Master Sergeant Amy Patterson *would mourn the loss of her mother, if the pain didn't still consume her.*

But a shared history may bind their hearts forever. A history known only to the Ghost of Willow's Past.

INTRODUCTION

This story is the first short story I ever wrote. It came to me after I'd been writing novels for almost two decades, but before I became a full-time writer. Here's how it happened.

"I want you to write a short story for my magazine," my good friend Kristine Kathryn Rusch informed me.

"I don't write short stories."

"Yeah…I'm tired of you saying that. It's for an issue entitled *Christmas Ghosts.*"

"I don't write ghost stories."

"Oh, and I want it to be a romance in your Night Stalkers world."

Kris, as you can see, is a very hard person to say no to. But I said: "No."

"By the way," she turned to walk away. "You're one of the lead names. I already have you on the cover design."

Let's just say I wrote the story. In fact, after twenty years of writing novels, I discovered that I *love* the short form. It was the first of what has grown to be over 80 short stories and many more to come.

It also didn't hurt that *Publisher's Weekly* had this to say about it:

"Among the standout (stories) is M.L. Buchman's *The Ghost of Willow's Past.*"

It all began with Christmas.

THE GHOST OF WILLOW'S PAST

"And Tomotada looked so long upon her face it grew rosy red from chin to forehead, and though she smiled, her eyes filled with tears."

-from "Green Willow" (an ancient Japanese folk tale of a samurai who marries the ghost of a willow tree)

Master **Sergeant Dustin James** nudged a clod of dirt back into place with the toe of his boot. The rich black soil of the Portland Oregon Rose Garden simply dissolved and left a blackish patch of mud on the worn leather. Today was the Winter Solstice. It was raining and about three degrees above freezing. Pretty typical. He stared down at the *Rosa canina*.

This rose had been propagated from a cutting of the oldest documented rose bush on the planet. The rose now huddled, dormant and pruned back for the winter. In bloom, it was the least assuming rose in the garden, a single layer of five pink petals around a yellow center. Four days before Christmas, it was a cluster of frosty twigs decorated by bright red rose hips.

Most people passed it by, but not his father, the head gardener of the nearby Japanese Garden. He had visited the rose every day after work on his walk home. Dusty and his mother had often walked up to meet him at the old Briar Rose.

"I met your mother by this rose. We married right here." Being a man of few words, his father never embellished the story. It wasn't the most scenic spot in the garden, but with ten thousand rose bushes in a couple hundred neatly tended beds, not bad either. The fact that they'd married here on the Winter Solstice when nothing bloomed had been a little odd perhaps, but then his parents had been rather eccentric.

Dusty had come home for this Christmas, even though his parents had been gone for three years. Their small condo now lay empty most of the year due to a crashed tourist helicopter. An old Bell 206 called in an engine failure and then auto-rotated right into an Icelandic volcano, no survivors.

That Dusty was a crew chief and mechanic on a Sikorsky Black Hawk for the U.S. Army's 160th SOAR had made the loss beyond ironic. His job was to fly, fight, and keep the Special Operations Aviation Regiment choppers running perfectly despite war conditions. His parents had died, probably from a broken fan belt.

So, any time that he was home, but especially on the Winter Solstice, he made a point of coming to visit their rose as his parents had done so often for their three decades together.

"I'm glad you went together, at least you got that much," he told the sleeping rose. With no ashes to scatter, he'd gathered some ash from the volcano and scattered it onto the rose's soil. His parents belonged together here. His father, a quiet man who loved visiting the garden's roses, such a contrast to his artistic Japanese garden, and his wild mother, a true child of the sixties, who had never understood Dusty's choice to serve. They appeared such an oddly-matched couple, the slight Eurasian and the tall, busty blonde. "She brings me to life like the spring warmth." "He keeps me steady with his deep roots."

When would Dusty find that? His own dreams had just been pruned back hard. He'd found out, on no notice, that he had a week's leave. He'd rushed back to Portland only to discover that Nancy had meant to Dear Dusty him, but forgotten, as usual, to follow through.

Another woman who hadn't understood his need to serve his country, his need to protect that which was so precious. She was living with some software geek named Ralph.

Dusty's few friends still in the area were busy with pre-holiday family stuff. Some invited him over for a meal, but being a third wheel in some other couple's holiday wasn't his first choice, nor his second or third.

On call, Dusty really didn't have time to go anywhere els—

The cry of pain echoing across the garden snapped him out of his damp reverie. His Special Forces training had him sprinting down the garden path before he even fully registered what was happening.

One hand slapped for his sidearm, and came away empty. The other slapped for the med kit on his SARVSO survival vest, but he wore only a rain slick over his heavy sweater.

The cry sounded again, a woman in agonizing pain. Halfway across the garden from his parents' rose, he spotted the source. Not that it was hard. On a rainy, winter Friday morning there was only one other person in the garden.

She knelt in the mud at the edge of a garden bed.

Dusty rushed up beside her. "Where are you hurt?" Seeing no obvious wounds he started unzipping her parka.

Her punch came out of nowhere.

She hit him square in the solar plexus so fast he had no time to block it. He tumbled backward among the pruned roses, the thorns carving painful scratches across his cheek and bare hands.

"What the hell are you doing?" the woman shouted down at him. Her hands were poised to strike another blow. He recognized a Taekwondo black belt when he met one and held his hands palm out.

Dusty rolled slowly from the rose bushes onto the wet grass and inspected his hands. "Ow! Shit, that hurts," he flexed a hand and felt every little scratch.

"Answer the damned question!"

He eyed her more carefully. It wasn't your average woman who issued commands to men half-again their size. He blinked the rain from his eyes. She had well-defined cheek bones, arched eyebrows that indicated brunette hair would be hiding under her hood, and eyes the brown of autumn leaves. He shook his head to clear it.

"You sounded like you'd been shot." "Soldier?" She watched him closely. "Yes."

She settled back on her heels in perfect balance, clearly poised so that she could attack easily if she decided it was needed.

"Okay. Maybe." She puffed out a breath.

"I'm fine."

"You look fine, but you didn't sound it." She did look fine. Not the white of porcelain, but refinement shone in her features. He considered mentioning how much he'd love to draw those features with the artist pencils his mother had given to him as a young child. He didn't know if he'd ever seen so much personality in a woman's features before. It was a face made to laugh and smile, but was now drawn grim and closed.

"I…" In the single word he heard all of the wounded distress return to her voice. She glanced back at the bed of roses she knelt in.

"They cut down the tree," she whispered as softly as the rain.

Dusty looked around, trying to picture this part of the garden in his memory. A tree had been here, a big one.

"It was their willow tree." That was it.

She pressed the heel of her palm against the center of chest.

"It makes my heart hurt."

Willow saw them in the rain. They reminded Willow of memories grown deep. Though so little remained beneath the soil, the past lay there in Willow's roots. The roses had still been young and new then. Their voices high and nattering. So sure of their beauty, judging themselves in the mirror of human gazes. Silly little things. Willow remembered a Winter Solstice that had been a lifetime ago. Willow knew the two squatting in the rain needed the story. Knowing the cost, Willow reached deep into its remaining roots and prompted the woman to tell the tale.

"IT WAS the summer of 1917 when Hiroshi Yamada and Amelia Patterson fell in love. I was named for her." Amy wrapped her cold hands around the large mug of coffee, though it did nothing to warm her hands. She wasn't ready to tell this story, and yet here she was.

Despite her best instincts, the man who had rushed to her rescue had coaxed her out for coffee. Amy had been about to refuse when he'd mentioned her mother's favorite bakery. St. Honore was a neighborhood place, a locals' secret. The *boulangerie* provided a small slice of France in the heart of Portland's oldest residential district.

They sat at the end of the long wooden table, a scattering of croissant crumbs on each of their plates. A couple of guys with laptops sat farther down the table, probably writers, as St. Honore didn't offer wi-fi. Two women, girding themselves with caffeine before picking up kids from kindergarten, occupied a tiny ironwork table crowded among a half dozen similar tables. One hardy soul sat outside at a steel table beneath the awning, turned to shield his book from the occasional gust of rain that spattered against the windows.

"Amelia, my great grandmother, was upper crust Portland Society, a founding member of the Rose Garden. There she met Hiroshi, an assistant gardener for the city. Such a marriage of course wasn't allowed. My great grandmother's diary was kept sealed until she'd been dead for as long as she and Hiroshi had been apart. We actually opened it a year early so that my mother could read it before she died."

Amy's hand shook and she set her coffee down quickly. How had she revealed that her mother died? To a stranger? She hadn't meant to say that. There was no way she was ready to face the loss.

Dusty slid one of his nice hands over hers. She wanted to pull away, but if she did she'd start crying. Actually if she didn't, she'd start as well. There'd been no one to offer her comfort in the last week since her mother's death. She'd been the one offering solace to her mother's friends and facing down bankers and insurance agents and...

She closed her eyes and did her best to close off her feelings. First she had to find her breath, focus not on thoughts but only on what was real, what was physical. From there find her center. From there find the calm.

But when Amy focused on the physical, she felt the warmth and strength of his hand over hers. That warmth drew her attention back off her path and she opened her eyes to look at him.

Dusty wasn't holding her hand, merely resting his over it in comfort. They were working hands, not like hers. No matter what she did, her hands were still long, fine, and delicate. Her mother and her grandmother both had the same hands. People commented on their feminine gracefulness, right before she used them to take the person down in sparring practice.

Dusty was soldier strong—it showed in everything about him—but not some overbuilt guy. His strong, working-man hands were simply backed up with good shoulders and a trim frame. It was his face that captured her attention. He had beautiful blond hair that rolled down just past his ears, unusual in a soldier. And dark eyes ever so slightly almond shaped.

"What are you?" It didn't come out right. His face was such an odd mix that somehow blended together so wonderfully.

He raised his eyebrows as he sat back and gathered the large porcelain mug into his hands. He didn't appear to take any offense. Nor had he appeared upset when she'd pummeled him into the thorny roses. There was a steady calmness about him that could weather any storm.

Amy missed his comforting hand the moment he withdrew it. *You're feeling way too vulnerable, Amy. Don't do anything stupid.* Her inner-voice guidance system was always wise, so Amy made a practice of following it carefully.

"What am I?" Dusty toyed with the question, again proving he had a great smile. That's how he'd convinced her to join him for coffee, he'd smiled at her. A genuine smile that reached those dark eyes so effortlessly. Amy hadn't realized how starved she'd been for even so simple a gesture.

"I'm my parents' son."

Shit! Amy could feel herself closing down again. She no longer had any parents. She needed to go now.

Willow waited. Willow knew how to do that. For as long as the life span of humans, Amelia and Hiroshi had met each other at Willow. Hiroshi had planted Willow on a Christmas Eve while Willow was still a mere shoulder-high sapling. Willow remembered each of Hiroshi and Amelia's meetings. In the summer's sun, if they met, they spoke only with their eyes. But Willow had waited eagerly for each Christmas Eve, when the roses' inane chatter had finally settled into mere winter mumbles. Then Willow watched and listened and stored those memories in the deepest roots. Willow saw exchanges of small gifts, a kiss, and heard sighs of two hearts broken.

"What the hell are you doing here?"

Dusty remained on the park bench under a massive Douglas Fir tree. He had his legs stretched out and crossed at the ankles, his arm stretched across the back of the bench. He'd layered up against the cold day.

He'd hoped Amy might come back to her willow tree, and felt pretty damned pleased with himself he'd been right. It wasn't like he had anything better to do.

"Enjoying the day." He tipped his head back. Yesterday's rain had washed the air clear, leaving the world a breathless blue. The air had a snap to it, his breath made misty clouds that caught the morning sunlight before dissipating.

He'd also enjoyed watching Amy walk down the steps into the garden. The way the woman moved was a thing of beauty. A confidence radiated from her, probably the martial arts training. He could now picture the short, sassy cut of brunette hair beneath the rose-red knit hat. Bet it would shine beautifully in the winter light.

"I wanted to see you again."

The words would probably scare her off, but they were blunt truth, just as his mother had always taught him to speak.

"You left a bit abruptly yesterday." He'd seen the pain, seen her try to explain. Unable to do so, she'd wrapped her dignity about her like a cloak of steel and lace, thanked him for the coffee, and departed.

He tilted his head. "You're not glaring at me or walking away. I'll take those as good signs."

Amy's slow smile crossed those perfect features and brought yet another aspect of her character to life. He'd decided that if Amy didn't show, he'd probably fly down to Reno and join Chief Warrant Clay Anderson at the casinos. Even if it didn't inspire him much, it would get him out of Portland.

But now that he'd seen Amy, he canned that plan. Maybe tonight he'd dig around his parents' place and see if he could scare up a sketch pad. He winced against that. Three years and he still thought of the place as theirs. They hadn't left him much in the way of possessions, but the condo was free and clear which gave him somewhere cheap to land on leave. It beat the Army barracks at Fort Campbell hands down. He hadn't even spread out from the small back bedroom he'd grown up in. Maybe he needed to deal with that.

"Dusty?" The smile slipped off her face. He wondered just what his expression had revealed.

"Sorry, I was just thinking. I really need to clean up my place."

"Oh, planning on dragging me back to your den?"

He laughed. He could really get to like this woman. "The thought crossed my mind last night a time or two, but no. It's clean enough. But the condo's still filled with my parents' stuff. I'd be glad to oblige you, by the way."

"Oblige me with what?"

"Dragging you off."

Her sad smile indicated that the answer was "not so much." He hadn't expected more, didn't really know what he was expecting. He'd simply wanted to see more of her; she was also the only other person alone at Christmas he knew in Portland. So he'd come to the garden at sunrise and settled in to watch the day awaken.

"You must be an early riser," he hadn't had to wait very long.

She settled at the far end of the bench, well clear of where his arm draped over the wooden back.

Willow listened. Did they know? Would they understand? Stories were like roots, they slide deep under the soil, reaching out and seeking for connection. Willow could feel Amy's heart and how it hurt. Different than Amelia and Hiroshi, but still, hurt. Willow's old roots lay deep under the bench, a whisper beneath the soil.

"STILL FILLED WITH YOUR PARENTS' stuff ? Where are they?" Even as she asked, Amy knew. That grim look clouded Dusty's features, the same as moments before. She knew the answer and wished she'd never asked, wished she hadn't come this morning. But her mother's ashes were still in her backpack. She hadn't scattered them yesterday because the willow tree was gone.

Last night Amy hadn't slept a wink, knowing even if the tree were gone, that spot in the garden was where her mother belonged.

"Mid-Atlantic Ridge, I guess." Amy squinted at him, but he just shrugged.

"They died in a crash, Icelandic volcano. At least it was quick and they were together which I guess was good for them. I was just thinking that I've never cleaned out their stuff at the condo, because it never mattered. That's just not where they are any more. They're now part of the Mid-Atlantic Ridge, a place where the earth's crust is born."

Amy watched his brows knit together as he looked somewhere far beyond the Portland Rose Garden. She'd had trouble throwing out the last napkin her mother had used, and here he hadn't cleaned house after three years. She had to be out of the apartment by year end. How in hell was she supposed to do that?

Her mother had hidden her disease from Amy until almost too late. They'd had three days together, most of it spent with her mother in drugged sleep, the rest with Amy reading aloud about Amelia and Hiroshi's yearly meetings at the old willow tree.

It had become a Patterson tradition. Each year since before Amy could remember, they'd come to the Rose Garden and left small presents at the foot of the old willow on Christmas Eve. As a child, Amy had made colored drawings for the tree. Once she'd covered its trunk with little gold and silver star stickers. In later years she'd often purchased a special Christmas ornament to dangle among the bare branches, or scattered a little vial of soil she'd brought back from her travels.

Reading the diary to her mother, they'd finally discovered the origin of the yearly visit tradition. Amy hadn't brought a gift for the tree this year, and with it cut down and gone, she didn't know if she should.

"Sorry," Dusty shook his head like a wet dog. "My mind has gone walkabout."

"I lost my mom five days ago." Again, words she'd never intended to speak had slipped out into the world as if someone had given them a nudge.

Dusty sat bolt upright and turned to her. No longer relaxed back on the bench, his whole attention was on her.

She waited for it, for the words she'd so come to hate. But he didn't speak. He didn't stare at her, though he was looking at her.

Finally she couldn't stand it any longer. "Say it!"

"No. I remember how angry I was at every person who said how sorry they were. It was so empty. Why would I go out of my way to make you angry at me?"

Amy shifted on the cold bench, wishing she'd worn another layer against the chill of the day.

"Who are you?"

His grin was easy. "I guess that's a step up from yesterday's 'What are you?'"

Had she really been so rude? Well, yes, she had.

"Master Sergeant of the 160th SOAR at your service."

"Which battalion?"

That stopped him. Now he really was staring at her.

"The fifth." His voice was now careful.

Amy knew why. SOAR was very secretive. A civilian knowing about the fifth battalion must be unnerving him a bit. She decided to keep her own military background to herself a little longer. She couldn't resist seeing if she could make him squirm. After all, he had stalked her this morning, sort of.

"What do you fly in?"

"DAP." He bit the word off.

The Direct Action Penetrator, the nastiest and most powerful rotorcraft in the world.

"Beale or Henderson?"

"How the hell do you know that?"

"Master Sergeant Amelia Patterson, I flew with Emily Beale in the 101st when she was still a Screaming Eagle. I just finished my five years in the service prerequisite before I could apply to SOAR. I report for testing next week." She held out her hand.

When he didn't respond, she reached out and took his nerveless hand and shook it. Slowly his fingers came to life and curled about hers.

Despite the layers of both of their gloves, she easily remembered the feel of his warm strong fingers covering hers.

He didn't release his hold as they talked. She didn't try to make him let go though the sun moved far across the sky.

Willow listened. It was harder, took more effort. No leaves, no branches, no trunk left. All that now remained of Willow ranged deep beneath the soil. The recent bite of the saw, the tearing of the stump both too painful to recall. But Willow still heard, still felt. He asked the ground to give up its heat and Amy and Dusty talked long through the cold day. It was warm only around that one lone bench in the Rose Garden.

"A FRIENDLY FACE, THANK GOD!" Dusty was deep in packing boxes when Amy dropped by.

"How's it going?"

He surveyed the damage. Bags of clothes for Goodwill lined one side of the living room. Bags of garbage lined the other. Boxes of books to take down to the used counter at Powell's bookstore blocked the couch. He'd kept his father's gardening books and the travel-picture books his mother had collected.

"Okay, I guess. I'm pretty much done. Anything that's too hard, I figure that I'm just not ready to let go of yet. Thankfully, this place is really small, so there aren't too many of those decisions." There'd been hundreds, though it felt like thousands of them, but the passing three years had given him some time to deal with the pain of loss. He'd make sure to offer to help Amy, so that she didn't have to face her mother's past while the wound of loss still bled.

"I've sworn that I'm going to sleep in the big bed tonight, but now I don't know."

He watched Amy as she hung her winter coat on a bronze hook by the door and moved to inspect the progress he'd made. She moved as if this were a military inspection, he followed two steps behind. He could see by her nods that she approved of what he'd kept. Some things she inspected more carefully, those that fit stories he'd told yesterday, others that fit stories not yet told. It was a finely honed and much appreciated assessment. He felt better with each considered nod. Hell, he felt better every single minute they were together.

The master bedroom had a pair of walnut dressers, a small desk, and a queen-size bed with fresh flannel sheets and a faded quilt. Two of his mother's oil paintings of the Rose Garden and a small collection of roses his father had pressed in glass hung on the otherwise bare walls.

She continued her silent inspection and led them into his old bedroom. He'd purged the kid crap long ago. Now it was book collection. Some drawings he'd made that his mother had liked enough that he'd pinned them to the wall half a lifetime ago. They weren't half bad, considering.

"Here." She picked up the couple of dinged-up Frisbees he'd kept from his days of playing Ultimate and handed them to him. She also took the two pillows and added that to what he was holding. She moved about the room picking up odds and ends and piling them in his arms.

Then she moved to unpin the art. "Hey!"

"Shh. It's all right."

He wasn't quite sure how it would be all right, but he subsided and watched as she gently took them down.

She gathered the art carefully, "Okay, let's go."

"Where?" Dusty was feeling a bit dense.

She nodded her head back toward the short hall then led him into his parents' bedroom.

He stood there with his arms full of his old belongings. "What am I supposed to do?"

She set the art on the foot of the bed. Then she took his parents' pillows and tossed them out into the hall.

"Your pillows go there. The rest is up to you to figure out." She turned back to his old drawings, spread them out across the quilt and then inspected the room's walls.

He started with the pillows. Set some comic books on an empty bookshelf. He dropped his sketch books and drawing pencils on the small desk. He glanced at Amy and then flipped the sketchbook open to a page he'd worked on while unable to sleep most of last night and set it back on the desk.

When he was done she told him to go get his bathroom stuff and move it into the tiny bath off the master bedroom.

After he'd finished, he leaned against the door jamb and watched Amy. that made her a pleasure to watch as she reached to pin each piece of art onto the wall.

He couldn't believe how much he enjoyed this woman. Not her beauty or elegance. Okay, not just her beauty and elegance; she truly had turned his head and his heart completely around. Things he'd avoided for years simply made sense in her presence.

He looked about the room. For the first time in three years it felt right. His mother's art now mixed with his own. Bits of his collection of science fiction and thrillers now leaned against his dad's gardening books.

Amy simply swept him away. The woman was impossible to resist.

Nor did he torture himself by doing so. He slipped up behind her as she noticed the open sketchbook.

He wrapped his hands around her waist in time to feel the shock of an indrawn breath. He laid a kiss on her neck between her turtleneck and soft hair.

"Is that me?" she whispered.

He nuzzled her neck again and ran his teeth over her earlobe where it just peeked out of her hair. Then he looked down over her shoulder at the charcoal sketch. Her face wasn't drawn from the front. He'd drawn her looking off to the side, as if only just noticing the artist. Her expression reflected a mixture of sadness and the very first hint of a smile. He'd set out to capture her beautiful features, and instead captured her shifting mood. He could still see a woman who had cried at the loss of a tree, but also the woman whose natural state was a quiet joy.

"Best I could do anyway." "It's wonderful."

"It's a start." He hadn't had as much fun as trying to draw her face in a long time. "You know, I can think of one more thing to help make this room mine."

She turned in his arms and didn't argue as he lay her upon the quilt and began making love to her.

Willow rested a little deeper into the dark soil, old roots slowly turning back into the earth itself. But Willow was aware of the bench where Amelia and Hiroshi had kissed and cried each year. And Willow had watched as Amy and

Dusty sat, kissing and laughing, the sound trickling into the soil and healing the old pains.

AMY HAD LEFT his bed reluctantly this morning and returned to her apartment to face cleaning out her mother's life. Knowing she was dying, her mother had dealt with most of it, but what remained was still too much. Amy had never felt so helpless.

Half an hour later Dusty had arrived bearing a dozen red roses under one arm, and boxes and garbage bags under the other. He didn't go until all that remained was the cleaning and deciding where to store her own meager belongings. They were all hers now. Maybe she'd ship them to Fort Campbell for lack of anywhere better.

Amy knocked on Dusty's door and waited, ignoring the pleasant tingle running up and down her nerves.

Dusty's invitation hadn't been a casual, "Hey, want to come over for dinner?"

Instead, as he left, he'd slipped a card among the roses. The note had read: "Master Sergeant Dustin James hopes that Master Sergeant Amelia Patterson will join him for a casual Christmas Eve dinner this evening at six." Dustin? Odd that she felt so close to him, had slept with him, and hadn't even known his full name.

The invitation didn't leave her a lot of choice, unless she really wanted to disappoint him. She considered that and decided she didn't want any other choice anyway.

He'd said casual, so, after trying on three different dresses she'd selected dark green slacks and a red silk top. Her hair was too short for her to do anything other than wash it, and she'd never been a fan of makeup. Casual he asked for, casual he'd get.

When he opened the door, she simply stepped into his arms. He turned her just enough to close the door and held her tight. Had she ever found a place she'd been happier than in Dustin's arms? Not a one that she could think of as she breathed in the wonderful smell of him. Man and...

"Is that roast beef ?"

"Not mine, though I can cook a mean one. I went down to Elephant Deli. Roast beef and Yorkshire pudding, and a treat for dessert. I did make the peas with those little onions myself."

"From frozen."

"Only the best for Amy."

She laughed and slid back into his arms. "So, tell me more about your parents' son, Dustin. He strikes me as an interesting chap."

"Well, there was a young boy named Dusty. He had a silent father who loved three things in life: his wife, his son, and his garden." Dusty led her toward the table in the living room. It was now cozy and friendly. While she'd been cleaning her mother's place, he must have been hauling everything out.

"And Dusty had a mother who loved laughing."

Willow waited. For almost a hundred years, every Christmas Eve someone had come. Willow waited, hoping. Old roots full of broken dreams could do no more.

"COME, WALK WITH ME." Dusty held out a hand. He didn't lead her toward the bedroom, where Amy would have followed him happily. He led her to the front door. "I hope you aren't throwing me out."

She slid against him reveling once again in the way their bodies fit together, in the way his lips now tasted of chocolate mousse and winter, the way he lost himself completely in her kiss.

With those strong hands about her waist, he pushed her back just a hand's breadth.

"No way would I throw you out. You're way to precious for that."

"God, don't ever stop saying stuff like that." He made her feel like such a girl, all soft and mushy.

"Deal. But I thought maybe we could go for a walk together."

That knocked the soft and mushy right out of her, but she nodded. Amy braced herself, knowing where they'd go. It was right, but no tree awaited her there. In a fit of sentimentality, she'd bought a small ornament that now rested in her coat pocket. Perhaps she'd hang it on one of the roses.

Dusty led her out into the night, up the winding paths beneath the silent Douglas Firs, and around the high, black wrought light of the full moon lit their breath in billowing clouds and cast brilliant pools on the trail separated by impenetrable shadows. They strolled the back paths leading to the Rose Garden as the silence of the night wrapped gently about them.

For a time they wandered hand in hand between the sleeping rose beds and finally climbed the stairs under the thorny arbors. In the bright moonlight, unbroken by a towering willow, rested the rose bed she'd always thought of as her family's.

"Oh my god!" her voice came out in a cry. "But how?" A slender willow tree, barely taller than she was, stood in the center of the rose bed just where the old willow had.

"I made a call to the Parks Department. My dad worked for them for over thirty years, so I may have thrown his name around a bit along the way. I got permission, and purchased the tree this morning. The master gardener, who my dad trained, came in from vacation and he and I planted it together. I figured, if you wanted, we could come back together in the morning and bury your mom's ashes here on Christmas Day. I already cleared it was okay."

Amy didn't fight the tears that slid hot down her cold cheeks. She wrapped her arms around Dusty and held him and laughed and cried some more.

She pulled the delicate bubble of blown glass from her pocket and hung it from one of the tree's slender branches. There it filled with moonlight and hope and joy.

"It's..." she had to swallow hard to speak. "It's the nicest thing anyone has ever done for me." She could only look at the young tree with its new bauble, for some reason she couldn't turn to look at Dusty.

"Well," Dusty considered Amy's profile and wondered for the hundredth time if he was about to do the stupidest idea he'd ever thought up. Of course that had never stopped him before. reported for basic training, his father had stood with him by the *Rosa canina*, the old Briar Rose. They had stood a long time in comfortable silence, the summer tourists flowing past the two silent men entranced by a single rose bush among ten thousand.

"Your heart knows it is right for you to go into the Army. If you always listen to it, you will make no mistakes, at least not about things that are important."

Dusty heard his heart clearly and knew it was the right choice as he gently turned Amy to face him and he looked down at the tracks of her joyous tears still glistening in the moonlight. He just hoped she thought it was right too.

Again he kissed her long and deep before setting his hands on her waist and stepping her back a half step so that he could form a complete thought.

"Amy?"

"Yes, Dustin?" He liked that she'd started using his full name.

"There's something I have for you that I hope you'll wear some day. It's far too soon, but I know it has to be here, on this night of Christmas Eve, in front of this young willow tree. I hope, Amy Patterson, that someday you'll want to wear this."

He reached into his pocket, then held out his hand before her. In the center of his palm lay the circle of gold with a square-cut diamond he'd chosen that afternoon. It caught the moonlight and glittered.

Amy studied his hand in silence for a long time. She pulled off her right glove and reached out to trace a tentative fingertip once around the circle of gold before withdrawing her hand.

Then she looked up at him, studying him, clearly thinking hard. Maybe he understood his father's silence a little better now, as Dusty found himself struck dumb, mute before this beautiful and amazing woman.

"I think..." Amy's face revealed nothing to him as she inspected his face.

Then that smile flowed across her features as she pulled off her left glove and held her hand out to him.

"I think I'd like to start wearing it now."

Young Willow liked the little bubble of blown glass that caught the moonlight, and the reflection of the people past and present. Amelia and Hiroshi. Amy and Dustin. Old pain might run deep, but Young Willow knew, this love would always run as fresh as spring rushing to brighten new leaves, born of the Christmas cold and the moon bright.

Young Willow knew that the ghost of Old Willow would agree that they'd done well.

For over ninety years Old Willow (actually a weeping beech which looks like a willow) stood in the heart of the International Rose Test Garden in Portland, Oregon. It was removed for safety reasons in early 2012 and replaced at the turn of the year in 2013 by a young flowering magnolia in the same planting bed (A89). This story lands in the middle of *Wait Until Dark*, the third book in M.L. Buchman's critically-acclaimed "Night Stalkers" series.

Praise for The Night Is Mine:
"A real treat for readers who
enjoy Suzanne Brockmann, Vicki
Hinze, and Merline Lovelace."
★Booklist Starred Review

Wait
UNTIL
Dark
THE NIGHT STALKERS
M. L. BUCHMAN

WAIT UNTIL DARK (THE NIGHT STALKERS #3)

(EXCERPT) - THE PREVIOUS STORY OCCURS WITHIN THIS TITLE

Sergeant Connie Davis felt the metallic stutter before she heard it. It broke the rhythm of the music that usually floated in the background of her thoughts when flying.

She began counting seconds… four, five.

Again.

A third time to be sure.

"Major?" she called on the Black Hawk helicopter's intercom.

"What!" Major Emily Beale's voice made it damn clear that whatever Connie wanted had better be more important than the firefight going on all around them.

The copilot and the other crew chief, Staff Sergeant John Wallace, kept their silence. It surprised Connie that she'd heard it before Big John. He was the most amazing mechanic she'd ever met.

"We have," Connie estimated quickly, "about five minutes until lift failure. We're losing a main blade." And without that, ten thousand pounds of U.S. Army helicopter and her four crew members were going to fall out of the sky far too fast.

"You sure?"

Connie leaned out the left-side gunner's window to unleash another spate of fire from her minigun on the bunkered-in machine gun nest that was giving them such trouble tonight. A hailstorm of spent brass spewed out the window as she pounded sixty-eight rounds a second of tracer-laden hell down on the aggressors. More raw power than the cannons in Tchaikovsky's *1812 Overture*.

For the three long seconds that the nest was in her range, the tracer-green fire whipped and coiled across the sky like a nightmare snake. In three seconds she hurled two kilos of lead. Four and a half pounds didn't sound like much until you pumped it along as three thousand separate pieces moving at three times the speed of sound. She raked her flying buzz saw back and forth twice over the enemies' position in the time they were in view.

"She's right. Maybe ten minutes if you ride it soft," Big John chimed in. He might not have caught the problem, but as soon as she pointed it out he'd found the vibration rippling through the frame of the Black Hawk helicopter, had counted the seconds, and he knew.

It was her first time in full combat with him. But already he was a man she'd learned to really admire during training flights. A man she had real trouble not noticing. She kept finding herself watching him when he wasn't aware. Big John Wallace fully deserved his nickname and was also perhaps the most handsome man she'd flown with in a half-dozen years aloft.

That she was a step ahead of him would have been satisfying in any less hazardous situation. One look out the window was enough to wipe any thought of a smile entirely out of her mind.

Even at night, the Hindu Kush mountains of northeast Afghanistan looked ugly. And tonight's mission had taken their flight in deep, way past five minutes to safety, or even ten. Base lay forty-five minutes away, with four good blades, and the area around that ranked almost as unfriendly as the people shooting at them now.

They might be the Night Stalkers of U.S. Special Forces, the fliers who ruled the night. But if they went down here, they wouldn't be ruling the night for very long despite being the toughest gunship ever launched into the night sky.

"*Viper*, this is *Vengeance*." The Major, the first woman ever in the

Night Stalkers, had long since proved her ability as a pilot and commander when fast decisions were needed.

Helicopters never flew alone into combat, and tonight's mission had paired them with *Viper*.

"We're losing a blade and running for home. Won't make it." Then she took one last turn, wide rather than her normal hard slam, giving Big John a final chance at clearing out the problem they'd been sent to solve. The copilot fired four rockets, and whatever they opened up, John drove home.

The shock wave hit them hard enough that Connie half feared they'd lose the blade now. ...Four, five, shudder, still right on cue. Okay for the moment. She puffed out a breath she hadn't known she was holding as the Major turned south by southeast.

They were through the smaller of two mountain passes while everyone on the ground remained distracted by the massive explosion that continued to roll skyward behind them. No one on the ground remembered to fire at the speeding helicopter until too late.

"Roger, *Vengeance*." The radio crackled in her helmet. "Heavy One is moving, thirty minutes."

Major Beale ran down the throttle to ease the load on the blade. They stayed low to avoid any stress from attempting a climb. That meant flying low through the next, very well-defended pass, assuming they didn't fold up and crash before then. Even with a good rotor, they'd already be up in high-hot limits. The combination of heat and altitude really knocked efficiency out of helicopters, the air was just too thin. With a bad rotor, they didn't dare climb out of harm's way.

The troops defending the pass less than a minute ahead were very unfriendly.

Connie thumped the ammo can with her boot, barely a quarter full. She opened her gun and tossed the ammo belt loose, snaking it back into the can. She snapped down the lid and pulled out a fresh belt from a new can.

Out of the corner of her eye she saw Big John, who sat back to back four feet away on the other side of the chopper's bay, making the same choice. Once again, they were in some sort of perfect synchronicity.

…three, four. Not good. She leaned out the window to spot the pass ahead. They were down in the gut of it. Open to fire from all elevations of both sides.

"Can I—"

"No." She and John cut off the Major in unison, almost making Connie laugh. No climbing, not on this rotor blade.

Connie switched on the night-vision goggles feature of her helmet. She'd turned off the NVGs to avoid being blinded by the rocket flare at the firefight. Now she needed any advantage she could find to see in the dark.

A wash of the world gone green projected across the inside of her visor. Leaning out the gunnery window to look ahead, she watched for the bright shimmer of gunfire or the sharp glow of running stick figures as fighters scrambled for position. They were there. A dozen or more. And several were higher than they were. She couldn't attack them, couldn't shoot upward, unless she wanted to take out what remained of their own rotor blades. Helicopters were designed to shoot down at things, not up.

"Major?"

"Stop asking and just speak!" Emily Beale was less steady than usual. Hard to blame her.

Connie swallowed hard and pictured it again in her head. She saw no better answer. It was either bet on the poor aim of the many gunners ahead of them or bet that the Major's reputation as the best Black Hawk pilot in all of the U.S. Army's Special Operations Aviation Regiment had been earned, rather than merely granted for being the first woman in SOAR.

"A roll is a neutral-gee maneuver." A slow barrel roll—flying straight ahead while rolling the copter over sideways, upside down, and back to right side up—actually placed very little stress on the airframe or rotor blades, if done correctly.

"Oh shit. She's right," John confirmed in that wonderful deep voice of his, making it almost sound rational even as the Major groaned.

Was it an act like this by some crazy or equally desperate pilot that had killed Connie's father? Why had she mentioned it?

"John, you'll be first. Then Connie."

Was this about to place her in the same unknown grave as her dad? Connie Davis. Just a name on the Night Stalker monument at SOAR headquarters. A short note in a secret file: Lost. Pilot, copilot, two crew chiefs. No survivors.

The Major aimed for the right-hand wall of the pass, almost head on. Moments before they would have hit the cliff face, the Major slewed the chopper back to the left. But not in a hard turn. In a long, slow roll.

The ground so close they nearly thumped their wheels on the rock passing at a hundred and fifty knots. At 175 miles per hour, death was only the slightest error away.

That was the moment Connie knew for a fact that Major Emily Beale had earned her reputation as the very best. Beginning the roll so close to the cliff wall reduced their availability as a target to those on either side of the pass. And it took advantage of the ground effect decreasing the stress on the blades. The Major had accepted the idea, planned the maneuver, and executed it all on fifteen seconds notice.

As the right side of the helicopter lifted, John's gun had a clear field of fire on the cliff face flashing by. He used the precious moments to rake the walls far and wide while Connie looked straight down at the ground racing by, going weightless in her seat.

They were so close that she watched the tips of the rotor blades swinging past sharp rock with bare inches to spare. She pushed back into her seat, her instincts taking control and trying to shove her body even another inch from impending disaster. The static electricity of the rotors striking dust in the air glittered in her NVGs, a green arc of brilliant sparks. So close to the rock, the sparks appeared to be inside it.

But with air-show perfection, the Major continued the roll, edging clear of the wall so that she didn't strike a blade. Now upside down, Connie had a disoriented moment to spot any fire John had missed.

She only tagged one on the wall racing by so closely before she faced straight up.

In the moment of rolling silence, as she stared at the heavens, she recalled hearing John's gun fire just a few short bursts while they were inverted. That meant any remaining dirty work on the left-hand wall of the pass was going to be her issue as they rolled back to level.

Anticipating the moment, she leaned forward and drove down the triggers the moment she saw rock instead of sky. An arc of tracer-green fire poured from the six spinning muzzles. She swept her M134 back and forth as the chopper rolled, taking her aim at the cliff face flashing by in the night. Enemy rounds spattered against the airframe with sharp thwacks barely detectable over the roar of her minigun.

The threat detector flashed target information on the inside of her visor, and with instinct born of a thousand hours of practice, she swept the gun over position after position, cutting them apart faster than they could duck and cover.

And then the *Vengeance* was through the pass. The targets were falling astern at eighty meters per second.

Beyond the pass, the front range of the Hindu Kush mountains broke like a thousand-meter-high wave, collapsing in deep rolls and turbulent clusters. The flat horizon of desert formed in the distance.

...two, three. A distance they weren't going to make.

"Now, Major," John announced. There was no questioning the man, not when he used that voice. Six foot four and mountain strong with a deep voice to match. It was a wonder he could cram into the Hawk's crew chief seat, but he did.

Connie had never felt short, but the top of her head would fit under his chin, comfortably. Odd thought.

And he was right. Now, or they were going to fall from the sky.

"This is *Vengeance*. Going down. Repeat. Going down. Beacon hot."

It was a risk. Lately, the bad guys were getting their hands on night-vision gear. A lot of it was first-generation crap, but even that wouldn't have any trouble finding the brilliant, infrared beacon now flashing atop their chopper.

...One, two. The ground was coming up awfully fast. Connie

glanced forward. Best not to interrupt the pilot at the moment, but she wondered at the woman's sanity. Major Emily Beale was a SOAR legend, but they were about to become just another footnote in the bloody history of the Night Stalkers. At her current rate of descent, they were going to dig such a deep hole in the desert that the sand might cover right over their impact crater.

Connie braced for the crash. This one was gonna hurt. And hurt bad. Assuming she was alive afterward to feel it.

Fifty feet up, she felt the shudder as the Major yanked the collective full up and cranked the throttle wide open.

Not crazy.

A calculated gamble.

The Black Hawk's twin turbines groaned in protest, then over five thousand horsepower roared to life. Connie heard them go right past redline, nearly six thousand. The blades howled in protest as they clawed the air like mad beasts. She and John chanting a mantra to the blade in unison, "Hang on. Hang on. Hang on."

Twenty feet. Ten. Slowing, five.

Then the blade let go. Twenty feet of laminated polycarbonate arced off into the night. Three blades remained, horribly unbalanced, but before they could turn twice more, the Hawk slammed into the sand. Not even hard enough to ram the shocks against the stops.

The Major dumped power, and the turbines collapsed from scream to cry toward moan. But not fast enough.

Another blade broke but didn't fly free. It slammed against the tail of the chopper, then the cockpit, then the tail again even as the rotor slowed. For ten seconds of held breath, they all waited while it dragged and beat the helicopter as it spun its way to a halt. The final scraping groan of wounded metal told Connie that half the bearings in the rotor head would need replacement and probably the swash plate as well.

"Everyone okay?"

"We're fine." Big John rolled free of his harness. "Now!" he called and snapped a monkey line to the steel loop by the cargo bay door.

Connie had to blink a few times. Was she fine? They weren't dead.

They hadn't been killed by the failure of one of these hell-spawn machines. What next?

Read this entire completed series at fine retailers everywhere:
The Night Is Mine
I Own the Dawn
Wait Until Dark
Take Over at Midnight
Light Up the Night
Bring On the Dusk
By Break of Day

M. L. BUCHMAN

3-TIME BOOKLIST TOP 10 ROMANCE AUTHOR OF THE YEAR

CHRISTMAS AT HENDERSON'S RANCH

A HENDERSON'S RANCH ROMANCE STORY

CHRISTMAS AT HENDERSON'S RANCH

*C***helsea Bridges'** *first trip to Montana lands her at Mark Henderson and Emily Beale's family ranch. In the past she pursued adventure from hiking the Continental Divide Trail to trekking in Nepal, but a horse ranch provides a whole new world of wonders.*

Doug Daniels *spent three tours in the Navy before he became foreman at the ranch. He has finally found his home.*

Nothing prepares them for the surprises that await during Christmas at Henderson's Ranch.

INTRODUCTION

The Night Stalkers grew into multiple series of novels and short stories. The first, *The Night Is Mine,* was listed just days before this writing in the American Library Association's *Booklist* compilation: "The 20 Best Romantic Suspense Novels: Modern Masterpieces." The main romantic couple in that story, Emily Beale and Mark Henderson, became very popular and went on to inspire multiple series. Along the way, Mark would often talk about his parents' ranch.

So, to put it simply, one Christmas I decided to go there to see what it was like. That turned out to be the five-story and three-novel series of its own...that starts here.

CHRISTMAS AT HENDERSON'S RANCH

"*This isn't right!*"

Chelsea Bridges leaned forward to see what Emily Beale was looking at. Chelsea didn't see a thing wrong, but then she'd never been to central Montana before. Out the small plane's front windshield were miles and miles of rolling green prairie. Streams crisscrossed the grassland in a bewildering maze. The backdrop was the foothills of the Rockies breaking the skyline with their snowy peaks and conifer-clad sides. The westering sun silhouetted the hills, but lit their tops with gold.

"It's absolutely gorgeous!" Then she clamped her mouth closed. She was trying to reel it in. Emily was always so even-keeled and understated that Chelsea was constantly stumbling to be less... Chelsea. Emily was this perfect woman with a drop-dead handsome husband and about the cutest kid on the planet. Chelsea had only been their daughter's nanny for a few months, but she'd seen the deference and respect that everyone at Mount Hood Aviation's firefighter airbase paid Emily. In return, the woman was kind, courteous, and utterly terrifying. Chelsea wouldn't mind being all of those things.

Her husband Mark, who sat up front in the other pilot seat of the small plane, wasn't much more effusive—except around his daughter. At least he had a sense of humor, though not as much a one as he thought he did; an observation Chelsea kept carefully to herself.

Chelsea looked over at Tessa who was strapped in beside her. She had her tiny version of her mother's elegant nose pressed up against the window. "Green," she announced. Out her window was nothing but the rolling grasslands of eastern Montana.

"It's wrong," Mark agreed solemnly but turned enough to wink at Chelsea, or at least she presumed that's what his cheek twitch was indicating at the lower edge of his mirrored Ray-Bans. "Not much snow in the hills. Means another drought year next summer."

"That's not the problem," Emily responded. "Okay, drought is a problem. But that's not the real problem."

"What is, Emma?" Again the sassy wink that said he already knew what his wife was talking about. It was amazing that the man had survived this long. Chelsea would never dare tease Emily Beale; she could probably kill with a glance if she ever took off her own mirrored shades.

"It's December," Emily took one hand off the plane's wheel—if she was on board, she was the one doing the flying—and waved it helplessly at the stunning scenery before them. "We came to Montana for a white Christmas."

"I thought it was to see Mom and Dad."

"It's still supposed to be white," she grumbled and set up to land the plane. It was as much emotion Chelsea had seen in her entire two months with them. Emily Beale was never unkind, but she was cold. Or at least chilly. But that wasn't right either. The woman was frank and forthright, as much with her daughter as with her husband. Yet Tessa was often in her lap, welcome not as child to adult, but rather as a piece of Emily that was simply back in the place where it belonged. The mother and daughter weren't close; they were simply one when they were together. It was about the most incredible thing Chelsea had ever seen. It made her ache for a family of her own; not a familiar feeling.

Again Chelsea strained up against her seatbelt to look down. A herd of horses startled and looked up at them as they passed by. They didn't scatter and run, but they eyed the low-flying plane carefully.

"Horsies!" Tessa declared delightedly when Emily shifted her flightpath so that the herd was visible outside her daughter's window. Not cold at all, just…inscrutable.

"Yes," Chelsea encouraged the toddler. "Those are horses. Aren't they pretty?"

"Pretty!" Tessa burbled, and they laughed together with delight.

Chelsea had never seen a whole herd of horses before. There were at least fifty in the group of every shade imaginable: grays, browns, whites, blacks, and mixes in patchworks, dapples, and who knew what all. They were gone behind the plane too fast to distinguish more. She tucked away the trail mix snack they'd been sharing to make sure Tessa's blood sugar was up.

Even after two months, Chelsea wasn't quite sure how she'd ended up in this situation. Not that she was complaining, Emily and Mark were great parents and it showed in their total sweetheart of a daughter. And flying with Mark over forest fires was often very dramatic.

It had started with Aunt Betsy who was a cook for the Mount Hood Aviation helicopter and smoke jumping firefighters. When Chelsea's degree in psychology hadn't led to any kind of a useful job, her aunt had asked if she liked to fly. She'd shrugged a yes because she'd flown in passenger jets any number of times to visit grandparents, and a trip to Nepal for a backpacking gap year.

She'd now spent most of the last two months sitting in tiny planes of six or eight narrow seats and been paid to enjoy the scenery and play with a baby girl. Best job she'd ever had by a long way.

Tessa was a fixture in Mark Henderson's plane when he was flying as the Incident Commander high above the fire. What was surprising wasn't that they'd added a nanny, but rather how he'd done the job for so long without one. Tessa was a pretty low maintenance kid, but she was also eighteen months old and quite intelligent.

It was a late fire season, Mark had said, and MHA had still been flying fire in the Southwest. But, finally released from the summer contract, they'd come north for a vacation and brought Chelsea along with them. She sure as hell wasn't going home. They'd known that.

As they flew closer to the ranch, more and more fences became visible, cutting the prairie into smaller pastures and training rings. There were several barns, smaller residences, and cabins surrounding the main residence.

Emily flew once over the grand log-built ranch house and waggled the plane's wings in a friendly wave.

Chelsea pointed to out to Tessa, "Isn't it amazabiling?"

"'mazbling!" Tessa called out happily. Emily sighed audibly as she circled wide of the barn.

Chelsea wondered if Mark's habits were rubbing off on her, but she couldn't resist messing with Tessa's rapidly developing language set. They landed on a gravel strip that ended close beside the house and a large out-building that turned out to be a hangar.

A big man strolled out to meet them, still buttoning up his sheepskin jacket. He was an older version of Mark; just as tall, just as broad-shouldered, his light hair going silver. But Mark's face was different. Darker, broader, and his hair was thick, straight, and almost midnight black, sharing only his father's gray eyes.

The clouds of mist puffing about with each breath of Mark Senior —Mac, she reminded herself, they'd said he liked to be called Mac— had Chelsea bundling up Tessa before the plane came to a halt in front of a hangar. The ground might be snow free, but it was far colder here than Oregon where they'd boarded the plane.

Doug Daniels had stuck his head out of the barn when he heard the plane come over low. The trademark gloss-black-and-red-flame paint job told him who was aboard. Some part of him had been alarmed that a client was in-bound for a ranch vacation even though they hadn't taken any Christmas reservations this year. But it was just Mark and his knock-out wife. He liked Mark fine, but he had trouble speaking around Emily Beale. It wasn't just the beauty, he knew how to talk to pretty women just fine; it was the fierce level of competence that she demonstrated at every turn.

He finished helping Logan pitch the hay into the stalls' feedboxes before heading out to greet them. The air had a sharp bite to it, wholly different from the horse-and-straw of the barn, but no moisture. As he stepped out of the barn, he noticed that there wasn't even a hint of cloud in the cobalt blue of the late afternoon sky. The temperature was already dropping though it was still an hour to sunset. It was going to get cold tonight.

Doug stuck his head back inside. "Hey, Logan. Open up the gates. If the main herd has any sense, they'll be coming this way by sunset."

"You bet, boss. Any horse that stays out there tonight needs his horse-sense meter checked."

Doug went out to help stow the plane. There was room in the hangar because he'd moved the helicopter tight to the side after the morning's flight to check the main herd and make sure there were no stray or injured. He hadn't been able to get an accurate count, but it had felt low and that was bothering him. Happened all the time. Still, it worried him.

He ducked through the hangar's side door, popped the release, and slid open the main door from the inside. It rattled and boomed in the cold air. A sharp squeal in one of the wheels had him adding "needs grease" to the infinite mental checklist that was running a working dude ranch.

Just emerging from the plane was a figure wrapped deep in a parka, with the fur-rimmed hood already raised as if it wasn't a merely brisk day, but rather a north polar night. She, for there was no chance of a guy wearing such tight jeans and making them look so good, carried an equally bundled child.

He came up and stuck his nose right into the child's hood, "Tessa, my love! Give us a kiss!"

"Kiss!" the little girl squealed and kissed him on the nose.

Then he rubbed noses with her until she was giggling before he pulled back. He'd ended up standing very close to the woman holding her. He could just see brilliant blue eyes, a freckled nose, and a bright smile in the narrow opening of the hood.

"Do you greet all the girls that way?" Her tone was light, almost musical.

"Sure." Never one to back down from a challenge, he stuck his face right into her hood until their noses rubbed and cried out, "Give us a kiss!"

Unlike the little girl, there was no squeal. Instead, there was a quick squawk of surprise.

Way over the line, Doug.

But before he could retreat, she gave him a quick kiss. Unlike Tessa's it didn't land on his nose, but right on the mouth. There and gone, but the lips were warm, soft, and tasted of peanuts and chocolate.

Once he was clear of the hood, the gloved slap that he expected to follow, didn't. He glanced again into the tunnel of the raised hood.

The bright blue eyes caught the low sunlight and weren't round with shock or narrowed with anger.

"Well," she blinked in slow motion, "okay then."

He laughed, he couldn't help himself.

Now that was his kind of woman.

CHELSEA HAD **no idea** what had come over her. She didn't randomly kiss men, even tall handsome ones who adored small children.

Men who then scooped a little girl out of her arms, slung her around with the ease of long practice until she was riding piggy-back, and—while Tessa shouted, "Horsie!" with glee—galloped about the yard with a protective hand wrapped awkwardly behind him. The man shook back his collar-length, sun-streaked hair the color of worn leather so that it brushed in Tessa's face. He let out a fierce whinny escalating her giggles of delight.

He trotted up to Mark and Emily then stopped with a sidle and a stomp that was thoroughly horselike and delivered the child to Emily.

Then he and Mark made quick work of pushing the plane back into the hangar.

Chelsea was still standing shocked into place when they'd finished and the men had returned carrying the luggage.

"A field pack, very practical," the man who'd kissed her held it aloft as if it contained only air rather than most of Chelsea's worldly belongings. Her camping gear was stashed at Aunt Betsy's and a dozen boxes of books at Mom and Dad's, but the rest of it was in that pack.

"It's my hiking pack, but I use it for everything. Really practical since I hike a lot," she was rambling; time to cut that out. She sniffed at the air and the cold made her nose hurt on the insides, "At least when it isn't sub-Arctic."

The man's jacket was fleeced-line denim, but he hadn't even bothered to button it against the frosty day. He smelled of hay and his kiss had been warm and fresh with the outdoors.

Mac greeted his son with a firm handshake, but gave Emily a deep hug that surprised Chelsea almost as much as being kissed by a total stranger. What had happened to the woman's backbone of steel? Emily leaned into Mac's hug as if she was the one related by blood and was happily come home. Then he led them toward the house, leaving Chelsea and her luggage bearer to trail behind.

"Do you have a name or should I just shout 'Sherpa!' when I want your attention? Or perhaps *daai?*"

"*Daai?*" he led her onto the wide porch and held the door for her to enter the mud room. There they shed boots and jackets. She was glad she'd been wearing a thick sweater against the damp chill in Oregon and kept it on for added warmth.

The others were talking happily enough together to be lost in their own conversation as they too stripped off the outdoor gear and pulled on slippers from the large basketful of them close by the inner door.

"*Daai* means *older brother* in Nepalese," she explained softly. "A sign of respect. Better yet, *bhaai* for *younger brother* as who knows if you're worthy of respect."

"You kiss me and question whether I'm worth respecting? That doesn't bode well for the morning after."

Chelsea was preparing a comeback, for she certainly wasn't the one who had done the kissing...or had she been, when she turned and saw the look on his face.

"What?"

He shook himself like a horse again. "If I'd known what was under that hood, I might have spent longer kissing you."

"Skin deep, *bhaai.*"

"Yes, but what a nice layer it is."

DOUG KNEW HE WAS STARING, but how was a man supposed to not? Thick waves of red hair cascaded down to her shoulders. Her cream-and-freckle skin only highlighted the brilliant blue eyes that were presently rolling at him. Her sweater must have been custom-made because it traced and enhanced the slender woman within. The rich green was finished with red zig-zags at wrists and waist. A small but elegant snowflake had been knit right over her heart.

"Frozen heart?" He teased to hide his suddenly dry throat.

She looked down where his attention had strayed. "I called this one White Christmas, *bhaai.* And watch where you're looking."

"I am watching where I'm looking, and very glad to be doing so," his made his voice pure tease. Then he wondered, "You name your sweaters?" Could he sound much stupider?

"Sure. At least the Christmas ones."

"You knit it yourself?" Apparently yes, he could sound dumber. But there was something about this girl—woman. She *liked* hiking? Major understatement. Her pack looked like it had been carried by an entire Army brigade, worn shiny in a hundred places. A very well-used piece of top quality gear. She knew terms of respect in Nepalese and could knit sweaters that made her look like a Christmas delight.

"I—" they stepped out of the mud room and into the living room. Her gasp of amazement echoed that of all who came here. Every ranch guest who entered the main house couldn't help but stumble to a halt.

"Quite something, isn't it?"

"It's gorgeous! A little daunting, but…" she did a slow twirl to take it all in. "But this is right out of a magazine. It's unbelievable!"

The large river-stone fireplace was a showpiece, big double-length logs crackled away on the grate. The flagstone hearth was surrounded by plush chairs and inviting sofas. An upright piano stood by a corner window overlooking the horse pastures and snow-capped peaks. And the high-beamed cathedral ceiling made the twelve-foot spruce that he and Mac had felled up on the northwest slope fit right in. The Hendersons always really did up Christmas. Coils of holly were draped from mantel and piano. Wreaths, garlands, winter-themed quilts on the walls…

"Quite the spectacle, isn't it?" And this nameless woman in a sweater named White Christmas fit right in.

"It's fabulous! My family does a totally lame Christmas, as in almost not at all. Once I got to college, I discovered it and turned into the Christmas loon of any group. You should have seen this poor pistachio tree I decorated one year in Puri."

"Puri?"

"India. On the east coast. I spent a couple months traveling there by train after I left the Himalayas."

Himalayas? Right, well, that explained where she'd picked up the Nepalese. What hadn't she done?

"I try to do up my place, too," he answered. "Same style of construction, but cozier. Bet you'd like it too."

"You do, huh?" Something was amusing her but he couldn't quite think what.

"Sure. I live on the far side of the meadow. I'm the ranch foreman."

"Your…place."

"They gave me a sweet little setup. Two bedrooms. Looks a lot like this, just on a smaller scale. A ranch house in miniature."

"You bet I'd like it?" Her tone had gone impossibly dry.

And her meaning finally sunk through his thick skull. "I didn't mean—" He'd just invited a woman whose name he still didn't know back to his place for a quick— Someone should just take him out to pasture and shoot him.

A wicked smile crossed her features. "Sure know how to make a girl feel welcome, *bhaai*."

Little brother. Suddenly that really wasn't the role he wanted to be cast in. Not even a little. Because he could certainly picture her clearly in that cozy little log house of his.

CHELSEA WAS CURLED **up** in one of the big chairs by the fire with Tessa on her lap. The girl was fading, but not out yet and Chelsea felt completely content working through the thousandth iteration of *Carl's Snowy Afternoon* picture book.

Mark's parents were relaxing comfortably in side-by-side armchairs. It was easy to see where Mark had gotten his good looks. His father had passed on his physique and kindly eyes. His mother Ama was half Cheyenne and had passed on dark skin and hair to her son. The three of them together were stunning.

Mark sat on an oak-trimmed leather couch and Emily was curled up against him with a woven throw of geometric tans and dark reds across her legs. She looked as sleepy as their daughter while the others talked about the ranch, and fires that MHA had flown to this season. Tessa had her father's gray eyes and her mother's fine features and blond beauty. When Tessa was grown, the three of them would make an equally stunning trio.

It was so unusual to see Emily relaxed, that it made Chelsea content to remain as long as she could in the room. Emily, the successful senior helicopter pilot of Mount Hood Aviation, the woman always in absolute control of any situation, lying against her husband like...well, like a woman in love. It was surprising and wonderful. Yet another thing that Chelsea put into her Someday List. Lie before a warm fire with her arms wrapped around a man she loved.

No. Scratch that. With *the* man she loved. She still had plenty of time to find him; she hoped. Mr. Wonderfuls weren't exactly hanging about for the picking, but it was a nice image.

It wasn't hard to picture what the man would look like in her fire-warmed daydream. He'd have casually long rough-cut hair, worn-leather brown just like—

There was a soft jolt in her lap. She looked down to see that Tessa had landed face first and fast asleep with her nose on Carl's finished snowman.

Chelsea slipped from the room with her and decided that it was time to put both Tessa and herself to bed before she became any more ridiculous.

Still, it was a nice image as she curled up in a guest room with Tessa on a low trundle bed beside her.

Doug Daniels was a *very* nice image.

Doug went for brash to cover his initial reaction to seeing a sleep-tousled Chelsea hunched at the breakfast table. He'd come in to refill his coffee and check up on her as Emily had asked. It looked as if he'd surprised the sleeping lion in her den.

Wrong image. Chelsea didn't strike him as dangerous, just enthusiastic. Like an Irish Setter. The dark red hair color wasn't a bad match. Except at the moment she looked like she'd been run over by warm bed and a soft pillow, and would still be a while recovering. Or like he'd want to sweep her right back into—

Cut it out, Daniels. But he'd lost a lot of sleep over her last night and her current state wasn't helping matters.

Chelsea was clutching a mug of hot chocolate like a lifeline. She wore a gold-colored turtleneck that proved the sweater hadn't lied last night. It revealed strength aplenty to carry a hiking pack and curves to…

He sighed at his libido's nudge-nudge, wink-wink.

"Where's Tessa?" she looked up at him through a screen of

unkempt hair that she didn't bother to brush aside. The ten-foot distance from the coffee pot to where he could brush it aside himself was a good thing.

"They all went into town; took her with."

"I should wait for them."

"They won't be back until dinnertime."

She squinted up at him again. "Where the heck is town from here?"

"Choteau is only thirty miles out, but there's not much there unless you fancy a good steak. They're headed into Great Falls which is eighty each way."

"You sure?"

"There's a note from Emily by your elbow."

She twisted her head to read it without relaxing the death grip on her mug. The long line of her neck was…something he shouldn't be thinking about. Mark and Emily might not be his bosses, but this was their guest. And thinking hot thoughts about Tessa's nanny was wrong in so many ways, not the least of it being that they'd be gone soon. Christmas was just the day after tomorrow; they'd be gone the next day.

"You eaten yet?"

She nodded.

It took him a moment to spot the pan and dish, already washed and perched in the drying rack. Neat and respectful too.

"Good. Dress warmly. I'll meet you at the hangar in five minutes. I need to go up."

"Or I could just kill you and go back to my cozy bed."

"You'd do that to *younger brother?*" he asked in horror.

"Absolutely," but he could hear the grin in her voice even if he couldn't see it clearly through her shield of hair.

"You'll miss a beautiful helicopter ride."

"*You* know how to fly one?" She was quick enough to take in that he must be the pilot and turn it around into a tease.

He didn't even condescend to answer as he headed for the back door. "Four and a half minutes."

CHELSEA MADE *it in* four and had spent three of that whipping up some instant hot chocolate in a pair of steel travel mugs.

"For me? Thanks."

When he reached for one, she pulled it away. "Mine. Two-fisted drinker."

It earned her that good laugh of his and she handed one over.

Doug had a pretty little Bell JetRanger pulled out of the hangar and was going over it carefully. Chelsea was taken aback for a moment. Two months ago she knew helicopters were the ones with their propellers on top instead of pointing to the front; now she recognized a JetRanger on sight. Furthermore, she thought of it as small compared to the massive Firehawk helicopter that Emily flew for MHA. When had that happened to her?

The pilot-plus-four-passenger craft was clean, but well worn. It looked well-maintained but hard used.

"I've never flown in a helicopter."

Doug looked at her aghast. "You work for two of the best helicopter pilots the Army has ever produced and you haven't been up in one?"

"I—" Chelsea hadn't known that about them. But rather than look foolish for the lack of knowledge, she just shrugged. "My job is to take care of Tessa. Mark is the Incident Commander Air"—she hadn't even known he could *fly* a helicopter—"so I fly with him and Tessa in the ICA plane."

"A helicopter virgin. Well, you're in for a thrill, honey."

"Watch it, *bhaai!*"

Again the merry laugh as he escorted her into the left-hand seat and made sure she was buckled in.

The ride was a real joy. The cabin heater kept the chill air at bay as they roared aloft. Headsets with boom mics made it easy to hear him as he pointed out the features of the ranch.

He let her look her fill, but she didn't know if she'd ever get enough. The green prairie stretched smoothly to the hills. The mountains broke from the grassland as if someone had drawn a line on the ground and said, "start them here." It was an abrupt and visceral shock. Only as they flew closer did the illusion start to break; secluded valleys intruded deep into the hills with small rivers sliding between sheer headlands.

"I love this land," Doug whispered softly after she'd finally managed to voice her awe at the rugged beauty. "It can be a hard land, but I never tire of looking at it."

"I wouldn't either," she said with a sincerity as if she was making a promise.

"Now who's being forward?"

She hadn't meant to be. Then she realized that she hadn't been. It was just Doug Daniel's mind twisting in…she sighed…much the way hers had been.

But the ranch was one of those places that simply felt right. Chelsea would start helicopter lessons tomorrow if it meant she could fly here. Doug flew with such an easy confidence.

"You've been flying for a long time," she finally turned her attention to the fine scenery inside the cabin.

"Navy. Did three tours, six years. That was enough for me and then some. A SEAL buddy hooked me up with Mac."

"A SEAL buddy? Like the diver guys?"

"Sure, Mac was one too," Doug shrugged easily. No wonder he flew with such ease and confidence. Except he didn't look confident; he looked worried.

"What's wrong?" She checked the narrow dashboard that rose on a pedestal between their feet. She recognized about half of the instruments that were like the ones in Mark's plane, but nothing looked wrong on them and nothing was flashing red.

"Lucy didn't come back to the barn last night. And she had a late season foal, so I'm a little worried about them."

Chelsea looked out the windshield but couldn't imagine how to spot a horse in such a vast area. Now at least she understood that Doug hadn't been sweeping back and forth over the ranch and the prairie simply to show it to her; he'd been quartering and searching the ground. She'd done search and rescue for lost hikers, but that was tromping through woods and over rough terrain.

"How do you find a horse in thousands of acres?"

"Well," he pointed down at a lush, pocket-sized meadow around a tiny lake. "I was hoping she'd be here. It's a favorite of the horses. Hold the collective a minute."

"The what?"

"The control on the left side of your seat. Just hold it steady, don't worry, you can't crash us."

She tentatively wrapped her hand around the control, until she had a firm grasp. "Okay," she barely dared whisper it.

Doug took his left hand off his matching control and reached back to scrabble around behind the seat.

Daring greatly, she pulled up on it ever so slightly, and could feel the helicopter rise. She eased back down until the altimeter said she was back at the starting level.

"Here," he dropped something heavy in her lap. "Put that on, would you?"

She opened the case and looked down at the contraption, for that was the only word for it. There were straps to hold it to your head. It looked like a pair of goggles from one side, and like a half-unicorn, half-bug-eyed monster monocular protruding from the other.

"What is it?"

"Night vision. Lucy and the foal will be significantly warmer than the background. She'll show up clearly. Mark gets us the best toys."

Chelsea straightened it out and leaned over to put it on Doug's head.

"No," he stopped her. "You wear it."

Doug was amused by her exclamation when she got it turned on. Chelsea took such pleasure from everything about her. The countryside, the helicopter—rather than showing fear she'd proved she had a good and light touch—and now the night vision was tickling her fancy. Last night he'd left early. Partly because it was a time for the family to be together, but also because the vision of Chelsea with Tessa in her lap had been so powerful. She'd made it too easy to imagine a red-headed girl sitting right there, curled up by his fireplace.

For the next two hours, he flew and she scanned. He filled the time with learning about her background. Deeply independent—with parents who had little interest in an intelligent child filled with dreams—she'd forged out on her own. Six years to get her degree because she'd spent two years traveling and hiking; first walking the Continental Divide Trail from New Mexico to Glacier Park, and then all over the Himalayas.

It both amazed and saddened him. She was incredible, had a much clearer view of the world and herself than most people. But he'd found where he wanted to be and she had adventure deep in her blood. She'd never be satisfied with…stupid fantasies of a demented ranch manager.

"There," her shriek almost blew his eardrums. Close beside the farthest fishing cabin, Lucy and her foal were huddled up against the side of the building. Lucy was lying down. Not a good sign.

He landed as close as he dared and rushed out to the mare. He'd brought a handgun, but not wanting to jar Chelsea's sensibilities, he'd left it stowed on the helo.

"We won't have to shoot her, will we?" Chelsea was right beside him.

Okay, so much for that worry. "Let's hope not."

Lucy was down, but had raised her head to watch his approach. Her whinny of greeting was encouraging.

He talked to her as he checked her out. No complaints as he tested for broken limbs. Same for the abdomen. Then she coughed in his face, a dry, hacking cough. He felt under her jaw and found swollen lymph nodes.

"Oh, crap!"

"What?"

"We vaccinated her against this."

"What?" Chelsea sounded deeply worried.

He sighed, "She has the flu. I can't do much for her here. She needs a warm barn and some rest. I'll have to ride back out, bring some high energy food and probably start her on a round antibiotics against secondary infection. With a little luck, she'll come back if I guide her. It will be a long slow ride."

THEY FLEW BACK, **and** when Doug saddled up a horse, she'd insisted he saddle two. She'd never ridden a horse, only a very recalcitrant mule when she'd sprained an ankle coming off climbing Imja Tse. She could have hobbled out faster than that Nepalese mule had carried her.

At Doug's guidance, she'd packed a pair of saddlebags with a change of clothes and several days of food. He packed clothes, camping gear in case they were caught out, horse meds, and a twenty pound sack of oats.

He led off at a light trot and she let him. Her horse, a big dapple gray male called Snowflake, looked at her strangely several times as she struggled to imitate Doug's easy saddle position. Every now and then he'd glance back to make sure she was still with him, and she always managed a plucky wave or nod as the saddle's hard leather slowly beat her to death.

They were about an hour out when he happened to look back during one of her barely-still-on-the-horse moments. Doug twisted his mount in a tight circle like it was the easiest thing in the world. He twisted again until they were side by side. He leaned over to grab Snowflake's reins and everything came to a blessed halt.

"Haven't you ridden before?"

She could only shake her head, because if she opened her mouth she might start crying from all the places she'd rubbed raw.

"You're either incredibly brave or ridiculously stupid!"

"Mostly," she managed through gritted teeth. "Except you got the adjectives backwards." Being at a blessed standstill gave her some tiny sliver of ease. "According to my parents, I'm ridiculously brave and incredibly stupid."

Doug regarded her for a long moment, then glanced in both the direction they'd come and the one they were headed, considering the options. If he tried to send her back, she'd…she didn't know what. But she hadn't gone through this much pain for nothing.

"Okay," he shook his head. "I've seen that look on plenty a stubborn horse and don't want an argument. Stand up in your stirrups, if you still can."

She managed it without crying out.

He unrolled an extra blanket he'd had tied to the back of his saddle. He folded it in quarters, tossed it over her saddle, and then pressed her lightly on the shoulder until she eased back down carefully. It wasn't too painful, and far better than it had been.

"I lead probably a hundred trail rides a summer, Chelsea. You know how many beginner riders could have pulled off what you just did?"

She shook her head.

He held up his fingers and thumb, tips together to show a zero.

"I deserve a prize then."

Chelsea only had a moment to see his grin before he leaned in and kissed her. This wasn't some quick peck through the shield of her parka.

Doug leaned into the kiss and, fool that she was, she welcomed it without even a little protest. He provided plenty skill and heat, but that wasn't what she was really noticing. What riveted her attention was how absolutely her body was galvanized by the simple act. Actually, ungalvanized. She melted against him despite the two horses that separated them. Leaning as far as she dared, she hung tightly onto the saddle's pommel with one hand and his jacket with the other and pulled them together. The kiss ran right down to her toes and made them curl in her riding boots.

When he finally eased back, Doug Daniels looked awfully pleased with himself. Of course she was feeling much the same way.

"I'm not sure," Chelsea was amazed she could even speak, "which of us you were just rewarding."

"At least you won't be *bhaai-ing* me anymore," his laugh was even more self-satisfied than his expression. "Now, let's teach you how to ride. First, take your reins like this."

She did her best to follow his instructions and pay attention, but he'd made a warm buzz between her ears despite the cool day only now breaking above freezing.

Doug Daniels was many things: handsome, male, and a heavenly kisser being only three of them. But *younger brother* he definitely wasn't.

It was four hours to the last turn up to the fishing cabin, less than an hour later than he'd planned. Chelsea was the most apt riding student he'd ever taught, and while Henderson's Ranch might be a working one, they made the majority of their income from all of the city folk guests who wanted a week or two of "country." Chelsea took to it as if she'd been born in the saddle...though she'd probably be too stiff to walk right for days. It had been cruel to keep going, but he couldn't afford the time to escort her back even if she'd have let him. He'd bet the chances of that were close to zero, yet another thing to appreciate about the beautiful woman. Tenacious as hell.

As it was, they'd be staying in the fishing cabin tonight. The sunset was only a few hours off and Lucy wouldn't be able to move quickly. It would be a far slower ride back tomorrow. On top of that, keeping Chelsea in the saddle through the night's journey back would be a cruelty, even if Lucy was up to it.

The final lap to the cabin at their quick walk should take about half an hour. Then Doug glanced back over his shoulder—more bad news. A squall was inbound. Blocked by the height of Wind Mountain, and the twisting trail up to the cabin, he hadn't seen it coming. He stopped them long enough to haul on ponchos, but he knew it wouldn't be enough. They were about to get drenched.

They'd galloped briefly on the flat trail, but they were now climbing up a harder route. The way wasn't dangerously narrow, but it would be far more challenging. Another eye at the rain front, now a gray curtain sliding down the mountain face, had him changing plans.

"Ease up out of the saddle a little bit," he told Chelsea. "Lean forward. Loosen the rein. Good!"

And he smacked Snowflake hard on the butt.

He nudged his own mount forward and in moments they were galloping together up the valley. The way narrowed and steepened until they could no longer ride side by side. Doug didn't dare lead from where he couldn't see her.

"Ride on!" he shouted as the first crash of lightning struck the mountain top and thunder rumbled down upon them, amplified by the echoes off the high rock cliffs.

Bless Chelsea, she leaned into it and flew up the trail. He watched closely, but she stayed solid, didn't even a grab the pommel. Her legs must be screaming fire, but she rode, if not like an experienced horsewoman, then plenty close.

The icy rain broke over them, but the trail was solid and drained well, so he left them at the run.

In five minutes they were drenched, but the cabin was in sight. He shouted ahead and they eased down through canter to trot and arrived at the cabin at a walk.

"Down you go," he slid off and helped her down from her horse. "Take their reins and walk them back and forth. It will do all three of you good. Slow is fine, just keep moving." He stripped the saddle bags and tossed them into the cabin. He heaved the saddles inside moments later, then waved her, holding their mounts' reins, down the valley.

Even aching and saddle sore the woman had a walk that stirred his blood. *Ridiculous!* That's what he was being.

He grabbed his medicine bag and the oats and circled around to Lucy who was thankfully back on her feet, but hanging her head miserably in the rain. Her foal was cowering against her. She'd been ten feet from the overhang and the big box stall, but had been too dazed—yet another symptom—to walk under cover.

He guided them in and checked her. He couldn't do anything for the flu, which was viral, but he gave her antibiotics against secondary infection and a booster shot of vitamins. She perked up a bit for her oats and water. He got blankets over her and the foal about the time Chelsea staggered back up to the stall with their mounts plodding along behind her.

"Is this enough?"

He ran a hand over them. No longer breathing hard, not hot. "You did good Chelsea. Go inside. I'll be in as soon as I get these two settled with the mare."

When he entered the cabin a few minutes later, Chelsea was on the floor in a fetal position.

Shit! He was an idiot.

CHELSEA HAD BEEN **this** cold before, she was sure of it. Like when she'd camped above snowline at the base of Chulu West and the zipper on her sleeping bag had broken. But in her memory it didn't feel colder. And when her knees had knocked together high in the Himalayas, she'd laughed at the novelty. Now she fought not to cry as the insides of her legs, rubbed raw by the saddle, sent shivers of pain right along with the cold shakes.

She opened her eyes when Doug entered the cabin and immediately began cursing. He looked furious! His dark hair matted flat and black with the rain, water cascading off his poncho. He hauled it off with a yank and dropped it on the rough wood with a wet splat.

Chelsea wondered if he was about to tear her to shreds because she'd collapsed, then realized she wasn't the one he was swearing at. He dropped to his knees beside her and began calling her name loudly.

"I'm c-c-c-cold, not d-d-deaf," she managed through rattling teeth.

"I'll start a fire," he jumped up toward the iron woodstove in the corner.

She tried avoiding the hard "c" of close, but found the "sh" sound little easier. "Sh-sh-shut the door first, you big lummox. R-raised in a b-b-barn."

Doug closed the door and then redeemed himself with his efficiency in building the fire.

"Heat? How long?" she managed.

He looked uncertainly from her to the stove. Not soon enough.

She tried to remove her poncho, but her hands weren't under her control anymore. This was bad.

"C-c-clothes. Off. B-b-bed," she instructed.

He stripped off the outer layers and hesitated until she stuttered out a series of curses at him. She cried out when he peeled her jeans.

Then he began cursing all over again.

She looked down. Her legs' normally pale skin had gone white with the cold, except for the insides from boot top to panties were livid red with abrasions. No wonder they hurt.

The goofball stopped at her soaking wet turtleneck as if embarrassed.

"C-c-come on. You know you want to s-s-see me naked."

He grunted and had the decency to try and look away as he finished the job and then scooped her up like a feather hard against his soaking wet jacket.

"Eww!" Yet even the tiny bit of heat that escaped through the denim felt so good.

The cabin was simple. Three bunk beds, several couches and plush chairs that had seen better days probably back at the main house, and a small corner kitchen with an impressive collection of cast iron pans appropriate for frying fish. Doug dropped her in one of the lower bunks and began piling blankets over her. She couldn't even clutch the blankets to pull them tighter.

"S-s-strip!" Chelsea ordered.

"But…"

"C-c-come on. You know I want to s-s-see you naked," she did her best to stammer it out the same way she had the first time. "I need heat."

He began peeling down and Chelsea watched as much as the shivers would allow.

"Wow! C-c-cowboys *are* built pretty."

He smiled at her for the first time since finding her on the floor. "This is a horse ranch. Not a cattle ranch."

"So get your fine butt in here, horseboy. Before I f-f-freeze to death."

He hesitated at shedding his underwear, someone please explain men to her, then turned away as he finally stripped off that last piece. His butt really was fine; topped by a narrow waist and broad shoulders with muscle that rippled across them with each movement.

Doug slid in beside her and, after a moment's hesitation, pulled her against him. His skin was so warm compared to hers that it burned, but she leaned into it as hard as she could.

"Christ! You're freezing!" He began chaffing those big hands of his up and down her back.

"D-d-duh!" Chelsea managed to get the covers completely over her head and concentrated on soaking up Doug Daniels' warmth.

*Doug held **her until** the shivers stopped. With his arms still around her, he could feel her breathing slow. Once she was deeply asleep in exhaustion, he slipped out of bed and dug out fresh clothes from the saddlebags, hanging the others to dry. He stoked the fire, made hot chocolate and wished for coffee, but the latter would make him even more awake than he already was.

A quick radio call back to Logan told him that the Hendersons weren't back from Great Falls yet. Logan wasn't a pilot so he couldn't bring the helo to fetch Chelsea. With the shakes gone, she probably just needed sleep...and time to heal. Gods but she was tough.

The windows were dark with the fading light of sunset happening somewhere beyond the heavy overcast. Lightning still shimmered through the heavy rain, though far enough off that the thunder was a rumble rather than a crack. The weather was still too nasty for a flight even if Mark was back. He had Logan leave a message on the kitchen table so that they wouldn't worry when they returned and found no Chelsea.

"Doug," Chelsea's voice was a whisper barely louder than the crackling flame from the glass-fronted woodstove. "Come back to bed." The firelight caught the blue of her eyes and the tip of her nose from where they peeked out of the blankets.

"You trying to kill me, girl?" Yes, he'd wanted to see Chelsea naked, from the first moment he'd spotted her climbing down out of that plane in those deliciously tight jeans. Even shuddering with the leading edge of hypothermia, she was beyond spectacular.

"Not girl. It's woman. And I think you trying to kill me once already today should be enough for both of us."

"I didn't—" But he had. He'd taken her skills for granted when she climbed up on the horse. And led her on a grueling ride through a storm. Sending her out on a cool-down walk in the freezing rain was about as dumb as it got.

Unlike so many of the guests who came to the ranch, Chelsea radiated skill. She'd triggered none of his high-season alarms that told him who to watch out for. Though she was certainly triggering other reactions.

"I don't think that's a good idea."

She rolled her eyes at him. "Get your warm butt back in here before I have to climb out and kick it. I ache right down to my joints."

Which told him just how dangerously cold she'd gotten.

Once again he stripped down, far more conscious of the woman who now wouldn't turn away than the earlier one whose eyes had been partly rolled back into her head.

She went to throw a leg over his, but jerked back and hissed at the pain.

"God I'm so sorry. Let me get some horse liniment," he climbed out of the bunk.

"Hello! Not a horse."

He grabbed a bottle from the kitchen shelf and returned to stand over the bed. How was he supposed to…

"Here," he held out the bottle. "Trust me. It works great."

CHELSEA FELT **as if** she was being a total wanton. She was in a cozy little cabin with no distractions of electricity. A very handsome man, momentarily unaware of his own nakedness, stood close beside her lit by the soft firelight that filtered through the woodstove's glass-paned door. And he was holding out the horse liniment the way you hold out a mouse for a dangerous viper to snack on.

The normal version of herself would have taken the liniment and tried to slather it on under the covers.

Instead, she watched Doug's face as she slipped a leg out from under the covers and twisted to turn it, inside-thigh up. His eyes didn't narrow suspiciously, instead they widened in alarm. She'd watched him handling the horses with a gentle but firm hand. A half ton of horse flesh didn't bother him at all, but the inside of a woman's leg had him totally flustered. Damn but he was cute.

"Come along, horseboy," she coaxed him in the same tone he'd cajoled the colt to follow its mother into the stall.

His gaze snapped from her leg to her face, and then his nice deep laugh rolled out. "Okay, you got me. I'm dying to slather some liniment on those fine legs of yours." And he knelt on the wood floor beside her and smoothed some on.

It was cold and sent a shiver up her leg. But the warm steadiness of his hand stroking in the thick liquid calmed the convulsive response before it could turn back into the shakes. She could feel his hard calluses and easy strength, but was surprised at the gentleness of his rough hands. Within moments a numbing warmth spread up her leg in a wave of relief.

"I'll smell like a horse," she complained to cover a moan of delight. The camphor was sharp in the cabin's warm air, but her attention was nowhere near her nose.

"A sweet smell to a rancher."

"How about to a horseboy?"

"Lady," he didn't even bat an eye. "You smell incredible to this horseboy, with or without the liniment."

There was no sign of any embarrassment by the time he'd ministered to both her legs and tucked them once more under the covers. He'd somehow transferred all of it to her. As he slid back under the layers of blankets, Chelsea was intensely aware of the narrow bunk and the warmth of his body pressed against hers. She was more of a long t-shirt gal, but it would be stupid to ask for one with a man she'd lain naked against for most of the last few hours.

Unable to find words, she simply nestled inside the curve of his arm. Then, against the fiery tension building so high that it roared in her ears, Doug began talking. He told her about the birth of the foal, who slept even now in the nearby stall with Lucy. He talked about the ranch and the spring wildflowers that colored the prairie like a paintbrush.

She fell asleep with the sound of his love for his life rumbling from his chest directly into her ear. It was the sweetest, safest sound she'd ever heard.

HE'D OFFERED *to call* the helo a half dozen times this morning, but Chelsea had turned him down cold, despite hobbling about like a geriatric case. Another round of liniment helped some, but he knew she'd be stiff for days.

Doug finally gave in. Partly because he knew Lucy wouldn't be up for more than a casual amble and partly because he wanted every single minute with Chelsea that he could get. He'd held her throughout the night, marveling at the rightness of it.

It had been like that when he'd arrived at the ranch fresh out of the service. After three full tours, most of them spent on ships in the Persian Gulf, he'd been sick to his heart of the unending heat, the limitless steel, and the noise—for a Navy ship was never silent. He'd been on the ranch for three years now and could still feel the Persian dust in his pores. But the ranch had fit him since the first moment he'd stepped on the soil.

He'd ridden plenty as a kid at his parents' place in Wyoming. When he didn't re-up, SEAL Commander Luke Altman had sent him up to see his own former commander outside Choteau, Montana. Mac had shown him around Henderson's Ranch and Doug had decided on the spot that he never wanted to leave. Mac and Ama had been looking for a foreman. Together, they'd transformed the aging ranch into a showplace tourist destination.

He'd worried a lot about "the son" coming home, until he'd met Mark and Emily. Mark had taken one look at the transformation and thumped him hard on the shoulder before walking away without a word.

It was Emily who'd translated for him. "He was so worried for his parents. You've really touched him." Then she'd kissed him on either cheek. "You done good, Doug. Keep it up." Then she'd gone after her husband. That's when he'd set his sights on the kind of woman he wanted. One just like Emily Beale.

And he couldn't have found one more different than Chelsea Bridges if he'd tried. Oh, a lot of the things that were right with Emily were just as right on Chelsea, especially her absolute fearlessness—the image of her galloping through a thunderstorm on her first ride still fired the imagination.

But where Emily was quiet, thoughtful, and soft spoken, Chelsea spoke her mind and laughed with a bright joy—even when on the verge of succumbing to hypothermia.

He imagined it would take years to fall for the right woman once he met her, because his ideal woman didn't fall that quickly. At least so he'd thought until he'd rubbed noses with Chelsea inside a parka hood and received a kiss for it. Now he was crazy about a sassy redhead who'd slept in his arms like she'd always been there.

Slept. And that was all she'd done. Hard to blame her, as her body had been through a lot of extremes yesterday. But the only extremes he'd been through had been treating Chelsea as if she was his injured sister. Everything had been perfectly chaste last night, if you didn't include his thoughts.

"Storm has passed," he did his best to distract himself. "Temperature is falling and there's another front moving in. Let's get ahead of it."

"Sure," she gamely picked up her saddle, that probably weighed half as much as she did, and headed for the door.

So much for a morning tumble, or even a kiss.

He'd escaped her bed early—because it was either that or he was going to do something wholly inappropriate—and bundled up to go tend the horses. Lucy had perked up overnight enough to greet him. She was still snotty with the flu, but it was clear so no secondary infection yet. Her breathing also sounded clear enough for the walk back to the ranch. The foal was more cheerful than the night before, which he'd take as a good sign regarding his mother's condition. By the time he was back inside, Chelsea was dressed in warm clothes and had made the bed. Oatmeal and coffee were simmering on the woodstove.

She'd looked as natural here as no paying guest ever really did.

They'd had breakfast together; Chelsea going on about the upcoming ride…and he hadn't jumped her. What was up with that? There was decent and there was ridiculous, and he'd definitely crossed that line somewhere in the night.

Then she'd washed the dishes, grabbed her saddle, and gone.

He'd already taken his own saddle out. So, he gathered up their saddle bags, double-checked that the woodstove was secure—the few remaining embers would burn themselves out—and gave the cabin one last look. All shipshape…damn it. Not a single tousled bed sheet. He hadn't brought any protection with him, but that didn't mean there weren't other options. But had they used them? Nope! Not a single, damned, inappropriately pleasant fondle had passed between them.

Closing the door, he stomped around to the horse stall and ran head on into a kiss.

This wasn't some little kiss through a parka or a taste of wonder when they were both up on horses. Chelsea wrapped herself around him and had him backed against the rail fence. With her arms tight around his neck, she was rapidly killing off fantasy after fantasy. Who knew it was possible to pack so much joy into such a simple act? Apparently Chelsea did.

When Snowflake came over to snort in his hair across the fence, Chelsea flapped a hand at the horse's nose.

"Busy here," she mumbled at the big gray.

Damn straight! was all Doug could think. All that soft and gentle warmth of last night had been replaced by the lively redhead who'd teased with him since the moment of her arrival. She didn't play coy or tease now; she delivered a kiss with her entire body. It left him shuddering with need when she abruptly released him and, as if his world hadn't just been spun around and dropped on its head, strode into the stall with one of the saddlebags that he'd dropped when she'd jumped him.

Unable to trust his voice, he focused on saddling them up. No need to rope Lucy or the foal. Lucy, he knew would follow them, and the foal would follow his mom.

Placing his hands around Chelsea's waist to help her up into the saddle was almost his undoing. With her arms raised to the reins and pommel, her jacket slid up and her waist was slender and warm in the circle of his hands.

Her smile was mischievous as he climbed up on his own mount.

"What?"

"I just wanted you to know, that kiss wasn't a thanks for how wonderfully you took care of me last night."

"Then what was it?"

She turned Snowflake and with a skilled nudge, sent her down the trail at an easy walk. "That," she called back over her shoulder, the only sound in the still morning other than the clopping of the horses' hooves. "That was just a preview. Like coming attractions at the movies."

Any ability to speak that Doug thought he'd regained was washed away. If that was a preview, he couldn't wait for the main feature. But the ranch was a long way off.

He looked back at Lucy and her foal who'd fallen in behind. "How fast can you walk?"

The horse declined to answer, instead settling into a slow shuffle.

"So, THE LOST IS FOUND," Mark greeted her cheerfully as Chelsea entered the ranch house kitchen.

"Seems so." It had taken seven hours to walk Lucy back. A long cold ride, but under a broken sky rather than a freezing rain. It was now mid-afternoon and the sky was once again darkening beneath an overcast. At least she'd be cozy and safe for the next storm.

"Tessa's down for her nap, so you can just relax. Where's Doug?"

"He's out at the isolation barn. He wants to keep the three horses and foal away from the herd until he's sure that they're not contagious."

"Good man."

"The best." Chelsea knew she'd never met a better one.

Mark looked at her curiously, and then headed for the door. "I'll just go and check on him."

"Do you know *anything* about horses?" She didn't know where the tease had come from. Women didn't tease men like Mark Henderson. But Doug had told her how Mark loved to fish, and almost always used an ATV rather than a horse to get there, so she couldn't resist.

He just winked at her and was gone.

Chelsea took a quiet minute to heat some leftover beef vegetable soup before sitting with it at the big kitchen table. It could seat a dozen without crowding. The kitchen was on the border between a generous farm kitchen and a small commercial one. It was cozy but also designed to feed a hungry hoard. She could imagine dinner parties here filled with laughter and good food.

"What would it be like to live here?" she asked the quiet kitchen. "How happy would it be?"

"Quite happy."

Chelsea startled and almost lost her soupspoon to the floor. For a startled second she thought the kitchen had answered her.

Then she spotted Emily Beale sitting quietly in a deep chair by the kitchen fireplace, a book in her lap. She rose smoothly and came to sit just around the corner of the table from Chelsea.

"The first time I came here, I was in absolute terror."

"You, in terror. Like I'm going to believe that."

Emily's smile was always a surprise and it was this time as well. "Seriously. I was engaged to my co-commander of an elite U.S. Army helicopter team—seriously bad from a regulation point of view—and about to meet his parents, one of whom had served twenty years as a Navy SEAL. I'd never gone fishing, never seen a horse up close, and never been to Montana."

Chelsea toyed with her soup. "This place is so amazing though; that must have helped."

"It did. Though not as much as realizing that Mark knew as little about horses as I did." Now Emily's smile turned rather wicked. "Mac and Ama bought the ranch after Mark had gone to West Point."

"So?" Chelsea tried to picture Mark not perfect at something and wasn't coming up with a good image.

"Let's just say that he ended up head over heels in the river and I didn't."

Chelsea held up a hand in salute, but was shocked when Emily actually high-fived it. "Women rule," Chelsea added weakly.

"We do," Emily agreed and offered her a smile of companionship that felt as crazy as everything else that had happened in the last two days.

"I've been very happy here," Emily continued though more as if she was speaking to herself. "It's a good place, as good as any I've ever been."

"I'll miss the ranch when we go."

Emily nodded, but was studying Chelsea carefully.

"What?"

Emily shook her head.

"Nope." Chelsea grabbed onto her bravery. "You don't get to do that."

"Do what?" Emily pretended all innocence.

Chelsea aimed her soupspoon at Emily, "Have that clear a thought and then not share it."

Emily considered for a long moment and then nodded at how that might be a reasonable demand. "Just remember."

"What?"

"You asked."

Chelsea swallowed hard. Why didn't she think she was going to like what came next? She nodded for Emily to go ahead anyway.

"It isn't the ranch that you'll be missing."

Her soupspoon slipped from nerveless fingers and landed in her bowl with a splash.

"Thought so," Emily remarked drily.

"Couldn't you at least have made it a question?"

Emily shook her head. "Why would I, when it isn't one."

"But we haven't even—"

"Doesn't matter. When it's the right one, the particulars don't matter. Trust me, I know."

"The right what? But—" Chelsea managed weakly wondering why she was trying to argue. She'd never met a man like Doug Daniels, a man who simply shone with the love inside him. He had such a passion for the land and the horses.

During the long, cold ride back from the fishing cabin, she and Doug had warmed the time with stories. He'd told her about his experiences overseas, so different from her own tramp abroad. In all of her travels, she'd never found anyone so easy to be with.

And the way he'd knelt before her in the cabin, naked and beautiful and so worried about offending as he treated her abraded legs with stinky liniment.

The way he'd held her last night. There couldn't be another man anywhere who wouldn't have taken advantage of the situation. But not Doug with his soldier's honor.

"I—"

But Emily was no longer there to explain things to. In the big kitchen was only the warm crackling of the fire, Chelsea, and a bowl of soup.

DOUG WAS SLUMPED *on* his couch. The grumbling in his stomach complained about missing dinner up at the main house; too frustrated to whip up something in his own kitchen. He hadn't been able to go because of what else he'd find there. What he was wanting so badly.

The knock on his front door had him racing to answer it. "Is Lucy…o…kay?" The only knock he'd been expecting had been Logan's if Lucy had a relapse. His nervous system was not ready for the vivid redhead standing on his front porch.

"Hi!" Her smile was big and again mischievous.

He had the feeling that he was suddenly in deep trouble.

"Do I get invited in? If not, I'm taking Emily's special homemade pizza back with me. She said that it's one of your favorites."

That's when he focused on the large covered tray Chelsea was carrying. Emily was an amazing cook, had won the hearts of Mac, himself, and every one of the ranch hands with a beef stew on her first visit to the ranch. But it was her from-scratch pizza that blew Doug away.

"Uh—" He looked back up at Chelsea. "I'd like to invite you in, but I don't think that's the best idea. Because if I do—" If he did, he couldn't be accountable for keeping his hands off her a second time. Last night he'd liked the brave and competent woman, and lusted after the redheaded knockout. On the long ride back, he'd also come to admire her deeply. She'd made some hard choices on her path, who hadn't. But hers had always come straight from the heart.

"—If you do invite me in," Chelsea picked up for him as she eased him slowly backward with the leading edge of a tray of pizza, "we just might enjoy ourselves beyond all imagining."

"Something like that," he managed.

"Good. I'm counting on it." She kicked off her boots, and carried the tray through his living room and into the kitchen as if she'd always lived here. "You were raised in a barn. Close the door; it's cold out there."

Helpless to argue, he did as she suggested and followed her into the kitchen.

"I'm sorry," she set the tray on top of the cold stove.

"Sorry for what?"

"The pizza and the tiny ranch house tour are going to have to come later. I can't wait any longer." She shed her gloves and jacket and dropped them to the floor. Then she walked straight into his arms.

THEY HAD **cold pizza** while sitting among their clothes on the kitchen floor. Doug reheated some after they'd made prolonged use of the living room sofa; long enough to have to restock the fire. They finished the last of the meal on their way upstairs when she went hunting for the bedroom; a search that was gloriously rewarded.

"Did we miss anywhere?" Chelsea lay sprawled over him, sore in so many wonderful ways. She'd never done anything like this. Never had so much fun having sex either. Doug's blend of powerful yet gentle, of roughly needy and deeply giving had enthralled and sated her like no one before.

"Uh, big bathroom, second bedroom, home office."

"Oh." They'd probably kill each other if they tried for all of them tonight.

"Back porch lit by June moonlight," he mumbled on. "There's a set of waterfalls with a hot spring about a three-hour hike above the fishing cabin that shouldn't scare off a woman who had hiked in the Himalayas. The open prairie on a warm May afternoon where you'd outshine the sun. I'll show you—"

She put her fingers over his mouth to stop him and he kissed the fingertips.

"I like your imagination," she propped herself up on his chest and looked down into his dark eyes. "So the sex is good."

"Incredible," he agreed.

"You love what you do?"

"I do," he agreed just as equably.

"And you've spent two days and two nights fantasizing about having me beside you forever."

"Yep."

She waited for it. Perhaps it was unfair. Giving a man his favorite food then making love to him multiple times; his defenses were pretty much gone.

But there was no shock of recognition at what she'd just said. No startled disclaimer that he wasn't dumb enough to extrapolate two days into a lifetime.

"Whoa there!" It was supposed to have been a tease.

"As the lady once said," he grinned up at her. "Hello! Not a horse."

"Hold on."

"The way I figure it," she could feel his chest rippling against hers as he spoke, "it's actually been two days and three nights. I think we're closer to sunrise than sunset. So, we've already made it twenty-five percent longer than what you said."

"Douglas," she warned him.

"Just Doug. Nobody calls me Douglas, not even Mom."

"Douglas!"

"Yes, Chelsea?"

"Does it make any sense?"

"Nope. Not a bit," and his voice remained merry.

"Aren't you even a little surprised?"

"Nope."

"Why not?" Chelsea's own thoughts were in such turmoil, they might as well be a wheeling herd of horses.

"Got over it in the barn while taking care of Lucy."

"A *horse* told you that we'd be spending our lives together? Even from horseboy, I'm not buying that one." *Spending our lives together* and still no flinch on his part. She checked in with herself. Even stranger, there wasn't a flinch on her part either.

"No, from Mark."

"Mark?" was all she managed.

"Yep! I was out making sure Lucy and the other horses were all settled in, when he came out to the barn."

"What did he say?" Chelsea was pretty sure she didn't want to know. She went to roll off Doug's chest, but he trapped her in place with a hand resting lightly on her hip. Just enough to tell her she was retreating, not enough that she couldn't get away. *Fine!* She could take it if he could, and rolled back into place.

"He said that you were one of the nicest young women he'd ever met and I'd never find any better. That part I agreed with readily enough," Doug nodded emphatically as if marking such an outrageous statement as simple truth. "And if I was too stupid to see that you were already in love with me, he'd be glad to pound some sense into me."

She let his "love" statement go by for the moment.

"Do you think they set us up?" She wasn't sure if she'd be angry or not, but wanted to know.

"My question too. Mark said no. Emily's not much sneakier than he is, so I'm guessing the answer there is also no. I suspect that we did this to ourselves."

"We…what?" But it was lame and she knew it. Emily had said the same thing, or why else was Chelsea here in bed with Doug?

This time when she pushed away, he let her go.

Chelsea wrapped a blanket around her shoulders and moved to look out the window. The yard rolled away into the darkness. Faint lights marked the barns, a lone porch light up at the main ranch house.

Could she be happy here? Working horses, sharing this gorgeous land with visitors? In a heartbeat.

With this man?

Doug slipped up behind her and wrapped his arms across her shoulders.

How was she supposed to know something like that so quickly?

Even if she already did?

Emily had said she recognized that he was the right one for her. As if she knew what love looked like. Well, if any woman did, it would be Emily Beale.

Chelsea leaned back against Doug—and the rightness was there. It ran so deep that she couldn't imagine being anywhere else.

"So I was thinking," he whispered in her ear.

She hummed with pleasure, couldn't help herself.

"How about we just try each other on for size? You and me."

"And the horses."

She could more feel his laugh than hear it.

"And the horses. We'll agree to make no decisions at all until the snow melts."

"But there isn't any snow," she waved a hand toward the window.

He didn't speak, instead he pointed. In the faint lights, she could see the first flakes spinning down out of the sky.

"A white Christmas," she managed on a tight breath.

He wrapped his arms around her a little more tightly.

Doug was right, they needed time to decide if what was between them was real or not.

But she knew. Her wandering days were done.

A white Christmas together.

Chelsea turned in Doug's arms and kissed him. She knew right down to her heart that this was only the first of so many to come.

REACHING OUT AT HENDERSON'S RANCH (HENDERSON'S RANCH #2)

(EXCERPT)

*H*e reached to console the frightened villager child.

Stan Corman knew it was dangerous, but he couldn't stop his hand. His left hand kept moving closer though some part of him screamed for it to withdraw, to fall by his side.

The boy, no more than five, could have been his nephew Jack. They had the same tousled dark hair, though Jack's skin was far lighter.

His hand continued to reach.

Deep inside himself, Stan cursed and fought, but his arm moved without his willing it.

No control.

Except his eyes. Though his hand remained out of his control, he could see with his eyes.

Stan could see the little boy's fear—his eyes so wide that the dark irises were almost lost in the vast field of white. He'd knelt so that they were eye to eye. Then Stan looked down and he could see his dog Lucy abruptly sit, close in front of the boy.

Lucy wasn't supposed to sit without a command unless—

Stan's hand brushed the boy's arm.

Lucy whined.

She was a military war dog and was trained to sit and be still when she smelled—

The boy disappeared in a cloud of light that slammed Stan into the void.

The scream tearing out of his throat ripped him from nightmare to darkness.

Absolute darkness...except for the afterimage of an exploding boy etched so deeply on his retina that it was all he'd been able to see when he woke in the hospital.

Now, months away, he tried to rub at his eyes as his pulse peaked somewhere past skyrocket and began a slow fall that Stan knew from experience would banish any hope of sleep for hours.

But there was no hand to rub his eyes with, only a fleshy stump remained of his left hand. His other hand was tangled in the sheets and for a long awful moment he was sure he had lost that one as well. Before he could scream again, he managed to pull it free and pressed his hand to his face.

Five.

He counted four fingers and a thumb pressed from jaw to forehead. Flesh and blood. He could feel them. Five. His right hand still remained intact.

As did the image of the exploding boy.

Stan's life had been saved because the boy's parents—or whatever total bastard had wired the kid up—had rigged the explosives too low. The alignment of explosive and Stan's life had been almost entirely shielded by Lucy's body.

The helmet had protected his head, the goggles his eyes, and except for nasty scarring on his left cheek, the rest of him had been behind armor and dog. Lucy had taken the hit and like a nuclear blast burn image, the shape of her had been imprinted on his lower face and chest in blood and bone fragments. The rest had healed: the dozen broken ribs where parts of Lucy had slammed into him, the concussion from the wall he'd been thrown into so hard that even his helmet hadn't saved him from that. They'd managed to save his left calf and knee with screws and titanium plates, but had warned him it would always be fragile. Just what every SEAL wanted to be labeled: fragile.

He lay in a cot. His pulse had slowed enough—though the rate of his breathing hadn't yet—for him to feel the hard chill of the cabin. The fire had gone out, which meant it was past three a.m.

It was a good sign. Usually the nightmare woke him by midnight in plenty of time to restoke the small cast iron woodstove for the long, sleepless dark watch. He considered waiting until dawn under the covers, but experience also had taught him to get up and build the fire now or the cabin would stay frosty until midday.

A North Carolina boy, his only experience with true cold before now had been on assignment. The Afghan winters had been brutal, but that's where Special Operations said to go—so he and Lucy went.

Lucy. Shit. They'd been together for two years in-country. She was six months dead and he still missed her every damn day.

He snapped on a flashlight, for all the good it did him. All he could see right now was the little Afghan boy etched in light. The doctors insisted that it was psychosomatic rather than retinal damage because doctors made shit like that up when they didn't know what was going on. The only part of his vision that he could use for the next hour would be in the one dark, dog-shaped patch that had been Lucy in the lower right corner of his vision.

He swung out of his bunk, tipped his head back and to the side so that he could see where he was going, and crossed to the woodstove. Grabbing the handle without a hot pad had him yelping again—not pain but a sharp, panicked sound that rang harshly in the small cabin. If he damaged his right hand he'd be beyond fucked. It was all he had left. He sucked on the slight warmth on his palm as if it was a second-degree burn, cursing the damn stove for still being hot to the touch, but not heating the cabin.

Reaching with his other hand didn't help. The paired titanium hooks of his prosthetic arm didn't care about the heat, but he hadn't pulled the rig on and all he had to wave about was his fucking stump.

Fumbling toward the woodpile, which was on the side he couldn't see, he found a small log and used it to whack the metal handle upward and swing the door open. For its duty and fine service, he chucked the log onto the few remaining embers inside.

Raising one knee, he propped a small bellows on his thigh and pinned its lower handle in place with his stump. With his remaining hand, he worked the upper handle until he coaxed a small snap of flame to life. It was bright enough to shine through the boy's afterimage. Carefully stoking the fire, he watched the flame grow as the boy faded.

The stove wasn't throwing much heat yet; all of the iron had cooled...except the goddamn handle. But he didn't move away. His bare skin rippled with goosebumps, but he remained to watch the flame.

When he'd first come to this small cabin in the Montana foothills, he'd spent many nights contemplating throwing his fake arm into the fire and then himself. At first he only resisted because he knew he'd piss off the ranch owner, and you didn't piss off a man like Mac Henderson or his son Mark.

Mac was a former SEAL—except he'd done his twenty years and retired. Being a SEAL, it was an easy bet that Mac would have followed Stan straight into hell and dragged him back to whup him good for throwing away the gift of life.

Gift of life, my ass.

It was early April. Back in North Carolina, the Sweet William would be blooming right now. The cherry blossoms would have already had their spring and the young cottonwood leaves would be unfolding to seek the sun.

Instead, he was squatting in front of a cold fire in a ramshackle cabin on the edge of the Montana wilderness surrounded by snow.

Keep reading this completed series at fine retailers everywhere:
Christmas at Henderson's Ranch
Reaching Out at Henderson's Ranch
Nathan's Big Sky

Welcome at Henderson's Ranch
Big Sky, Loyal Heart
Finding Henderson's Ranch
Emily's Christmas Gift
Big Sky Dog Whisperer

M.L. BUCHMAN
AUTHOR OF THE NARA REACTION
Relive the DAY!
a time travel story

RELIVE THE DAY!

A story of New York-

***Katrine Feinberg** is an acclaimed artist. Her mother's death reveals a true surprise. She too was an artist, in her youth.*

A new technology offers Katrine the chance to go back and live for a time in her mother's memories. A chance to learn how art could be lost.

But can she handle the truth when she chooses to Relive the Day!

INTRODUCTION

This is a very curious story for me in many ways.

I love science fiction, I read little else for over fifteen years of my youth. I'm also a moderately rabid fan of SF movies and television series. But until recently, I've written very little of it.

Relive the Day! is one of my very early ones.

One of the real curiosities of this story is that while genetically I'm 100% Ashkenazi Jew, I've actually had very little exposure to the culture.

I feel that in writing this story, it is perhaps the closest I've ever come to understanding that lost piece of my heritage. Not in the choices the character makes, but perhaps in why she makes them.

RELIVE THE DAY!

" *R*elive the Day!"

Katrine Feinberg would rather be shot than relive this one. She looked away from the damned billboard that drew the eye no matter how often she refused its brilliantly cheerful design. The things had sprung up like weeds over the last year, a whole new market… billboards over graveyards.

"Before it's too late!" The unwritten half of the phrase forced its way into her mind despite her best efforts to avoid it. She was too tired, that was all that was going on.

Turned from the sign, she was once again forced to look at what lay before her. Beneath the dull gray and drifting snowflakes of the December sky, spread the vast array of a quarter-million Jews all lying under the soil of the Mt. Zion Cemetery in Queens, New York.

Thanks for the Christmas memory, Mom. Okay, perhaps that was a sacrilegious thought considering where her feet were shuffling back and forth trying to stay warm, but the two had now been tied together in her mind. Dead on Christmas Day. Who knew what it would take for her to unblend those two brushstrokes on the canvas of her life.

A tattered black ribbon pinned over her left breast fluttered in the chill breeze. It symbolized the rending of clothes and marked her as one who had lost a parent. The other mourners wore the black ribbon over their right breast, mourning a friend.

Her mama didn't draw much of a crowd. Mrs. Zimmel and her sister from the brownstone walkup in Brooklyn where her mother, Rachel Feinberg, had lived most of her life until her husband had died and she'd moved in with Katrine two years ago. Three people from the art supply store on Atlantic Ave where she'd worked until just weeks before the tumor took her. That was all that could get the afternoon off at the same time. The owner, Herman Motz, had called and offered to pay for part of the service, but she'd turned him down. He had his own sick mother to tend. A couple of Katrine's friends had come despite her asking them not to, including the curator of the SoHo Gallery who sold much of her artwork, each of them attending had surprised and touched her more than she expected.

Dead just twenty-four hours and her mother was already sent into the ground. No other family to fly in. No reason to delay what the faith said to do quickly. Katrine had not seen her mother again after they pulled the sheet over her face in the hospital, one did not look upon someone who could not look back. A simple wood casket, no embalming, and only a small spread of her favorite winter jasmine, blooms of yellow resting on the unfinished pine, as it was lowered into the earth. Each mourner spread several shovels of earth into the dark hole, their offer of assistance to the deceased.

Katrine spoke the eulogy in her turn, her voice flat upon the air. What did one say of the dead? She was a good mother. She was proud of my success and supported me in my art when my father had turned his back upon us. She was a quiet woman. She even went to temple on most of the high holidays, more than Katrine could claim. She was content with a simple life.

The Rabbi read the psalm in a nasally voice and it was done.

They all waited despite the cold and the snow while the gravediggers finished filling the grave. They stood to witness that all was properly done as it should be.

It was an atonement on behalf of the dead, this standing in the snow while listening to the rapid, slick sounds of the shovels and breathing shallowly in caution against the biting air. A final offering for the one who could no longer see, act, or show thanks on their own behalf.

When at last her mother was buried beneath the fresh-turned earth, Katrine looked back up into the fluttering flakes that floated like down and landed on her cheeks like frozen kisses.

"Relive the Day!"

KATRINE'S MOTHER had organized everything. Knowing her death was imminent, they had together sorted through all of the papers, sold books, and discarded memories that belonged to Rachel Feinberg and not to her daughter Katrine. All that remained were four boxes that her mother had made her promise to not throw out while she lived and not open before throwing out after she died.

Katrine now stood in the back bedroom of her Brooklyn Heights apartment and stared at the four boxes. They were too heavy for her to pick up. She had her mother's light build. Appropriate for a painter, but not for moving heavy boxes. She should hire someone to take them to the dump for her, but that didn't seem respectful.

With an apology to the departed, she knelt and opened the first box, the tape crackling with age, a roll of garbage bags beside her.

Yet one more last act of atonement.

"SO HOW DOES THIS WORK?" Katrine had read the website, but she'd wanted to look someone in the eye while she asked her questions.

The representative of "Relive the Day" was about what she'd expected. A perky, sharply dressed blond-haired, blue-eyed man in his mid-twenties named Ricky who hit the gym most days but clearly was never exposed to direct sunlight. Barely able to contain himself, he expounded on this "lightyearsleap," he made it one word, of technology. The incredible breakthroughs. Reliving the momen…

She waved him to silence. Katrine hated to think that she was so jaded in her early forties. The Internet had "arrived" while she was in college. E-mail, website, laptops, tablets, the first interface glasses from Google…she'd been an adult for all of that. But these guys claimed they were selling time travel.

The on-line customer reviews were unprecedented solid fives. And there was no arguing about their financial success. Their office space, perched on the ninety-fifth floor in the barely finished One World Trade Center, offered an expansive view of New York. The Empire State Building in mid-town was down and below, the Chrysler Building almost invisibly small but for its distinctive art deco spire.

"Most people think it's a trick," the man sipped his mocha from the fine porcelain mug bearing his company's logo.

The artist in her had to admire the design, the shapes invited, the colors soothed. There really was no way to not be captivated by the "Relive the Day" logo, even when wrapped around a container for hot liquids.

"It really isn't," his insistence was heartfelt. He was a believer. "Your mind does travel back in time. Though your body remains here, your mind is truly back in time."

"Suspended animation?"

"More like sleep." His words were as neatly punctuated as his sentences. "But it is real. Your mind actually travels, though your body remains in this time. You can touch, feel, interact. Your subject will not be aware of you, but you can guide them. Not every choice will be yours, it appears that actions must remain within the ethical bounds of the person you are reliving with. You will know their thoughts. You will have a clear vision of what are now but hazy memories. You will feel their feelings, experience what they experience. First kiss. First, well…" He tapered off as if being tactful but clearly this was one of their hot selling points.

How many wouldn't like to redo the first time they made love? *If only I knew now what I didn't know then, it surely wouldn't have been with Robbie Berkowitz.* Jeffrey Hamilton had been equally willing, but he'd been a *goyim* and she knew her father wouldn't approve if she made love to a non-Jew. Not that he'd have approved of his only child having unmarried sex at seventeen no matter who was between her legs. She'd been careful to make sure he never found that one out.

By the time she was out of college, he'd given up on her because of her choice of art and of the lovers she'd eventually chosen to flaunt at him. His hopes for a good Jewish grandson to carry on his bloodline had slowly scraped away beneath a long line of European, African, and Asian men who had graced her bed, though she'd married none of them. She'd considered bringing home one or even two of her lesbian friends just to tweak him, but had never quite had the heart to be that pointlessly cruel.

"How about travel into another person's memories?"

"Who would you like? Shakespeare? Jesus? Mata Hari?" He managed to grin without making it salacious, a look he clearly had practiced with care. "I'm sorry, but we are confined to approximately the last hundred years for technical reasons that I don't understand."

"My mother."

That stopped him. "We don't typically received such a request. Moment of your conceptio—" He cut himself off. In his momentary lapse revealing quite how one track his mind, and that of most of his clients, might be.

"Before that."

"Oh," was all he could think to say.

"How is it that someone can go back, make changes, relive a different past, and not change the future?"

"Good question. Most people don't think about that." He picked up a small remote control, nearly the only adornment on his desk. Of course they already had a neat presentation on that. In moments, the view of Manhattan had dimmed as darkened glass slid into place. Smooth, silent, very expensive.

A hidden projector came on, aimed at a white sidewall that they could both conveniently turn to without leaving their chairs.

"The solid line is the past. It is unchanging, immutable." He traced it with a bright red laser a few times as if that made it more real. "Then, we inject your mind back in time."

A sparkle appeared in the timeline and a date popped up of her eighteenth birthday. Obviously a popular moment, lifted and programmed from the simple pre-interview questionnaire they'd had her complete.

"At this moment, you begin a new timeline." The timeline jogged to the side, and was brightly labeled in a rippling run from left to right, "New Experiences." Whoever did their graphics was awfully good. It was the correct pace to draw the human eye and also raise her pulse rate ever so slightly.

"We have determined that there is only a singular flow of time and that time is very resilient. So, when you return..." Another click and the new timeline stopped abruptly. A thin arrow sent her back to the present. Then the timeline that had jogged to the side, rippled right back into the main flow of time and was reabsorbed.

"We can determine no offset value. You recall both your real past and your relived past, but only the real one will have occurred. If you choose to remain in the past for minutes or years, murder your grandfather... It doesn't matter, time will heal itself once you depart."

"You said years, but how..."

He smiled at her with his over-whitened teeth. "Quite simple, really. Again, recall how resilient time is. You are locked in the present by the on-going existence of your body. When you dream, the dreamtime may appear to last for hours though we know in reality that it will last mere seconds to the sleeping person. If you stay in the past a day or a decade, it is only a matter of a few moments here."

"And I can return when I wish by...?"

"We provide a pass-phrase, you must use it to return. When you do, your 'Reliving of the Day' is terminated."

❄

IT WAS while reading the paperwork that Katrine noted the "hold harmless" clause.

"Oh that? Standard lawyer stuff. Most people just sign it," Ricky assured her.

She recalled the one time a particularly gorgeous Greek man had convinced her to jump out of a plane on a tandem parachute jump. The paperwork had been very explicit regarding their complete lack of liability if you died, were dismembered, disabled, and a long list of various, but very clearly detailed, bodily and mental injuries. She had neither jumped that day nor the Greek man ever again.

"Does any of this happen?" The list was not as gory as the parachute list, but it did include total brain death.

"One in a hundred thousand," was the whispered answer when she pushed. "Ten times safer than riding a motorcycle." Overly bright and cheerful.

That was probably any injury on a motorcycle compared with total brain death riding the "Relive the Day" road into the past. The fact that he had that figure on tap did not bode well.

She signed the form.

AFTER THAT, it had been so simple. Swipe the credit card, sign the little tablet, and lie back in the chair. Like a dentist's chair with a 1950s hair dryer conehead on it. They taught Katrine the ridiculous but impossible to forget code phrase and recorded the brain wave patterns it generated. Think it three times in a row with no interruptions and she'd be back.

She closed her eyes and opened them to stare upon a canvas.

Rachel Steinmetz was not dead beneath the cold earth in Queens, New York. She did not yet bear the name on the stone planted above her head, the name of her husband not yet met, not of her daughter not yet born.

It was 1970. She was eighteen. And she stood considering a canvas she had just finished painting.

Katrine looked out through her mother's eyes. The painting was vibrant with color. Life slashed across the cloth. But anger mixed in with it. Katrine recognized the blood of war, the angst of battle, the pain of death, all tangled in a field of grass green and fall golds.

She had found it, while sitting on the floor of her own Brooklyn apartment. Her mother had taken it from the frame and folded into one of the four boxes that even now sat over forty years in the future, their contents spread about the back bedroom and tacked to the walls.

The painting's oil-based paint had cracked along the folds; the canvas, gone stiff with decades of storage, had unfolded only reluctantly. Across the back had been taped a fading copy of *Where Have All the Flowers Gone?* A date had been scrawled across the bottom of the typewritten page, scrawled in a hand Katrine knew almost as well as her own. It was one of the few dates on any of the works in the four boxes and Katrine had chosen it as her target date to relive her mother's memories.

Now the two women artists contemplated the brand new painting together. The mother artist well satisfied, at least as satisfied as she ever was with a painting. The daughter artist in awe of a facet of her mother she'd known about for less than forty-eight hours. Not once in all those years had her mother mentioned art except in supporting her daughter's desire to paint, but she'd left behind four boxes packed with paintings, sketches, charcoals, and pastels. Stacked layer upon layer, they had shown the evolution of an artistic talent.

This piece, Katrine recognized, as being near the end of the cycle. Only a few dozen more pieces had followed, ending abruptly as if the artist had been snipped off, cut out of existence only a few months after this painting.

Pleased with the painting, Rachel turned.

Katrine did not recognize this room. It was a New York artist's loft, studio and living space combined. Out the window, a peekaboo view of the Brooklyn Bridge revealed itself between a red brick apartment building and the deep red clock on the top of *The Watchtower* building. Old wooden floors suggested a partitioned warehouse. The twin mattress on the floor, bookshelves of apple crates, and primitive kitchen told that the art didn't pay well. But Katrine could see the potential, certainly as much or more than she'd shown at that age.

When her mother crossed in front of a mirror, Katrine had to stop and stare and her mother's body had responded without any unusual thought.

Katrine saw herself in the mirror. Just as she'd looked at twenty. Same fine face. Same slight body with good breasts. Though unlike her own severe, studied style in black, her mother wore a thin peasant blouse dropping off one shoulder and spattered with stray blotches of paint and no bra. As exposed as any risqué runway model forty years in the future. So much for perceived changes of social mores.

It was the hair that stunned her. Rather than a sharp cut as befit Katrine the urban artist of the future, it billowed in a glorious, dark, ever-widening ruffle down to her butt. Her mother was a hippie artist.

Katrine did little to direct her mother. Instead they simply lived together.

Her mother was a world of contrasts. In old age, she had been a quiet woman who sold art supplies and cooked for her husband and her daughter on the few occasions her child bothered to come home. In her youth, she had been an artist filled with vitality, at least on the outside.

Rachel Steinmetz was often at the center of political debate, attended every anti-Vietnam War demonstration she could, read far more widely than most and hence carried a force of argument that few others could match.

But inside, in a place others didn't see but Katrine now lived, her mother was a quiet, thoughtful woman. On Friday evenings, when she could slip away from her friends, she covered her hair and her body and attended Shabbat service at Temple. She didn't believe in a God who could allow war. But she was drawn by the sense of past and connection to who she was.

Katrine had rejected her past as strongly as possible, though she'd balked at changing her name, often boasting that her art had become known before she'd had a chance to do so. Her rare trips to Temple were always to accompany her mother, never for herself.

Her mother had begun to find a peace, a place that she might belong in the world. Katrine still fought for her place every day seeking to be edgy, *avant-garde*, different. Katrine wondered at how her mother's inner quiet might change Katrine's own art after her return. According to *The Village Voice* Katrine was already known as, "a visionary offering a sharp critique on passé modernism." Collectors said much the same and her prices had risen accordingly. She'd worried about trends in art, not in the world around her. Her mother was the opposite.

It took Katrine weeks to understand the possibilities. She could discover how her experiences were shaping her art through her mother. At first her mother was awkward about it. Her hands and her eyes had not been trained in techniques that didn't yet exist, some of which Katrine herself had developed. However, working together, they slowly discovered new form, new richness, new depth.

Rachel Steinmetz had always sold her art at street fairs or in Central Park. Now she'd been spotted and when she had her first joint show in a tiny Brooklyn Gallery with three other artists several pieces sold.

Katrine knew the business world, knew which galleries, even now in the past, were run by the innovative thinkers who would shape the future, but she didn't have Rachel pursue them. This timeline would cease to exist when Katrine finally departed, all that mattered was the art and the relationship with her mother.

RACHEL TRIED POT, but didn't like it anymore than Katrine would in college. It blurred the inner vision rather than enhancing it.

They took casual lovers and sweat and moaned together on the thin mattress in the artist's loft.

Eventually, the Manhattan gallery owners discovered the new visions of Rachel Steinmetz.

At her first solo show, at a very "in" gallery at the heart of Greenwich Village. Rachel and Katrine, despite all of the doctrine against outer appearances mattering, had fussed for hours choosing the right skirt, even considered a mini but decided against it. They'd chosen yet another off-the-shoulder peasant blouse, a soft blue one, open leather sandals, and bare legs.

She'd left her hair long and full. Rachel had been in favor of hacking it off, even to an outrageously short Twiggy style, but Katrine had insisted. It billowed and swirled and everyone remarked on it. Including a handsome, energized man.

At first Katrine did not recognize Zalman Feinberg. When had her father gotten so stern and conservative? This man wore a sharp tweed blazer and had ridiculously in-fashion sideburns. He had dark eyes and, once spotted, was on a clear mission to bed the artist.

Katrine couldn't decide at first if she wanted to relive this particular conquest. It was only as he had nearly shuffled Rachel out of the door of her first major show that Katrine woke up. They actually made it to the threshold before Katrine was able to dig in her heels and stop her mother from being charmed.

This was the moment. Perhaps this was why Katrine had returned to relive this time, to stop this one instant from happening.

If Rachel slept with this man tonight, she would become pregnant.

A pregnancy that would lead to a marriage.

A daughter named Katrine would be born, but an artist would die and turn into an old woman selling art supplies to others.

Katrine actually wrapped one of Rachel's hands around the door frame and held on until she could turn from the powerful steamroller that was a young Zalman Feinberg. She did not know how he became such a conservative, why he had such a need to control and destroy the very artistic energy that had drawn him to choose Rachel Steinmetz as a conquest.

Perhaps it was Katrine herself who had changed him. Perhaps Zalman Feinberg became as trapped by Rachel's pregnancy as Rachel became trapped by an enforced marriage.

Not this time.

Katrine did not allow Rachel to let go of the door frame until Zalman Feinberg had stormed off, disappointed in his night's lack of victory.

TOGETHER RACHEL and Katrine made art that bloomed.

The "First True Voice of the '70s" had stunned the art world, partly with her innovative techniques, but mostly with her depth of vision. When her mother painted, even without Katrine's participation, or perhaps especially without it, all the power of a sharp mind and a deeply caring heart glowed upon the canvases.

Katrine was constantly stunned at the power that surged from the depths of her mother's soul and her mother's art. She had given Rachel Steinmetz the techniques to express what she was feeling, but her mother created the art that Katrine could never have imagined despite her future success.

KATRINE SPENT a lot of time considering her choices. She often forgot that she was but a visitor to this time.

But then she would recall that her journey was not real and would only last until she repeated a phrase three times in her head. The loss to her mother and to the art world made her sad beyond imagining, beyond tolerance. She was enough of an artist that she could recreate her mother's work in the future, but she would never be able to produce the freshness and power by herself.

What would happen if she stayed? If she never repeated that phrase three times?

The "complete brain death" clause of the contract and release form filed at "Relive the Day" would probably come into effect. Not long after, an even smaller crowd would visit the gray cemetery and stand witness to the internment of one Katrine Feinberg who had showed such promise.

What would happen to this timeline, the one in which her mother thrived, if Katrine didn't end it? She wished she could go back and ask that question, but perhaps they didn't know.

Of course they would know. Too may "failures to return to the present."

Or was the human spirit strong enough to maintain that timeline if it wasn't ended by her own conscious departure?

ROGER CARLSON HAD STARTED as a casual lover. Not one drawn by Rachel's art, but rather by a chance meeting over lox and bagels at a small coffee shop just off Carroll Gardens. On their third date, Rachel took him to her small loft studio, a place she spent most of her time despite the much nicer apartment she now kept a few blocks away.

He claimed not to understand art, but he thought hers looked nice.

They made love for the first time surrounded by her paintings.

THE ART WORLD commented quietly on the change in the art of the great Rachel Steinmetz. Richer, deeper, full of dreams and joy.

It was an element Katrine had never brought to the canvas, never thought to, never imagined such a thing existed.

Katrine could feel herself fading. As if she became thinner and thinner, or slept more and more as her mother's life continued.

Except in this timeline, Rachel Steinmetz had not married Zalman Feinberg for an unplanned pregnancy. Instead, she was three months pregnant and six months married to man she had fallen in love with.

Katrine had wished that she had eyes to cry with aside from her mother's, tears of her own loss for never seeking the love that her mother had found. A love so true that it soared into her art each day. It made her mother more whole than Katrine, despite all her superior attitude about an old Jewish woman. Rachel Steinmetz became more than Katrine had ever imagined, never mind achieved.

Katrine had a theory.

The reason that "Relive the Day" never knew about what happened to those few who didn't return was because they had all reached a similar conclusion to her own. By remaining in the past, by forcing their timeline to continue, the true past would realign ever so slightly to include the new version of the past.

By remaining in her mother's past, she had known more joy, more art, more truth, and more love than she ever find if she returned. And if she remained, her mother's new life would follow its path and continue as a part of the one real line of time. Her daughter would never walk into Relive the Day hoping to even Live the Day.

"Relive the Day" was indeed a true time machine. She had entered the past and now understood how to change it. The operators in the future would never know, because it was their one true past she would be changing.

Katrine allowed her thoughts to fade, allowed herself to forget the return phrase, and to not care when she did.

When the time came, when the tiny, squalling girl was born, Katrine roused herself for one final act. It would be the ultimate act of atonement, the gift to the living that only the dead could give.

"I THINK we should call her Katrine," Rachel Steinmetz said to the man crushing her hand in his, his face abashed with wonder and love.

M.L. BUCHMAN
NPR and B&N Top 5 Romance Author of the Year
"Will blow the readers' minds and leave them awestruck."
Romantic Times, Pure Heat
4-1/2 stars
Firelights of Christmas
a Firehawks romance story

THE FIRELIGHTS OF CHRISTMAS

atsy Jurgen's first season as foreman of a wildfire hotshot crew burns up her nerves. She fights to do her best for her crew and to create the firefighting career she always dreamed of. Falling in love? An unwanted distraction.

***Sam Parker** bought the bakery in the mountain resort town of Leavenworth, Washington. He intends to bury all memory of his last relationship in an avalanche of Bavarian treats. Woman-free? Definitely the way to go.*

But neither of them counted on the heat of the Firelights of Christmas.

INTRODUCTION

I had a mentor tell me years ago, "No one wants to watch average characters. We want to watch the exceptional character, even when that person is just the kid next door perhaps discovering just what she can be."

Emily and Mark, who eventually launched the Henderson's Ranch series, had first launched the heli-aviation wildland firefighter series, Firehawks. But as I was researching these amazing fliers, I couldn't help but learn about the smokejumpers, so I wrote the Firehawks Smokejumpers trilogy. Then I had to write short stories about the Lookouts who watch for the fire, the Hotshots who hike in to fight wildfire face to face, and even a smaller heli-aviation outfit that I named the Firebirds.

This next pair of stories, set in the Hotshots world, are both Christmas romance tales. I included both of them for two reasons.

One, this is a collection of my Christmas stories.

But two, I find it fascinating that they were written just two years apart. I almost find it hard to believe that I wrote both of them.

I enjoy the first story, but how much I grew as a writer and a person in those two years is amazing to me. I find that growth to be incredibly affirming and hopeful. It is something I worked to teach my kid: practice *can* work wonders.

The first story is good, but the second is one of my top five favorites of the more than eighty that I've written to date. Maybe it's more than just practice. Maybe it was "meeting" the lead character.

THE FIRELIGHTS OF CHRISTMAS

"Rise and shine," Patsy Jurgen swept down the hall of the Cascade Hotshots barracks. This was their first wildland firefighting season, the newest hotshot team in the country. And the worn-out, board-and-batten building was their new home. She thumped the side of her fist once on each wooden door, making them rattled loudly on old hinges.

She smiled to herself. It had taken her six years to make foreman of an Interagency Hotshot Crew and this was about the nicest place she'd ever lived. She'd heard some of the new recruits griping good-naturedly about a "hardship post." Once the fire season hit, they wouldn't be in residence here in Leavenworth, Washington all that often. And after their first month or so walking to the wildfires, they'd bless having running water, a cot, and a roof that only leaked a little.

After two weeks of recruit selection and three more of intense training, the twenty hotshots had really come together. The old hands and the new were blending well. They had yet to be tested by anything more strenuous than a prescribed burn to cut fuel levels in untended fields around the mountain town, but she knew the real thing would be happening all too soon.

Not soon enough for her.

Candace Cantrell's phone call that she was forming up the Cascade IHC had brought Patsy running. Cantrell had been a kick-ass foreman on the San Juan IHC and Patsy wanted to lead her own crew someday. She couldn't ask for a better slot that being Cantrell's foreman, her Number Two. Of course she had to share that particular slot, one super and two foremen to a crew.

Jess Monroe, the other foreman, opened his barrack door before she could thump it.

"Yeah, yeah! I'm up already, Jurgen." He didn't look it, but she knew from overlapping him on various crews over the years that he wasn't a morning person and the only thing that really woke him up fast was a fire. He wore shorts, and nothing else. He was hotshot fit, muscle rippled along his legs and chest.

"Day one, Monroe." Candace had just informed her team last night that she'd let the Forest Service know the Cascade IHC was ready for call out. A real testament to her skill as a superintendent that they'd trained up so fast, because Patsy agreed. They were ready.

"Day one," he looked down at his watch. "Still early yet. Wanna come in and celebrate?" He held the door a little wider. As foreman, he had a room to himself instead of a two-bunk, just as she did.

"I think you're still dreaming, Jess." The man would flirt with a burning tree. He never pushed; teasing women was just some kind of a game to him. Most flirted back and they all seemed to have fun with it. A skill she'd never had nor wanted. She reached out and pulled his door shut—with him on one side and her on the other.

It wasn't *that* early. She'd woken everyone just early enough to ease into it and eat before the day's planned exercise.

Candace and Luke Rawlings, one of the newest recruits, had gotten a small apartment also close by the fire station. The heat between them was amazing to watch; it was just so…right. Candace had always been deadly serious about hotshotting; fire chief's daughter, no big surprise. But with Luke she glowed like, well, like she was happy.

Patsy hadn't seen that one coming at all. Candace was so dedicated to wildfire that she had become a role model for Patsy. Her suddenly finding love was like a crack in Patsy's worldview—one she still didn't know what to do with.

Patsy had woken before sunrise, an old habit, and gone outside to watch the day break before waking the others. The sun had lit the towering peaks of the Cascade Mountains which climbed up to the west of Leavenworth eventually topping out at Stevens Pass. The line of sunlight had moved down the conifer and gray rock-covered slopes like the slice of a knife, the line was so clean. To the east, the mountains fell away into hills headed for the rolling sagebrush and orchard steppes of Eastern Washington.

On the silent air, broken only by a blue jay's call, the scent of pine washed through the river valley. Dry pine. It was only June, but already she knew it was going to be a hot summer and a busy fire season. They'd been smart to sponsor a hotshot crew here.

Now that everyone was awake, but not moving yet, she was suddenly at loose ends. So she walked the couple blocks into the sleeping town; hadn't had a moment to breathe during training to give it the once over. All of her prior postings had been pretty far out into the nothing. "Town" usually meant a church, a grocery store that was also a gas station, and a pizza joint that was more importantly the sole bar. But here, the Cascade hotshots had been formed by Chelan County and posted in a resort town surrounded by towering timber.

Leavenworth was…bizarre. A failing timber town in the 1950s, it had resurrected itself as a Bavarian Alps village in the 1960s and been a tourist mecca ever since. The kitsch was so complete that it was almost believable. She wondered if even Bavaria looked this German.

Coming east from the fire station, just a block off Route 2—the second biggest east-west highway across the Washington Cascades— she walked right into the heart of "old town." A gazebo on the village green. Red brick cobblestone paving with ornate black cast-iron streetlights. White buildings with that zig-zag dark wood accenting. Generous balconies that dripped with massive red geraniums.

Every building that didn't boast a beer garden was lush with souvenirs. There was a lederhosen store for crying out loud and, she'd seen in the few breaks they'd had from training, that it did a serious business. Tourist kids tromped around town with an ice cream cone and wearing attire right out of *The Sound of Music.*

The only thing open at this hour was the Bavarian Bakery. She was missing breakfast, eggs and bacon no doubt, most of them taking white toast. Why was it that hotshots had no imagination about food? They certainly had to eat enough calories to survive a fire season, but they always went for the fastest and the easiest.

As she walked by the bakery's window, someone slid a tray of delicacies into the display. When the baker saw her hesitation, he flashed her a big smile and waved her to come inside.

The tray looked fantastic.

SAM PARKER WAVED at her again.

The woman watched him for a long moment, then shrugged and turned for the door.

"First customer and not a tourist. For that you get an extra special treat," he greeted her before the bell even stopped jangling. Not a local either. He'd only bought the bakery a month ago, but there was something in the way she moved that was different.

A tourist rubber-necked and wandered, and if they were up at this hour of the morning then they'd be wearing their runner's togs. Seattle folks who didn't know how to slow down for even one second.

A local would be moving with purpose and direction. This woman had been out strolling at sunrise for the sake of strolling.

"Smells good," she'd stopped one step inside and sampled the air. Most went straight to the big display cases brimming with confectionary. Or headed straight for the register to order their triple-shot skim macchiato, which wasn't a macchiato at all.

Instead she remained where she was long enough to let him really get an eyeful. Her honey-blond hair was short-cropped, and offset her dark eyes. Her face was thin and well-tanned though it was still more late spring than summer.

She wore a yellow shirt and cargo pants with big thigh pockets and serious boots. He could see the power of her despite the loose clothing just in the way she stood.

"I give up." Nobody back in Providence, Rhode Island had ever come into his shop looking like this. He couldn't make sense of her outfit.

She slanted a look over at him, but didn't say a word.

"What are you?"

She raised an eyebrow.

Okay, maybe not the best greeting, so he waved a hand at her attire rather than risking more words. He ran a bakery, words were almost as important as sugar to making a success of it, but he didn't know which words to use with this woman.

She inspected herself carefully and then looked back at him, again raising that single eyebrow. Without the least hint of a smile, she answered, "*Homo sapiens,* female of the species."

At Sam's burst of laughter, she barely blinked.

WHILE HE LAUGHED, Patsy turned back to inspect the display cases. Most bakeries smelled of sugar, sugar, coffee, and more sugar. But just as a wildfire had hints of cedar, redwood, pine, maple, and a hundred other clues, the air of the Bavarian Bakery was deeply nuanced.

The sugar was there. And the chocolate. But she could smell the butter in the croissants, the apricot in the Danish before she spotted it, the smoothness of rich Bavarian cream, the sharp cinnamon in the baked apple strudel. Hotshots were always lean, there was simply no way to consume more calories than you burned during a season; often there simply wasn't time to do so. But this was a place a woman just might have to be careful. It all looked as incredible as it smelled.

The baker hadn't gone back behind the counter, but instead had remained out front with her. She knew what he'd meant of course, had received the question so many times over the years that the straight answer had long since worn out any interest for her.

A hotshot? What's that?

I fight wildland fires.

Forest fires? Like a smokejumper?

Yes, but without the parachute.

I thought that was a guy thing, jumping out of planes.

As if she hadn't just said…

Sure, hotshots were predominately male. The upper body strength required meant a woman had to want it twice as badly as any man to make the grade—had to bust her ass to overcome genetic predisposition.

Not as unusual as it once was.

It was common now for a hotshot crew to have at least a couple women. The even more strenuous smokejumper roles were starting to see women on the crews as well.

She'd grown so tired of all the stupid follow-on questions, that she'd stopped answering the first one. But usually the men knew she was avoiding a straight answer, grew offended, and left her alone.

This one had laughed, a good laugh. It made her glance back over when she didn't intend to. He didn't look like a German baker: round-faced, blond-haired, and all of the other stereotypes in her brain. He was as lean as she was, an inch or so taller, and his big hands and powerful arms showed a hundred small burn scars and a few older ones that weren't so small. Working with fire. She knew how that looked; had her own fair share of them.

"*Homo sapiens,* male of the species," he answered her apprising look.

She could feel a smile tugging up one corner of her mouth. The man had a sense of humor, and he worked with heat. Even if it was in another form, it was intriguing in its own way.

SAM PUSHED himself up the trail. He'd left the bakery at noon, after a typical nine-hour day, baker's hours. And he enjoyed unwinding on the hiking routes that abounded so close to Leavenworth that he could walk to the trailheads. In Rhode Island, the biggest hill had been eight hundred feet and been a half-hour drive away. Now he lived at twelve hundred feet and couldn't turn around without seeing a half dozen eight thousand footers.

During his one month here, he'd learned that hiking the Cascades was a different challenge than back East, and not just the elevation. A wrong turn there could lead you back to the highway miles away from your car; do the same thing here and you could walk a hundred miles without ever seeing another human, or a road. Wilderness that even jets took a while to cross over. Lost on foot? Very bad news.

Today, he headed off across the flats to the south of town. He'd spotted a plume of smoke up on the hills and used it as an excuse to hike in a new direction. A boxy truck was parked at the base of the trail. Light green with shining golden script, *Cascade Hotshots.*

It was an odd vehicle. The back was a short box with four windows down the sides, like a bus that had its back end sawed off. But instead of being on a bus frame, it was on a very heavy duty truck form, like a cement delivery truck—robust enough to tackle serious loads. Or, he noted that it was parked well across the fields from the nearest street, to negotiate rough terrain. The ride did not look comfortable.

He continued up the trail, the breeze and sun at his back as he climbed. The trail became steep and tough, but he'd learned, and now wore solid boots rather than light walking shoes.

Sam rapidly ascended above the meadow line into the wooded hills, and thought of the woman from this morning.

"Funny how someone can stick in your mind," he told a nodding bush, pulling out his guide long enough to identify it as a huckleberry. He'd have to come back and pick some once they were ripe. He often talked to himself, or at least to the surrounding wildlife as he hiked.

And though he didn't want to be noticing a woman, any woman, she really had stuck in his head. Christi had left him with a gaping wound after a brutal divorce that had sent him all the way to this remote mountain village seeking a bolt hole. Last thing he wanted was to be noticing a woman.

But when he'd watched her eyes flutter shut in appreciation as she bit into his apricot almond bear claw…

Then snap open when her pager buzzed loudly. A quick glance at the small device on her waist and she completely changed.

The slow-moving, slow-smiling woman evaporated as if she'd never been. Now she was pure business. She folded the bear claw in half and stuffed one end of it into her mouth but didn't bite it off. With her hands free, she dug out her wallet, tossed him a ten dollar bill, and bolted out the door without either her hot chocolate or her change. Maybe she was an ambulance EMT or something. Whatever, she'd simply evaporated.

"Maybe that's what was so intriguing," a chipmunk looked at him doubtfully from its hesitant perch atop a boulder. "My woman of mystery."

The chipmunk laughed and scooted.

So much for that idea.

He rounded a bluff and stumbled to a halt.

He'd been hiking steadily upward through thick conifer forest. His East coast brain would call it a pine forest, but his assistant at the bakery informed him that it was mostly fir trees out here. He'd rounded a boulder in the trail, and the world changed. Before him lay a scene from Dante's *Inferno* so jarring that the transition made little sense.

The low grasses and tall trees were gone, replaced by black char. The trees up ahead were tangled with fire. Flames circled and swirled up the tall trunks, heaving ash into the dark cloud of smoke overhead. A gust sent a spray of embers aloft that danced like fireflies against the black smoke and shining flame before reluctantly winking out. It was beautiful and horrible at the same time.

He looked back over his shoulder. Sun-dappled forest.

He turned ahead once more…

There were figures moving about the base of the flames, people in yellow hardhats and coats.

The souls of the damned!

Another shower of sparks swirled aloft.

It was Hell!

PATSY WORKED DOWN THE LINE, checking in with her half of the crew —she and Jess each had nine crewmembers. For their first fire, they were doing well; not that it was a big one. It made for a perfect introduction.

The fire had climbed into a dead-end ravine. Candace had sent scouts both to left and right in case it tried to jump over to the neighboring ravines, but it wasn't big enough to make the leap—again, just good training. They'd think to go themselves next time after checking in with her on the radio. The fire already was dying against the walls and the only ones who didn't know it were the rooks.

The rookies saw the old hands remain calm around them—she'd alternated them down the line so that the rooks couldn't feed off each others' fear—and they had stayed calm in turn. Now it was just a matter of letting it burn out the available fuel in this narrow slot.

She broke out three rooks and a three-year veteran and led them back down to the base of the fire.

"Get a one-and-a-half inch hose into that stream over there. Start working this line. We don't want to leave a single hotspot. When this is done burning out in a couple hours, we want to have the mop-up mostly finished or we'll miss pizza back in town."

That got them moving. Nothing like the promise of real food and a place to brag about your first fire to motivate a hotshot.

A lone figure with wholly insufficient hiking gear stood at the base of the "black," as the charred area of a wildland forest fire was called, looking like he'd been electrocuted standing up. She considered climbing down to him, but decided to make him hike his pretty, clean gear up through the base of the black and save her the walk. It would stain up his boots and socks pretty good. Then maybe she'd rid herself of yet another gawker to worry about during future blazes.

She waved him up the hill to her.

He hesitated, unsure of himself until she signaled again.

As he approached, she recognized the face from somewhere. Oh, his eyes going wide as she stuffed his delicate pastry into her mouth like a some squirrel stuffing its face full of acorns.

She sighed. Graceful had never been one of her strengths.

SAM WAS ONLY a few paces from the firefighter before he realized it was a woman. The charcoal smeared shirt might have once been yellow. Close-fitting sunglasses hid her eyes. Her hardhat was blue… and smeared black. The rest of the crew's were yellow.

"Why is your helmet a different color?"

The way she tipped her head when she looked at him seemed familiar, and then an eyebrow arched between her sunglasses and helmet.

"Female of the species…" came out half statement and half gasp. It was his woman from the bakery this morning. Firefighter. Wilderness firefighter.

He also recognized the half smile that tugged at her left cheek as she acknowledged him.

"Helmet is blue because I'm a foreman."

"*Foreman?* Wouldn't that be the male of the species?"

"Assistant superintendent if you prefer. The superintendent is the one over there under a hot pink helm. Also a female of the species, though she's taken." He had little more than the impression of someone moving quickly *toward* the inferno until he lost sight of her in the smoke.

Then he glanced once more at her. *She's taken* implied that the woman he was talking to wasn't, and had made a point of it. He was about to ask, but he saw the look of chagrin at her own statement, so he went for a subject change.

"Shouldn't there be helicopters and smokejumpers here?"

She glanced over her shoulder and shrugged, "It's just a baby. I wouldn't want it getting an over-inflated sense of importance. We probably wouldn't even be on it except it's a good training opportunity for a new crew."

If this was a baby, he was completely out of his league. His knees felt loose, so he sat down on a handy rise in the ground. It felt warm through his pants. Even..Hot! He jumped to his feet and brushed hastily at his butt; his hand came away black.

That smile was pulling up the side of her mouth once more.

"Okay, don't play with fire. Got the idea." The ground looked burned and black here just like anywhere else in the vicinity. He reached down to touch the ground by his boots. It felt cool by comparison.

She didn't look so amused anymore.

The woman eased him back a step and then moved forward and kicked the spot where he'd sat. A small flame burped up and was gone.

Sam swallowed against a dry throat.

She was signaling her people to come over, "Okay. See this spot?"

Her crew nodded and studied it.

She waved them back a step and used the flat hoe-like blade on the back of her fire axe to drag a gouge in it. Flames leapt upward taller than she was.

"That's what you're looking for during mop-up. Doesn't look like much, but they can be a real pain when they reignite, especially if they're behind you. Now, give me some water from the hose."

One of the people had a hose the size of their wrist that trailed back toward the stream.

As she dug into the mound, flames leapt, water shot in, steam erupted.

Sam backed off slowly, finally turned back downslope and headed away. But he kept looking back at the woman casually mopping up a fire, as fearsome as a witch on Hecate's Heath stirring her caldron.

A world of fire and steam he'd never imagined.

PATSY HADN'T MEANT to ignore the man, hadn't meant to be rude, but he'd been gone before she finished the training opportunity. And fire always took precedence. They'd done well and were, indeed, back down off the mountain in time for pizza and a beer.

Candace had led them to Maxine's Pizza, a hole in the wall that had no hint of Bavarian from the outside. The insides only confirmed this was a strictly locals' joint. No waitresses in cute Bavarian skirts, no pomp and oom-pah-pah from the jukebox; the Stones were rocking it over the speakers. She went up to the faded "Order Here" sign, and saw that the options were slices or a whole pie and a pint or a pitcher. No burgers, no soups or salads, just pizza that smelled incredible. Worked for her.

Twenty hotshots, first day on the fireline, she ordered eight large pizzas but only three pitchers—they were big here. Maxine returned her change with a smile.

"One beer each, maximum," she told the team. "You never know what tomorrow has for us." She took a diet Coke and a slice of pepperoni to wait for the pizzas to come up.

Patsy was looking for the logistics needed to pull a bunch of tables together in the crowded dining room when she spotted him. She threaded her way through the noisy area, dodged aside before one of Jess' crew took her out with the back end of a pool cue, and made it to the small table close by the stairs to the upper dining area no worse for the wear.

"May I?" He was reading something in German. Might have been a cookbook.

He blinked up at her in surprise, "Female of the species."

"Patsy Jurgen."

He said something in German that her grandmother might have understood, but was meaningless to her.

"I speak English, bad English, and worse Spanish." It wasn't that her Spanish wasn't fluent enough, it was that while she'd started her education in that language during high school, she'd finished it on the fire line. Vulgar would be putting it politely.

"Oh, sorry. Sam Parker."

"Nope!" she told him as she sat and took a bite out of her pepperoni slice, which really was as good as it smelled.

"What do you mean, *nope?*"

"You read and speak German, and you bake the best apple-cinnamon bear claw I've ever tasted. Does that sound like a Sam Parker to you?"

"Can't say that it does," he sipped a beer. "However, Patricia Jürgen," he said it with a thick German accent, "sounds like a wildland firefighter."

"Thanks, I think. By the way, only Grandma ever called me Patricia." Conversations with attractive men often stumped her, but this one with Sam Parker...

"So, that was really a 'baby' fire?" he waved in exactly the right compass direction indicating a good sense of where he was both indoors and out. He had strong arms, looked very fit; give her a month and she could make him a damn fine firefighter.

"Good for training. This crew was only formed up five weeks ago and the season is just starting up here. Arizona is the one being hammered right now. New Mexico and Colorado will be next. Nevada and Utah don't really have enough to burn. But that's only general patterns. We could light up tomorrow. Normally we would have let the locals deal with something the size of this morning's fire, maybe send a couple of guys to assist."

He looked right and left. Looked down at his beer for a moment.

Patsy had seen this reaction before. Despite Candace's falling for a guy on her crew, that had never been her style. The problem was that someone who wasn't a firefighter never knew what to do with a woman who was.

"So you fight wildfires?"

Why did they always state the obvious before the brush-off. She nodded. Here it came.

Patsy got her feet under her so she could stand and go back to her crew. There, at least, she fit in.

Then Sam grinned at her, "Did I mention that I'm a baker? That's pretty dangerous work you know. Leave out the baking soda and you can be in a world of hurt."

In general Patsy didn't laugh much, but Sam made it easy to join in.

SAM WASN'T QUITE sure how it had happened.

"Sleep deprivation, gotta be," he told the cold strudel dough he'd put in the fridge yesterday, and now pulled out onto the marble slab.

"Up way past my bedtime," he mentioned to the ovens as he lit them off so that they'd be ready for today's bake as soon as he was.

"Damn but that was a hell of a kiss," he told no one and nothing in particular.

Sam usually hit the sack at seven or eight at night and was up and in the kitchen by three at the latest. It was four now and he was behind.

Last night at eight o'clock he'd been watching Patsy risk her life as she went to snag several pieces of pizza from the ravenous group at the hotshots' table. He noted that she picked them up easily though they were still oven hot, usually a trick that only a baker could do. That she returned from her raid unmaimed by the hoard made her all the more impressive.

They'd spent most of the evening bumping knees at his small table and discovering quite how different two people's pasts could be. Even her mom had been in the fire business; the fire house clerk who had married the captain. Both her brothers rode city engines—he noted the slight scoff in her voice—in Seattle and Boise.

He'd never been to Montana, or was it Idaho. Idaho he decided during his second beer around ten at night. He was the only son of a Boston lawyer and a socialite mother who had married into a prominent Rhode Island family, and then gone to court to get out of it much to his mother's dismay.

They spent most of the evening laughing together. By eleven p.m. and his third beer, it was harder to stop laughing that to start. He noticed she nursed only one glass through the night, but in the laughter department she'd kept right up.

Maxine's Pizza was closer to the fire hall than his small apartment above the bakery. So, he'd walked her through the chill night air, cold enough in June to see his breath despite the lack of streetlights. They were few and far between off the main tourist strips. Whether the city fathers were being cheap or maybe they were trying to encourage tourists to stay in their part of town so that the locals could have some peace and quiet; he wasn't sure which yet. He suspected the latter.

The nearest light had been a block away when they reached her door.

He'd considered saying some cliché about enjoying the evening.

Then he'd considered a different cliché about she was welcome in his bakery any time.

Then he'd kissed her and she'd met him halfway.

It wasn't even a first date, and he'd known her name for only three hours. But he had wanted to discover the taste of her. And though he could still scent the day's fire in her fresh-washed hair, he'd tasted the merriness of her kiss. It was as neatly hidden beneath her serious exterior as the hotspot had been beneath the char this afternoon.

It hadn't started as a friendly little kiss and it certainly hadn't ended like one. They had shared a mutual hum of pleasure before it was done.

"Good night, female of the species."

"Sleep tight, not Sam Parker."

He hadn't noticed the cold at all last night on the five-block walk home from the hotshot's barracks front door—which might have been closer to ten by the time he and his third beer were done with it at midnight. He'd been feeling very mellow and a little lost, in several ways.

For one thing, his ex-wife had left him pretty well convinced that no woman would ever want him. He'd convinced himself that he'd never again risk being with a woman. Yet he'd been here less than two months and just kissed one.

Last night. Just over that way. He glanced in the direction of the hotshot barracks and saw his walk-in refrigerator.

The three a.m. alarm had been a shocker, but he soon lost himself in the dough and date filling, the flavor and texture, trying not to think about how much he'd like to kiss her again.

PATSY WAS unsure if she was disappointed that the fire season was off to such a slow start, or pleased that it allowed her to pursue her new morning ritual.

That second morning, returning to the bakery, had caused her to hesitate. She didn't hesitate around men, but Sam Parker's kiss the night before had been as sweet as his confections and as powerful as his flavors. It was the power of him that had surprised her, baker's arms and hands meant something, as much strength as a firefighter.

Like a good hotshot, she'd forged ahead through the door and Sam had put her at ease with his immediate smile.

Their initial greeting had been interrupted by an early jogger wanting their coffee fix.

His invitation to come to the back door the next morning had her climbing out of her bunk while the night still ruled the valley and the stars burned above.

A morning kiss, a tall hot chocolate, and the first baked good out of the oven all served on a flour-dusted counter, while she perched on a high kitchen stool was an excellent way to start the day. He was smart, funny, and enjoyed hiking. She loved his childhood memories as he prepped and baked. Day after day she'd leave him at sunrise to roust the team.

During the evenings, rather than joining the other hotshots, they would wander around town together, as if they couldn't get enough of each other. Trying out different restaurants from waffles to schnitzel. Sometimes they'd go for hikes through the lower hills in the softness of the late light once the sun had plunged beyond the tall peaks to the west. Other times they poked through the souvenir shops, marveling at the things that tourists seemed so eager to own.

There was even a year-round Christmas store right on the main square that was unbelievable. Towering trees, so thick with ornaments and lights for sale that the fake needles were barely visible except as a green backdrop. Vast Christmas villages of tiny ceramic buildings and figurines, even a miniscule skating pond with skaters. It soon became their favorite shop, as there were always new layers to discover. They would meet there before heading off to find a new place to eat. A town of two thousand people and two million tourists boasted an incredible variety of food.

Last night they had visited the animal ornaments display corner of the store and later shared a surprisingly authentic Mexican fajita. Their goodnight kiss had been the third and best element of the evening, parting at sunset as she'd adapted to his hours.

This morning Patsy had woken very early and was at the back door waiting for him when he wandered down the stairs from the apartment above the bakery.

He looked warm and sleepy and rumpled—irresistibly delicious. So she didn't resist.

Sam awoke quickly enough at her welcoming kiss in the kitchen. There was a need that had been building in her over these last weeks, gathering heat and starting to burn.

"I want to take you upstairs," he whispered against her neck.

"I want you to take me right here."

And he did. She wasn't sure what had inspired her to slip some protection in her pocket that morning, but she was glad she had. With her back against the warming ovens, his heat filling her until it felt as if she was burning as brightly as a flame-wreathed tree. His powerful hands were not gentle, but neither were hers. After they'd initially sated their bodies in a fast, bright flare, he moved his mouth over her. As he did, he tasted and tested like she was a fine treat until she climbed once more over the delicious peak and long slow waves of heat rolled over her.

He was late to start his baking that morning, but neither of them was complaining.

It was their first real call up of the season and it was a hot one. Patsy's pager went off just as she was leaving the bakery feeling particularly loose and pleased with herself—and with Sam Parker.

A quick jog to the fire station and she'd found the whole crew loading up into The Box. Patsy made sure that all the gear was stowed properly from yesterday's trail-clearing work and climbed aboard with her team.

Three hours of jostling around in the back of the heavy truck later, they arrived at the base of Mt. Rainer National Park and looked up. The glacier-topped dome of the mountain was a shining beacon of light as the mid-morning sun glittered off the snow.

The fire wasn't on the mountain, but rather on the neighboring Silver King Peak. The fire had at least six heads, probably from multiple lightning strikes, that had already joined into a burn of a thousand acres. They couldn't just let it burn, because if it climbed up and over the mountain, it would take out the Crystal Mountain Ski Resort, the largest one in the state.

The primary approaches were already engulfed in the fire.

Patsy had been gearing up for the long hike in, seething with frustration at how long it would take them to get to the fire going over rough country on foot. There were no roads for The Box, not even bad ones.

Candace took one look at the situation and pulled out her radio.

"Incident Commander. This is Cascade Hotshots requesting helitack."

Of course. That's why she was the boss. Candace rocked.

Minutes later a pair of big, black-and-flame painted Firehawk helicopters from Mount Hood Aviation descended through the smoky sky and landed in the same clearing as The Box.

A man jumped down and moved past the rotors quickly, pausing just a moment to snap their photo. He looked like a goof with the two cameras—a handsome goof—but he walked like a hotshot. MHA was a top outfit, maybe he was both.

"Hi, name's Cal. Ten of you with Jeannie and me, ten with Emily," he waved at the other helicopter. "Rugged terrain up there, so you're going in by rope."

"Harness up," she shouted to the team. As soon as she had hers on, she checked her team, pleased with how little she found to correct.

Now, they were soaring aloft, packed in the back of the Firehawks like firewood, and Candace asked her, "Who is he?"

"I—" Patsy closed her mouth, unsure what to say.

"Oh, yeah. I recognize that look," Candace shouted over the helicopter's roar.

Patsy studied her boss' face, but couldn't read what was there.

"Same thing happened with Luke. There I was, going along ever so happily, and then snap!" she made a twig breaking motion. "The whole world changed."

Patsy didn't know about the whole world, but certainly a portion of it had.

She surveyed the fire as they climbed skyward alongside the steep ridges, looked at how it was moving along the hills.

Patsy pointed and Candace nodded, their first point of attack was obvious from this height—a few hundred meters from the north flank of the fire; keep it from going any wider here. Candace leaned forward between the seats to tell the pilot.

The other thing that Patsy could see was that she wasn't going to be back in time for dinner, perhaps not for days.

She pulled out her cell phone, probably no reception once they hit the ground out here in the National Park, and certainly no time. She caught two bars off a tower somewhere and dialed Sam's number.

Patsy had never had anyone to call before, when going to a fire. She'd simply go, for a day, a week, a month; it didn't matter. Once a week she tried to let Mom and Dad know she was alive, but they understood if she didn't check in during a busy fire season. They'd taught her to be safe around fire by the time she entered kindergarten. And how to fight it while still in middle school.

She got Sam's answering machine.

"Hey, this is Patsy. I'm off on a fire. Will let you know when I'm back." She didn't know what else to say. Nothing appropriate except how much she'd enjoyed having sex in his kitchen this morning. And meeting him in the evenings. And eating his delicious creations. "Uh, thanks," was the best, lame-ass thing she came up with.

Patsy hung up the phone and tucked it away as the helicopter circled down on their chosen position.

She'd be the first one down, so she clipped her rappelling harness onto the line tied off to the loop outside the cargo bay door.

Candace was back beside her and double-checked Patsy's gear.

"He's a baker," Patsy told her. Which explained absolutely nothing about him.

The helicopter was sliding to a halt just above the treetops. Patsy tossed the coiled line out the cargo bay door and watched as it snaked down and disappeared through a narrow gap in the trees.

Candace's bland look told her that wasn't nearly enough explanation.

"He's really good with his hands."

At that Candace smiled and nodded enthusiastically, "Don't you just love men with good hands?"

Patsy leaned forward out of the cargo bay, then she slid down beneath the battering wind of the rotor, the fire's radiant heat powerful on her face even at this distance.

Heat. A man who worked with heat and generated it as well with those nice hands of his.

Love? She wasn't there yet, but for the first time in her life she could imagine getting there. Much the same way she could imagine beating this fire, though they hadn't even begun.

She hit the ground and disengaged from the line, but her feet were still floating somewhere up in the sky.

❄

Six days.

Sam was amazed at how many emotions had churned up within him in six days.

First, disappointment that Patsy was gone and he didn't have an immediate opportunity to test if what had been between them that morning was real...or even repeatable.

This near stranger, naked and unabashed in his kitchen, had been a revelation. His first time with her had been better than any time with Christie—and throughout their marriage they'd both always remarked on how good they were together physically. Until she was also good, and unrepentant, with her married boss.

Patsy had been incredible, responding in ways he'd never imagined. And where Christie had been delicate, cultivating it into a fine, fragile art form, Patsy was powerful. She definitely gave back as good as she got, and she was impossibly, fantastically real. He'd also had no idea how amazing the body of a "female of the species" could form up until he'd had a chance to appreciate Patsy Jurgen's immense degree of fitness.

Besides, she wasn't a stranger. In their evenings together, he'd found it easy to spill out tales of his past. At first he avoided his marriage, divorce, and abandoning his job. But that too eventually came out in the comfortable world they'd created between them.

"I always wanted to own my own bakery instead of cooking in someone else's. That was about the only good thing I got out of the whole mess."

It was only after he'd said the words that he thought of how they might have sounded to this woman he was now seeing. They certainly wouldn't have met if not for his moving across the whole country to get away from Christie.

But Patsy hadn't taken some unintended offense. Instead, she'd remarked that if his business sense was as good as his food sense, he was set for life. It was good, but he'd signed up for an on-line business course that night to make sure of it.

She was more reticent than he was, but once she started a tale, she told it without any attempt to evade or be embarrassed by it. She told the good with the bad as if the past was of no consequence at all.

He worried less about the past the more time they spent together.

What he hadn't expected was to, once more, start looking forward to the future. That was a skill Christie had taken in the divorce that he was only now rediscovering.

He went through disappointment that he didn't hear from Patsy. Then anger. Surely the woman could find the damned time to text the man she'd just had sex with. Maybe that's all she'd wanted, one good screw, and was now done with him. He knew that was wrong about her, but it didn't stop it from swirling through his mind like folding a meringue time and again until it was totally flat and useless—an immensely frustrating twenty-four hours.

When he still didn't hear from her, he shifted over to fear that she'd been injured or killed and no one would know to tell him.

After two nights in a row of lost sleep, he went down to the Leavenworth fire station for lack of any better idea.

Captain Carl Cantrell was in his office.

Patsy had talked a lot, for her, about Candace Cantrell—the fire chief's daughter and head of the Cascade Hotshots. Practically worshipped the ground the woman walked on.

"Patsy?" Cantrell had offered him an easy smile. "She's still off on the Silver King Fire. Just heard from my girl last night on the radio. She thinks they'll have it contained in another day, two max. Once they can hand it off to a Type 2 mop-up crew, they'll be back, unless there's another blow-up."

On the radio. Not somewhere she could call, which could explain why Patsy hadn't called. No phone service.

Type 2? Not a clue.

At least he knew what "mop-up" looked like, columns of fire erupting from ground that pretended to be black and dead.

Blow-up he definitely didn't like the sound of.

"You the one put that smile on her face?"

Sam was tempted to avoid answering, but could feel the smile of relief on his own, knowing she was fine, just out doing her job.

"I hope that's because of me."

Cantrell just kept grinning, "Keep it up, son. That smile looks good on her. She takes it all far too seriously."

"Well, she fights fires for a living," he felt himself getting deeply protective of her.

The man held up his hands in a placating motion. "Do some of that myself."

Right, this is the Fire Chief, you dolt.

"She's a good one and I've seen enough to know. Maybe as good as my Candace, though if you say in front of my daughter I'll deny it. Just needs someone to lighten her up a bit."

Deeply comforted by the news and the Captain's words, Sam headed back into town to wait. He wanted to get her something. Something to tell her that he thought she was incredible.

As he passed the Christmas shop, he knew just what to get.

BACK IN TOWN Patsy crawled out of The Box and into the shower. Eight days on the first fire of the season. She'd slept...hmm, she was sure she'd slept at some point. They'd *coyoted* for much of the fire, lying down in their gear right where they finished a shift—usually twenty-four to thirty-six hours long—and slept until the fire made an aggressive move and you were on your feet again—usually way too soon.

She plunged into her first shower in all that time and let the stink wash down the drain with the char. Clothes in the wash.

She came to, standing upright and staring down at her bunk. Yes, she should just do a faceplant and hope nothing burned in the next twenty-four hours. But she didn't want to.

Instead, she was halfway to town before she knew what she wanted. Her brain was definitely moving slower than her body.

Eight days.

All Sam Parker had gotten from her in eight days was silence. Would he still want to see her? She thought so. She hoped so.

It was amazing how much he'd been in her head through all that time.

Instead of just living the moment of the fire, she wanted to tell him about it. The little victories, the staggering defeats, and the return to battle until it was won. There was no option, winning is what hotshots did, engaging the fire until it was down and done.

She didn't think that Sam would need a bribe in order to want her back. But she wanted to take him something to let him know she'd been thinking of him.

SAM HAD DECIDED to hang out late in the bakery that day even though his assistants had it covered. Late morning he'd gotten a call from the Fire Chief.

"They're home. Doesn't look like they've slept much, probably shower and sack time, but I thought you'd want to know."

He left the back door open as he worked in the kitchen. It was after lunch when a shadow cut the light pouring into the kitchen, even as he made some notes to try next time on the banana muffins.

He turned to see her, for he had no doubt it would be Patsy. Something inside him just knew.

She stood there, framed in the sunlit doorway. Instead of her fire gear, she wore shorts and sneakers that revealed those powerful legs that had been clamped so tight around his waist that one morning.

Her t-shirt was bright red with a jagged yellow line like mountain peaks, but also like fire. Block letters spelled out, "Silver King Fire" and the year. It hugged her curves in ways that just begged for him to explore them.

Her golden hair caught the sunlight like a halo of fire.

"I got you something," she held up a small bag that he recognized.

Sam reached under the counter and pulled out a similar bag, "I know it's only June, but it just seemed right."

He actually felt awkward as they exchanged bags; it was a

surprisingly intimate moment. They began to open them together on the steel prep table.

He pulled out a string of lights and couldn't help smiling. It was a totally ridiculous string of tiny baked goods: cakes, éclairs, and cookies.

Sam waited while she finished upwrapping her own set of "Fiery Twinkle Lights." He snagged the plug and put it into the outlet under the lip of the counter, then he plugged in his string to hers. Together they all flashed on and hers began to flicker like fire.

"They look good together," her voice was soft, on the verge of that rare laugh he'd so come to enjoy.

"They do," he agreed. Then he looked up at her, "You look incredible."

"So do you," she took a step closer and nodded toward the steel prep table, the reflection doubling the lights. "It looks like between us we have a good start on a Christmas tree."

"A very good beginning," Sam moved in a step, could feel the warmth of Patsy Junger's heat spreading through him as that lopsided smile of hers broke free.

"I bet that between us, we could make an incredible tree by December." She slid into his arms and wrapped her own arms around his back. She rested her head against his shoulder.

"I'm sure you're right."

And she was.

There had never been a gift so perfect as this woman in his arms.

M.L. BUCHMAN
NPR and B&N Top 5 Romance Author of the Year
"Will blow the readers' minds and leave them awestruck."
Romantic Times, Pure Heat
4-1/2 stars
a Hotshot Christmas
a Firehawks Hotshot romance story

A HOTSHOT CHRISTMAS

*Heavy equipment driver **Sheila Williams** got blown up one too many times. The Army kicked her loose for that idiot reason. How the hell she ended up in a tourist town for the holidays makes even less sense.*

***Hotshot Randall Jones** fights wildfires for a living. The adrenaline fits him like a fire in the forest.*

They both feel the heat on a Hotshot Christmas.

INTRODUCTION

This story, which I've mostly introduced already, I'll just say one more thing about.

Sometimes a character just steps onto the page fully formed. The writer, at least this writer, doesn't get to know where they came from or why.

Sheila simply arrived.

My Delta Force story, *Her Silent Heart and the Open Sky* is another one of those (still perhaps the best story I've ever written). And Dilya, who you'll meet later, has a whole history of her own that I'm still only starting to discover though she's been in and out of novels for over ten years now.

Here's Sheila.

A HOTSHOT CHRISTMAS

*S*heila inspected the heavy dark beams and white plaster of the restaurant. A hostess—in a bad Bavarian costume of ruffled sleeves, low-cut above blousy, cotton-cupped breasts—smiled at her as she sashayed across the hardwood floor in incongruous heels.

"Table for one?" Just one notch too perky for her to swallow.

"No, thanks. Just looking in." Sheila turned abruptly and nearly trampled a couple and their kids coming in the door. *Civilians! Too close!* She kept the epithet to herself and stepped around them and back out into the crisp darkness.

To her left was the snow sprinkled faux-Bavarian town of Leavenworth, Washington, so perfect it was like a goddamn life-sized snow globe. To her right was a McDonald's with a wood and plaster Germanic facade. She'd promised herself that she'd do better than McD's for a Thanksgiving Day dinner, but crowds were kind of a problem for her and the town was packed.

Saddle up, girl.

She didn't even bother raising her camo jacket's collar as she turned to tromp through the snow—even the damned falling snow was picturesque—and into the heart of the town. Somewhere there had to be a bar with a burger, a brew, and a minimum of Bavarian.

She'd been driving to…well, nowhere. She'd been driving *away* from the family Thanksgiving in Seattle. Five hours through packed city roads and over slick mountain ones.

Not a soul understood what it meant that she was out of the Army. No one got that a TBI diagnosis didn't mean she was nuts. Traumatic Brain Injury meant that she'd been blown up one too many times for the Army to trust her at the wheel of her big transport truck. Didn't meant she was crazy. Please let it not mean she was crazy.

Which totally explained why she was in a resort town, that looked about as inauthentic as most of the ones in the real Bavaria did, looking for a quiet place to get drunk on Thanksgiving night.

A polka band playing out on the town's square made her wonder how the tuba player's lips didn't freeze to his mouthpiece. Children skidded around despite all the salt and sand laid down on the sidewalks. One ran into her legs hard enough to fall back on its butt.

She stopped, knelt down, and picked up the kid to put it back on its feet. *See, acting perfectly normal. Helping out.*

It took one look at her, burst out crying, and raced away.

Sheila closed her eyes for a moment…before standing and continuing through town. She crossed the street to get clear of the square.

Bavarian Bistro. Not a chance.

Soup Cellar. *O Tannenbaum* playing on the juke because Thanksgiving was over in another half dozen hours. She didn't even make it halfway down the stairs.

She closed her eyes to get past the garish Christmas store and let the tourists bounce off her until she was clear.

King Ludwig's. The Mad King. Not a freaking chance.

She jostled and was nudged along until she fell out the other end of the town. Four blocks. She'd survived four blocks. *Sometimes the victories are small.* She hated when the psychs were right, especially when it felt more like defeat.

At the far end of the tourist strip, the town collapsed back into small American town. Dimly lit, cold. She leaned against the concrete wall of a closed warehouse and did what she could to catch her breath.

"Been following you," a deep male voice.

She really didn't need this shit right now. She rested her hand on her sidearm, but the Glock 19 wasn't on her hip where it should be. Where it *used* to be.

"No need for that," the voice continued as she started a hand up to her concealed shoulder carry. Her back was turned, he shouldn't have been able to spot her motion.

Sheila risked a glance.

Big guy. Ten feet back. Standing planted on the sidewalk. No one behind or to the sides. Alone. She recognized the stance.

"You got somewhere to be?" His voice was soft, steady. She could deal with that. "I can help you get there."

Sheila could only shake her head. No, she had nowhere to be. Might never again.

He waited a while before continuing, like he was studying her and thinking.

"What?"

"Got a place you might like."

"Shit! Not looking for a goddamn roll in the hay."

"More like snow, this time of year," he said it with barely a hint of smile. "Besides, it's not that kinda place. And my wife would kick my ass."

"Must be some tough wife to keep you on a short leash."

He shrugged, "Works for me."

Sheila stared at him, but he just waited. Military recognized military. She could do worse. She offered him a shrug. Didn't really matter anyway.

He pointed past her.

She waved for him to lead the way.

Being a smart man, he also saw that he should circle wide out onto the empty street rather than try to come by her on the sidewalk.

RANDALL SAT close beside Jess and Jill. They were about the funniest damn couple on the whole team and who better to sit with while Thanksgiving dinner was cooking. The two Js met on a wildfire in the middle of last season and Jess had somehow swept her up before she'd even hit the damned fire line. Or maybe she'd swept him up. Randall had long since learned that being five-four, blond, and cute as hell had nothing to do with Jill's skills. The woman totally rocked it, offering her sunny smile the whole time.

"Sure you don't have a twin sister?" He asked for the hundredth time.

"Nope! My moms only had the one kid."

"Crap!" They shared a smile. He'd met her moms at the wedding, two of Seattle's finest firefighters.

A cold gust of air crawled up his back.

"Close the goddamn door!" Randall shivered. He really should move, but this crew area of the Leavenworth fire station was maxed out. The volunteer firefighters and their families would have made it crowded enough. But Captain Cantrell had invited his daughter's entire Interagency Hotshot Crew to his Thanksgiving Feed. No wildfires in the winter in the Cascade Mountains, but half of them had found ways to keep busy and keep local. Candace was the kind of superintendent who helped make good things like that happen.

"Happy Thanksgiving to you too, asshole," Luke smacked him on top of the head as he came through the door and they both laughed.

Then a shadow slipped in behind him and did close the door. She was close to six feet, not gaunt, but not far from it. She had dark hair that fell in soft waves past her shoulders and narrowed her pale face even more. Her fists were jammed deep in the pockets of her unzipped hunting jacket. She wore a turtleneck and a thin white sweater that flowed down her slender frame, apparently oblivious to the biting cold.

She wasn't exactly beautiful, but she was as dramatic as hell.

"What's your problem?" Her voice was low, rough.

"Breathing around you," was all Randall managed.

Somewhere in the background Jill laughed. He couldn't tell whether or not it was at him, but he sure wasn't going to risk looking away to find out. She might evaporate if he did, or stab him.

Her dark eyes studied him for a long moment, then glanced aside to look out the door's frosted window.

"Sorry. Rude. I know. Never think first. You'll have to get used to that if you're going to hang around me. I'm Randall. Randall Jones," he held out a hand.

Again those piercing eyes studied him for a long moment. Then she cursed emphatically.

He started to draw back his hand, but she reached out and shook it once. Solidly. With a damned strong grip. And her fingers were cold as ice.

"Sorry. I'm having trouble around people at the moment."

"Oh, then you're fine here. No people at all. Only firefighters and a couple folks stupid enough to marry them." *And you're babbling, dude. Rein it in.*

"Okay," and the ghost actually smiled—a thin one, but definitely there. It looked amazing on her. "As long as there aren't any actual people."

"Scout's honor," he did his best Boy Scout three-fingered salute.

She snapped upright and was most of the way to a hard salute before she froze, went momentarily wide-eyed, then rammed her fist back into her pocket hard enough that he was surprised she didn't punch through the fabric.

"Sorry," he didn't know what else to say. "I'm…" Maybe it would be better if he just introduced her around or… "Are you hungry? We can go see if it's done cooking." Even though he could see by the long table that the turkeys weren't out yet.

She studied him again, then glanced sideways at Luke.

Randall hadn't even noticed that he was still there, watching them.

Luke gave a shrug to her as if to say, "Up to you."

Sheila turned back to him. Again that long pause before she spoke, as if she had to practice it in her head first before speaking.

"Food would be okay," she finally managed. "A beer sure wouldn't hurt."

Searching for a possible path through the crowd, and seeing the way his ghost was still hanging close to the door, he decided for expediency. He grabbed his jacket off the back of his chair.

"It's quieter that way," he pointed out the door.

Again, her first look went to Luke, who nodded that it would be okay.

He held the door for her and led her outside.

RANDALL'S GRIP had been strong, solid. What Sheila would expect from a firefighter.

"Were you a SEAL too? Like Luke." He asked as he led her toward the back of the building. It was dark except for the distant lights of the town reflecting off the snow, but the path was shoveled. She could smell the thick pine of the trees growing close behind the station.

He didn't move like a trained hand-to-hand fighter. She'd wager she could take him down if necessary, even without her sidearm.

Shoulder carry, not hip. She still needed to change that habit.

"He's a SEAL?" That fit. The silence and the arrogant level of self-assuredness. An unarmed man who simply said, "No need for that," as she'd prepared to draw on him. SEAL? Unarmed? Not likely. "No. Not like Luke. There aren't any SEAL women. I was in the Army. A HEMTT driver."

"A what?"

"Big trucks. A Heavy Expanded Mobility Tactical Truck. Also just called a 'heavy.' I carried anything lighter than an Abrams tank." That shut up most men.

"Did you like it?"

Not Randall. He continued on cheerfully as if they were having an actual conversation and it was okay that she'd driven a massive Army transport for a living…until she couldn't anymore.

He held open a door for her at the rear of the building and she saw that they were entering the back of an equipment bay. A line of shining fire trucks and a pair of polished ambulances were lined up in a neat row. At the far end, one of the doors was rolled halfway up and she could see some guys standing around a big closed-top grill nosed just outside the open door. No crowd pressure in the vast bay which was a good thing. By their feet was a cooler and most of them were nursing a beer. *Target acquired.*

"Yeah," she looked at the beautiful rigs all lined up. "I liked it a lot." Maybe too pretty for her taste. She preferred a machine built to get down and dirty, but the ladder truck could definitely tempt her.

He led her up to the group.

"Captain Cantrell," he began introducing her around. "And Candace is the super on our IHC team."

Father-daughter. Obvious right down to how they stood—sure of themselves but without any real ego display.

"You met her husband Luke."

Which explained just who could keep a SEAL on that short leash.

"And this is Patsy, one of our two foremen. Her husband's the town baker and is around somewhere."

Again, a solid grip and a questioning eye. IHC. Interagency Hotshot Crew. That meant that Randall wasn't just some firefighter. He walked into the wilderness to fight wildfires with a chainsaw and an axe—a very real form of hand-to-hand combat. She suspected it took some serious balls despite his easygoing manner. It also meant "team," which explained the outsider looks she was getting. They were being nice about it though, so she tamped down any need to get out. Especially when "out" would mean going back among the flocks of happy tourists. Families. Candace handed her a beer from the cooler so she'd definitely stick for a bit.

"And I still don't know your name. Sorry." Firefighter Randall Jones was a guy who couldn't stop apologizing. Very strange.

"Sheila Williams."

"And this is Sheila," he introduced her to everyone else.

He didn't mention the Army, which she appreciated. But he did mouth her name a few times to himself to make sure he had it down. Which was kind of cute.

RANDALL SHADOWED her the whole evening. At first because he wanted to, but later she seemed to appreciate it. She didn't exactly open up, but she did appear to relax. When a plate was offered piled high with grilled turkey and all the fixings, she took it. When he pointed to the fire station donation box and told her they were all kicking in a ten, she slipped in a twenty.

Luke floated by on occasion, but made no big deal of it. He'd expected to lose her to Luke, some form of ex-military bonding, but Sheila didn't seem inclined to leave his side which worked fine for him. Even if it was just for the evening, it was nice to have a date. Of sorts. Eventually she told him the story of the Seattle family dinner she'd bugged out of. He couldn't get her to laugh, but he raised that soft smile a couple of times and called it good.

Sheila hung around right through the cleanup chores, earning her a round of thanks that she did her best to shrug off.

"Where are you staying? I'll walk you there."

She shrugged, "Gotta find a room. And I know how to walk myself just fine."

"Won't find one on a Thanksgiving in Leavenworth." Randall glanced at Luke who seemed to be making a point of not watching them. "I've got a couch. Not much of a place, but you're welcome to it."

She didn't do that sideways check-in with Luke that had punctuated so much of the evening. Instead she looked at him carefully. "Just the couch."

His nod of agreement settled it, at least until they were headed to his place through the cold night air. It was late enough that all of the tourists had gone to bed. He liked the town at these times—still all bedazzled up, but only the occasional local walking by with a friendly nod and a "Hey."

"No luggage?"

She swung open her still unzipped coat, fists again in pockets. "Left in a bit of a hurry." By the sound of her family dinner, he would have too.

"I can lend you a t-shirt, maybe scrounge some shorts," he unlocked the door to his apartment and led her up the stairs. And did his best not to picture how she'd look in them.

THE RESULT WAS FAR MORE incredible than he'd imagined. Her narrow shoulders made his "Firefighters Bring the Heat" ride low and expose a lot of neck and collar. Even though it was his longest one, it rode barely past her hips. A pair of gym shorts revealed long, powerful legs.

He did his best to hide his astonishment with a cough and knew he'd completely failed. He enjoyed strong competent women…if he didn't, he was on the wrong crew. Candace had drawn more than the standard share of women to her team—one or two women was still the exception on a twenty-person IHC, and they had five. But not a one was like the dark-haired soldier standing in the middle of his small living room.

"You want to do it, I don't mind."

"Want to?" He gasped it out on a half laugh. How could a man *not* want to; she was stunning. Randall didn't know what self control had him walking up to her, placing his hands on her shoulders, and looking her right in the eyes. "Let me know when *you* want to. Then we'll talk."

He waited for that odd processing lag that she had. Finally she just nodded and turned for the couch. He got out of there before she bent over to adjust the blanket and made the t-shirt ride up higher than it already did. Besides, he'd seen the size of the handgun she'd slipped under her pillow.

SHEILA STAYED on the couch that first night and puzzled at Randall's comment. What did *she* want? There was the thousand-dollar question.

The door to what she wanted had been closed. The Army offered to let her stay in if she would drive domestic, but no foreign action. She'd told them just how far out of the daylight they could ram it. Their ever-so knowing and tolerant smiles—they'd all read her psych profile after all—almost earned them a personal demonstration. The black ops contractors didn't need drivers, they needed operators— she'd checked. As far as "want" went, she hadn't looked any further than that.

Three more days and nights with Randall didn't add a lot of clarity. During the days they went on long cold hikes through the crisp mountain air. In the evenings, they'd sometimes meet up with a few of the others in a locals' bar—the kind of place she'd been trying to find that first night—or they'd end up back at his apartment playing backgammon or watching some action flick.

Sunday night, end of the weekend, she went to lie on the couch when the first bit of *want* seeped into her brain. She didn't care about the sex one way or the other, but it would be nice to be held. What was more, it would be nice to be held by Randall. Somehow all the care she had to take to not be offensive to civilians didn't matter around him.

For once not thinking deeply, she turned aside and followed him through his bedroom door. She'd checked out the place the first day, had the layout clear in her head (including all exits), and could walk right to the bed in the pitch dark.

When she slipped under the covers, it earned her a grunt of surprise, but no more. She lay against him. For a long frozen moment he lay perfectly still unsure what to do next—it was a moment she knew well. He didn't paw at her or jump her, both of which she was ready for; just part of the price.

Instead, he pulled her in and held on tight.

Somehow he knew that this was what she wanted. No, he wasn't some freaking telepath like those damned Army psychs thought they were. Randall waited while she figured out what she wanted. For a long time, it was exactly what he was giving her.

When she decided it was more, he seemed pretty okay with that as well.

RANDALL KNEW HE WAS DREAMING, but four weeks hadn't been enough to wake him up so far and he was starting to hope it never would. Just as she had that first night, Sheila had started on the periphery, staying in town when he went to work on the Monday after Thanksgiving. That had lasted her active nature about two days.

By the end of the week she had fully integrated into the small business that he and Patsy had set up with Jess and Jill. WUI Cleaners —the name made them laugh even if no one else seemed to get the joke. They specialized in cleaning up the Wildland-Urban Interface around homes, securing them as well as possible against the dangers of wildfire. They dropped dead trees, or ones too close to a house. Around homes pushed into thickly wooded areas, they trimmed off all of the dead lower branches that could act as ladder fuels to take a fire from ground to crown. They'd recently expanded from burn piles into prescribed burns, clearing brush and deadwood from the forest floor with carefully controlled small fires.

Sheila—still oblivious to the cold—started out dragging branches and tending burn piles. It wasn't long before she picked up saw work and finally harness work climbing in the trees. The general lack of snow let them keep busy in Leavenworth, only occasionally shifting down the dry eastern slopes of the Cascades to Cashmere or Wenatchee.

She didn't really open up around the others, but her hesitations shortened over time. They'd talked about the whole TBI thing, looked up the symptoms together, and it didn't quite fit.

"As you just demonstrated, it's not that you think any slower than I do," Randall observed one night as they lay exhausted together. A good work day around the Kitchner farm, followed by an equally thorough workout with only a short break for delivery pizza in bed. Slow thinking was one of the main signs of a traumatic brain injury and Sheila had shifted over the month from an active lover to an immensely creative one. Combined with her magnificent body, he was a complete goner.

Her silence was her usual answer but he could feel her listening. She was like that when they were making love as well, completely silent but gloriously present.

"It's more like we're all speaking a foreign language and you need time to translate it."

She buried her face against his shoulder for a while before finally responding, "God, I hope you're right. It feels that way. Even as familiar as you feel, there's a strangeness I can't seem to get around."

"Familiar, huh?"

SHEILA COULD HEAR THE TEASE, but she could feel the pain.

Randall felt so much more than "familiar" but she didn't know how to say it. He had welcomed her into his world with no questions asked. A dinner, his couch, his bed, his job, his life.

And what had she offered in return? Her body. There should be more than that.

She considered using it to demonstrate quite how much more than familiar he felt. But it wasn't that simple or that crass…because it *was* more than that.

"You feel…"

And he waited while she searched for the word. It wasn't that sluggish feeling she'd felt back when the Army was giving her the medical discharge. It wasn't even the foreignness issue, though that was the best explanation she'd heard of it.

"I feel…" That was the real problem. Her feelings—other than anger at what had happened, at the raghead who'd blown up her truck, with her inability to say what she meant—were distant, almost vague. She didn't know what she felt and had no idea how to put words to that.

So, she fell back on showing it with her body. But it wasn't merely great sex this time. It was more. It was deeper. She groaned aloud as the layers of defense broke loose inside her. Randall eased his way past more than the barricades of the flesh, he also shattered the massive walls she'd built around her own emotions without realizing.

This time, as her body shuddered with pleasure, it wasn't a release. It was a cleansing.

THE FIRE HIT and it hit hard. December had been unseasonably dry, less than a foot of snow and a series of warm afternoons that had melted what little fell. The town had brought in snowmaking machines so that they could have a white Christmas.

Patsy's call wrenched them out of deep sleep. Just breaking dawn outside the window.

"We're activated. Move!" And she was gone. Hotshot teams were never mobilized in mid-winter.

He punched Tori's number, remembered that she was wintering with her famous writer husband in Seattle, mumbled an apology for waking her, and hung up. Next on his leg of the phone tree...nobody who was still in town.

Time to move.

He was pulling on his cotton long johns as Sheila stripped off her t-shirt and began doing the same.

"What are you doing?" Other than escalating the hell out of his pulse rate. Not in a hundred years could he get used to the look of her.

"There's a fire." No hesitation at all. No question either.

"You're not..."

He stopped when he saw her baleful gaze.

...a firefighter. Though he'd trained her in all he could and she'd learned fast, she wasn't trained for wildfire—didn't have her Incident

Qualification System "red card." However, he'd long since learned that changing Sheila Williams' mind once she set it was not something that mortal men should attempt. There was no hesitation when she was in work mode. The same thing had happened when they were working for WUI Cleaners. When there was action, Sheila didn't pause for a microsecond. No more wrong with her brain than her stunning body.

Fine. Let Candace try to face her down about the "official" certification.

He watched her pulling on the Nomex fire retardant gear he'd given her as a gift when she'd proved she was going to stick with WUI for a while. A powerful woman climbing into firefighting gear. And not just any woman, but Sheila Williams.

Randall knew what he wanted to see for the rest of his days, and he was looking right at it.

"You're still naked," she said without looking up from lacing her boots.

"Shit!" He finished dressing at firefighter speed.

When they arrived at the station, Candace took one look at Sheila and growled, "I don't have time to argue this shit. Fine. You're attached to Randall's hip. I find you more than ten feet apart, I'm gonna kick your ass off the fire and out of this town."

Then she turned to him, "She dies, it's totally on you." Then she rushed off to ream someone else's ass about something.

"Wipe the surprise off your face, Randall." Sheila gave him a gentle shove to get him into motion. "Let's go."

He led her to the type 3 wildfire engine that hadn't seen a job since October. Built on a truck frame, it carried five people, five hundred gallons of water, and could blast a hundred-and-fifty gallons per minute out of fifteen-hundred feet of hose. The big diesel, rear dualies, and four-wheel drive also meant it could cross over seriously rough terrain.

Sheila went for the driver's door, then stopped with her hand on the handle. "Sorry, old habits." She circled to the passenger side.

Randall had learned that it was easier to just let her drive the work truck, but there were special insurance issues here and he was glad that he didn't have to force it.

Captain Cantrell came by and slapped an address in his hand. "Remote as hell. None of my engines can make it up there. It's up to your team to lead. My men are right behind you."

Randall could see teams of firefighters loading the backs of their four-wheel drive personal vehicles with fire gear and piling aboard. Jess, Candace, and Patsy slid into the back seat of his truck's cab. It was odd having Sheila in Tori's usual seat beside him, not that he was complaining.

Jill actually chirped the tires on the other wildland engine as she pulled out ahead of him along with the rest of the Leavenworth Hotshots wintering in Leavenworth. Ten people. Half their normal crew. They'd need Cantrell's people fast. The problem was that though they were good guys, they were volunteers and would need to be watched like hawks. Along with Sheila...though he'd never found watching her to be a burden.

Together, he and Jill raced the big engines down Highway 2 toward the small town of Dryden.

SHEILA WASN'T ready for the scale of a wildfire or the scale of the change that washed over her easy-going and affable lover. She barely recognized him. Deep in a valley beyond Dryden, a fire was ripping apart the landscape.

"Goddamn winter hunters," his unexpected snarl came from deep in his chest.

"What's wrong with hunters?"

"They're big on exploding targets. Doesn't matter that the damned things are outlawed on state forest land; they love seeing the flash and bang during target practice. Then, if they start a fire, the hunters scram so that they don't get caught and have to pay for the firefight. Not the primary cause of our manmade fires, but it's climbing."

"What are the primaries?"

"Campfires and arsonists. But there aren't any hiking trails back here and arsonists like showier fires than the back hill country. There also hasn't been any lightning lately, which says numbskull hunters. They were probably bored because the elk are staying in the higher pastures due to the mildness of the season." Randall sounded seriously pissed. Army-style pissed, something Sheila didn't know he had in him.

She was already discovering a soft-spot in her head for Randall Jones; this just amped up the developing pile of mush that was her brain. She'd *never* been mushy about a man or anything else before—except maybe her truck before the roadside bomb dismembered it. Actually, she cared more about him than anything before which was a surprise. If you'd asked her a month ago, she'd have said she was past caring about anything ever again.

They swooped off the end of the gravel road they'd been following into the backcountry and the big truck jounced and jostled as he headed into an area that was a combination of meadow and trees. All conifers—mostly scattered—except low in the valley, where the water would accumulate. They made thick clumps down there. Higher on the dry slopes they spread out, and the brown grasses dominated. The fire was climbing both valley walls simultaneously and sending a plume of smoke soaring upward like a line of JDAM bombs. She kept expecting to feel the shockwave slam into the truck. But the smoke just kept rolling upward in a continuous gray sheet, dark with ash above and bright with flames below.

"Flanks first," Candace called from the back of the truck as Randall slammed it to a halt over two hundred yards away from the fire. Everyone piled out of the back.

"What are they…" Then Sheila stopped asking. Stay in the truck. Watch and learn, just like in the Army.

The firefighters who piled out of the two trucks spread out in a short line. In moments they were swinging their Pulaski fire axes, digging a line across the meadow. Great clumps of grass and dirt were peeled up. They moved in a fast, coordinated action.

The townie firefighters drove up and were soon put to the same task with varying degrees of effectiveness. Just like a fresh shipment of boot camp privates arriving on the line, the main thing they did was make it really clear how skilled the hotshots were at what they did.

Randall dropped the wildland engine into four-wheel low and continued toward the fire until she thought he was going to drive straight into it. She could see Jill in the other engine driving down into the valley ahead of the fire and climbing back up the other side.

The smoke was thicker here. They were close enough that she could see the fire crawling up the trees like a living thing. It crept through the grass beneath the trees, like an orange serpent until it reached the next tree and then raced upward: a flicker and a snap at first, but soon a rush high into the boughs. He drove along the front as if it was no more than a guardrail on the highway. At the end, he turned along the flank, the truck tipping ten degrees sideways due to the grade.

"Here. Take over the wheel." Randall slid out the uphill-side door and closed it, even though the truck was still idling forward. By the time she slid across, he had fifty feet of one-inch hose pulled off the back and connected to the on-board pump.

"Just roll ahead slow," he spoke calmly over the radio.

"Sheila better not be driving my truck," Candace called back in response from her position on the front line.

Randall shot her a grin and Sheila decided that they'd both ignore her.

Sheila had to flex her hands a few times before she could bring herself to grab onto the steering wheel. Randall walked up to the fire, the flames off the deep grass were as tall as he was. With a casual flick of his wrist, he opened the nozzle and began spraying the fire down.

She was surprised at how easily the flames died. It took her a while to see why. Randall ignored the black area that had already been burned. He concentrated only on the burning line which was truly not very wide. Whenever he reached a tree burning along the line, he'd spray it for an extra moment to kill the fire, but never slowed.

As she became oriented to his world, she learned more of what to watch. In the rearview mirror, she saw a patch still smoking. She tapped the horn and pointed back when Randall looked at her. He slashed the spray at the smoke, thoroughly inundating it, then continued ahead without breaking stride.

He was so clearly in his element. She appreciated the casual skill with which he and the others of WUI had dealt with everything. But watching him have the same attitude toward an active fire was a real sight to see. He might not be Army, but that didn't stop her from feeling better just for being in his presence.

Over the next hour they traveled a couple of times down to the stream at the bottom of the valley and pumped aboard another five-hundred gallons.

"It's a surreal place. We call it The Black," Randall explained as he rode easily in the passenger seat while she climbed the engine back up the slope through the burned-out char to the fire line. "Part of the natural life cycle in this kind of environment. The grass and the trees know what to do; we're the problem. There are power lines over that ridge," he pointed one way. "And homes over that one," he pointed the other. "So we have to kill it off even though it's just a baby fire."

"Just a baby?"

"I half think the Captain must have been bored to call us out on this one. Maybe he knew Candace was getting antsy; she's always happiest when she's fighting a fire. Doesn't matter. We'll kill it in plenty of time for dinner."

ONCE THEY HAD the flanks doused, Randall drove the truck around to the head, trading with Sheila because he figured he shouldn't flaunt in Candace's face who'd actually been driving all morning.

The crew had been busy and had a long line sliced through the soil. The trench ran twenty feet wide and from his flank, all the way down to the creek, and well up the other side.

"Spray the line behind us," Candace instructed when he pulled up. The look she gave him said that switching drivers hadn't fooled her for a second no matter how hard Sheila tried to look innocent in the passenger seat.

"Sure," Randall eyed the grassy slope beyond the trench. "Just as soon as you get these amateurs to move their vehicles."

Candace looked over her shoulder and swore. His path was blocked by a tangled array of the volunteer firefighters parked far too close to the line. It only took moments before she had firefighters racing off the line to move their vehicles. Totally overestimating the danger, the volunteers then drove five-hundred yards away. It would take them a while to trudge their way back.

"Better light the backfire soon," he nodded toward the nearly empty line now manned by only a half dozen hotshots along its half-mile length.

The fire head wasn't more than a few hundred feet away and was going to arrive at the line before the stray volunteers did.

A backfire had to be lit right now on the fire-side of the trench they'd cut. Unable to cross the trench, it would slowly burn up the fuels back toward the main fire, robbing it of heat before it hit the line.

"Shit!" Candace got on the radio to the other hotshots and raced off to start the fire.

"Darn it!" Jill's voice came over the radio. She really was too sweet, though with Sheila beside him he was no longer wishing she had a twin sister.

"What?" Candace's voice was harsh, in no mood for additional problems as she sprinted to gather up her own fire torch to ignite the line.

"I'm in the creek," Jill called. "Stuck trying to get back to your side."

Randall looked down the slope and saw the big red engine down in the bottom of the valley. The fire was still running hot through the trees, headed her way. This first fireline was only to get the fire off the slopes. The second battle would be down in the those trees, so there was nothing set up there yet to protect her.

He slammed into gear and raced down the hill toward her, barely remembering to warn Sheila to hang on before he slammed over a foot-thick fallen tree.

"I stuck it good," Jill called out as he drove up. She already had a length of chain hooked up to her front bumper, but the slope was steep and he wouldn't have a lot of extra power to pull her free while trying to climb. Hopefully it would be enough because she was wheel deep in creek water and the fire was on the move.

He backed down as close as he dared, already feeling the first of the fire's heat through the window. Jill shot him a thumbs up as soon as she had the chain hooked up and raced back to her truck.

They eased into first gear together, but it wasn't budging. The fire wasn't going to give him time to unhook, circle around, and try pulling her back the other way.

Sheila cursed from beside him and then was gone with a slam of her door.

He didn't have time to deal with whatever snit-fit she was having. In the rearview mirror he kept an eye on Jill in the stuck fire engine's driver's seat as they tried once more to dislodge it without success.

The warmth of the fire was now up to a hot summer's day and climbing fast. Even with both engines pumping, the flames would be too big to fight directly.

Then, shortly before he was going to call her to abandon her engine, he saw Sheila stalk up to Jill's driver-side door. She yanked it open and, with little ceremony, shoved Jill over into the passenger seat.

"Give me five feet of slack," her terse command snapped over the radio.

Randall glanced once at the flames. He should call for them to abandon the engine. There would barely be time to undo the chain and get the hell out.

"Don't think. Do it!"

Randall smiled to himself as he eased off the chain. That sounded just like his Sheila.

She began rocking the truck back and forth in the creek. The slick rocks gave her little purchase, but she was getting some motion as she slammed back and forth between drive and reverse.

"On five. Give me everything you've got, Randall."

He shoved in the clutch, shifted into first, and revved the engine. It had better work on five because by ten the fire would overrun both of them.

Sheila counted down her increasing rocking motion.

Her shout of "Now!" came just halfway between a rear swing and a forward one.

Anticipating her, he came off the clutch hard and slammed down on the gas.

The five feet of slack jerked out of the chain, jarring him hard against his seatbelt.

He kept his foot down and the big diesel groaned with power.

As if the creek didn't want to let go, the other engine emerged a foot at a time, sheeting water to the sides.

There was a moment when their momentum hung in the balance as grass and mud sprayed off their spinning tires, but his front pair found some traction on good soil and it was enough to drag them both forward and up the slope.

He checked the rearview and watched as a burning tree crashed down where the engine had been stuck just moments before.

"THAT FELT GOOD," Sheila couldn't stop saying it. "That felt soooo good."

"Hey!" Randall complained. "You're only supposed to be saying that about me."

Sheila grabbed Randall and shoved his back against the rear wall of the fire station. He stopped complaining when she kissed him. The joy that coursed through her ran deep and hot and she poured it into the kiss.

His strong arms clamped tight around her just as they had that first night she'd climbed into his bed. Except now it wasn't about being held—it was all about who was holding her.

"You don't feel good, Randall," she nibbled at his neck making him squirm. "You feel incredible!"

He laughed at her crow of delight.

"Will you two cut it out?" Candace stuck her head out the back door of the equipment bay. "We can hear you right through the wall."

"Nope," Sheila had no intention of stopping with Randall any time soon.

Candace looked at her watch. "I figure you have one hour to get home, shower, and get back here after picking up the pies at Sam's place. Get a move on, I don't like my pies or my hotshots to be late." And she slammed the door.

Randall laughed and tried to pull her back into a kiss, but she held off.

Her mental processes really weren't slow. They didn't feel slow anyway. Maybe that was all part of the issue. But she'd heard something that...

"Did Candace just say 'hotshots'? Plural?"

Randall sobered and turned to study the closed door.

Then she felt his shrug.

"Could be..."

THE SHOWER WAS fun as always.

Sheila almost felt shy sharing it with the firefighter that Randall had turned into, but shy had never been a thing between them. Still, now that she knew the hard-core firefighter that lurked beneath his easy-going demeanor, it was like she was with someone else. Someone even better than she'd thought she was with, which was astonishing as she'd been counting herself damned lucky of late.

And Randall got her to smile as they went into the Bavarian Bakery to pick up the pies for dinner; the place was such classic

German kitsch. But the sample cinnamon rugelach they'd split had been splendidly authentic.

It was so different walking through town now than it had been a month ago. It didn't matter that the snow was artificial; the town glittered with tiny ice crystals. The polka band was in full swing as were the chaotic crowds of children. She managed to dodge all collisions this time, so there would be no test of their reaction to her —something she still wasn't ready for.

"Damn, I keep forgetting to buy twinkle lights."

He hesitated in front of the Christmas store window, and she didn't even cringe.

"When I told my sister that I was in love, she said I should get some twinkle lights for the bedroom," he set off walking again.

"When you told your sister…*what?*" Sheila ground to a halt. *In love?* Some chattering tourist couple slammed into her from behind and bounced off.

Randall simply smiled at her. "I think making love to you by the light of twinkle lights would be a very good thing."

"No. What's that other thing you said?"

"See? I told you there weren't any issues with your reaction time," he kissed her on the nose and then kept walking toward the fire station with his armful of pie boxes.

Sheila wasn't used to having to scramble to keep up with a man.

Luke came out of a side street not a dozen steps ahead. There were some things that she definitely wasn't going to discuss in front of *him.*

Or at all.

And the crowd built from there.

Or was she?

By the time they reached the fire station, more firefighters and families had joined them. They all greeted her by name, made her feel welcome. Sheila realized that she knew all of their names as well. Had eaten at several of their houses. Knew most of the kids' names too. *When did that happen?*

With no privacy, she could only puzzle at Randall's statement. The problem was that the more she did, the less strange it became. She cared for Randall. She really did. Is that what love felt like? If it was, how in hell was she supposed to know.

It was halfway through the dinner before she was able to track down Candace and ask her what that "hotshots" comment had meant.

"One of the main things I look for when I'm building my hotshot team is what you showed today."

"What's that?"

"You're not afraid of fire. You keep thinking even when it's right on top of you. Damned hard to test that without a real fire."

Sheila had driven through enough shellings and bombardment that the fire hadn't fazed her at all. "What are the other things?"

"Saving my damned engine," Candace grinned at her. "Work with Randall, get your red card. Tryouts are in the spring, not that you need to worry about that." She punched Sheila on the arm like guys did and strutted back into the crowd. It was no longer a surprise that she had married a Navy SEAL and was keeping him happy.

It was only at the end of the night, as she and Randall were walking arm in arm back through the sleeping village that Sheila really connected that this was Christmas Eve...she checked the cuckoo clock in the window of Der Markt Platz...no, Christmas Day. She'd known it was close. Obligatory call with Mom about whether or not she was coming home for it, etc. etc. But the firehall dinner had just been a Christmas party. Not the official Eve of.

"I didn't get you anything, Randall. Please tell me that you didn't get me a present either."

He looked aside as if seeking a subject change.

"Oh no! What did you get me? Are there any shops open past midnight?" The empty street answered that one. "Maybe McDonald's up on the highway is open and I could get you some French fries."

Now he seemed to be the one having trouble connecting words. After a few slowing paces, he turned and led her away from the shops to the small park where the band had been playing Christmas carols earlier. She could still hear them on the night air. That should have reminded her to get him something, would have if they hadn't been playing them since the moment of her arrival back at Thanksgiving.

He led her to the little gazebo and sat beside her on the bench.

"I got you something," his voice was low and rough. "Probably pretty damned stupid, but…" His shrug showed his sudden unease.

"Just, I don't know, just give it to me and I'll get you something equally stupid when the stores reopen. Then we'll be even." It came out in a mad rush. She didn't know why she was feeling so nervous. It wasn't like her.

"Equally stupid?" There was a tease in his voice that she'd come to like. There was never a hidden agenda behind it; it was more his way of laughing with her rather than at her. And he took her return teases in stride just as easily as he took her silences.

"I promise," Sheila raised her right hand. "Equally stupid."

"Okay," he blew out a hard huff of breath that made a brief cloud in the chill air. He dug into a pocket, pulled out a small box, and opened it.

Inside was a golden ring with a small ruby the color of fire. "It's beautiful. Simple and perfect."

"It's yours, if you want it."

"Of course I do, it's—" and with those words her brain seized up.

I do? Randall hadn't offered her a present. Well, not a present like a present present. Her brain was babbling.

She looked up into his dark eyes and studied him carefully by the soft street lighting. He didn't look away. Didn't shy off.

"You said to just give it to you," he explained. "I had a speech, which I can't remember. I'll kneel if you'd like. But the important part is that every one of my days has been better for having you in it. I'm betting that isn't going to change. I know it won't."

Sheila wanted to protest that she was a wreck, but she didn't feel like one. Not when Randall was around. She felt capable, strong…

She looked at the ring once more. It wasn't as simple as it had first appeared. The band was twisted, like a mobius strip. All one side, the inside becoming the outside and the outside in. It was an elegant piece of work.

And it was who she was, all twisted up, the inside and the outside blurred until they became one because of the man waiting patiently beside her.

Well, not altogether patiently. She knew him well enough to see the strain, but he'd never pushed her to be other than who she was. That's when she knew that the ring wasn't the gift, Randall Jones was. A life-long sized gift.

She leaned forward and kissed him lightly.

"Something equally stupid..." she whispered against his lips. "I promise. I really do."

WILDFIRE AT DAWN (FIREHAWKS SMOKEJUMPERS #1)

(EXCERPT)

ount Hood Aviation's lead smokejumper Johnny Akbar Jepps rolled out of his lower bunk careful not to bang his head on the upper. Well, he tried to roll out, but every muscle fought him, making it more a crawl than a roll. He checked the clock on his phone. Late morning.

He'd slept twenty of the last twenty-four hours and his body felt as if he'd spent the entire time in one position. The coarse plank flooring had been worn smooth by thousands of feet hitting exactly this same spot year in and year out for decades. He managed to stand upright... then he felt it, his shoulders and legs screamed.

Oh, right.

The New Tillamook Burn. Just about the nastiest damn blaze he'd fought in a decade of jumping wildfires. Two hundred thousand acres —over three hundred square miles—of rugged Pacific Coast Range forest, poof! The worst forest fire in a decade for the Pacific Northwest, but they'd killed it off without a single fatality or losing a single town. There'd been a few bigger ones, out in the flatter eastern part of Oregon state. But that much area—mostly on terrain too steep to climb even when it wasn't on fire—had been a horror.

Akbar opened the blackout curtain and winced against the

summer brightness of blue sky and towering trees that lined the firefighter's camp. Tim was gone from the upper bunk, without kicking Akbar on his way out. He must have been as hazed out as Akbar felt.

He did a couple of side stretches and could feel every single minute of the eight straight days on the wildfire to contain the bastard, then the excruciating nine days more to convince it that it was dead enough to hand off to a Type II incident mop-up crew. Not since his beginning days on a hotshot crew had he spent seventeen days on a single fire.

And in all that time nothing more than catnaps in the acrid safety of the "black"—the burned-over section of a fire, black with char and stark with no hint of green foliage. The mop-up crews would be out there for weeks before it was dead past restarting, but at least it was truly done in. That fire wasn't merely contained; they'd killed it bad.

Yesterday morning, after demobilizing, his team of smokies had pitched into their bunks. No wonder he was so damned sore. His stretches worked out the worst of the kinks but he still must be looking like an old man stumbling about.

He looked down at the sheets. Damn it. They'd been fresh before he went to the fire, now he'd have to wash them again. He'd been too exhausted to shower before sleeping and they were all smeared with the dirt and soot that he could still feel caking his skin. Two-Tall Tim, his number two man and as tall as two of Akbar, kinda, wasn't in his bunk. His towel was missing from the hook.

Shower. Shower would be good. He grabbed his own towel and headed down the dark, narrow hall to the far end of the bunk house. Every one of the dozen doors of his smoke teams were still closed, smokies still sacked out. A glance down another corridor and he could see that at least a couple of the Mount Hood Aviation helicopter crews were up, but most still had closed doors with no hint of light from open curtains sliding under them. All of MHA had gone above and beyond on this one.

"Hey, Tim." Sure enough, the tall Eurasian was in one of the shower stalls, propped up against the back wall letting the hot water stream over him.

"Akbar the Great lives," Two-Tall sounded half asleep.

"Mostly. Doghouse?" Akbar stripped down and hit the next stall. The old plywood dividers were flimsy with age and gray with too many showers. The Mount Hood Aviation firefighters' Hoodie One base camp had been a kids' summer camp for decades. Long since defunct, MHA had taken it over and converted the playfields into landing areas for their helicopters, and regraded the main road into a decent airstrip for the spotter and jump planes.

"Doghouse? Hell, yeah. I'm like ten thousand calories short." Two-Tall found some energy in his voice at the idea of a trip into town.

The Doghouse Inn was in the nearest town. Hood River lay about a half hour down the mountain and had exactly what they needed: smokejumper-sized portions and a very high ratio of awesomely fit young women come to windsurf the Columbia Gorge. The Gorge, which formed the Washington and Oregon border, provided a fantastically target-rich environment for a smokejumper too long in the woods.

"You're too tall to be short of anything," Akbar knew he was being a little slow to reply, but he'd only been awake for minutes.

"You're like a hundred thousand calories short of being even a halfway decent size," Tim was obviously recovering faster than he was.

"Just because my parents loved me instead of tying me to a rack every night ain't my problem, buddy."

He scrubbed and soaped and scrubbed some more until he felt mostly clean.

"I'm telling you, Two-Tall. Whoever invented the hot shower, that's the dude we should give the Nobel prize to."

"You say that every time."

"You arguing?"

He heard Tim give a satisfied groan as some muscle finally let go under the steamy hot water. "Not for a second."

Akbar stepped out and walked over to the line of sinks, smearing a hand back and forth to wipe the condensation from the sheet of stainless steel screwed to the wall. His hazy reflection still sported several smears of char.

"You so purdy, Akbar."

"Purdier than you, Two-Tall." He headed back into the shower to get the last of it.

"So not. You're jealous."

Akbar wasn't the least bit jealous. Yes, despite his lean height, Tim was handsome enough to sweep up any ladies he wanted.

But on his own, Akbar did pretty damn well himself. What he didn't have in height, he made up for with a proper smokejumper's muscled build. Mixed with his tan-dark Indian complexion, he did fine.

The real fun, of course, was when the two of them went cruising together. The women never knew what to make of the two of them side by side. The contrast kept them off balance enough to open even more doors.

He smiled as he toweled down. It also didn't hurt that their opening answer to "what do you do" was "I jump out of planes to fight forest fires."

Worked every damn time. God he loved this job.

THE SMALL TOWN of Hood River, a winding half-an-hour down the mountain from the MHA base camp, was hopping. Mid-June, colleges letting out. Students and the younger set of professors high-tailing it to the Gorge. They packed the bars and breweries and sidewalk cafes. Suddenly every other car on the street had a windsurfing board tied on the roof.

The snooty rich folks were up at the historic Timberline Lodge on Mount Hood itself, not far in the other direction from MHA. Down here it was a younger, thrill seeker set and you could feel the energy.

There were other restaurants in town that might have better pickings, but the Doghouse Inn was MHA tradition and it was a good luck charm—no smokie in his right mind messed with that. This was the bar where all of the MHA crew hung out. It didn't look like much from the outside, just a worn old brick building beaten by the Gorge's violent weather. Aged before its time, which had been long ago.

But inside was awesome. A long wooden bar stretched down one side with a half-jillion microbrew taps and a small but well-stocked kitchen at the far end. The dark wood paneling, even on the ceiling, was barely visible beneath thousands of pictures of doghouses sent from patrons all over the world. Miniature dachshunds in ornately decorated shoeboxes, massive Newfoundlands in backyard mansions that could easily house hundreds of their smaller kin, and everything in between. A gigantic Snoopy atop his doghouse in full Red Baron fighting gear dominated the far wall. Rumor said Shulz himself had been here two owners before and drawn it.

Tables were grouped close together, some for standing and drinking, others for sitting and eating.

"Amy, sweetheart!" Two-Tall called out as they entered the bar. The perky redhead came out from behind the bar to receive a hug from Tim. Akbar got one in turn, so he wasn't complaining. Cute as could be and about his height; her hugs were better than taking most women to bed. Of course, Gerald the cook and the bar's co-owner was big enough and strong enough to squish either Tim or Akbar if they got even a tiny step out of line with his wife. Gerald was one amazingly lucky man.

Akbar grabbed a Walking Man stout and turned to assess the crowd. A couple of the air jocks were in. Carly and Steve were at a little table for two in the corner, obviously not interested in anyone's company but each others. Damn, that had happened fast. New guy on the base swept up one of the most beautiful women on the planet. One of these days he'd have to ask Steve how he'd done that. Or maybe not. It looked like they were settling in for the long haul; the big "M" was so not his own first choice.

Carly was also one of the best FBANs in the business. Akbar was a good Fire Behavior Analyst, had to be or he wouldn't have made it to first stick—lead smokie of the whole MHA crew. But Carly was something else again. He'd always found the Flame Witch, as she was often called, daunting and a bit scary besides; she knew the fire better than it did itself. Steve had latched on to one seriously driven lady. More power to him.

The selection of female tourists was especially good today, but no other smokies in yet. They'd be in soon enough…most of them had groaned awake and said they were coming as he and Two-Tall kicked their hallway doors, but not until they'd been on their way out—he and Tim had first pick. Actually some of the smokies were coming, others had told them quite succinctly where they could go—but hey, jumping into fiery hell is what they did for a living anyway, so no big change there.

A couple of the helo pilots had nailed down a big table right in the middle of the bustling seating area: Jeannie, Mickey, and Vern. Good "field of fire" in the immediate area.

He and Tim headed over, but Akbar managed to snag the chair closest to the really hot lady with down-her-back curling dark-auburn hair at the next table over—set just right to see her profile easily. Hard shot, sitting there with her parents, but damn she was amazing. And if that was her mom, it said the woman would be good looking for a long time to come.

Two-Tall grimaced at him and Akbar offered him a comfortable "beat out your ass" grin. But this one didn't feel like that. Maybe it was the whole parental thing. He sat back and kept his mouth shut.

He made sure that Two-Tall could see his interest. That made Tim honor bound to try and cut Akbar out of the running.

LAURA JENSON HAD SPOTTED them coming into the restaurant. Her dad was only moments behind.

"Those two are walking like they just climbed off their first-ever horseback ride."

She had to laugh, they did. So stiff and awkward they barely managed to move upright. They didn't look like first-time windsurfers, aching from the unexpected workout. They'd also walked in like they thought they were two gifts to god, which was even funnier. She turned away to avoid laughing in their faces. Guys who thought like that rarely appreciated getting a reality check.

Keep reading this completed series at fine retailers everywhere:
Wildfire at Dawn
Wildfire at Larch Creek
Wildfire on the Skagit

M.L. BUCHMAN

B&N and NPR Top 5 Romance Author of the Year

"One of our favorite authors."
Romantic Times Book Reviews

Androcles the Christmas Lion:
Betsy

a Seattle romance story

ANDROCLES THE CHRISTMAS LION:
BETSY

etsy searches for her true Christmas wish on the ferry ride to Seattle. Mama is taking her to see Santa and there isn't much time left.

Androcles, her stuffed lion friend, wears his favorite Christmas bathrobe against the harsh Seattle winter. He works on an idea of how he can fulfill Betsy's wish and heal her broken family.

Sometimes you just need to discover the right wish and ask for help from Androcles the Christmas Lion.

INTRODUCTION

I actually have Androcles. He's my muse.

He's a foot-high lion who wears a bathrobe all day, as I often did when I was writing. (I get dressed now for the twenty-second commute up the stairs to my office, though I'm not sure when or why that changed.)

Androcles was a gift from my family. He's a stuffed animal who came from a mall store called Build-A-Bear. And while he wasn't a bear, he sat there waiting for me. Being a "symbol" kind of family, we put a little stone inside him that we had picked up on the Scottish island of Iona during a research trip for my fourth-ever novel *Monk's Maze.*

I named him for the folktale of Androcles and the lion.

For over a decade, Androcles has watched over my shoulder as I write. He has a little cluster of plush friends who keep him company including the platypus from my first novel *Cookbook from Hell: Reheated,* Harold the parrot from *The Nara Reaction,* and Licorice the tiny, all-black writing cat who just showed up one day but has been too shy to join a story—at least so far.

Androcles likes adventures. He's traveled all over Oregon, posing for pictures in every single covered bridge in the state and rode in my pack as we traveled to the East Coast and drove through five states and a hundred towns looking for a new home. He was always happy to consult on the advantages of the different possibilities we visited.

This story is about a journey that Androcles decided to take one Christmas. I'm sure he'll voyage forth again soon.

ANDROCLES THE CHRISTMAS LION: BETSY

I watch the snow fall and the big waves outside the window of the ferry. Except I don't really. I'm thinking very hard about my Christmas wish. Mama was taking me on our special trip to Seattle to see Santa. We were having a girls' day and I had to think hard about what to ask for. Most of my friends would ask for a video or a doll or a bike. But not me. I wanted those, but it seemed like a waste of a whole trip across the water to see Santa.

"That's a pretty fierce-looking lion you've got there."

I look up at the man who stands in the aisle near my seat. Maybe something was wrong with him. Mama had warned me about talking to strangers, but he looked nice. And we were on the ferry. I sat in my safe seat. It's right against the window across the aisle from the place where the people who run the ferry work. Mama lets me sit here by myself for a minute while she got a cup of coffee.

The man doesn't take Mama's seat. He doesn't come any closer. I make sure I have a good hold on Androcles in my lap. Maybe the man thinks Androcles really was scary.

I look down at my lion. He's a big lion, for a stuffed animal. But sitting on my pillow at night, his feet don't come near the edge. Maybe he's not that big a lion. And he is wearing his white bathrobe and his

195

red-and-white Christmas hat. How could you call a lion fierce when he's wearing a white bathrobe and a Christmas hat?

I wrap my arms tighter around his soft fur, his fuzzy mane tickles my chin. I remember what Mama said about talking to strangers, but Androcles thought I should say something.

"He's very fierce," I warn the man. I imagined Androcles bearing big nasty teeth and snarling like a lion on the television shows. "Very." I try to make my voice low and serious like my kindergarten teacher, Mrs. Brown.

"I can see that. Does he have a name?"

I look down, but my lion doesn't say anything.

"Yes."

For some reason, the man thinks that is very funny. He laughs at me. But it isn't like the boys at school when I tripped and fell on the playground. He laughs nice. As if I'd said something funny.

"Will you tell me his name?"

The ferry hit a big wave and the boat tilted. Not bad. But I would have to take a step to keep my balance if I stood up. I try to keep my feet steady, but the big waves make me step sometimes. I have watched other people. Everyone has to step. Some have to grab on to something. A big wave like this, and some people half-fall into a seat. I'm better than most, Androcles tells me it would be easier if I had four feet, but I tell him I don't. Sometimes his ideas sound good, but really aren't.

The man doesn't step. He doesn't grab on. He shifts. It's like he stays still and the boat moves around him. The only people who do that work on the ferry. They watch out for me and Mama. He must work on the ferry, even if he doesn't wear a uniform.

I decide I will tell him.

"Androcles. Androcles the very fierce lion," I remind him.

He squats down until his face is down at my level. He holds out a hand, and I pull mine back. I see the ferry man in the doorway watching me, so I try to be brave. But the man doesn't reach for my hand. He reaches for Androcles' paw, then he shakes it.

"Pleased to meet you, Androcles."

Androcles doesn't bite him. I can feel in my arms that he is shaking the man's hand back.

This close I can see his eyes are very blue. Not like Mama's, which are the color of the sky, but like the middle blue in my crayon box.

"And do you have a name?" I ask the man, Androcles wants to know.

"Yes," he answers.

It is my turn to laugh. I get why I was funny before. Androcles and I laugh together.

"Will you tell it to us?"

He looks very serious. Another big wave rocks the ferry. It's very stormy now. Even squatting down, the man stays still while the boat moves around him, moving me with it.

"I don't know if I should. After all, it can be a dangerous thing to tell your name to a very fierce lion."

Androcles growls. It's a deep growl, but a quiet one. He does that one when someone outsmarts him. Not many people are smarter than Androcles, and no grownups except Mama. And even with Mama I have to shush him to be quiet sometimes.

"It will be okay." I half tell the man and half tell Androcles. I want to know his name, then I can ask him how he knows so much about lions. Then maybe he can teach me not to move when the ferry boat does. I hold Androcles extra tight so that he can't jump at the man.

"Can I help you?" That's Mama's angry tone.

She stops right beside him. I didn't see her come back.

The man doesn't get to his feet and act all funny like they usually do when they see Mama's cane. He looks up at her with the same serious smile he had when he shook Androcles' paw.

"I was worried about this girl. It seems to me that she can tame lions at a very young age. I wanted to be sure that the rest of us were safe around her."

I like how it sounds. Me, a tamer of fierce lions. Not that Androcles was very fierce, but I could pretend.

Another wave, and Mama had to step quickly sideways. A big splash of brown coffee, and her cane hit the floor with a loud whack!

Before I could jump up, the man rose, caught her arm, kept her steady, and then guided her to her seat. He was taller than Mama.

"Thank you." Mama's voice still sounds tight and angry, like when I've been bad.

But she didn't look at me. And she didn't look at the man. Not even at Androcles. She looked down at where her cane lay on the floor between them and clutching her coffee cup in both hands.

The man squats down and hands Mama back her cane.

"Do you need some paper towels?"

Mama had worn her good white coat special for my trip to go see Santa because I told her that she always looks like a beautiful snow princess when she wears it. The spot is all brown on her nice snow princess coat.

"No, thank you." She reaches in her pocket and takes out a napkin, but it doesn't do much to help.

"Or a fresh cup of coffee?"

"Definitely no."

The man looks so sad, like Androcles when he can't help me with my making letters.

Mama glances at me. Usually I can tell what she's thinking. I can get her things before she even asks. But I don't know what she wants.

"Thank you for keeping my daughter company."

"My pleasure." And I saw him look closely at Mama, but try to pretend he wasn't. Like when Androcles is watching something he wants, but doesn't want to give anything away by looking right at it.

The man starts to get up.

"Wait." I say.

He squats back down.

"Wait."

And he does.

But I can't think of why I want him to wait. Now he and Mama both watch me. That's when I feel Androcles watching me without looking at me.

"Oh. Androcles still wants to know your name."

"Tom. Tom Jacobs."

"TomTom," I say it like one word. I don't know why, but I do. We all laugh. Even Mama. Mama has a wonderful laugh, all shiny and bright. Even if she doesn't use it very much.

TomTom talks to us while the ferry gets closer to Seattle. The snow whirls all about outside the window like a fairyland. When Androcles reminds me, I ask him how he stays still when the ferry moves around him.

He learned on his sailboat. It's little, like the ones I see scooting away from the ferry on nice days.

He shows me. We stand side-by-side while Mama and Androcles watch. I keep my knees loose. Like in ballet. When the ferry moves, I keep my body still and let my feet move. I let my knees bend. It takes practice. Soon, only TomTom and I keep standing whenever the ferry tips.

Mama applauds. But she won't try. She looks sad when I ask. Her eyes again go to her cane and I remember. She can't walk pretty. Not since the accident. The one I don't remember. The one that took away my dad, who I don't remember.

I hold her hand while the ferry docks. Sometimes it bumps hard when it lands.

TomTom makes sure we get down to the taxi okay. It's mostly inside, but he stays close anyway.

He wishes her goodbye, then he squats down to face me and Androcles.

"Maybe he isn't such a fierce lion."

"No," I tell him. "Androcles is very fierce. I'm a really good fierce lion tamer."

He shakes Androcles' paw and says very seriously, "You protect her, now. You hear?"

Androcles growls that he will.

THE STORE IS EVEN BETTER than I remember. People are everywhere. There are Christmas lights and wreaths and trees everywhere we look. The decorations are all so pretty and it smells like the pine woods near our house only better. There's a big star shining on the outside.

Mama is happier as we go from one end of the store to another. We try on dresses we would never wear. I get a necklace of pink glass beads. She gets one that matches.

The toys. The toys go on forever. I see the doll that Juby wants. And the truck that Davey wants. The perfect dress for Debbie. But I can't find what I want.

What I want.

I ask Androcles, but he is just quiet and thoughtful the way he gets sometimes.

He's watching Mama. And I watch her too, without watching her. Just like Androcles taught me. She's so pretty. But so sad. She tries to hide her cane, but needs it to walk. I want to tell her it doesn't matter. She's so beautiful.

And I think about how TomTom looked at her. Watched her. Caught her so easily, and didn't look at her funny when she dropped her cane.

I'm starting to get an idea. But I can't figure it out yet.

THERE ARE a lot of kids waiting to see Santa Claus. I can just barely see where he sits in his big chair with his reindeer. A very tall elf, Androcles always thought elves were short, told us why they didn't move.

"The real reindeer are resting at the North Pole. They want to be all ready for Christmas eve. So we made statues of each one to keep Santa company while they rest."

I like the idea, but Androcles thinks the elf is pretty silly. Reindeer have had most of the year off. Why would they leave Santa alone?

As I get closer to Santa, I start to wonder. I watched carefully out the taxi windows and counted seven other Santas before we got to the store. All of those Santas must be statues of the real Santa. They could move. Maybe they were helpers. If they were, how could I know if this was the real Santa?

I worried about that. I didn't want to ask Mama. She seemed so excited that I was going to see Santa. He must be the real one.

But Androcles and I weren't so sure.

All of a sudden it was my turn, and the tall elf lifted me up and sat me in Santa's lap.

I hadn't thought of my wish yet.

Santa laughed. And said, "Ho Ho Ho!" so happily that even Androcles liked him with hardly any growl at all.

Santa has the bluest eyes. The same color as the middle blue in my crayon set.

I now knew exactly what I wanted for Christmas. I leaned down to whisper my idea to Androcles.

But Androcles was busy shaking Santa's hand with his paw.

When I look up at Santa's face, he isn't looking at me.

He's looking at Mama.

I've never seen her look so happy.

Wow! Santa really does make dreams come true.

M.L. BUCHMAN
3-TIME BOOKLIST TOP 10 ROMANCE AUTHOR OF THE YEAR
DELTA MISSION:
OPERATION RUDOLPH
DELTA FORCE ROMANCE STORY #9

DELTA MISSION: OPERATION RUDOLPH

*I*n three days, **Betsy** *retires from a decade as a Delta Force tracker and shooter. But a training mission gone wrong...or perhaps "strange" is a better word...sets her one last challenge.*

St. Nick's lead reindeer, whose name is actually Jeremy, has gone missing. The dangerously handsome **chief herder elf, Horatio,** *needs the best tracker in any world.*

Is Betsy hallucinating?

Can Christmas be saved?

Is there enough time left for: Delta Mission: Operation Rudolph?

INTRODUCTION

Earlier I mentioned that I don't write ghost stories...right before I wrote my first ghost story.

Well, I *really* don't write elf stories. Not elves, brownies, pixies, hobbits, ogres...none of them.

But how could I resist Horatio the Christmas elf in charge of Santa's reindeer when he decided to recruit a Delta Force operator to help him save Christmas?

This is totally not the story I set out to write, but it was so much fun that I can't remember what story I *did* start with. There's even a guest appearance by Mark Henderson. The shooting that he refers to is in Henderson's Ranch #5, *Big Sky, Loyal Heart.*

DELTA MISSION: OPERATION RUDOLPH

*L*ive-fire training.

She didn't need any blasted live-fire training. Especially not during a freak snowstorm that was inundating Range 37 at Fort Bragg, North Carolina. Betsy's personal thermostat was currently set to Congo jungle, not three-days-before-Christmas blizzard.

Okay, the pretty white flakes fluttering down on the rifle range didn't count as a blizzard—though she'd grown up in Arkansas and it was more than she was used to—but it was cold enough that they were sticking to everything, including her. And her breath showed in puffs. She focused on breathing only through her nose to cut down on the clouds that might give away her position to the instructors.

The fact that she was out of Delta Force and the Army in three more days didn't matter to them. She'd done her decade in the field and Christmas Day would mark her release from service. But when command said you did a training, you did one. She was theirs to order about until the moment she walked out the gate.

Betsy kept low behind a stone wall and pondered the enemy's next move. She'd barely had a glimpse of the artificial town that was the core of the training range's purpose. The Fort Bragg training squadron was always rearranging it in unexpected ways. She'd been in the field for a full year on her latest deployment, so the hundreds of hours she'd spent here over the years were now irrelevant.

The hundred-plus acres of Range 37 was a 360-degree, live-fire shoothouse. Some parts were modern urban, others Kandahar Province-low-and-crammed-together.

What kind of idiot training scenario sent a solo soldier on a snatch-and-grab mission? Minimum for that type of operation was a four-man team: two to grab, two to guard. Instead, they'd sent her in on her own without any explanation.

The only way out is through. Old axiom.

Of course solo was the story of her life. Dad gone from the beginning. While her high school classmates had been discovering friends and sex, she'd been caring for her mother through a fatal bout of cancer. Delta Force, the true loners of the US military, had been as natural to her as breathing. One of the only women there? Sure. Whatever.

But a one-woman snatch-and-grab operation? She was probably the best they had for that—no matter how stupid an idea it was. Perhaps they were using her to test some crazy scenario just to see how it worked.

Fine! Time to show them just what she *could* do.

She lay down in the snow and fast-rolled across the gap between the stone wall she'd been crouched behind and the brick building next over. As she rolled, she kept her rifle scope to her eye. Her best moving shot for rooftops was actually on her back, not her stomach— an unlikely trick she'd learned by accident in Mosul. Head tipped back, HK416 at the ready, she spotted two hostiles atop the wall on the far side of a broad courtyard. She hit both from her back, rolled onto her stomach, double-tapped an armed bad guy target crouching by a plywood maple tree, then two more into the mannequins on the roof from her back just to make sure the targets stayed dead.

The six hard clangs of bullets striking metal targets registered only after she was safe behind the red brick.

She held her fire as two children mannequins peeked at her from a nearby window. A dummy woman rushed across the street, her form gliding on a hidden track. A rough-painted man close behind her, using the woman figure as a shield, had an AK-47. Two harsh rings of metal echoed between the buildings as Betsy shot him twice in the face—all she could see of him—and one more as she hit his knee through the fluttering back of the woman's dress.

A particularly large snowflake plastered itself across the lens of her shooting goggles. It left a wet smear when she brushed it aside.

Betsy had tracked her quarry off the edge of the map somewhere, slipping out of simulated Afghanistan into a quaint French village setting that she didn't recall ever seeing before.

The next building over, probably just painted plywood, was an exceptional imitation of rose-and-gray stonework, medieval arches, and cobbled streets barely wide enough for two donkeys to pass. It would make a resting place for the Merovingian French kings back before the Dark Ages. With the snow, it looked perfect for finding a little Provençal bistro with a mug of mulled wine and a cozy chair by a stone fireplace.

Of course the best that would be waiting for her after this would be a hot cup of coffee and a burger at the SWCS DFAC—the Special Warfare Center and School Dining Facility. If she didn't freeze to death first.

A glance back the way she'd come to make sure no one was behind her and—

Betsy blinked hard, as if that would clear away the obscuring snow.

There was no longer an Afghan town behind her, though she knew she'd just been through one. She was at the center of a French village that looked too authentic, even for Range 37. Alleys twisted. Yew trees, so old and gnarled they truly might have been planted by some ancient French king, rose before a two-story, stone, row house. A cluster of dormant rose vines climbed a nearby wall, some of the stems thicker than her arm. They'd been there a while...a long while.

An actual donkey, pulling a tiny cart bearing a large wine barrel, clopped along, his unshod hooves muffled by the fallen snow. The hard rattle of the two ironclad, wooden wheels sounded from the cobbles.

She spun back to look down the street where she'd just shot the target with an AK-47. More people flowed across the courtyard now, but not gliding on any hidden rail. Some carried gigantic woven baskets, others wooden platters of food—all hurrying this way and that as if preparing for some event. Their clothing was loose and broadcloth.

And puffs of breath were coming out of their mouths.

There weren't supposed to be any real people in a live-fire training except the attackers—in this scenario, just her. If she made a mistake, she could kill an innocent, not that she ever had. She'd always scored perfect marks in target discernment. A man came out a doorway close beside where she lay in the snow and almost stepped on her.

"Excusez-moi." He definitely spoke before hurrying down the road. Not a mannequin.

She sat up carefully, keeping her eye out for potential shooters. All of the people on the streets—and there were more with each passing moment—were dressed for some form of medieval village reenactment like the Norwegian Folk Museum in Oslo, only more French-Grand-Master-painting-come-to-life than simplistic-Nordic.

Not a one looked at her. She glanced down at herself to be sure that she hadn't changed as well. Army boots, camo pants, Kevlar shooter's vest filled with spare magazines for her rifle and a Glock still in its holster. She indeed still held her HK416 rifle and could feel the helmet on her head. Another blink, and she could feel her eyelashes brushing on the inside of her shooter goggles.

"What the hell?"

Even the air smelled different. Baked breads, wood fires, roasting meat that made her stomach growl.

Only one man was out of place now. He stood in the exact center of the courtyard and was looking directly at her.

Out of place! The alarm went off in her head. Instinct kicked in and she aimed and fired, only at the last moment realizing that he held no weapon. She tried to shift her aim, but knew it wasn't enough.

The man leaned slightly to one side and the bullet missed his cheek by a hair's breadth, smacking into a stone arch behind him and releasing a puff of rock dust as it pulverized itself.

Then, as calm as could be, he looked back at her.

Nobody, but nobody dodged a round fired from an HK416.

BETSY COULD ONLY STARE at him as the villagers continued to mill about without paying any attention to either of them. By now the donkey had drawn even with her position. She reached out to touch it. Though she wore thin gloves, it felt real enough.

The man, however, didn't look real. Six feet tall, but slender as a willow branch. He didn't look unfit or misproportioned, just impossibly slender. He had glorious black hair that fell to his waist, whereas her own blonde was short-cropped and barely reached her jawline. He had a long face with high cheekbones, pale skin, and the bluest eyes she'd ever seen. He was dressed in form-fitting black leather that might be appropriate for a chick on a motorcycle calendar. It did look very fine on him, so maybe she finally understood why guys went so ape over those kinds of calendars. A little. Not much really.

One thing was for certain, though. It made him look even more out of place in Medieval France than she did.

She couldn't react, couldn't find it in her to move as he stepped among the hurrying townsfolk until he was standing just an arm's-length away. A thin red line scored his cheek.

He noticed the direction of her attention and raised a hand to brush at it.

"I'll have to remember to move faster in future encounters."

"Move. Faster." People didn't step aside from bullets moving at 890 meters per second.

His smile was brief, but dazzling and she could only blink in surprise.

"But..." She didn't know "but" what, but it was the only sound she could make.

"I'm Horatio."

"Horatio?"

"Yes," his voice was impossibly deep and sounded more like flowing water than spoken words.

"Is that like 'Go West, Young Man' Horatio Alger? Or 'Alas, poor Yorick' in Hamlet?"

"Nor Captain Horatio Hornblower. Just Horatio the Herder."

"The herder of what? Who..." No. "*What* are you?" She forced herself to look away from his dazzling blue eyes. Her gaze landed on a prominently pointed ear where the chill wind blew aside an elegant length of his hair like some runway model's. He was both the handsomest and the prettiest man she'd ever seen, even if he wasn't one.

A group of children, ones she'd have labeled as beggars, gathered together in a group and began to sing in Latin. As a child, she'd chosen to do her confirmation into the Roman Catholic church in Latin. As an adult, she could only wonder why she'd bothered with any of it.

Orientis partibus
adventavit asinus,
pulcher et fortissimus,
Sarcinis aptissimus.

"From the east, the pretty Advent donkey carries the sacred baggage?" Maybe not so much with her Catholic school Latin.

"It is an ancient Latin Christmas carol, popular in twelfth-century France," the man waved his long-fingered hand negligently about as if that was somehow where they were. "In your language it is called *The Friendly Beasts* and relates the legend of the animals who helped with the birth of Jesus. That verse is the donkey telling of carrying Mary to the manger."

"Oh." What else was she supposed to say to such a crazy statement. She considered for a moment. This *definitely* wasn't Range 37. She rose to her toes and tried clicking the heels of her Army boots together three times.

Nothing changed.

Maybe it only worked for ruby Army boots.

Horatio smiled at her as if he knew exactly what she was doing.

"Allow me to escort you elsewhere," he turned sideways to her and offered his arm. At a loss for what else to do, she shifted her rifle to her other hand—in shooting, all Delta operators were ambidextrous—left the safety off, and slipped her fingers about his elbow. He felt as thin as he looked, but he felt as strong as a seasoned operator who could hike fifty kilometers with a full pack, just to get *into* battle.

He led her down the street to a doorway that had a wooden sign hung above it depicting a cluster of grapes, and led her inside. The smoke from the big, ill-vented, stone fireplace stung her eyes and there was a rank smell like an entire Delta platoon that had been in the field for a month without bathing. But beneath that, the cinnamon and nutmeg of mulled wine and the richness of mutton stew filled the air.

Horatio sat with the elegance of a powerful man at a small, rough table close by the warm fire. She propped her rifle against the wall close to hand and sat across from him. Their knees brushed together comfortably. He didn't draw away, but neither did he press. It was merely comfortable, friendly even. Not something she was used to with men. For the most part they either wanted sex or wanted her to get the hell out of the boys' club military unit. Horatio the Herder was harder to read and she rather liked that bit of mystery.

In moments, they were served with clay mugs of wine—enough to plow her under the table if she tried to finish it—and a steaming bowl of stew.

"The wine is quite acceptable, but I would exercise a degree of caution regarding the stew," Horatio winced as if it was bad memory.

She sipped at the wine and decided that if *this* was good wine, she'd definitely be avoiding the stew.

Betsy pinched herself, no change.

"Any chance that you'd know how badly I was injured or when I'm getting off these drugs? Or are you just a gorgeous hallucination named Horatio?"

Horatio hid a smile with a big draught of wine, but his blue eyes twinkled. They *actually* twinkled. It made him look very merry. If he really was in full elf-character, which his pointy ears indicated was likely, maybe it was part of his job to be merry. But that didn't explain how he'd made those pretty blue eyes twinkle. Of course "Elf: identification and interaction with" wasn't in any part of Delta Force's Operator Training Course.

Maybe she didn't want off these drugs, whatever they were. She'd had morphine after being shot up in Nigeria once and been completely loopy but calm as well. She still remembered portions of that helo ride while the combat search-and-rescue medics struggled to stabilize her. An incredibly handsome stranger, even in a seedy medieval pub, was a far more interesting reaction.

"I can place you back in Range 37 at any moment you should choose to request it. But I would like to discuss a special mission with you prior to such an eventuality."

"A special mission?" She tried the wine again while considering where he might have learned such speech patterns. British sit-coms came to mind. The second sip of wine slammed the back of her throat with its tannic bite. This time it only made her want to gag rather than rip her throat out, which was an improvement. She could also taste the high alcohol content. That, she decided, could be a good thing in the current situation and managed to brace herself through a third taste, but couldn't manage a fourth.

"Yes," Horatio spooned up some of the stew, apparently ignoring his earlier warning—at least until he put it in his mouth. Then looked as if he didn't know where to spit it out.

"In the fire."

He did so, creating a brief flurry of sparks.

"Back to my question," Betsy nudged her own stew bowl a little farther away as a safety precaution. "What *are* you and why am I hallucinating you?"

Not finding anywhere to wipe his mouth, he used his fingers, then wiped them on the edge of the table. "You are *not* hallucinating."

"Just what I'd expect a hallucination to say."

Horatio sighed before forging on. "This is real. Or mostly real. We see each other, but the locals merely observe a pair of strangers in locals' clothing."

"Uh-huh." Betsy could only assume this was one of those accidents that was bad enough for amnesia to kick in. Most of this she wouldn't mind losing, though Horatio himself was a real pleasure to look at. She'd been in the field a long time and dallying with a squad mate just wasn't an option. Horatio however... He looked far yummier than the wine.

What *had* happened?

Maybe a stone wall of Range 37 collapsed onto her? Or perhaps one of her shots at the metal targets had ricocheted back. At this point it wouldn't surprise if one of the targets had *shot* her back. Talking to a reindeer herding elf in a twelfth-century pub made anything seem possible.

"And as pertains to your earlier question, I am an elf—of the Christmas variety. The one entrusted with the care of Santa's reindeer, if I may be specific."

"Hence, Horatio the Herder," Betsy didn't think her imagination was strange enough to cook up this one, which was tipping the scale— impossibly—toward the side of this experience being somehow real.

"Precisely. My dilemma lies in the fact that it is only three days to Christmas and I can not find the lead reindeer anywhere. I have need of aid from a professional."

"Me?"

"You."

"You need me to track down...Rudolph?"

"Well, his name is Jeremy, but essentially yes."

"Jeremy the red-nosed reindeer. Doesn't exactly have the right ring to it, does it?"

"Robert L. May was prone to agreeing with you, which is why he changed the name for the Montgomery Ward children's book he wrote regarding Jeremy's tribulations as a young reindeer."

"Wow!" Betsy managed a large swallow of wine to fortify herself. "You actually delivered all that as a straight line. I'm impressed." Then she stared down at the wine and wondered what exactly was in it that she almost believed him.

"So, lay it out for me."

"Lay *it* out? What needs laying out of it?"

Betsy pulled out her Benchmade Infidel knife, thumbed the release, and the four-inch, double-edged blade snapped out the front of the handle. She began carving the Special Operations Command shoulder patch into the wooden table with the point—a stylized arrowhead with a knife up the middle.

Horatio eyed her carefully. "I expect that you are a hard woman to buy Christmas presents for. What's your Christmas wish?"

"I gave up on wishes a long time ago."

Horatio looked at her aghast.

She held up the blade. The black-coated D2 steel appeared bloody in the dim firelight. "This one did nicely as a gift to myself. Start talking, Elf." She returned to her carving.

"We permit the reindeer to run wild during the summer season."

"I could do with a little running wild myself." Betsy could feel her inhibitions slipping away. She hadn't had that much wine. But knowing that you were injured and in some drug-induced dream made it difficult to care much about propriety. And if she was going to run a little wild, who better to do it with than a gorgeous man-elf-herder-thing.

"They always return when the fall lengthens the wavelengths that leaves reflect."

"Lengthens the wavelengths? Oh, reds and golds. Never mind.

Keep going." Keeping her gaze averted from his intense eyes didn't help much. His slightly hoity-toity way of speaking didn't diminish the fact that his voice was just as beautiful as he was. She couldn't be so shallow that a beautiful man with a liquid voice was getting to her, even if he was.

"Jeremy has failed to return."

"That was the fall. And you're just contacting me three days before Christmas? That is not what we'd typically call adroit mission planning." She began digging the arch of the upper tab of the shoulder patch. What if she carved in the word "Airborne" as it should be and the table was discovered eight hundred years from now? Cause a hell of a stir. Perhaps she should drop into wherever this village was in the real world and find out for herself.

"Actually, yesterday was the final day of fall. We have now traversed the threshold of the winter solstice and such matters are suddenly come to a head."

"Maybe a hunter got him."

Horatio actually flinched. His oddly light complexion paled even further.

"Sorry, but you have to consider all of the possibilities."

"That is one I shall not be considering until all other hope is lost."

"So, where do we begin?" It wasn't often that an impossibly beautiful man asked her to do something so highly unlikely. Usually it was requests for sexual favors, which wasn't something she doled out to any Tom, Dick, or Horatio.

"At the stables, I suppose."

"Of course. Because why wouldn't Santa's reindeer have stables. Are you nuts, Horatio? I was thinking it was me, but maybe it's you."

"I have not considered the possibility," Horatio's beautiful brow actually furrowed for a long moment as he studied his wine, then shook his head, causing his hair to flutter attractively. "No, I find your premise unlikely."

Could she ever be with a man prettier than she was? If he looked like Horatio, in a heartbeat.

"Do elves kiss?" It was amazing what could be done within a drug-induced haze.

"We do," the color returned to his cheeks, brightly.

"Do they marry?"

"Is that a proposal, Betsy?"

Now it was her turn to scoff. "I just don't like my fantasies to already be married before I kiss them."

"Then you may do so without further concern if that is your wish." The bright color high on his cheeks wasn't going away, which was rather cute.

It would be a little like kissing a movie star. He was too perfect. But that wasn't exactly a complaint worth filing with the Fantasy Dream Department—a division of the US Army Personnel Services Branch she'd never thought of submitting a requisition request to before.

Betsy reached across the table to snag the lapel of his body-hugging black leather suit and pulled him closer. She leaned in and briefly tasted the mutton stew on his lips. Thankfully, she was past that before it could put her off completely. Past that, he tasted of cinnamon and the wild outdoors of a snowy night. Of luscious hot cocoa and a crackling fire.

Horatio's kiss was warm, attentive, thoughtful...and masterful.

If she hadn't been dreaming before, she most certainly was now. Dreaming of how fast they could go somewhere there weren't any other people, just the two of them and a big, warm bed.

Her pulse was soon chattering faster than an M134 Minigun on full auto, yet Horatio was still only exploring the first steps of a kiss.

"Get me out of here," her own voice sounded desperate and needy.

"As you wish."

THE COLD SLAPPED her so hard that she lost her breath—as well as her lip lock on Horatio.

"What the hell?"

"The stables."

"You brought me to a freezing cold barn?"

"I brought you to the source as you requested. These are the reindeer stables of St. Nicholas of Myra."

Betsy could only look around in astonishment. A long line of stalls appeared to be made out of living yew trees, all trained into walls and stable dividers. Their roots were lost beneath a luxuriant layer of living grass—the brightest green she'd ever seen. The stables were lit by fireflies swarming among the branches.

And the sky.

The ceiling was of glass so clear that she could hardly tell it was there between her and the magnificent night sky. As she blinked away the worst of the pub's smoke and her eyes adjusted, she began picking out constellations.

"That's the North Star."

Horatio looked up as well. "It is."

"It's directly overhead."

"Point six seven degrees from directly overhead to be precise. We are at the celestial north pole rather than the magnetic or geographic one. Nice, isn't it?"

"But the North Pole isn't over land. It's over sea ice."

"It is, in most planes of reality."

Betsy couldn't think of what else to do…so she hit him. Not hard—it had been a very nice kiss after all. Just squarely enough in the solar plexus that he wouldn't be able to speak for a few moments so that she could do some thinking.

Horatio dropped to his knees and wheezed a bit.

North Pole.

A missing reindeer named Jeremy.

An elf, a very handsome elf who could kiss better than any human—a kiss that also left her wondering what else he could do better.

St. Nicholas beneath Polaris the North Star in some very adjacent reality.

Real? Surreal? Digital? Drugs?

No way to tell.

She sighed, and helped Horatio back to his feet.

The only way out is through. Old axiom. There were times she hated old axioms.

"Last spring. Did anyone see which way Jeremy went?"

IT HAD TAKEN the CIA years to find bin Laden. And another half-year to actually get around to taking him down after "Maya" had found him.

She had three days to track a reindeer. Her total assets? One elf who didn't want it to be known that he'd lost Santa's most famous reindeer, Jeremy.

The first break came when they were questioning the other reindeer. They didn't like having her around and were very standoffish, until she dug around in Horatio's larder and found a bag of carrots. They warmed up to her quickly after that. Who knew that reindeer had a major weak spot for carrots.

A small portion of St. Nick's deer herd—mostly the younger set—had gone south and west last spring, rather than south and east to their normal habitat in Finland. It turned out that reindeer had a particularly low-brow sense of humor—even worse than most Delta operators. They liked spending their summers mingling with the Finnish herds and teasing them about not making the cut to become a Christmas reindeer. They also weren't above tripping them into mudholes and the like.

The breakaway herd had crossed down over the Canadian tundra, mingling with the caribou herds in some sort of convention. But they quickly grew bored as the Canadians had even less of a sense of humor than their Finnish counterparts.

That had led to any number of fights and endless head butting. The younger members of the herd whined about it no end.

"Teenagers," she scoffed to Horatio after he'd translated that for her. "Hard to deal with."

"Gift cards." Apparently that was his harshest epithet. "It is the only way St. Nick has found to deal with them at Christmas."

Betsy had been such a good girl as a teen, of course taking care of her ailing mother had made that an obvious choice. She'd even been well behaved as an Army grunt then a Delta operator. And now, just three days from freedom, she'd been injured and was drugged up in some Fort Bragg hospital. It didn't seem fair.

She tossed out some more carrots to get the rest of the story. Most had continued west to roam with the big herds in Alaska. But Jeremy had turned south once more, toward the heat and bright sun. He'd said he was headed to a place called Mont-a-land or something like. None of them had ever heard of it.

"Montana?"

Some of them thought that sounded right, but were more interested in carrots than answering questions. She took the bag with her when she left. When they protested, she simply made a show of resettling her rifle across her shoulders…which proved most effective. About time they did some growing up.

She and Horatio started in the Canadian Northwest Territories at a place with the unlikely name of Reindeer Station. Eight or nine houses located along the edge of the sprawling Mackenzie River delta less than fifty miles from the Arctic Ocean. It wasn't all that much warmer than the North Pole with just two days to Christmas. The river was iced over and was crisscrossed with snowmobile tracks. She'd borrowed a brilliant red parka with a white sheepskin lining to keep her warm.

It took most of the morning to track the region's sole remaining reindeer herder to his remote cabin. It was a gruesome affair. Not merely well away from even the hamlet of Reindeer Station, it was also the butchery for bulls thinned from the herd. Reindeer meat was stacked outside in the Arctic chill and quick-frozen beneath hides. Inside the hut, the tools of the trade dangled from hooks on the wall. Yet the herder also had a young reindeer on a leash as a pet.

Horatio was shivering even more than the temperature could account for.

Betsy held his hand tightly to calm him, which she didn't mind doing at all, while she was talking to the man. Even while shivering from disgust or distress, Horatio's hand was as warm as a handmade quilt. He appeared perfectly comfortable in his body-hugging leather despite the Arctic temperature.

The herder's English was limited and apparently Horatio was only fluent in English, French, and reindeer, so he was of no help. The herder, speaking mostly in some Inuit language, allowed as he might have seen a rather curious animal that had stood aloof from his herd of three thousand reindeer. A magnificent bull with more points than he could count. He waved south.

"Inuvik?" That was the next town, some twenty miles away.

He shook his head and waved again.

"Fort McPherson?" It was the only other town she knew in the Northwest Territories.

Again the wave south, "Mont-a-land."

But going directly to Montana was too big a leap. It would take forever to pick up Jeremy's track again. So they worked south in stages following the rumors of an aloof, many-pointed bull reindeer.

"I thought Jeremy was supposed to be a cute little guy."

"Indeed he was, seventy-five years ago when Robert L. May wrote about him. He has matured somewhat over the years. He is still a sweetheart though as he never allowed the success to go to his head."

"How long do reindeer usually live? Maybe he died of old age."

"Fifteen to twenty years, typically, unless they are in the employ of St. Nicholas. Then their lives are rather extended."

Betsy eyed him carefully. There was an agelessness to Horatio's clear features. He would have been as classically handsome a thousand years ago as he was now. Perhaps there were some questions that it was better not to ask.

Besides, time was running too fast.

"Can't you slow it down?"

"Not even St. Nicholas can do that."

Thirty-six hours remaining.

Jeremy wanted her to eat something after they'd chased leads all the way down the frozen Mackenzie to the small town of Yellowknife on Great Slave Lake. From there, they'd run the ice road over to the hamlet of Detah and were now sitting in a small barn. The owner had told the story of the most "magnificent bull" he'd ever tracked while hunting. Best he'd ever seen, but apparently his shot had gone wild.

"Jeremy is very wily," Horatio's whisper had tickled her ear like a warm breeze.

She tried a carrot, but they'd frozen hard. "Give me an MRE and let's get going."

So, he gave her a pre-heated Meal-Ready-to-Eat. She didn't ask how. Next time she'd ask for a roast beef dinner with Yorkshire pudding and see if her friendly neighborhood hallucination could deliver.

"Maybe you should rest." The small barn had a hayloft, and the hunter had returned to his ice fishing on the frozen lake. It was tempting. So very, very tempting. She couldn't remember the last time she'd been this tired.

"When the mission is done." She chowed down on the Southwest Beef and Black Beans while Horatio massaged her shoulders. Now that was something she could become very used to—far better than the cold, lack of sleep, and the utterly ludicrous situation.

His fingers were strong enough to ease even her soldier-hard muscles until she felt ready to melt against him. She tossed aside the empty MRE package and decided that a little melting wasn't completely outside the mission profile.

She'd forgotten—mostly—about the kiss in the ancient French bistro. The memory did nothing to prepare her for what happened next. Horatio felt luscious as he pulled her tightly against him. In mid-clench, she tried to rub herself even more tightly against his incredible body.

Horatio grunted, and not in a good way.

"Your vest," he managed to gasp.

Betsy paused and looked down between them. She wore her Glock sidearm, as most Delta did, front and center for a fast draw. Above that, pockets of ammo and emergency supplies made hard edges that had left scrapes on his smooth leather.

"Sorry." Vest. Mission. Ludicrous scenario.

The only way out is through.

She sighed, sat up, and patted Horatio's cheek. He had the decency to look disappointed despite the gouges she'd been digging into his chest.

"Your colonel," Horatio nodded to the south, "said that you were the hardest-driving scout in his entire team."

"You spoke to Colonel Gibson about finding one of Santa's reindeer?" She tried to imagine how the stern colonel took it.

"Perhaps I may not have asked him quite directly, but he was very impressed with your skills."

That was news to her. She hadn't known that Delta Force's commander even knew who she was.

She sighed to herself that some overwound inner drive wouldn't even let her enjoy a hallucinatory snuggle.

They left the tiny Detah barn and they turned south across Alberta.

THEY HAD pizza in Banff and she spent three delicious hours mostly passed out in the curve of Horatio's arms in a snowed-in hiking cabin high in Glacier Park. She didn't ask how Horatio moved them from place to place. It seemed that they flowed, glided, perhaps simply morphed from one destination to the next. It was a dream, so it was easy to not question the transitions.

But she would miss her time with Horatio. No, she'd miss Horatio himself. Even strung out on whatever narcotic was giving her this extended dream, she was becoming very attached to him.

Yes, he'd started out all strange and mysterious and mostly concerned about a missing reindeer. But he had shifted. More slowly than their jumping from one place to another, but just as steadily.

Still wrapped in her parka, she lay in his arms in the chill cabin and felt…right. As if it was where she was supposed to be. Perhaps "content" was a better word, though it was not one that had ever come up before in her life.

He hadn't asked about her past, which was just as well. She didn't want to talk about it. But neither had he talked about his. Did elves have pasts? Did elves have regrets? She hoped not as she had enough for both of them.

"What is an elf's life like?" She could feel him shift as if he was looking down at the top of her head in some surprise.

"Normal enough. The reindeer usually do a good job of taking care of themselves, that's why I didn't think to worry. Generally I spend but one month a year tending them. It's a good life for them as well." And he began telling her about their grazing habits, and the practical jokes they liked to play.

One year they'd started at the South Pole rather than the North, forcing St. Nicholas to act like a Dumpster-diver as he dug out successive presents from the bottom of the sleigh's pile instead of working top-down. Or the year they'd switched all of the rabbits' stockings with all of the squirrels'—the rabbits had ended up have a grand game of ice hockey with the acorns and walnuts but the squirrels had never figured out what to do with the sudden bounty of cabbage.

It was only as they were trekking south into the Flathead Wilderness of Montana that she realized he'd told her nothing of himself. Perhaps it was fair, she'd said nothing of herself either, but it rankled. Of course, with his voice, she'd happily listen to him reading the naughty and nice name list—especially the naughty if he gave some of the details.

Dawn broke hard.

She couldn't think of how else to describe it. While traveling through Canada, they had been in and out of snowstorms beneath gray skies. This morning, they'd left the cabin in Glacier Park beneath the last stars of the night, almost as brightly perfect as those from Santa's reindeer stables. It had been a relief that the North Star had shifted well down the sky, so they were indeed well to the south.

But standing atop the Castle Reef ridgeline and looking down at the Montana Front Range in one direction, and up into the heart of the snow-capped Rocky Mountains in the other, dawn began with a snap as sharp as the cold.

The sun lanced over the flat horizon from impossibly far away and the entire world was catapulted into a limitless blue bowl of sky.

"I take it this is why they call it Big Sky country," Horatio sounded breathless.

"I guess." Betsy also couldn't catch her breath. It might be the eight-thousand-foot elevation or the slicing cold of the morning wind driving ice crystals into her face like blowback from Barrett .50 cal sniper rifle.

It might be the view.

But it was more the realization that this was December 23rd. One way or another, their quest would be over today. As soon as sunset hit the International Date Line in roughly twelve hours, St. Nicholas would be flying off to do his job—with or without the errant Jeremy.

Yet she could feel that he was close. Some instinct, honed over the years by Delta training, told her their quarry was nearly in sight.

She flagged down a rancher passing by in his helicopter, who settled it neatly atop the peak. Clearly ex-military by how he flew, despite the fact that he now commanded a small Bell JetRanger with a herd of horses painted along the side.

"How can I help you, ma'am?" He drawled it out in a Texas accent so fake that it would get him lynched in certain states. "Need a lift off this here hilltop?"

"No, we're fine."

"We?" He tugged his mirrored sunglasses down enough to squint at her strangely.

She glanced aside at Horatio who just shook his head.

Fine. Whatever. So he was invisible or something. Had he shown up for anyone else, or had she just crossed Canada as a solo crazy lady talking to herself? She'd bet on the latter, but didn't have time to deal with it now.

"Have you seen a reindeer that—"

"Reindeer? We have moose and elk in these parts. Even a few caribou, but no reindeer."

"Reindeer and caribou are the same animal," Horatio prompted her.

When the pilot didn't respond, she repeated the information.

"Wa'll, ain't that a wonder."

"Have you seen a particularly impressive one lately?"

He rubbed his chin thoughtfully. He'd have been the handsomest man in any crowd that didn't include Horatio.

"Might have heard mention of one. Over to a hot spring up along the North Fork Deep Creek. My wife said she saw one when one of our guides and a guest shot—"

"Shot?" Betsy grabbed the pilot's arm in a panic.

"Shot two *young* bulls," the man looked down at his arm in some distress and tried to shake her off. At least the awful Texas accent was gone.

She shook him by his arm to keep him talking.

"She said it was the biggest old bull she'd ever seen. Had himself a couple of does and a fawn. Guess they didn't want to break up the family. Ease off, lady." He wiggled his arm a little and grimaced.

"Jeremy has a family?" Horatio's blue eyes were almost as wide as the Big Sky. Then he looked at her and his gaze shifted as if asking if she also had a family.

She had no one. No one on the outside, and in just another day, she'd be out of Delta and have no one on the inside either. This definitely was *not* the moment she wanted to be thinking about her future.

"Do you know where that hot spring is?"

Horatio nodded.

"Of course I do," the pilot looked at her strangely. "I'm the one who just told you about it. Are you okay all alone up here?"

"Not really." She let go of the pilot who began massaging the arm she'd had a hold of. She was hunting for one of Santa's reindeer and absolutely falling for a hallucination named Horatio, but she didn't want to talk about it with some rancher pilot. "But I can find it on my own."

"I can't just leave you here, lady." The pilot looked around. There was nothing to see from the summit of Castle Reef except snowy mountains, dusky plains, and the biggest blue sky ever.

"Fine, *I'll* leave *you*, then. Thanks for the help."

She walked past Horatio. For the first time, she could feel one of his spatial shifts slowly wrapping around her before it actually happened.

"What the hell?"

She liked that she left the pilot with his own hallucination to figure out. Misery loves company.

THE HOT SPRING WAS UNOCCUPIED, but it didn't take her long to pick up the fresh tracks through the snow.

"By the tracks, it's a big bull, two does, and a half-grown fawn."

Horatio let her lead the way. It was a hard slog through the deep snow, even though the herd had broken the path.

At one point, an avalanche had erased their tracks. It took them several anxious hours to pick them up again on the far side of the damage path.

It was barely an hour to local sunset—and only four or five to Global Flying Time—when she found them. The small herd was grazing near a copse of Douglas fir that had blocked much of the snow. They were kicking aside the little snow that remained and eating the frozen grass.

"Jeremy!" Horatio's shout of joy shook loose an entire cascade of snow from one of the trees that she barely managed to dodge.

The two of them—elf and reindeer—ran to each other and were

soon chattering away in reindeer which sounded like grunts and squeaks to her untrained ear.

Betsy ducked under the low-hanging branches and found a small spot clear of snow where she could lean back against the trunk and wait.

Exhaustion rippled through her as it always did after a hard scouting job. But it wasn't just that. She was leaving Delta because she could feel that she was losing the edge and, with how far past it Delta normally operated, that was an unacceptable change. One far too prone to death. For the first time since she'd joined the Army, she didn't belong anywhere. Yet over the last three days…

Betsy watched Horatio as he was introduced to the rest of Jeremy's family.

For the last three days, Betsy had started to belong. Not merely due to her skills either. When she was with Horatio even something as crazy as searching for Santa's missing reindeer made sense. Anything…*everything* somehow made sense when she was with him. She hadn't truly belonged somewhere that she could ever recall, but she could see herself belonging with a fantasy named Horatio.

She must have dozed, though the sun had barely shifted when Horatio kissed her awake. That gained her undivided attention, but he was too excited for it to last more than a moment.

"He has a family. But he couldn't get them back to the stables on his own. He needed an elfin herder to transport them the first time. Jeremy is a good man—"

"Reindeer," she corrected him.

"Reindeer," Horatio readily agreed and kissed her on the nose. "He didn't want to abandon his family, but didn't know any of the locals who could send me a message. Apparently love at first sight happens for reindeer as well."

As well? Is that what had happened to her? It didn't seem very likely, but neither did anything in the three days since she'd last stood on Range 37.

Now Horatio was looking at her very intently. "You're the most amazing human I've ever met, Betsy."

"Human?" But that said nothing of the amazing elf women he'd surely known. Why was she pining for a drug-dream fantasy?

"Woman. Of any breed or species. I've been watching you for days and can't believe your tenacity and skill. Or your beauty. Can all human women kiss the way you do?"

Betsy could feel herself becoming overwhelmed by his compliments. But nothing overwhelmed a Delta soldier. They were trained to keep their thoughts under control in any situation.

She slipped her fingers into his magnificent mane of hair and tugged it lightly to pull him closer.

"Perhaps I won't give you any excuse to find out."

"Mmm," he made a happy sound as he leaned into her kiss.

She could feel it supercharge her, ramp her up even the way a decisive victory couldn't achieve. There was a feeling of vitality, of joyous triumph at being alive at the end of a hard battle.

Horatio made her feel that ten times over. His kiss filled her thoughts until they overflowed and radiated back to him. She wanted him to take her right here, right now. Under the trees. In the snow. Even with the reindeer watching. She didn't care.

She opened her eyes to look up into his amazing eyes the color of the Montana Big Sky, just as a particularly large snowflake plastered itself across her shooting goggles she didn't recall putting back on.

It left a wet smear when she brushed it aside.

And once again she was in the heart of a mock Afghan village, dusted with North Carolina snow.

A mannequin bearing an RPG leaned out of a doorway.

Only habit had her shooting it twice in the face and once in the chest.

BETSY FINISHED the Range 37 course with the same high marks she always did, but felt none of the victory at the score—even though she'd managed to snatch-and-grab the bad guy on her own.

The next two days were a slow slog through the bureaucracy of leaving a service she'd given a decade to. Quartermaster this. Housing that. Personnel records the other thing.

She couldn't equate the Range 37 exercise and the two days of bureaucracy involved in leaving the service with the three days she'd spent with Horatio the Herder tracking a stray Christmas reindeer.

At each step she took through her Fort Bragg reality over the same three days, she could feel the other reality fading into memory. The three days with Horatio had passed so quickly and now time crawled.

December 21st: Quartermaster this. Horatio's strong hands resting on her shoulders a moment longer than needed as he helped her into a red-and-white parka while they stood in the most magnificent stables she'd ever seen.

December 22nd: Housing that. Holding each other close in a small hayloft in Detah on the frozen shores of the Great Slave Lake. A feeling of belonging she'd never known.

December 23rd: Personnel records the other thing. Waking in his arms in a Glacier Park cabin and knowing she had never been anywhere so safe or so...important before in her life.

December 24th: nothing but a blur. Horatio the elf would be with his reindeer, making sure they performed their annual flight, preparing the stable for their return. Bedding them down when they were done.

No one that she'd served with was currently rotated into Fort Bragg from abroad, so she passed her final days in the US military in silence. Alone.

The snow had melted and new teams were working their way through Range 37. No twelfth-century French village with bad wine and poisonous stew would be awaiting them any more than it was awaiting her. She'd go back if she could, just to see Horatio once more. Once she was out, maybe she'd take her motorcycle to Europe and go searching for a French pub with an Airborne shoulder patch carved into one table's surface.

But there wouldn't be. Hallucinations didn't work that way. It had taken a long and lonely Christmas eve to convince herself that was all it had been.

Early Christmas morning, she turned in her firearm, was issued her DD 214 Honorable Discharge form, and was issued a temporary visitor badge that would see her to the front gates. She bundled up against the chilly day, missing the warmth of the North Pole parka, though she didn't really feel the cold anymore. Climbing on her Yamaha YZF superbike, Betsy rolled out the Manchester Gate by Pope Airfield.

Maybe she'd swing south and see a bit of the country. She had no real plans until summer. But then her course would be certain. This summer, she'd be chasing the melting snow north, starting with the Flathead Wilderness. Even if it hadn't been real, she'd retrace the path as far north as she possibly could, right up to Reindeer Station on the banks of the Mackenzie River.

Perhaps there would be a reindeer, a small fawn grown into the grand bull that would at least remind her of Jeremy and she could pretend that he would lead her north to a stable made of yew trees.

At the Fort Bragg gate, the corporal took her temporary pass, and saluted her smartly. She returned the gesture for the last time, then rolled out the gate. Out Manchester Road, she'd pick up North Bragg Boulevard and punch south.

For now.

Then she'd—

Betsy slammed on the brakes and tried to make sense of what she was seeing.

Just off base, along the wooded lane, stood Pyrates Sports Bar. It wasn't much of a place: pool, beer, and a decent burger.

And leaning against one of the big maples stood an impossibly thin man with black hair down to his waist and eyes the color of the Big Sky.

She couldn't release her death grip on the handlebars as Horatio strolled up to her and reached out to raise the visor on her helmet.

"Hi."

"Hi? *Hi!* That's what you have to say for yourself? I've spent three days convincing myself that you were just a hallucination. What are you doing to me? Is this some kind of weird drug experiment or—"

Horatio leaned in and kissed her.

She dropped the clutch. The Yamaha lurched then stalled, and broke the kiss. She'd already forgotten his taste of cinnamon and the great outdoors. How had she possibly forgotten that?

"Does that feel like a hallucination in your consideration?"

Betsy could only shake her head.

"I know this is a little abrupt, but how would you like a job?"

"No way, Horatio. You evaporated at the end of the last one."

"I would not this time."

"And I'm supposed to trust an elf hallucination on that?"

"Absolutely," and Horatio's smile lit his eyes to a merry twinkle, just as they did every time.

"Why?"

"Because I could use the assistance of a skilled reindeer herder."

"You want me to live at the North Pole with you?"

"We would travel a lot. I only tend the reindeer around Christmas. An elf's main job during the year is rather global: spreading good cheer wherever he can."

"Can you promise me that you're not a hallucination? I really want you to not be a hallucination." Even if he was, Betsy had the feeling that she wasn't going to care.

"I've been wracking my brain to find an appropriate Christmas present for you. That wish will do nicely. I promise you that I am completely real."

She hadn't thought about a Christmas wish in a long time, but if there was ever one she wanted to come true…

Betsy kissed him lightly, then nodded toward the back of the bike.

"Climb aboard, Horatio. We've got some good cheer to spread."

BETSY LEANED against the yew tree that made one side of the stable's main door and pulled her red-and-white parka more tightly about her as she watched Horatio with the herd. It was Christmas Eve and once more the excitement practically shimmered through St. Nick's stables.

Harnesses with bright polished bells were laid upon well-curry-combed backs as the reindeer pranced with delight. A small elf choir stood up in the hayloft singing about Good King Wenceslas, Little Drummer Boys, and Friendly Beasts. She noted that Rudolph was nowhere in the repertoire—Jeremy was *not* a fan of Robert L. May. He'd grown to be a very dignified reindeer.

"Especially now that he has a family to look after," Horatio had whispered softly in her ear one night.

And his nose was definitely not red, his main point of contention.

Before Jeremy was harnessed into the lead position, he clopped over to her and faced her silently.

Betsy's grasp of reindeer language still sucked, though she was improving.

But he didn't say a word.

Instead, he tipped his head down, and shifted his face gently against her chest and simply rested it there. His great rack of antlers framed her protectively to either side.

She hugged him, wrapping her arms around his head.

"Merry Christmas to all," she whispered to him. "And have a good flight."

He snorted a soft laugh at her twisting of the last line of Rudolph's story before pulling away to stride over to his position to be harnessed in.

With a stamp and snort and a prance and a paw, the herd was soon aloft, towing St. Nick and his sleigh on their merry rounds.

The silence seemed to be a long time settling over the stables once they were gone. But in time, even the fireflies had settled and only the quiet stars of the Arctic night lit the stables.

Jeremy slipped close beside her and wrapped his arms about her. She rested back against him and marveled at how her life had changed. How she would never be alone again.

Last Christmas, Horatio had given her a gift beyond imagining, she was no longer alone in the world.

She rested her hand on her own belly.

Tomorrow, Christmas morning—after the reindeer had completed their flight, then gone to bed for the night—she would tell him the news.

Her gift to him would be—she tried not to think it in the same rhythm as the Rudolph poem, but being married to a Christmas elf was changing her in many wondrous ways—that quite soon they'd be three.

WILD JUSTICE (DELTA FORCE #3)

(EXCERPT)

The low hill, shadowed by banana and mango trees in the twilight of the late afternoon sun above the Venezuelan jungle, overlooked the heavily guarded camp a half mile away. But that wasn't his immediate problem.

Right now, it took everything Duane Jenkins could do to ignore the stinging sweat dripping into his eyes. Any unwarranted motion or sound might attract his target's attention before he was in position.

From two meters away, he whispered harshly.

"Who the hell are you, sister? And how did you get here?"

"Holy crap!"

He couldn't help but smile. What kind of woman said *crap* when unexpectedly facing a sniper rifle at point-blank range?

"Not your sister," she gained points for a quick recovery. "Now get that rifle out of my face, Jarhead."

Ouch! That was low. He wasn't some damned, swamp-tromping Marine. Not even ex-Marine. He was ex-75th Rangers of the US Army, now two years in Delta Force. And as an operator for The Unit —as Delta called themselves—that made him far superior to any other soldier no matter what the dudes in SEAL Team 6 thought about it.

That also didn't explain who he'd just found here in *the* perfect sniper position overlooking General Raul Estevan Aguado's encampment.

It had taken him over fifteen hours to scout out this one perfect gap between the too-damn-tall trees that made up this sweaty place and, with just twenty meters to go, he'd spotted her heavily camouflaged form lying among the leaves. It had taken him another half hour to cover that distance without drawing her attention.

Where was a cold can of Coke when a guy needed one? This place was worse than Atlanta in the summer. The red earth had been driven so deep into his pores from crawling over the ground that he wondered if his skin color was permanently changed to rust red.

Why did evil bastards like Aguado have to come from such places?

More immediate problem, dude. Stay focused.

The woman's American English was accentless, sounding flat to his Southern ear. Probably from the Pacific Northwest or some other strange part of the country. But there was a thin overlay that matched her Latinate features—full-lipped with dark eyebrows and darker eyes, which was about all he could tell through her camo paint. The slight Spanish lilt shifted her to intriguingly exotic.

But she wasn't supposed to be here. No one was.

"Keeping you in my sights until I get some answers, ma'am," Duane kept his HK MSG90 A2 rifle aimed right at the bridge of her nose—a straight-through spine cutter if he had to take her down. It would be serious overkill, as the weapon was rated to lethal past eight hundred meters and they were whispering at each other from less than two meters apart. With the silencer, his weapon would be even quieter than their whispers, but he hadn't spent the last sixteen hours crawling into position to have her death cry give him away. If she so much as squawked as she went down, every goddamn bird in the jungle would light off, giving away his presence.

She sighed and nodded toward her own rifle that rested on the ground in front of her.

He shifted his focus—though not his aim—then let out a very low whistle of appreciation. A G28. Even his team hadn't gotten their hands on the latest entry into the US Army's sniper arsenal yet. Not quite the same accuracy as his own weapon but six inches shorter, several pounds lighter, and far more flexible to configure. A whole generational leap forward. Richie, his team's tech, would be geeking out right about now. The fact that he wasn't here to see it almost made Duane smile.

"A Heckler & Koch G28. What's your point, sister?" He drawled it out for Richie's sake, who'd be listening in on Duane's radio. Then the implications sank in. If his Delta Force team couldn't get these yet, then who could? Whatever else this woman was, she would be tied to one of the three US Special Mission Units: Delta, SEAL Team 6, or the combat controllers of the Air Force's 24th STS.

Or The Activity.

That fit.

The Intelligence Support Activity served the other three Special Mission Units. If she was with The Activity…that was seriously hot. It meant she was both one of the top intel specialists anywhere *and* a lethal fighter. And that meant that *she'd* been the one to put out the call that had brought him here and was sticking to see the job through. That at least answered why she was in his spot. It also said a lot that she hadn't taken any of several easier-to-reach locations that were almost as good.

"It is about time you caught a clue. Welcome to the conversation." She picked up her rifle as if his wasn't still aimed at her. Very chill. "You are being a little dense there, soldier." At least she got the *branch* of the military right this time.

"Hey, they don't call me 'The Rock' for nothing, darlin'," Duane lowered his barrel until it was pointed into the dirt. "They actually call me that becau—"

The moment his weapon was down, he suddenly was staring down the dark hole of the G28's silencer.

"Uh…"

"The Rock certainly isn't because you are a towering black movie star. It must be for your thick head."

Duane swallowed carefully, unable to shift his focus away from the barrel of her weapon to see if the safety was on or not.

"He spells his name differently. He's Dwayne 'The Rock' with a w and a y. I'm more normal, D-u-a-n-e T-h-e R-o-c-k." He made it sing-song just like the theme song from *The All-New Mickey Mouse Club* that he'd been hooked on as a little kid.

"M-o-u-s-e," she gave the appropriate response.

He couldn't help laughing, quietly, despite their positions—him still staring down the barrel of her weapon—because discovering Mickey Mouse in common in the heart of the Venezuelan jungle was just too funny.

"Normal is not what I need here," the woman sighed and there was the distinct click of her reengaging the safety on her rifle.

"Only thing normal about me is my name, ma'am." Always good to "ma'am" a woman with a sniper rifle pointed at your face.

"Prove it," she turned her weapon once more toward the camp half a kilometer away through the trees. Her motions were appropriately slow to not draw attention. However, it was too even a motion. A sniper learned to never break the pulses of nature's rhythm. She might be some hotshot intel agent—because The Activity absolutely rocked almost everything they did—but she still wasn't Delta, who rocked it all.

Duane breathed out slowly and spent the next couple minutes easing the last two meters toward her. Having the camp in view meant that one of their spotters could see them as well, if the bad guys were damned lucky. He and the woman both wore ghillie suits—that's why he'd gotten so close before he spotted her. The suits were made of open-weave cloth liberally decorated with leaves and twigs so that the two of them looked like little more than a patch of the jungle floor. He'd dragged his on backcountry jungle roads for twenty miles to make sure he smelled like the jungle as well. Having a jaguar trounce his ass wouldn't exactly brighten up his day.

Even their rifles were well camouflaged except for either end of the spotting scopes and the very tips of the barrels. If he hadn't recently been lusting over the new specs, he wouldn't have recognized her HK G28 at all in its disguise.

Getting into position as a sniper took a patience that only the most highly trained could achieve. A female sniper? That was a rare find indeed. The two women on his Delta team were damned fine shooters, but he and Chad were the snipers of the crew. A female sniper from The Activity? This just kept getting better and better. He'd pay a fair wage to know what she really looked like beneath the ghillie and all that face paint.

"Maybe you and I should go to the party as a couple." At long last he lay beside her, close enough that he would have felt her body heat if not for the smothering sauna of his ghillie suit.

"What party? And we're never going to be a couple."

"Halloween. It's only a couple weeks off. We could sneak in and nobody would see us in our ghillies. People would wonder why the punch bowls were mysteriously draining."

"And why the apples were bobbing on their own," she sounded disgusted. "What I want is—"

"Let's see what y'all are up to down there," he cut her off, just for the fun of it, and focused his rifle scope on the camp below. He was a little disappointed when there was no immediate comeback, though there was a low muttering in Spanish that he couldn't quite catch but it cheered his soul.

The general's camp was a simple affair in several ways. The enclosure was a few hundred meters across. An old-school fence of wooden stakes driven into the ground, each a small tree trunk three meters high with sharpened points upward. Not that the points mattered, because razor wire was looped along the top. Guard shacks every hundred meters—four total. The towers straddled the fence. Not a good idea. The structure should have been entirely behind the wall to protect it from attack. Unless…

"You got a name, darling?" Lying beside her, Duane could tell that she was shorter than he was. Her hands were fine, but her body was hidden by the ghillie so he couldn't read anything more about her looks.

"Yes, I have a name."

"That's nice. Always good to have yourself one of those," Duane could play that game just as well as the next person. He turned his attention to the camp. "Our friendly general isn't worried about attack from the outside or he'd have built his towers differently. He's worried about keeping people inside."

SOFIA FORTEZA HAD ALREADY KNOWN that from her research, but she wondered how Duane—spelled the "normal" way—did.

She'd spent months tracking General Aguado. Cripes, she'd spent months finding him in the first place. He was a slippery *bastardo* who did most of his work through intermediaries and only rarely surfaced himself. Tracing him to this corner of the Guatopo National Park—so close to Caracas, the capital of Venezuela, that she'd dismissed it at first—had taken a month more.

Duane had taken one look at the place and seen...what?

He'd have built his towers differently.

She leaned back to her own scope and inspected them again. It took a moment to bring the towers into focus because her nerves were still zinging as if she'd been electrocuted. Somehow, in all her training, she'd never looked down the barrel of a rifle or even a handgun at point blank range—perhaps the scariest thing she'd ever seen.

Scariest other than Duane's cold blue eyes. He was the most dangerous-looking man she'd ever met, which is why his jokes and his smooth Southern accent were throwing her so badly. He sounded half badass, macho-bastard Unit operator and half southern gentleman. It was the strangest combination she'd ever heard. One moment he was wooing her with warm tones, obviously without a clue of how to woo a woman, and the next he was being pure Army grunt with a vocabulary to match. She simply couldn't figure him out.

Finally she shrugged her emotions aside enough to focus her scope properly. *Stay in the jungle, not in your head.* She rebuilt it in layers. The strange silence of the wind—not a single breath of air reached the jungle floor, instead it stagnated, adding to the oppressiveness of the heat. Macaw calls alternated between chatter and screech. Monkeys screamed and shouted in the upper branches. Buzzing flies had learned to leave her alone and the silent ants were no longer creeping her out. All that was left after she canceled each of those out was the man breathing beside her and the compound of that bastard Aguado that she'd been staring at for the last twenty-four hours.

The guard towers were supported by four long, tree-trunk legs, two inside the fence and two outside. Outside! Where they were vulnerable to attack. General Aguado hadn't built a fort in the depths of a national park—he'd built a prison.

All of her research had only uncovered his location, not his purpose here. Because she hadn't cared. Cutting the head off the snake one target at a time worked for her.

She looked again at the camp. Wooden shacks for the most part—workers' cabins. What else had she missed?

"Locks on the doors," Duane answered the question she hadn't asked in a whisper that was surprisingly soft for such a deep voice. He ignored a fer-de-lance pit viper as it slid up and over the ghillie covering his rifle barrel, slowing to inspect them with a flick of its tongue before continuing on its way in search of mice. If he could ignore the snake, so could she. Mostly. A little. She watched long after it had slithered out of sight.

Sofia looked at the shacks' doors again. Locks on the *outside*. She'd been watching the camp for twenty-four hours and had missed that. The dozens of armed guards weren't being lazy on patrol as she'd thought. They didn't care about the outside world—they were worried about the inside one. And because they were the only armed personnel in the camp, and everyone knew it, they could afford to be nonchalant.

Back to the towers. The guards were leaning on the inside rails looking down, not the outside ones looking out. All of her work to slip into this position was probably meaningless. If Duane was right, she could walk right up and knock on the front gate before anyone would pay her the least attention. A band of red howler monkeys working their way noisily through the jungle canopy above the camp didn't even attract a glance from the guards.

Still, Aguado was here. She'd seen him arrive with his entourage. And he was never going to leave. Not alive.

"Not a nice place," Duane observed quietly.

"Not a nice man."

"Sure I am. You just don't know me yet, sugar."

Sofia brought her knee up sharply. Lying side by side, she was able to bullseye the Charlie-horse nerve cluster on his outer thigh. Her nana hadn't raised her to be a target.

"Shit!" He didn't sound so almighty pleased with himself any longer, though he did manage to keep it to a whisper as he continued swearing.

Why did guys always think they were so charming? With her looks, she should be used to it by now. Except her looks were hidden by the ghillie suit. What had kicked Duane-spelled-the-normal-way into such a guy mode? Just that she was female? When did Delta start recruiting cavemen as their standard? Actually, that one she knew the answer to—since Day One if past experience meant anything.

She hadn't ever deployed with Delta before, but she'd met enough of them to know the type. They were the rebel super-warriors of the US military. Everyone thought that their team was the baddest, but Delta Force, more commonly called "The Unit," completely owned that title. Somehow they drew the people that didn't fit anywhere else in the military. But where they'd been troublemakers in their old units, 1st Special Forces Operational Detachment-Delta collected them and honed their skills. They were like a barely controlled reaction just bubbling along, waiting for an excuse to explode.

"So, what's the general's story?" Duane, once he was done nursing his thigh, went for a subject change proving he wasn't stupid.

"Deep in the drug trade. Known to have called for at least three high profile murders, including a Supreme Tribunal of Justice judge (that's their version of the Supreme Court) even if he didn't pull the trigger himself."

"Oh, so *he's* the one that's not nice," as if Duane only now was figuring that out.

She was not going to be charmed by him. His every tone said that just because she was female, he'd switched into some weird-ass flirt mode. She'd had enough of that coming up through the ranks to last a lifetime.

"This isn't slave labor, so you'd better add human trafficking to your list." With the speed of a light switch, all the charm was gone from Duane's voice.

As if to prove his point, at that moment a couple of guards exited a small building, readjusting their pants and laughing. They kicked the door shut behind them and snapped the lock closed. No question what they'd just been doing to some poor women—one of the perks of their job.

Numerous guards. Locks on the outside of the cabin doors. No large central building that might be an illicit drug lab or slave labor textile sweatshop. This was a holding pen, hidden deep in the jungle of a national park. The few people who were circulating around, aside from the guards, were almost all women. Women who were keeping their heads down and trudging about their tasks. The sickness that twisted in her stomach had nothing to do with lying still for the last twenty-four hours.

Sofia wasn't even aware of raising her rifle until Duane reached over and casually pushed it back down.

"Not yet." It was all he said, but she could hear the anger beneath the soft words.

Well that wasn't shit compared to what *she* was feeling at the moment. This place needed to be erased from the map. Scorched to the ground, removed permanently from existence!

"Why are you here? I sent for a goddamn team, not some Southern Rock."

He flashed a smile at her, "If you've got me, you don't need a team." All of his macho bravado was back. As if she'd misheard his momentary anger. He sounded too much like her useless brother and the rest of her useless family. She couldn't be rid of him fast enough.

As the last of the sunlight faded from the sky and the bird calls tapered toward silence, Sofia wondered who she was going to want to shoot more by sunrise: General Raul Estevan Aguado or Duane The Rock?

This completed series is available at fine retailers everywhere
Target Engaged
Heart Strike
Wild Justice
Midnight Trust

M. L. BUCHMAN

3-time Booklist Top 10 Romance Author of the Year

The Christmas Lights OBJECTIVE

a Night Stalkers 5E romance story

THE CHRISTMAS LIGHTS OBJECTIVE

elsey "Killjoy" Killaney can track down the worst drug lord of a Mexican cartel. But of all stupid days, why must it be on Christmas? Her least favorite day of the year.

Jason Gould flies with the very best, the Night Stalkers 5E helicopter company. Christmas ranked as his best day every year, until this one.

When the mission comes to take out a drug lord on Christmas Eve, maybe they can both track the Christmas Lights Objective.

INTRODUCTION

This story is actually kind of autobiographical. I wanted to really think about my past and present views of Christmas.

It's obvious which character fills which role.

What isn't obvious was that I thought I still had a lot of "Killjoy" Killaney in me.

Maybe not so much.

THE CHRISTMAS LIGHTS OBJECTIVE

"This sounds as much fun as an air raid at Christmas… Wait, that's what it is." The guy in the goofy Santa hat cut Kelsey off after her opening line of the mission briefing: *This mission flies tonight.*

"Dashing through the air," the senior crew chief of the Night Stalker Chinook helicopter team began singing in her bright soprano. "In a two-rotor heli-sleigh."

"Over the jungle we go, a-fighting all the way," another joined in—an off-key tenor.

The various members of the operation's primary helicopter crew began adding in verses. Soon both pilots and three crew chiefs were rocking to the beat just as if they were in their massive, twin-rotor Chinook.

Sergeant Jason Gould—loadmaster on the *Calamity Jane II* and the man wearing the goofy Santa hat—joined in with a rich baritone. She didn't know why she should be surprised.

But she *was* surprised. He looked like a New York Jew from her own Brooklyn neighborhood. His speaking voice, while pleasant in the few words she'd been willing to exchange with someone in a Santa hat, hadn't foreshadowed the bone-melting baritone that quickly became the anchor of the song.

She could almost like him, except his hat sported a blinking-nose Rudolph on it. In her book, it was a target saying, "Please shoot me here." Though since they'd just met, and they were both US Special Operations, she left her sidearm in its holster.

They sat in a meeting room in the team's residence building. It stood beside a large hangar—labeled as abandoned. Abandoned deep in the woods of Fort Rucker, Alabama. She'd been directed down a tiny access road that was marked as closed and had looked disused. The gray afternoon, dripping with December rain, made both the building and hangar appear even more sad and weather-beaten. She'd almost turned around—until she noticed the cutting-edge surveillance and security system tucked in the corners of the structures.

The inside of the residence, once she'd gained admittance, was immaculate and comfortable with all of the latest conveniences. She hadn't seen the inside of the hangar yet.

The meeting room's walls were covered in brilliant travel posters —so many of them that they were starting to overlap: Costa Rica, Honduras, and Venezuela were understandable. But there was also Afghanistan, Iraq, Somalia, Libya…

It was the strangest briefing room décor Kelsey Killaney had ever worked in.

"It's my Christmas, too. Not my call." She grimaced as her protest cut off the singing. *Killjoy Killaney.* Once again, the old high school nickname was definitely her. If it *had* been up to her, she'd have scheduled the flight for Christmas Eve anyway, just so that she didn't have to think about "the happy season" for one more millisecond than necessary. But it had been circumstances, not orders that had brought them together on Christmas Eve afternoon.

This morning, everyone at her office in Fort Belvoir, Virginia had been buzzing with the "Best Wishes" and merry yeah-whatever. She'd wanted to lie on the floor and throw a tantrum as if she was nine, not twenty-nine—the little girl wanting everyone to just shut up. Her worldview was more mature now. Now, she was a grown woman who just wished everyone would go away.

Another Christmas wish gone bust. Not that any of the ones as a child had paid off.

This morning, Michael Gibson, the commander of Delta Force, had appeared at her desk inside The Activity's headquarters without warning—not even from security who were there to make sure such things didn't happen. The Intelligence Support Activity worked in one of the most secure buildings on a fort made up of twenty major intel agencies. The Activity's sole purpose was serving the Special Operations Forces, but that didn't mean they were supposed to be able to just walk in.

"There's a jet waiting for you at Davison Army Airfield," had been his idea of a pleasant Christmas Eve morning greeting—which actually worked for her. "Here's your team and mission file to read on the flight."

He'd handed her a slim folder that she wanted to handle as much as a live snake. It had a yellow fly sheet with a dark red border. In large type it only had an identification number and two of the scariest words in the intelligence business: Eyes Only. She'd checked the back of the fly sheet. Her name had been added in the second position, countersigned by Colonel Michael Gibson himself. Theirs were the only two names on the file.

She'd looked back up at him, but he'd been gone. If not for the file clutched in her white-knuckled fingers, she'd have doubted he'd ever been there. One look at the first page and she was on the move. On her way out the door to grab the scram kit from the trunk of her car, she'd stopped off at the front desk. Just as she suspected, he never *had* been signed in...or even seen—Delta Force guys were just creepy sometimes.

Reading the mission portion of the file Gibson had given her, made her the obvious choice for the operation. Actually, the only choice.

Reading the portion about the 5E was just...headshaking.

The 5E had an unprecedented number of missions with an

unlikely success rate—even by the Night Stalkers' stratospheric standards. Yet the details of most of their missions had been redacted from the file now sitting in the locked briefcase at her feet.

With their song cut off, they were all sitting and waiting. Waiting and ready for their latest mission assignment. That's when she looked at the posters again.

"Duh!"

Jason, happy in his Santa hat, looked over but she just shook her head to ward him off. She hoped he would look away before she was forced to attack Rudolph's blinking nose. The last thing she needed was to explain herself to a Night Stalking Christmas elf, no matter how nice a voice he had. Why was a New York Jew singing Christmas carols anyway?

Except he wasn't a fellow Brooklynite. According to the file, Loadmaster Jason Gould was from Florida no matter how much he sounded New York.

Kelsey understood now. She didn't need the list of redacted missions—they were right there on the walls. These people collected travel posters of everywhere they'd ever had an operation. Now she could start putting some of the pieces together.

Each poster was a snapshot of a mission file.

"Find Beauty in Honduras." A black ops Honduran mission last year that had shaken the corrupt banking-military cooperative to the core. It had significantly stabilized the duly-elected government—but no hint of who had done the mission. The answer sat in this room.

"Surf Kamchatka." The 5E had done the Russian drone mission.

"Hike the Negev." The disastrous Negev Desert, Israel, mission that had shaken The Activity itself to the core, somehow salvaged by the field team. By this team.

She tried to catch her breath, but wasn't having much luck. No wonder she hadn't heard of the 5E, though they were the logical extension of Henderson's and Beale's D Company. The 5D had been hugely innovative in their approach to military tactics. The 5E, however, were the tactical equivalent of Delta Force—silent and dangerous as hell...or Christmas.

"Damn it!" Jason complained. "Christmas Eve! Shit, man! And I was going to get my nails done tonight." That earned a laugh around the table. The team was apparently unflappable.

Despite her clumsiest efforts, their spirits remained high.

She got along with data, not people.

Activity agents were rarely in on the final mission. They might go out into the field a dozen times themselves gathering intelligence, but operations were generally left to the action teams. But tonight there was no choice.

Kelsey couldn't stop herself from glancing down at Sergeant Jason Gould's hands as he made a show of inspecting his nails critically. They were cut short, uneven, and showed that he made his living with those hands—which made sense for a ramp gunner on an MH-47G Chinook. As one of the three crew chiefs, he'd have a dozen roles to serve—all of which said competent and strong. He was several inches taller than her own five-seven with an attractive leanness. She knew from his file that his family had a sportfishing business out of St. Petersburg, Florida. Curly dark hair and nearly black eyes.

She'd almost been attracted—if not for her hopelessness with attractive men. And the stupid hat.

"We'll go together, Jason. I need a mani-pedi anyway." Carmen. Dark red hair. Crew chief of the Chinook. Married to the co-pilot on the same craft. What a crazy outfit.

Five aboard the Chinook and four more aboard each of the two DAP Hawk gun platforms that would be flying protection. With her that made a total of fourteen flying tonight, plus two assets who had yet to arrive.

As Kelsey had no more control over the crew selection than the mission, she started the briefing. They might appear carefree, but the moment she began laying out the details of the mission, she had a hundred percent of their attention.

IT WAS STILL mid-afternoon by the time the short briefing ended and they were into the hangar. The soft rain had turned downright wet.

Jason had been searching for an excuse to talk to Kelsey Killaney since the moment she'd hit the pavement at the 5E's compound. He found it when they stepped into the hangar.

"Stealth, ma'am. Every last bird." Their big Chinook, two DAP Hawks—Black Hawks turned into the world's most advanced gun platforms, and two Little Birds. The last wouldn't be on this mission, and the crews hadn't been called.

"I see that," she sounded a little breathless. "I've simply never heard of them."

"Must admit that we like it that way."

"It explains how," she looked at him puzzled for a moment, as if surprised to find herself talking to him. "How you do what you do."

"That, and the best crew flying." He still couldn't believe that he was here. He supposed it was just being in the right place at the right time. After the Negev Desert disaster, they'd needed a new bird. The Army had provided them with the stealth configured *Calamity Jane II* and shipped them down to the 5E's team at Fort Rucker. Their mission pace had doubled and the complexity as well. He'd always simply been glad to be flying, but in the 5E he'd become more than he'd ever imagined.

And now, with Kelsey Killaney standing so close beside him that he could smell her fresh scent, like a strange winter flower, he started to understand just what he'd achieved. He was a goddamn flyer on the best bird in the sky, anywhere. Maybe, just maybe, he was good enough to stand next to a woman like her and not feel out of place.

They were following the rest of the crew up the rear ramp of the *Calamity Jane II*, prepping it for the first leg of the flight.

Her light brown hair was back in a severe ponytail that emphasized her large eyes. She was fair-skinned and had one of those smiles that looked as if it was always ready, even though she hadn't used it yet that he'd seen. The fact that she worked for The Activity said she was screamingly intelligent—an assumption borne out by the concise style of her briefing. If smart was the new sexy, she was a chart breaker—not that she wasn't by the old measure as well.

He'd truly done his best to pay attention at the briefing, but it had been hit and miss. He'd managed to sit next to her, by the simple stratagem of holding out a chair for her. But, no matter what he did, he couldn't get her to laugh. That hint of a smile hadn't even shifted when he'd started a whole riff about personal grooming tips off Carmen's mani-pedi remark—which was more Zoe the drone pilot's thing than Carmen's anyway.

Danny and the Captain were already in their seats running through checklists. Carmen and George were still outside pulling off pitot tube and air intake covers. So he had a moment and intended to use every second of it to his advantage.

"You need anything, ma'am? If so, I'm your man." He tried not to wince. Smooth as descending staircase on a tricycle—a trick he'd only tried once, but possibly where he got his taste for flying. He was getting no points for subtlety on this effort.

"Do you have a reality check somewhere?" Her question caused him to do a doubletake. So she did have a sense of humor behind her ever-so-serious facade.

"Somewhere, sure." Jason began patting the pockets of his flightsuit, peeked inside a couple of the pouches on his survival vest, and finally pulled a small pack of candy out of his medical supplies. "Will these do?"

Her expression turned into a dangerous scowl, "Hell no!"

He looked down to see if he'd mistakenly pulled out a grenade or a breaching charge, but he hadn't. "Who doesn't like Skittles?"

She sighed and rested a hand on his arm a moment as if apologizing.

Her fingers were almost delicate, but he could see a strength to them. She was so fit that he'd have guessed she was the sort who went to the high-end gym three times a week with a gaggle of girlfriends and had an impossibly handsome aerobics trainer named Julio—*except* that she was Activity. The agents from The Activity were just as likely to go into the field to gather their own intel from behind enemy lines as they were to work at a desk in Fort Belvoir. They were known for being ruthlessly competent. Another thing he liked in a woman. If competence was the new sexy, then—

"Thanks for the offer and, yes, I do like Skittles. I just have this thing about Christmas, so thanks but no thanks."

He looked down at the little pack. It was clearly labeled Holiday Mix and showed only red and green flavors rather than the normal rainbow.

"Seems like you're putting a lot of weight on a little bit of seasonal packaging."

She nodded, "No argument from me. It's the one topic I'm a complete lunatic on."

"Christmas?"

"Christmas," she confirmed as if it was an incursion by an entire battalion of Taliban.

"Completely rational about everything else?"

"Everything!" Kelsey's tone was dry enough for him to laugh, which had several of the crew turning to look at him.

He squinted at Carmen, who had just come aboard and was checking over the internal systems, and mouthed, "What?"

Carmen shook her head, keeping her thoughts to herself, as she continued the pre-flight check.

Fine!

He tried to turn to give Carmen the cold shoulder, but she gave him an I-caught-you wink that blew his timing, even if he didn't know what she was on about.

"Even rational about men?" Jason turned back to Kelsey.

"Always," then she grimaced, "for what good it has ever done me."

"I'm not sure if I should ask if that's a good sign or a bad one for me."

"As long as you're wearing that hat? Bad sign."

He looked up enough to spot the white, furry trim just above his eyebrows and remembered the blinking Rudolph.

"Nope," he looked back down at her and made a point of shaking his head hard enough to make the little bell at the end tinkle brightly.

"Even being a gorgeous Activity agent, I'm not giving up my hat for you."

"Your loss," and finally that smile of hers came out. She did a quick turn and hair toss worthy of any disdainful supermodel, then strode up the cargo bay. But it was the smile that slayed him. From pretty to radiant faster than a heat-seeking missile.

He could only wonder what it would take to make her smile like that again. Taking off his hat? No. She'd smiled while making a joke because he had it on. He'd stick with a winning hand, no matter what she said about Christmas.

There had to be a reason behind it, but he wasn't sure how comfortable he felt digging for it with a complete stranger, no matter how attractive. It wasn't just her beauty. Something in her drew him—deeply. Not a feeling he was used to.

Done with the exterior inspection, George boarded as well and began checking his Minigun just as Carmen began going over hers. His own M240 hung out of the way in its bracket close by the rear ramp.

Kelsey sat in the observer's chair just behind the pilots' seats. That should be safe, they were both married: the Captain to the unit's hot Italian drone pilot and quiet Danny—impossibly—to the vivacious Carmen. The only other crew member was the portside gunner and George was too British to try poaching where Jason had showed interest.

Out of excuses, Jason started his own preflight checks of the *Calamity Jane II* for a mission. Ammo full-stocked after the last mission was still fully stocked. Emergency supplies of food, water, and first aid were fully stocked and inside the refresh date. Enough to feed the whole crew for a week if they went down hard somewhere.

Then he started in puzzling on Kelsey. She must have her own reasons for being so *Bah Humbug!* But it didn't fit her. She seemed… happier than that.

Quiet. Which among the screaming extroverts of the 5E must be a shock. But there was something more. As if—

A high whine of fast-moving tires was all the warning he had to dodge out of the way before a pair of Polaris MRZRs came racing up the rear ramp. He jumped aside, clinging to the inside of the Chinook's hull to stay clear. The MRZRs were four-seater ATVs on Special Operations steroids. Tough, lightweight, fast, electric-quiet, and able to carry a thousand pounds of soldier and gear at sixty miles an hour or scramble over rough terrain at twenty. Except instead of the usual Army tan, they'd been painted like blue and red hotrods. Blinking Christmas lights had been wound around the bars of the roll cage which didn't make much sense unless...undercover as civilian hotrod dune buggies.

Right. Low profile mission. But had the woman who hated Christmas thought of the Christmas lights? Jason suspected that she was the sort of woman who thought of everything and left nothing to chance.

The way the MRZRs raced aboard told him it was either SEAL or Delta at the helms.

Once they were in, he dropped back down. Both drivers wore clip-on fuzzy antlers.

"Duane? Dude! Haven't seen your ugly face since you left the Rangers for that wimp-ass Delta outfit." They'd stayed in close touch, but in four years had never managed to be in the same place at the same time.

"Jason, you Night Stalker piece of shit!" They thumped each other's backs hard enough to hurt.

"Cool antlers. Too bad they aren't half as cool as my hat." Then he spotted the gorgeous Latina stepping out of the other rig. She looked *very* cute in her antlers.

"You must be Sofia. I can't believe that you fell for a lump of coal like this one."

"He is all mine," she said in a happy, lushly Spanish accent, as she gave him a hug. "I have heard so many good things about you. I would know you anywhere by your so very silly hat."

"And if it hadn't been Christmas?"

"By your *very* good looks," she didn't hesitate to laugh.

Then she turned to Duane but kept an arm around Jason's waist so he kept his around her shoulders.

"I do not know," Sofia said thoughtfully. "Jason is *so* handsome. Why didn't you ever tell me this. Maybe I should be with a Night Stalker man and not a Delta boy."

With all the speed Jason would expect of a Delta operator, Duane hip-checked him into the emergency fire extinguishing system and separated Sofia with a quick hand about her waist—a move so smooth that it had all three of them laughing.

KELSEY SAT at the far end of the helicopter's shadowed cargo bay and tried to look away. What would she give to be a part of that laughing circle of three? They looked so easy together, so effortlessly happy. That was a part of working for The Activity—she and the other analysts were a collection of loners, brought together by a fascination for the intricacies of information and an ability to turn it into actionable intelligence.

The folder that Colonel Gibson had provided was a perfect example. The first page had contained just three lines of information that suddenly brought her last six months of work into sharp focus.

Delta Team and 160th SOAR 5E, Ech Stagefield, Fort Rucker
Juan Zavala, Christmas Eve
(and an address in Cozumel)

It was Christmas Eve Day and Colonel Gibson had given her the first actionable lead on the elusive Juan Zavala that she'd seen in six months of hunting for him.

Zavala was one of the kingpins of the ultra-violent Jalisco New Generation cartel that she'd been tracing. The Jalisco were the former armed wing of the Sinaloa cartel and were rapidly gaining precedence in the Mexican drug scene. Under the kingpin theory of "take out the top and the internecine battles will do the rest of the cleanup," Zavala was a prime target.

She even recognized the address. It was a beach house that she had researched as one of his likely safe houses, but had never been able to trace him to.

Then the woman separated herself from the two men as they turned to arranging the two MRZRs more carefully and tying them down for flight. She moved through shadows until she was almost at Kelsey's side.

"Sofia?" She'd never expected to see Sofia Forteza again since she had left The Activity.

"Kelsey!" And Sofia gave her a hug as well which surprised her completely. Sofia had been one of her few friends at The Activity before she'd made the unlikely shift to Delta Force. But they'd never had a hugging kind of friendship.

"You seem happy."

"Ecstatic! I didn't know how much I loved being out in the field. Actually, I did know that. I know it better now. And Duane certainly helps," she was practically glowing as she aimed a happy look back down the bay.

"How do you know Jason?" Kelsey wasn't sure why she was asking. She'd watched them hug and felt… She didn't know. As if she wished it was her instead?

"I don't. It is the way that Duane talked about him, I seem to already know him. They served in the US Rangers together. They've stayed very close."

Another skill Kelsey didn't have. She'd lost touch with Sofia the moment she'd headed over the horizon.

"Is this mission yours?" Sofia's effortless manners didn't give Kelsey enough time to feel uncomfortable.

She nodded.

"Good," Sofia nodded her head emphatically in return as the APU screamed to life and then the twin turbines began spinning up. "Then I know everything will go fine."

"You do?" Kelsey must have heard wrong over the building noise.

A backwash of hot exhaust rippled through the cabin—it would clear as soon as they were moving. She'd been worrying about the mission every second since Colonel Gibson had handed her the file then evaporated or dropped through a trap door or whatever he'd done.

Sofia dug into her pocket and pulled out a pair of earplugs as the engine noise escalated. She shouted as she slid them in. "You were always the best planner we had when the terribles hit the fan. Except for me, of course. We all knew it and it made you a little scary to work with."

"I was?"

Past words, Sofia simply nodded before heading back down to rejoin the men.

People were scared of her?

Actually, that explained some reactions she'd observed. Rooms did seem to go quiet when she stepped into them, as if she was checking up on everybody. Except the 5E's briefing room. They were so skilled that maybe nothing daunted them.

What would it be like to work with them more? On occasion, an agent was permanently embedded with an elite team to facilitate operational communications more tightly with The Activity's specialties regarding human and signal intelligence. To be embedded with the 5th Battalion E Company would be both a challenge and… fun. Fun? That wasn't something she was very good at and erased the thought from her mind.

But she couldn't help glancing back down the cargo bay. Jason in his blinking Rudolph hat hadn't been afraid of her—just the opposite. He'd continued talking to her even after she'd snapped at him for offering her Christmas candy. Killjoy strikes again.

Kelsey Killaney's plan sounded simple on the surface. Jason now knew that the surface appearances had nothing to do with one of Kelsey's plans.

She'd only outlined the basic approach strategy back at Fort

Rucker: length of flights, refueling stops, necessary equipment. Per her instructions, beneath his flightsuit he wore slacks, a dress-shirt, and running shoes, though she hadn't explained why at the time. Under his shirt he wore a vest of lightweight Dragonskin armor for a bit of invisible protection.

She'd laid it out on the four-hour flight down to Naval Air Station Key West and refined it on the three-hour crossing to Cozumel after they'd eaten a hurried dinner while refueling. He'd never been to the small resort island off the Yucatan coast. Bringing a hot babe down here for a winter vacation had definitely been on his bucket list.

He'd never imagined that when he did it, he'd be unloaded after nightfall onto an empty stretch of beach ten miles across the island from the city of San Miguel de Cozumel. The weather was perfect. They'd left the storm somewhere over the Florida Keys and now drove out beneath a canopy of stars. Shirt sleeves were just right for the warm evening, though he could have done without the extra layer of the Dragonskin.

Night Stalkers usually didn't deploy on the active part of the mission, that's what Ranger door kickers and Delta operators were for. His job was to get them there, then shuffle away and hide until it was time to come fetch them.

Not on a Kelsey Killaney mission.

"I need an expert in flight operations on the mission team in case something goes wrong."

He'd considered arguing, until she said she was going as well.

"There isn't time to sufficiently brief everyone on the layout. We only have tonight, so I have to be there. I've spent too long hunting Zavala to let him slip away."

Which explained why she'd only requested two Delta operators rather than a full team.

"Can you drive?" Kelsey had asked as they were releasing the tie-downs on the vehicles.

"Sure." Of course he could.

"I mean really drive?"

"Dad ran sprint car races for a hobby. If he paid the entry fee, then got a sportfishing client, I'd drive the race for him. I was a much better driver than I was a fisherman." Then he climbed into the driver's seat of the MRZR and buckled in to settle the point. An MRZR was a close relative of a sprint car. Four seats instead of one, no airfoil on the top, and an MRZR had an engine that could only go sixty, not a hundred and sixty. But those were the differences. In common, they both had: an open metal frame with a serious roll cage, a very low center of gravity, demon-like cornering abilities, and were made for running in the sand and dirt and being fast while doing it.

In the far back, an MRZR had an extra space like a miniature pickup. It could carry two extra soldiers or a pile of gear. Right now, they had massive tourist drink coolers—coolers that were loaded with all of their tactical gear and most of the weapons they had just illegally smuggled into a friendly country. Due to corruption, the results on these types of missions were often better if the foreign government wasn't notified. The challenge was to not be caught in the process as that tended to upset them badly.

It was only as they rolled off the back of the Chinook and onto the deserted beach, that the truth clicked in.

"You already knew that I could really drive. That's why you didn't get a second driver for this mission from Delta."

"Maybe I just like your hat," Kelsey said it as if she was all innocence. No, she said it like a tease—like maybe the first tease she'd ever made.

He drove up the beach and over the berm onto the Quintana Roo road, then waited for Duane and Sofia to join them in the second MRZR. How had that lucky bastard gotten a woman like that? Sofia was beyond beautiful, right up there in Kelsey Killaney's category. And she was a Delta Force fighter. As far as he knew, they had like three women in the entire unit, yet somehow Duane had won her heart. And not just a little. Married if that didn't beat all. The only man less likely to get married in their Ranger platoon than one Jason Gould.

That got Jason thinking about why he himself was that way. Because he was stupid? Or because he'd never met the right woman?

He'd take answer B any day. Any day before now. He wasn't sure why she fascinated him so much, but that was a question he was willing to pursue.

"You hate my hat," he reminded her.

"You're right. I hate your hat."

"And how important is it that we go low profile undercover here?"

"Why do you think we repainted the MRZRs in hotrod colors and are wearing civilian clothes?"

"But you hate my hat."

She glared over at him.

"That's too bad." He wasn't quite sure why he'd grabbed the extra accessory when getting civilian clothes out of his room, but he had.

"Why? Because you so *love* your hat?"

"I do, but that's not the problem," he tried to shake his head as if she was pitiful.

Duane and Sofia cleared the berm and pulled up beside them on the empty highway as the helos disappeared back into the night: the big Chinook and the two guardian DAP Hawks. They'd fly out well beyond radar range and refuel from a circling C-130 tanker while they waited.

"Then what's the problem, Jason?" Kelsey's guard was down just enough that if he was quick…

He pulled out his second hat, triggered the flashing nose, and pulled it onto her head. Her hair was impossibly sleek, so smooth it might have been ice, but was so warm and human that it seemed to burn his hand. He yanked his hands away before he could do more.

"There," he declared. Stomping on the gas, he unleashed the MRZR. It leapt down the road with Duane and Sofia close behind. "Now you're low profile."

"I'm going to have to kill you, Jason," she shouted over the racing wind.

"Wait until after the mission, okay?"

KELSEY TUGGED the hat down against the speed-generated wind and hated herself for it. Hated that she hated Christmas. Hated that she still didn't know how to be nice to Jason when he'd been nothing but nice to her. Wearing his stupid matching hat was the first concession she'd managed.

He looked over and grinned at her as he turned left onto the Carretera Transversal to cross the island.

"So, tell me why you're irrational about Christmas?" He shouted over the wind noise. The electric MRZR itself was quiet, but there was roaring wind and the tire noise as they raced the 9.3 miles across the island in a vehicle with no windshield. The wide two-lane road ran straight as an arrow between two uninterrupted walls of green—their headlights well-focused on the road ahead so that they'd be hard to spot from any distance.

Not a chance. "Tell me why you're so crazy for it that you have not one but two Rudolph hats."

They covered a mile in silence before he spoke. He slowed a little, but the road noise barely changed.

"Mom bought them for Dad and I last Christmas. This one is his," he tapped his forehead. "You're wearing mine."

"Why do you have *his* hat? Thief!" She was suddenly very conscious of having Jason's hat on her head. It was so…personal. As if they were together—somehow a couple.

Again the mile-long pause.

"The cancer killed Dad by Valentine's Day. Mom followed him, of a broken heart by July Fourth."

Kelsey felt as if she'd just been punched. She reached out and clamped a hand over his arm in sympathy. Could feel his muscles rippling beneath the surface as he drove. His strength a comfort, when she should be the one providing that.

"Sorry," he steadfastedly stared ahead without a glance toward her. "It just slips out sometimes. When I'm not being careful."

Kelsey could only look at him in amazement. His ridiculous hat and teasing her about it had more meaning than should be possible. In an instant he transformed from a ridiculous man who had been kind to her, to a kind man who didn't mind being perceived as ridiculous—even if he wasn't.

How was he so comfortable in his own skin that he could do that?

She was on the verge of asking, but knew that wasn't right. He'd just laid his heart out on the cross-Cozumel road. His honesty demanded the same.

"My parents hated each other. I still don't know why they stayed together."

Kelsey's hand still rode lightly on Jason's forearm, but she was reluctant to take it away. Through it, she could feel a listening stillness come over him.

"But they didn't fight all year. Instead, they saved all of their bitterness for one 'special season,'" she wished she could do this softly rather than shouting it in short choppy sentences with no ability to gauge her listener's reaction. "The Christmas tree. Mom thinks they're pretty. Dad hates them as a waste of money, space, time... I don't know. It's not like we were poor. Maybe he hates them because Mom likes them. Dad would pick the fight starting in October. Stretch it into February when he was on a roll."

Jason's stillness continued as the lights of San Miguel de Cozumel city began to light the road ahead of them.

"Christmas is nothing but bad memories."

Jason slowed as they entered the outskirts of the city. He hadn't said a word as she'd told him something that she'd never told anyone. She'd always managed to keep her *Bah Humbug!* to herself before. Somehow was never dating anyone when Christmas came around, always opting out of Secret Santa at work. She'd stressed herself into actual illness before any number of Christmas parties.

And Jason just drove.

"Look."

She was looking, to see what his reaction to her was. For some reason it seemed to matter, but she couldn't read it.

Then he nodded to either side of the road.

She looked. There were breaks in the trees. Houses that were little more than hovels were tucked in among palm and avocado trees. And each one had bright Christmas lights. Sometimes just a doorway, sometimes a spiral climbing a palm tree, and frequently a lit creche of the birth in the manger in gaudy plastic. The closer they got to town, the more extravagant the displays.

They turned southwest on the Avenida Rafael E. Melgar.

The waterfront was a wonder of lights. To her right lay the sea. Cruise ship docks jutted out into the dark ocean—the ships lit like cities of their own. Hundreds and hundreds of people strolled along the seawall. Most holding hands or in close groups chattering happily together.

The street was divided by a narrow median with a palm tree every hundred feet or so, and each was brightly wound in Christmas lights. The one- and two-story whitewashed shops along the inland side of the street were a bounty of Christmas displays.

Jason continued to drive in silence.

People waved at them in their two colorfully lit MRZRs, dressed up so that they looked like high-end dune buggies. She waved back.

They passed a tall lighthouse close by the cruise terminal. It cast no light. Yet even from here, in the brightest heart of the promenade, she could see the tall beacon to the south that had replaced it—two white flashes every five seconds.

Was that herself? A decommissioned lighthouse amidst an abundance of light?

She turned back to Jason as he continued easing along in the southbound traffic. Was he the beacon that now flashed so brightly ahead? Somehow he was holding onto the joy that his dead parents had taught him while she was still wrapped up in the darkness that her parents had tried to teach her.

It was a crappy metaphor, especially if it was true and she was the decommissioned lighthouse.

Up ahead there was another light, far taller and flashing brightly. That looked like a much happier metaphor, if she could figure out how to live it.

❄

"I DON'T WANT to feel decommissioned any more." Kelsey slipped her hand off his arm and he missed it. He missed the comfort. He missed the connection.

"What?" Jason wondered where that had come from. He was still trying to shake off the memories of last Christmas, his dad already past being able to speak, but smiling as he wore his goofy hat. Meager presents opened on a hospital bed because no one could find the energy to shop for more.

"The lighthouses," Kelsey pointed upward.

Jason hadn't even noticed them. He could barely see anything other than the withered man who took up so little space on the vast bed.

"You think you're a decommissioned lighthouse?"

"Can't prove otherwise by me."

He'd heard her story, about her idiot parents. Had they somehow pounded into this beautiful woman's head that she wasn't worth better?

Jason had asked Sofia about her, when it was clear they knew each other.

"Not much to tell. Brilliant, driven, the very best in very tough crowd. But she really keeps herself to herself, if you understand what I am meaning. She never talks about anything outside of the missions. So it's not as if I'm giving anything away because neither will she."

But Kelsey just had. To him.

"Kelsey?"

"Uh-huh."

"How could you get something so completely wrong?"

"What? I know where Zavala is. I know the layout of the house. We are the perfect assets to do this fast and quiet." She was back on the mission, and she was right. They'd rolled past the flashing lighthouse, leaving behind traffic, another cruise terminal, and once more were into the outskirts of the rapidly disappearing town.

"There," she pointed. They dropped down onto the narrow shore road past the big resorts, the Chankanaab Beach Resort being the last of them. He had a quick glimpse of a quiet lagoon and thatched huts.

It was the sort of place he'd imagined bringing a woman, though not with a load of weapons, rather with a bikini and a lot of time with nothing planned.

They continued south along the shore. The low beach and berm were usually close by, except when lush estates pushed the access road inland.

"Here," Kelsey pointed again.

He turned off into a vacant lot. It made a gap through the scrub trees and palms connecting the road to the beach. He stopped before they reached the sand. The electric MRZRs were silent and he could hear the gentle splash of the waves picked out in the headlights. He and Kelsey here, together. It was very easy to imagine.

Duane and Sofia rolled up quietly behind them, but Jason ignored them.

Instead, he turned to Kelsey. Her face was randomly lit by the blinking Christmas lights on the roll cage. The shifting shadows made it hard to read her expression.

"It's Christmas Eve," he said, for lack of any better ideas.

"It is," she looked down at her folded hands.

"Got a present for you."

"Better than this hat?" Then he saw her bite her lower lip because she now obviously understood the importance of the hat. He'd only been teasing when he put it on her, but it had gained so much meaning in the last half hour.

"Well, okay, it's not *that* cool, but I'm making this up as I go."

She only nodded, but it was quick, accepting. Then she appeared to brace herself.

He dug in his pocket and pulled out the bag of Christmas Skittles, handing it across solemnly.

Kelsey stared down at it for a long time before taking it gently from his hands.

"To hell with your past," he told her. "To hell with mine. New beginnings. Though I figured I was safer to start small." It was also the only thing he had to give at the moment.

She looked up at him with her dark eyes so wide that they seemed to catch all of the colors of the Christmas lights at once.

Then she clutched the little packet of candy to her chest with both hands, and nodded for him to continue down the beach.

The plan was fiendishly simple—he wondered if all of Kelsey's plans were like that. If so, she absolutely belonged in the 5E. It was beyond stealth...it was cool! And so much better than the home invasion that was their backup scenario.

They drove the two Christmas-decorated MRZRs slowly down the beach. In front of each beach house before Zavala's, they stopped and sang Christmas carols. When her clear soprano joined in, it really brought it to life. The owners came out, offered punch and apple fritters at one house and orange sugar cookies at the next. Each stop drew out the owners of the next residence along the beach front.

At Zavala's, the last in the row, the pattern held. Zavala came out to hear them and brought a bottle of rum. On the last stretch of darkened beach, they knocked out his two guards with dart guns they'd stashed under the seats, drugged Zavala and his equally dangerous brother as well before tying them in back of the MRZRs, and continued on their way as if nothing had happened. His capture only took seconds.

Just inland was the little-used Aeródromo Capitán Eduardo Toledo. A small field used for tourist flights during the day, and nothing at night. The Chinook slipped in and they drove up the cargo bay ramp so fast that the helo barely stopped.

Once they were aloft and clear of Cozumel, Kelsey came to find him where he was leaning against the angle of the raised rear ramp— his normal post as tail gunner.

She still wore the hat.

And she opened her joined hands for just a moment to show that she still clutched the little packet of candy, before once more holding it to her chest. And her eyes, those wide, lovely eyes looked ready to take on the world.

Then she leaned in to kiss him. Not some quick thank you peck, but soft, lush, so full of warmth that for a moment he felt as if he was indeed lying on a sunny Cozumel beach with her.

"Thank you," she whispered from mere inches away.

Jason tried to come up with some quip. Something to ease the moment for the lady in the blinking Rudolph hat. But all he could think to whisper back was the same, "Thank *you*."

He'd assumed this Christmas would be hell, because of the memories of the last one. Instead, she'd given him the gift of hope as a present.

When she kissed him again, this time letting herself curl up against him, he had hope for the many Christmases to come as well.

M.L. BUCHMAN
3X BOOKLIST TOP TEN ROMANCE OF THE YEAR
5E
NIGHT STALKERS
TARGET
OF THE Heart
NIGHT STALKERS 5E ROMANCE #1

TARGET OF THE HEART (NIGHT STALKERS 5E #1)

(EXCERPT)

Major Pete Napier hovered his MH-47G Chinook helicopter ten kilometers outside of Lhasa, Tibet and a mere two inches off the tundra. A mixed action team of Delta Force and The Activity—the slipperiest intel group on the planet—flung themselves aboard.

The additional load sent an infinitesimal shift in the cyclic control in his right hand. The hydraulics to close the rear loading ramp hummed through the entire frame of the massive helicopter. By the time his crew chief could reach forward to slap an "all secure" signal against his shoulder, they were already ten feet up and fifty out. That was enough altitude. He kept the nose down as he clawed for speed in the thin air at eleven thousand feet.

"Totally worth it," one of the D-boys announced as soon as he was on the Chinook's internal intercom.

He'd have to remember to tell that to the two Black Hawks flying guard for him...when they were in a friendly country and could risk a radio transmission. This deep inside China—or rather Chinese-held territory as the CIA's mission-briefing spook had insisted on calling it —radios attracted attention and were only used to avoid imminent death and destruction.

"Great, now I just need to get us out of this alive."

"Do that, Pete. We'd appreciate it."

He wished to hell he had a stealth bird like the one that had gone into bin Laden's compound. But the one that had crashed during that raid had been blown up. Where there was one, there were always two, but the second had gone back into hiding as thoroughly as if it had never existed. He hadn't heard a word about it since.

The Tibetan terrain was amazing, even if all he could see of it was the monochromatic green of night vision. And blackness. The largest city in Tibet lay a mere ten kilometers away and they were flying over barren wilderness. He could crash out here and no one would know for decades unless some yak herder stumbled upon them. Or were yaks in Mongolia? He was a corn-fed, white boy from Colorado, what did he know about Tibet? Most of the countries he'd flown into on Black Ops missions he'd only seen at night anyway.

While moving very, very fast.

Like now.

The inside of his visor was painted with overlapping readouts. A pre-defined terrain map, the best that modern satellite imaging could build made the first layer. This wasn't some crappy, on-line, look-at-a-picture-of-your-house display. Someone had a pile of dung outside their goat pen? He could see it, tell you how high it was, and probably say if they were pygmy goats or full-size LaManchas by the size of their shit-pellets if he zoomed in.

On top of that were projected the forward-looking infrared camera images. The FLIR imaging gave him a real-time overlay, in case someone had put an addition onto their goat shed since the last satellite pass or parked their tractor across his intended flight path.

His nervous system was paying autonomic attention to that combined landscape. He also compensated for the thin air at altitude as he instinctively chose when to start his climb over said goat shed or his swerve around it.

It was the third layer, the tactical display that had most of his attention. At least he and the two Black Hawks flying escort on him were finally on the move.

To insert this deep into Tibet, without passing over Bhutan or Nepal, they'd had to add wingtanks on the Black Hawks' hardpoints where he'd much rather have a couple banks of Hellfire missiles. Still, they had 20 mm chain guns and the crew chiefs had miniguns which was some comfort. His twin-rotor Chinook might be the biggest helicopter that the Night Stalkers flew, but it was the cargo van of Special Operations and only had two miniguns and a machine gun of its own. Though he'd put his three crew chiefs up against the best Black Hawk shooter any day.

While the action team was busy infiltrating the capital city and gathering intelligence on the particularly brutal Chinese assistant administrator, Pete and his crews had been squatting out in the wilderness under a camouflage net designed to make his helo look like just another god-forsaken Himalayan lump of granite.

Command had determined that it was better for the helos to wait on site through the day than risk flying out and back in. He and his crew had stood shifts on guard duty, but none of them had slept. They'd been flying together too long to have any new jokes, so they'd played a lot of cribbage. He'd long ago ruled no gambling on a mission, after a fistfight had broken out about a bluff hand that cost a Marine three hundred and forty-seven dollars. Marines hated losing to Army no matter how many times it happened. They'd had to sit on him for a long time before he calmed down.

Tonight's mission was part of an on-going campaign to discredit the Chinese "presence" in Tibet on the international stage—as if occupying the country the last sixty-plus years didn't count toward ruling, whether invited or not. As usual, there was a crucial vote coming up at the U.N.—that, as usual, the Chinese could be guaranteed to ignore. However, the ever-hopeful CIA was in a hurry to make sure that any damaging information that they could validate was disseminated as thoroughly as possible prior to the vote.

Not his concern.

His concern was, were they going to pass over some Chinese sentry post at their top speed of a hundred and ninety-six miles an hour? The sentries would then call down a couple Shenyang J-16 jet fighters that could hustle along at Mach 2—over fifteen *hundred* mph —to fry his sorry ass. He knew there was a pair of them parked at Lhasa along with some older gear that would be just as effective against his three helos.

"Don't suppose you could get a move on, Pete?"

"Eat shit, Nicolai!" He was a good man to have as a copilot. Pete knew he was holding on too tight, and Nicolai knew that a joke was the right way to ease the moment.

He, Nicolai, and the four pilots in the two Black Hawks had a long way to go tonight and he'd never make it if he stayed so tight on the controls that he could barely maneuver. Pete eased off and felt his fingers tingle with the rush of returning blood. They dove down into gorges and followed them as long as they dared. They hugged cliff walls at every opportunity to decrease their radar profile. And they climbed.

That was the true danger—they would be up near the helos' limits when they crossed over the backbone of the Himalayas in their rush for India. The air was so rarefied that they burned fuel at a prodigious rate. Their reserve didn't allow for any extended battles while crossing the border...not for any battle at all really.

IT WAS pitch dark outside her helicopter when Captain Danielle Delacroix stamped on the left rudder pedal while giving the big Chinook right-directed control on the cyclic. It tipped her most of the way onto her side but let her continue in a straight line. A Chinook's rotors were sixty feet across—front to back they overlapped to make the spread a hundred feet long. By cross-controlling her bird to tip it, she managed to execute a straight line between two mock pylons only thirty feet apart. They were made of thin cloth so they wouldn't down the helo if you sliced one—she was the only trainee to not have cut one yet.

At her current angle of attack, she took up less than a half-rotor of width, just twenty-four feet. That left her nearly three feet to either side, sufficient as she was moving at under a hundred knots.

The training instructor sitting beside her in the copilot's seat didn't react as she swooped through the training course at Fort Campbell, Kentucky. Only child of a single mother, she was used to providing her own feedback loops, so she didn't expect anything else. Those who expected outside validation rarely survived the SOAR induction testing, never mind the two years of training that followed.

As a loner kid, Danielle had learned that self-motivated congratulations and fun were much easier to come by than external ones. She'd spent innumerable hours deep in her mind as a pre-teen superheroine. At twenty-nine she was well on her way to becoming a real life one, though Helo-girl had never been a character she'd thought of in her youth.

External validation or not, after two years of training with the U.S. Army's 160th Special Operations Aviation Regiment she was ready for some action. At least *she* was convinced that she was. But the trainers of Fort Campbell, Kentucky had not signed off on anyone in her trainee class yet. Nor had they given any hint of when they might.

Keep reading at fine retailers everywhere:
Target of the Heart
Target Lock on Love
Target of Mine
Target of One's Own

M. L. BUCHMAN

CHRISTMAS COOKIED CHEF!

A DEAD CHEF
THRILLER STORY

CHRISTMAS COOKIED CHEF!

When gingerbread competitions are played for the highest stakes!

Connell *will soon rule the world of prime-time cooking shows. He possesses the chops, the charm, and the winning recipe.*

Or so he thinks until he ends up murdered by his own gingerbread village during a live Christmas broadcast.

Kate Stark's team of heroes *will never look at Santa's North Pole workshop the same way again.*

INTRODUCTION

Yes, I write a series of light-hearted foodie thrillers, called the Dead Chef series.

Let's see, what are the common themes:

- A chef dies gruesomely in the opening scene.
- She/he may well deserve it.
- At least one of them dies on national TV.
- It creates life-changing havoc for everyone around them.
- Cooks Network is probably not the safest place to be a contestant on a reality cooking show.

What can I really say? These tales are just plain fun.

CHRISTMAS COOKIED CHEF!

*H*e should have practiced under studio lights before the actual competition. Then Connell would have accounted for the heat of the big television spots. It over-softened butter. It slowed the cooling rate of the hundreds of pieces of gingerbread cookie he had to bake, causing several of them to overcook just from residual heat. It even increased set times for the royal icing that he was counting on to glue his walls and roof together.

The heat also made him sweat on national television. He wasn't going to be one of those guys who sweat into his food during a cooking show and grossed out the television audience.

Instead he tied a dishtowel across his forehead like a white boy playing kitchen samurai. How was this look supposed to get him his slot on national TV? Unless he made it a thing. So, he would try making it a thing when the interviewer came around the next time and hope that it worked.

Paul Stark was Mr. Genial Host. Tall, blondly handsome, and a notorious playboy, he was also half-owner of the most successful cooking television network out there. Connell wanted a piece of that. Maybe he should dye his carrot-red hair to match Paul's. Though he

297

wasn't the one Connell had to impress, but rather his twin sister Kate Stark. She was the real force behind the network's success.

Here he came, working down the line. Geoffrey, Oliver, himself, and then the delectable Juliana—the showgirl piece of the grand finale. She hadn't gotten in just for looking hot, he had to keep reminding himself. She was an artist in the kitchen, fast and meticulous. The only real threat to his win.

A cute little Asian chick trotted along behind Stark with a closeup camera. Would he get one, too? A tiny, tight-bodied servant of his own? Easy money said Paul got himself a piece of that.

"I like the look," Paul picked up another kitchen towel, hot pink instead of plain white like Connell's, and tried wrapping it around his own forehead before turning to the camera to model it. "Think it's me?"

The camera girl rolled her eyes at him, even as she filmed his antics. Maybe he wasn't getting a piece of that.

"So not!" Connell didn't want anyone stealing the look if it worked for him, but he remembered this guy was the host in time to make it funny.

Paul made a pretend pout. "Looks good on you though. Why is that?"

"We already had an Italian contender, Ralph Macchio in *The Karate Kid*." One of Dad's favorite movies watched repeatedly over his ever-increasing beer belly.

Coulda been me.

Sure, Dad, if you ever got off your ass to do more than burp and fart. His dad could have also been the CEO of GM and the President of the United States according to him. Instead he was a marginally-employed longshoreman, with a secretarial wife, a son, and a daughter who all hated his guts.

"Maybe it's time we had a red-headed Irish Kitchen-Towel Samurai," Connell suggested. *Kitchen-Towel Ninja? Nah, Samurai sounded better. Not bad for a first shot at an onscreen trademark.*

It earned him a laugh from Paul that had all been for the camera but had somehow felt as if it was all for him as well. Asian chick didn't even crack a smile. But a glance at the judge's table showed that all three of them did. A *very* good sign.

Too bad one of them wasn't the great Kate Stark, but it was a sure bet that she was watching the show for new talent.

Right here, lady!

He got back to work on his gingerbread scene.

RIKKA ALBERT DIDN'T PUNCH the twerp's nose. But if he ogled her ass or her breasts (such as they were) one more time, she might reconsider.

However, second, it would probably be bad form for a cameraperson to take down a contestant on national live television. And first, she didn't want to risk hurting her new hundred-thousand-dollar toy.

Kate always gave her the best presents, this time a RED Weapon 8k camera with Zeiss optics. The camera was massive overkill for a cooking competition, but the *Cooks' Christmas Gingerbread Grand Finale* show made for a good shakedown test and Rikka was loving it.

She often joined Kate in the field for her more complex shoots for Cooks Network shows and, in those cases, resolution could really help bigtime. Why if she'd had this while they were filming at that G-8 meeting... But they hadn't. However, if her RED baby kept performing this well, she'd sure be ready the next time Kate stumbled into some international disaster.

Assuming Kate kept keeping her around. Rikka had never had a friend for more than a passing moment or two. The Black Hat hacker part of her was in the past, technically, but it didn't lend itself to trusting others. Twice now Kate had washed her through the Witness Protection Program and no way was she going to screw it up this time. There were too many good things going for her. Kate actually treated her like a friend, which Rikka still didn't know how to process.

Focus on the show.

Paul had been working down the line: Geoffrey, Oliver, and Connell.

Then he moved on to flirt with the elegant Juliana. *Why couldn't she be tall and elegant like that?*

Rikka would normally move in to act as a buffer to Paul's unstoppable charm. Rikka had considered talking to some genetic engineers to see if it could be excised, but she doubted it. Besides, was emasculating Paul really worth the trouble? Probably not.

Before she could step over to Juliana's work area, she felt the room pressure change. No one should be allowed in or out of the studio except during commercial breaks, but she looked up and there he was.

Sam Fierro was six-foot-a-jillion of lovely Marine Force Recon (retired) who ran the best butcher shop in Brooklyn. Of course he could enter the studio anytime he wanted to—because if he chose to be clandestine, all the guards in the world would never see him go by despite his massive frame.

He stopped just inside the door and crossed his arms.

Waiting.

For her!

If she was the swooning type, she'd swoon right here and now. She wasn't, but considered doing it anyway just to watch his reaction. They'd been lovers for over a year, but Sam never pressured her for more than she was willing to give. He was just there. A new inexplicable constant in her life, just like Kate.

Rather than fainting with delight, she sent him a big wink and wondered how fast this show would be over. Maybe if she punched the Connell twerp, who she could again feel staring at her ass, that would end it sooner. But Kate wouldn't be amused, which was actually the real reason she didn't attack him.

Paul was busy hustling Juliana, so Rikka scooted over and slipped her aptly named RED Weapon camera right in between Paul and the harried contestant.

CONNELL TOOK a moment to shake out his hands and unkink his back from bending over the counter for almost six hours. Just ten minutes left, precisely on schedule, he allowed himself a few seconds to scan the scene.

Clearly Geoffrey and Oliver belonged to a whole other subclass of baker and he didn't even waste time looking in their direction.

However, to his left, Paul Stark was now on his shit list even if he was half-owner of the network. The guy should never have been hitting on Juliana. That was going to be his turf. Thankfully, Paul and little Asian camera babe were now moving on for the "final word with the judges" segment.

Juliana's perfection made her the one to beat—and he wasn't thinking of only her body. Her design work was really pretty. Not that he was actually worried or anything.

After he won, he'd ask her out for a celebratory dinner. If he played down his own win and kept focusing on "We're the top two!", maybe he could upgrade it to a celebratory fuck. She was one hot Latina and her dark skin looked damn good in a white chef's coat—it would look even better spread beneath him on white sheets. She was the only one of the four finalists whose coat was still spotless, because she was just that precise. But he'd bet she was super hot in bed, just like that movie star Michelle Rodriguez who kicked so much ass in the *Fast & Furious* and *Avatar,* and all those other Caribbean babes. Let just the women across the border—that was his solution to the immigration crisis—but only the hot, single ones without kids.

He turned back to his own creation.

He'd considered taking on the definitive Herculean task of making the White House. But then he'd be compared to each of the ones produced by those Presidential master chefs over the decades. In these turbulent political times—was there any other kind anymore?— he'd thought about "honoring" the "good old days" and recreating Mount Rushmore. But the carved granite was so monotone.

The International Space Station with massive solar wings covered in edible gold had been tempting.

Ultimately, targeting maximum audience appeal, he'd gone for the humorous. He'd created the North Pole.

Santa's home with red walls made with food dye in corn syrup-blond gingerbread. A smoky curl of brandy snap coming out of the red velvet cake chimney. Happy scenes visible through each window…except he'd left the bedroom dark where he imagined Mrs. Claus with her white-fur trimmed red dress hiked up to her waist and her jolly ass raised high waiting for Santa's return. Did the man have a candy cane for a prick? Maybe it was a great big one like the pole planted in the center of Connell's North Pole landscape. *Hey Santa. Got your big dick right here on display.*

The reindeer barn was a fanciful world of Finnish-carved gingerbread. The elves' workshop a fantasy of a chocolate-worked roof with sea salt seasoning sprinkled over the top, that seemed to float above see-through sugar lattice walls revealing marzipan elves at gingerbread workbenches making over a dozen kinds of to-scale cookies. His favorite were the fingertip-sized chocolate chip ones.

Santa's candy cane "Pole" towered above them all.

BY PLAN, Sam had arrived for just the last half hour of the show, right when the broadcast had switched from pre-recorded to live.

The first five hours of the competition were edited on the fly to fill the first half hour of the hour-long broadcast. Then, from one commercial break to the next, the show had shifted to a live format, which always increased the tension and hooked the viewers. The sprint to the finish and the judging were live. It was a format that Kate had perfected and the other networks still hadn't figured out how to pull off decently.

He stayed by the door and appreciated the magnetic attraction that had Rikka turning to flash one of her electric smiles at him before he'd even stepped all the way through the door. He was always equally aware of her.

His muscles felt good; they still burned from the long day of butchering. He'd started at four this morning so that he could be free for dinner and an evening with Rikka.

He scanned the studio: audience spread in a single row of chairs to either side of the exit door he waited beside.

Just ahead stood the two floor cameras. They were free-rolling and came up to his chin. Each camera head about the size of a FIM-92 Stinger shoulder-fired missile, with twin control handles dropping to the rear. The operators steered them a bit like motorcycles.

The sixteen-foot-high studio space had a simple metal pipe grid mounted close to the ceiling—lighting instruments hung down from it. They were on the 29th floor of 30 Rockefeller Plaza in the heart of Manhattan, so the floor above would be the Cooks Network corporate offices, including Kate's. For a moment he wondered if Paul ever actually used his.

The show was a surprisingly small operation, just two floor cameras and Rikka's close-up rig. Two producers on the floor, two operators in the control room, eighteen guests, four contestants, three judges, Paul as emcee, and himself. It always looked so much bigger on TV.

The whole focus was on the four contestants of course.

The leftmost contestant's entry was a trainwreck—literally. His gingerbread locomotive was five-feet long and over a foot high. No detail was missing: crank arms, steam whistle, even an engineer leaning out the window. Sam had learned enough from hanging out with Rikka to know that he'd taken a real judging risk—he'd used silver dragées for the rivets which the FDA declared as inedible even though they were listed as a food item. And he'd scorched the gingerbread for the wheels, which were now cracking and breaking as he tried to place them alongside the engine. Even as Sam watched, a cry of horror sounded from the small audience and Rikka's camera was zooming in. The coal car collapsed sideways like an empty box folding flat. The black currant "coal" spilled off the table and across the floor as the baker cursed fluently and began sliding about on them as they squished.

The second one had gone for height, an intricate reproduction of the Chrysler Building. Probably trying to stick his brown nose right up to Kate's ass. He was always amazed when people thought that would work on Kate. It might on Paul, but never his sister. They lived together in a fabulous multi-level condo, tucked into the top three floors, inside the fluted Art Deco taper of the Chrysler Building's pinnacle. Unlike the first contestant's train, it was standing—six feet tall and architecturally accurate. But, even to Sam's untrained eye, it looked like a seven-year-old had built it: spilling seam glue and crooked gargoyles.

The third guy in the row had clearly gone all out with an elaborate North Pole village that he'd have to move closer and inspect later. Lots of detail there.

And in the last one. The pretty Latina had made a snowy cottage scene with a fanciful little gingerbread home. Like the woman, utterly elegant. It had far more taste than the more elaborate village beside her. It had sparkling coconut snow, with melted-candy windows, that actually had images of the happy scenes inside. Her "stained glass" was lit by a tiny indoor Christmas tree. Outside, she had a far larger one adorned with tiny macaroons in a dozen colors. The snowy rooftop even had Santa's sleigh and eight tiny reindeer.

He had no say in the matter, but he'd vote for the tiny snowbound cottage.

Sam wondered if it was the sort of place Rikka might like to go some Christmas. *That* was an interesting thought.

CONNELL BRUSHED the last of the royal icing over Santa's roof where Santa would be getting his later tonight just as he himself would—in the form of the hot Juliana—definitely a Christmas treat for himself. He'd already teased her into tasting several of his micro-cookies, the last right from his fingertips (he'd timed his request for her opinion for when both her hands were covered in dough). Like a well-trained girl, she taken it with those lush lips and told him how good it was— he'd worked hard to get a big flavor punch in each tiny cookie.

If she was really good to him, maybe he'd invite her as a guest on one of his shows as a consolation prize. Maybe, if he played his sugar right, he could get the tight-assed Asian camera girl too.

The consistency of his last batch of royal icing was strange—maybe he'd mis-measured the amount of glycerin that he'd added for extra shine. Or maybe it was the heat from those damn studio lights. He was out of time to tinker with it, so he spread it more thickly over the main slope of Santa's roof than he'd planned. Connell wanted the finishing touch to be the final surprise, so he'd timed this last task to the second during practice.

On the final slope of the roof's surface, he quickly set ten-millimeter Sixlet sugar pearls. Each almost a half-inch across, he was able to rapidly transform the roof into a flag for the North Pole that he'd designed—a slightly surprised looking Rudolph face on a field of white "snow" with an oversized red jawbreaker for a nose. He'd premade cookie cutters in the right shapes so that he could frame a section, like Rudolph's fur, and rapidly fill in brown Sixlets in an even layer. Another frame, filled with snowy whites for the background. It let him place hundreds of them in just minutes.

It was the total "Awww!" moment. As the camera chick shifted to get the best angle on it without getting in the way, Connell knew it was replaying on the big overhead monitors when he heard just those exact sounds from the audience and judges.

The colored Sixlets settled into the royal icing. They were sliding a little due to the runniness. Not enough to distort Rudolph's expression yet, but it might. And his nose appeared to be dissolving.

Connell glanced at the clock.

Seventeen seconds.

Geoffrey was weeping over his trainwreck.

Oliver's nose actually was brown from where he'd smeared some gingerbread on it as he struggled to make his Chrysler Building less feeble.

Juliana was raising her hands above her head to show that she was finished. Her generous breasts pushed against that immaculate white chef's coat in a luscious curve.

Connell snapped on his hair dryer to set the royal icing and leaned in close to watch against overheating.

UNKNOWN TO CONNELL, the heat was the final factor in the chemical reaction.

The jawbreaker had been replaced with a thinly coated shell that dissolved rapidly in the citric acid of the orange juice that Connell had added to the icing for flavor. Once the surface was breached, it released a small flood from its interior of combined sulfuric and nitric acid. These acids mixed quickly with the excess glycerin in the icing.

The application of heat was sufficient to complete the reaction.

Had the roof of Santa's bedroom been less well supported, or made of thinner gingerbread, the result would have been little different.

The imperfect admixture of nitric and sulfuric acids with glycerin, and the application of heat, was still sufficient to ignite as it formed nitroglycerin.

Three seconds to go, the unstable compound blew up explosively.

At two seconds, the sugar-coated chocolate Sixlets launched from the sturdy roof in rough formation. Five hundred and seventy-three brightly colored, hard candy pellets with tasty chocolate centers ripped off the parts of Connell's face that the explosion hadn't already burned away. The sixty-two that entered his open mouth didn't kill him, but the thirty-eight that punched out his eyes and entered his brain would in just a few more seconds.

At one second, Connell knew he wasn't going to get Juliana naked after all.

The revelation was cut short when he collapsed forward as the final buzzer sounded, shattering his gingerbread display and impaling himself on Santa's candy-cane dick.

He was so screwed.

SAM WATCHED THE PANIC UNFOLD. Some people didn't take well to bloody deaths at close quarters. Almost twenty years in Marine Force Recon had inured him.

The audience, a small cluster of the competitors' family and friends, screamed and ran. Not a one of them ran toward the bleeding chef. *Man must have been* real *popular.* A few clustered around each of the other three. The rest rushed toward the exit door—where Sam stood, casually blocking it with crossed arms and a no-nonsense military presence.

The people at the lead of those seeking escape tried to stop before they slammed into him, but the crowd pressure was too much and they were knocked forward.

With a quick forward swing of his crossed arms, he tipped them back.

Because they were so tightly packed, they mostly fell over backward like dominos. The people at the very rear managed to stumble to a stop before they too were caught up in the cascade of flailing humanity.

Rikka Albert set aside her camera and soon had everyone herded back into their seats. Though she was a head shorter than anyone else there, they soon discovered that the tiny Japanese woman was a force to be reckoned with and was only running the camera because she enjoyed playing with expensive toys.

Damn but that woman was amazing. Nothing flapped her confidence.

Of course, you had to be at a serious kick-ass level to be Kate Stark's right hand. She should be the pint-sized heroine in one of those old Kung Fu movies, except she wasn't much of a fighter. However, she was a sushi master, something his third-generation butcher heritage could really appreciate, in addition to being one of the world's top five computer hackers.

However, it appeared that his plan of taking her out to dinner right after the show wasn't going to happen.

The studio was still in chaos.

Floor producers rushed around as if they could make a difference.

The cameramen knew their jobs and made sure that the control room had feeds from the finished gingerbread projects in case they needed something to broadcast other than bloody death.

Paul, for once in his life, wasn't being Mr. Useless, but was keeping the judges and the other three contestants calm. Relatively. Shock was still running pretty high.

Thankfully all cell phones had to be checked outside the door, so no one would be pumping this imagery straight from the studio to the world.

Sam rocked back on his heels to consider the situation.

What if the person hadn't been caught on camera?

That would require someone who understood camera angles well enough to avoid them. They would also need access to the prep materials to have rigged the explosion. A suicide on national TV seemed unlikely, which meant the dead chef was murdered.

He could feel Kate Stark rushing up behind him. Something about her he could always sense despite her ability to move so silently. Tall, as lovely as her brother Paul was handsome, and always in control. Even though she rarely cracked a smile, the camera loved her as did the network fans.

"What this time?" She stepped up beside him.

He glanced down at her, but she wasn't looking to him for an answer. Instead she did a quick scan of the room and assessed it for herself.

"Oh, Kate," Rikka rushed up. "You missed a good one—well, in a horrible way. Connell's entire roof blew up in his face, literally. It's too bad. He was a contender. Definitely had second place tied up and might have had a shot at winning, though my vote would totally be with Juliana. Besides, she has much better camera appeal. You could tell that Connell was gunning hard for Juliana—took me some tricky camera work to not show that. Keep playing off Juliana's innate kindness. He was sort of a slime mold."

"Did you see anything out of place, Sam?"

He was touched that Kate asked him. Their relationship over the years had rarely been an easy one. Regrettably, he could only shrug.

There'd been something that his Marine Force Recon training had sensed while he'd been busy watching Rikka move about the studio, but he wasn't sure quite what.

"I'll watch the door," Kate nodded for him to go ahead and inspect the scene while she took over blocking the door.

It was a hell of a concession. Sure he had twenty years of serving in Marine Force Recon, but Kate Stark had made it all the way to the vice-presidential protection detail before she'd lost a protectee. Didn't bother him any—guy had been an asshole. Had bothered Kate a lot, so she'd quit the Secret Service and taken over her parents' television network instead, turning it into a major operation along the way.

SAM WAVED Rikka forward and she began describing what she'd seen as she moved toward him.

"The two contestants to camera left were wholly focused on their own creations. They barely looked at each other once things started going wrong. Seeing the quality of work that Connell and Juliana were doing kept them really focused."

Sam glanced at her. Her observation skills were as sharp as her computer ones.

"Connell is the victim. Juliana is the pretty one. She had several interactions with the victim."

If the culprit had indeed avoided the camera… The EMTs and police would be only minutes out. Whatever he was going to learn, he had to learn it fast.

He glanced again at the pipe-grid ceiling. It seemed unlikely that any reasonable delivery point for incendiaries could come from above, so he dismissed it.

It would have been too obvious if one of the cameramen had left his post, so he dismissed them from consideration and stepped past the two primary camera positions. Rikka and Paul had the best access to all the workbenches as the roving interview and close-up team— but he'd trust Rikka with his own life.

And, reluctantly, he crossed Paul off the list. He didn't trust the guy enough to even consider using him in a throwing comparison to see if he trusted him more than how far he could throw him—about 175, Sam could probably get twenty-five feet of clear air before Paul landed, and Sam definitely didn't trust him that far. But the guy was Kate's brother and would never do anything, intentionally, to screw up his twin sister. In his own weird way, he was very protective of her.

Predictably, Paul had moved over to console Juliana. *That* was his specialty—women wilted around him. All except Rikka.

"Hey, Stark," Rikka called out to Paul so that everyone in the studio could hear. "No hitting on freaked-out contestants or I'll bust you into little pieces."

"Speaking of freaks, Rikka!" Paul retorted out of habit but he was holding out a handkerchief to the weeping woman.

Sam noticed that he didn't argue that Rikka *could* bust him into little pieces, which showed he had some brains.

Juliana had also had reasonable access to Connell's workstation.

Had anyone in the audience?

Unlikely.

He didn't trust the other two contestants. Too stone-faced.

But none of them were the pattern he'd somehow felt.

RIKKA STEPPED up to the edge of the wreckage caused by the blast and Connell's collapse. She'd liked the cozy miniature North Pole scene and it was sad to see it crushed. As she'd filmed its creation, she'd imagined curling up there alone where no one would ever find her again. Thanks to Kate she should be safe now, but the Witness Protection Program had guaranteed that she had no past. Not that it had been so wonderful as to be worth remembering but, still, not having one sucked.

Of course, Connell's little scene had been coldly calculated to please. Now he was a bloody mess that only moments before had been an asshole.

Her inner creep detector had been highly tuned by her past. At that level, people like Paul Stark didn't even make the grade—he wasn't even a bad one, just full of himself. Connell had definitely rung Rikka's "Bad" bells. Whereas Sam Fierro rang her good bells in ways she hadn't known existed. She could almost regret her past as a Black Hat hacker because he was such a fine upstanding example of everything she wasn't—third generation butcher and third-gen Marine Force Recon.

"What's up with that shit anyway?" Rikka turned to face Sam squarely.

He raised an eyebrow at her.

"Okay, question for another time. I know. I know. I'm making about as little sense as ever. But one of these days, you're going to have to explain why you're with me. Or maybe I need to explain *myself* to me. I don't know. Something. You know that I—"

Sam tipped up his bare wrist as if looking at a watch.

Too kind to cut her off verbally. She rested her hand briefly on where the watch would sit to acknowledge his kindness.

Deep breath, Rikka. Focus. Not exactly her best skill when away from a keyboard.

"So what blew up?"

Sam leaned in, sniffing the air, then nodded to himself.

Kate joined them from the door, Building Security was on site now.

He tapped his nose, Rikka and Kate leaned in together.

Rikka didn't smell anything except something that made her want to sneeze.

"Acid," Kate knew what it was, of course, because she was so awesome.

Sam pointed at a line that had been burned into the model's snowy "ground" where some liquid had drained off the roof's edge and burned a long thin line into the marshmallow fluff.

"Sulfuric acid fumes are what's making your nose itch," Kate explained. "Not exactly your typical baking ingredient. Mixed with a few other things, including the glycerin in the royal icing, Connell created nitroglycerine. The moment he added heat," she of course had noticed the hair dryer even though she hadn't been here, "he was doomed."

Rikka stepped back to grab her camera, then filmed the details in the snow. Which was a little gross, because of how Connell still lay impaled by his winter wonderland.

"Wait a minute. If something blew up in his face, wouldn't he fall backward rather than forward?"

In answer, Sam poked a finger hard enough in her belly to have her doubling over forward in surprise. Before she could fall flat on her face, he smacked a hand against her forehead. He didn't do it hard, just enough to slow her forward momentum. Just when she almost had her balance back, Kate hit her behind the knees.

"Hey!" Rikka would have dropped to the floor if Sam hadn't wrapped those big hands of his around her shoulders.

Kate continued as if she hadn't just been all sneaky, "The blast itself wasn't all that powerful, just enough to launch a lot of small candies. The ones that blew into his brain probably cut his autonomic nerve system. His knees gave out when he lost control of his whole lower body. He didn't fall forward, so much as collapse down before he could pull away."

Kate definitely freaked Rikka out sometimes. She seemed to know even more about how to kill people than Sam. Herself? Rikka could cut up a dead fish like nobody's business—she'd earned her title of *itamae* sushi master fair and square. But the fish was already dead and clean before it arrived on her cutting board.

"So, who drops a cookie chef on national TV? Like...a ginger snap." She cracked herself up and laughed, even if there was still a bloody corpse lying before them.

SAM LISTENED to all of the interviews. The police had tried to do those individually with no other peripheral witnesses. Sam had simply leaned against the back wall of the conference room they took over for interrogations and crossed his arms over his chest.

When one of them had tried to engage him, he'd rolled up his shirt sleeves. One forearm had the skull and crossed oars of Marine Recon. His other forearm had the Latin motto: *Celer, Silens, Mortalis*—Swift, Silent, Deadly.

He didn't need to translate it for them, they seemed to get the idea and left him alone.

But still no satisfying the itch of the broken pattern he'd seen somewhere.

Every audience member had been accounted for as a particular contestant's relative or friend.

It wasn't until they were done and the forensic guys were gone, that Kate's crew was authorized to come in and clean up the studio. A special team took care of the murder scene, but they had to reset the other workstations as well for the next show being filmed tomorrow —if the contestants dared to show up.

"Let's get out of here," Rikka looked exhausted. Being the close-up camera operator, she had been questioned last and longest. Longer even than Paul Stark or Juliana.

It was past midnight, so getting her to eat something and tucking her in bed was going to be their evening together. Or rather their early morning.

He didn't mind. Sam enjoyed watching her sleep. Her vibrant energy would taper off slowly, until she was simply at peace. That was why he'd spent twenty years in Recon, so that people like Rikka Albert could sleep in peace.

As they headed out of the studio, he glanced over his shoulder before stepping out the main door.

Like a galvanic shock, there was the pattern he'd been missing.

"What is it?" Rikka had made it well down the hallway before she noticed he was missing from her side and doubled back.

Together they watched the suppliers set up for a sugar sculpture competition. The multiple ovens and cookie sheets for baking the big pieces of gingerbread were quickly rolled away. In their place, a wide variety of pots and thermometers were set onto cooking ranges for the melting of sugar.

Everything moved like clockwork, with the smooth efficiency of a Marine Force Recon team preparing for a mission far behind enemy lines.

Except for one person. Her movements were just a little out of sync.

"Should I call someone?" Rikka saw it as well, which confirmed his assessment.

The police and coroner were long gone. Kate had returned to her offices. Paul had escorted the lovely Juliana out the door, and probably straight up to the family penthouse. Sam knew from the stories that Paul would actually be in love with her and treat her royally for as long as it lasted. Then he would mourn until the next "love of his life" came along. He'd even make sure that Juliana got a fair audition with his sister—for Kate made all of the station's casting decisions herself. Her instincts about what worked and who was sympathetic to the camera were impeccable.

In answer, Sam simply walked back into the studio. Walked until he was standing directly in the way of the woman setting up the replacement for Connell's workstation.

When the woman sighed, Sam reached out a finger to brush at her hair. The goth-dark wig shifted aside to reveal brilliantly red hair. He'd wager that the thick makeup would also cover fair and freckled skin like Connell's.

"You're such a good man, Sam Fierro." Rikka curled up against him. It wouldn't be for long; she had another show in a few hours. Trading in her old life—with both the FBI and foe-hackers always chasing her tail—had turned out to be one of the best things she'd ever done. And soon, before the sun rose, she knew that Sam would leave his bed to return to his butcher and charcuterie shop. At least until the next time trouble came their way, then he would turn into the biggest, staunchest ally any woman could ask for.

She pictured how he had simply stood dead still in the studio and waited until the young woman had started to speak on her own.

Rikka's slimy jerk detector had been right on the money about Connell.

His sister had given herself a Christmas present: freedom from her soullessly evil older brother. Apparently he'd been a morality-free zone since childhood.

When she finished her confession—right down to the chemistry she'd studied and finagling the job for Connell's show—she'd offered herself to Sam to take to the police. He'd instead, after she'd washed off the makeup and tossed the wig, led her up to Kate's office.

Kate had still been there, as if she'd been waiting for them. Maybe she was.

She'd offered a Sam-style silent-and-questioning look before gesturing Connell's sister to take a chair.

Rikka answered for the girl's sake, "She decided it was time to stop living in the past." Sam had then guided her out the door and left the two women to talk about the future. It didn't seem as if either one was interested in talking about the past.

Maybe that was good advice, even if she didn't know how to apply it to herself.

Sam had taken her home, to his home above the butcher shop, and they'd curled up together.

"I don't quite get why you let a murderer go. I mean she *did* kill her own brother. I'm not saying you were wrong, I liked her, but isn't it still murder?"

Sam didn't stop with his slow smoothing of her hair down her back as she continued to lay on him with her ear to his chest. It was as if he was too mesmerized by her feel to think of anything else. She liked having that power over him.

"Of course, in a way, I suppose that she was just...sort of the instrument of his own death. If he hadn't molested his own sister all those years, she never would have killed him. And she was smart enough that she would have gotten away with it if you hadn't noticed how she didn't quite fit in. I suppose that in a way, he did commit suicide on national TV."

Sam patted her butt in acknowledgement that he agreed. The sex had definitely left him far beyond speech, but it typically wound her way up. He was a man of hidden talents and she did her best to return the favor.

Imagine! Christmas with a lover. With *her* lover.

Rikka had never spent Christmas with anyone, but knew she would this year. Not just with her friend Kate at the Starks' notoriously fabulous and exclusive Christmas party, but also with Sam.

A home for Christmas. Juliana had built one out of gingerbread and Connell's sister had blown a path to a new one of her own.

A home? It was too big a thought for now but, for the first time, Rikka could think about the future rather than the burden of her own past. She wanted to let Sam know just how special he was for giving her such a gift.

"What would you like for Christmas, Sam?"

He curled one of his arms about her waist and crushed her against him.

"I mean in addition to that." She wasn't the giggling sort, but could definitely feel him squeezing a happy sigh out of her.

He shrugged, then brushed a finger down her nose and she knew that she was enough for him just as he was for her. But she wanted to show him that as well.

"I'll bake something for you. Something yummy and…Christmasy," she teased him.

Sam froze.

She kissed him before leaning down to whisper in his ear. "I promise—no gingerbread."

That earned her one of his wonderfully rare, slow, deep laughs as he held her tight. The best Christmas present of all.

M.L.
BUCHMAN
B&N AND NPR TOP 5 AUTHOR OF THE YEAR
ONE
CHEF!
A DEAD CHEF THRILLER
"A fabulous
soaring thriller!"
—Midwest Book Review
on Take Over at Midnight

ONE CHEF! (DEAD CHEF #2)

(EXCERPT)

Marianne Rimaldi scooped a scant teaspoon of the Gran Marnier chocolate ganache and drizzled it atop the single bite of truffle cheesecake. The perfect final bite for the meal she was creating.

A glance at the competition clock.

Two minutes.

She plated three more desserts for the judges. The television cameras filming *Kate's Kitchen from Hell* hovered close by—two on her, two on her competitor as the final seconds ticked away. One glass-eyed lens had an angle that showed the cameraman wasn't focused only on the food.

Precisely according to plan.

Marianne needed the win on America's most popular cooking show, which meant winning over at least two judges. More than that, she lusted after that *Kate's Kitchen* "Golden Knife" stamp of approval on her career, which required all three judges. For that she wasn't above applying other…ingredients.

The heat of the competition kitchen—the flaring burners and blinding stage lights—had "forced" her to pull at the cross-shoulder buttons of her confining chef's jacket which now hung half open. She wore a loose-necked satin blouse beneath, no bra. She'd chosen a emerald green to contrast with the fire-red of the winner's jacket that she hoped to be awarded at the end of the show. It also stood out well against her unadorned ash-black jacket of a contestant, but she wanted the red.

However, mere party tricks wouldn't work on the show's main judge.

Marianne had to capture Kate Stark's attention. With her, nothing would count except the food itself.

Kate Stark, the blue-eyed goddess of television food on the nation's most popular cooking network, was also founder and perennial judge of the show. Always front and center on the final panel.

Deep down Marianne didn't want to just win Stark's vote, she wanted to impress the hell out of her. She'd sell her soul to Devil if needs be; it was *Kate's Kitchen from Hell* after all.

Don't think! Focus on the food...but don't forget the theater.

Marianne was slightly built, so even the least view down her blouse from above was a very revealing one. She bent over her dessert plates and the satin draped away from her body allowing a deliciously cool ripple to course down her front. Her build might be far less substantial than the one that had made her mother such a success on the "wrong" side of Hollywood. But she'd certainly watched her mom and learned what sold. It had been an educational upbringing, if not a typical one.

Three judges.

Two of them were easy.

The guest taster was Zania in the role of the "every person's" palate so necessary for engaging an audience. Someone for the viewers to identify with, among all those professional chefs. Of course her palate was about the only thing on Zania that wasn't extraordinary.

Zania was the hottest new Hollywood starlet—who Marianne would bet was a closet butch. It wasn't too dangerous a bet because Zania's mother worked the same side of Hollywood as Marianne's and word got around of what really happened after the bedding was rumpled in erotic film.

During her intro, Tinsel Town's hot new box-office draw had announced she was centerfolding for *Playboy* next month in the same sultry breath as promoting her new tight-leather, sci-fi thriller movie. Marianne knew that anyone who pegged Zania as an airhead had a nasty surprise coming; she absolutely knew how to market herself. In all ways.

However, hinting to the actress that there was a chance of some woman-on-woman bonding that would allow Zania to prove just who was the "ultimate female among women" offered real possibilities for leveraging the star's vote. It definitely looked as if she'd bought into Marianne's careful seasoning of her performance with hints and suggestions.

Marianne's own tastes however, were for the second guest judge; the professional chef.

Harold Merritt, with his Michelin-starred *Chicago's Merritt* restaurant, was both very handsome and notoriously single. Win or lose, she'd make a point of chatting him up after the show. All that broad chest and short dark crew cut gave him a deliciously tough look; she could find many uses for him outside the kitchen, or in it—a little oil, two bodies, maybe some chocolate sauce...

A careful peek from behind the screen of the jet-black dyed bangs of her blond hair revealed Zania and Harold were staring hard at their monitors of the show's live feed rather than gazing benignly over the competition kitchen floor. Their attention was right where Marianne wanted it. On her.

The head judge was a different problem.

Kate Stark—the number one slotted television chef on any network, not just the one she owned—also watched the monitor, but with a slightly amused smile that Marianne would pay a lot to understand. Kate with her direct blue eyes and straight brunette hair that brushed her shoulders and framed the well-defined cheekbones and aquiline nose that made her one of the most attractive faces in television, cooking or not.

She was a notoriously deadpan judge, at least on this show, so that wry smile must mean something.

For good or ill, Marianne would not find the answer to that this side of the judge's table.

The camera that was spying down her jacket still hadn't wavered, so Marianne "accidentally" dribbled a large dollop of the orange-chocolate ganache onto the back of her hand. She licked it clean as if too hurried to wipe it away, making sure the camera could see the pleasure on her face at the success of her own work without losing the angle on her blouse.

Damn! It really was good. Marianne would win on taste alone. But she'd have to play the meal presentation very carefully, spiking the odds even further in her favor with both of the two guest judges.

The competition buzzer sounded as she shaved the last of the zest of a blood orange using a nutmeg rasp. Even as Marianne held up her hands to show she was done, the camera focused in on the cloud of orange dust still sprinkling down like the first snowflakes.

Her shiny dark green satin blouse made a perfect backdrop, which had "somehow" slipped out of another button. Somehow...because she'd enlarged the buttonhole last night to ensure that the button popped when she raised her arms.

Nailed it.

She had to close her eyes for a moment to steady herself.

Light-headed.

She needed to eat.

Her normal technique of shrugging it off didn't work. Even lowering her arms and subtly bracing herself against the table didn't help clear her head.

Her hands were shaking.

Her hands never shook.

Keep reading at fine retailers everywhere:
Swap Out!
One Chef!
Two Chef!

M. L. BUCHMAN

3-time Booklist Top 10 Romance Author of the Year

Flying Beyond the Bar

a US Coast Guard romance story

FLYING BEYOND THE BAR

US Coast Guard Rescue Swimmer Harvey Whitman lives to save lives. The unit's motto, "That Others May Live", defines his life's goal perfectly.

Helicopter Crew Chief Vivian Schroder, newly assigned to Astoria, Oregon, cares only for her career—and flying clear of her family.

When a storm-tossed nighttime rescue goes desperately wrong fifty miles offshore from the hazardous Columbia River Bar, they must rely on each other's instincts in ways they never imagined.

INTRODUCTION

This story actually embraces three holidays, beginning with Christmas.

For six years, I lived along the Oregon Coast. It is one of the most treacherous stretches of the entire Pacific Ocean. Our dozen-mile stretch often claimed the same number of lives each year. And the Colombia River Bar, where the big river pours out, is generally ranked as the most dangerous shipping waters anywhere in the world.

For that reason, the US Coast Guard presence is very strong there. Almost daily, sometimes twice daily in the summer, the bright orange Dolphin helicopters slide along just a few hundred feet above the vast beaches, proactively looking for people in trouble.

This story arose from a Christmas walk along the chilly beach as I watched a helo patrolling by overhead.

FLYING BEYOND THE BAR

The beat of the Dolphin's rotors pounded into his body and Harvey Whitman did his best to tamp down the automatic adrenaline charge. The orange US Coast Guard HH-65C "Dolphin" search-and-rescue helicopter was hustling due west out of Astoria, Oregon and straight into the darkness of a Pacific Ocean nighttime gale. Blowing forty knots was so normal out here for a chill February night that the pilots hadn't even remarked on it as they'd loaded up. Something about the wild smell, the taste of the salt spray that a good storm kicked up into the air, always charged him up.

"Sea state is very rough," Vivian called out from her position as crew chief close behind the pilots but facing backwards into the cargo bay. A single strand of her dark curly hair had escaped the neatly formed bun to show between the lower edge of her flight helmet and the upper edge of the international orange survival suit they all wore. He'd always liked that curl. Even back before he knew Vivian Schroder's name, it had captured his attention. Not that the rest of her didn't, but there was something special about that renegade lock on the otherwise perfectly squared-away petty officer.

"Like that's news," Harvey didn't need to be able to see the nighttime ocean to know that. A Douglas Sea Scale State of 6, or "very rough" meant six-meter waves. Two-story high, wind-shredded surf rated as a typical dose of ugly for this stretch of the Pacific. "Just another day at the beach."

Vivian laughed over the intercom. Something she'd done every time he spoke his dad's ritual phrase.

"Just another day at the beach," Harvey recollected. *Sure, Dad. Except you were a Navy clerk for two years in San Diego and never spent a day on the water no matter how many tales you'd spun for all those years—before I figured out how to look up your service record.* Actually, confronting his father hadn't changed a thing: Dad's stories or his complete lack of interest in his son.

"Ten minutes," one of the pilots called back.

As the helo jounced through the storm, Harvey was glad to be doing the prescribed routine tasks. Thinking about his dad was never a good sign. He started prepping in case he had to go into the water. He double-checked the ankle, wrist, and neck seals on his wet suit. He'd already pulled the long beaver-tail of his jacket between his legs and attached it to the front of his jacket. Tapping the closures of his harness assured him that everything was in place. A habit-trained series of slaps located: radio, flashlight, knife, hammer for shattering glass with a hook for cutting straps, diver's knife, and magnesium flare. All in place.

He could see Vivian's eyes following the same pattern as she visually confirmed everything he touched.

"Anything new?" He knew that they would have told him if there was. That he would have heard the call coming in over the intercom. It didn't stop his need to know what he was getting into. Despite the drama in the movies, rescue swimmers didn't enter the water all that often and he wondered if tonight would be one of the exceptions.

"Nothing new," Vivian offered a lopsided smile at his need to know. Her smirk was almost as much of a tease as the stray curl of hair. "Fishing charter *Albatross*. It's a Bayliner 35."

He groaned to fill the pause she'd left for him to do just that. They all knew that Bayliners were designed to look good sitting at the dock. Smooth-water boats, they were never meant to go for deep-water halibut fifty miles offshore in February. Most of the Coast Guard's rescues were in the turbulent waters of the Columbia River Bar or hunting for people dragged out to sea by the coast's vicious rip tides. Where the river hit the Pacific was rated as the most dangerous shipping waters in the world and called for frequent assists within easy reach of the Guard's forty-seven-foot motor lifeboats. Not tonight.

"Six aboard." Which would load up the Dolphin to its capacity: the four crew aboard now plus the six rescued from the Bayliner. It was going to get tight in here fast. And that was assuming everything went well.

Of course they might not need rescuing at all. Most of the time it was a matter of telling them they were fine. If the situation was bad, their Dolphin's flight would pinpoint the endangered boaters so that a motor lifeboat or cutter could come out and give them a can of fuel or a tow. Only if it was dire would the USCG send a rescue swimmer into the water to help airlift them out.

A Bayliner 35 in two-story waves—they were probably just all too seasick to stand up.

"THEY WERE PROBABLY BLIND DRUNK." Vivian recalled Harvey's declaration about her parents at their first meal together two months ago.

"They probably came here first," she responded, because it was about the most unlikely circumstance on the planet. Her parents in an Astoria, Oregon bar was never going to happen. Especially not one like this.

Besides, it was Christmas Eve, always a big affair at the Adler mansion. Instead of surviving Mother's endless matchmaking, it was her third day in Oregon and Vivian had nowhere else to go. It was calm and unusually cold for the Oregon Coast—just below freezing, her breath had clouded on the night air as the whole team hustled out to Workers Tavern. It lay on a dirty back street under the Astoria-

Megler Bridge that spanned the Columbia River between Oregon and Washington on the Oregon side.

The place was a total dive, and the owners were proud of that. Just in case there was any doubt, "Dive Bar" was prominently displayed in the front window below the glowing red-and-green "Breakfast All Day" sign and the blue Pabst neon. Inside was deeply marine: dark wood walls that might have been ripped off sunken ships, life rings, oars, funky art, a mounted five-foot-long fish that she didn't recognize but definitely declared "we grow them big here", more craft beer logos than you could count—though none so prominent as the big circular Buoy Beer Co. sign.

Most of one wall was covered in small currency bills from all over the world stapled to the wood. One of the pilots had inspected them carefully and declared that a third of them no longer even existed. The Australian pound, the Taiwanese yen, Israeli lira—he listed off a bunch of them. "And that's before you get into the nineteen countries now using the euro."

"The place has been a port dive bar since 1926. Get a lot of drunken sailors from a world of ports in that time." Harvey had explained for her benefit.

Vivian wished she could get drunk. But both of their crews were on call so they all had tea or coffee with their prime rib—apparently a Workers Tavern specialty. The air was thick with the smell of grilled burgers and fries from the tiny corner kitchen tucked behind the massive U-shaped bar. She, Harvey, and the six other Coasties of their two helicopter crews had taken over one of the battered tables close by the front windows.

The lead and backup crew didn't have to sit out at Air Station Astoria, but they had to be available for immediate deployment—which meant, "Don't leave town and you'd better be stone cold sober." Quite how that had turned into Christmas Eve dinner in a dive bar was something that still eluded her.

Sylvester and Hammond, her assigned pilots, had sworn this was the greatest place in all of Astoria. Having only just made it into town from the Aviation Training Center, she had nothing to judge by. The

ATC, located in Mobile, Alabama, had also been far warmer. She'd wanted out of Alabama before another summer hit and had filed her request five days ago, knowing it could take months to fill. USCG thinking had figured that meant she should be posted to Oregon within the week in the dead of winter.

Astoria, Oregon? It was the sort of place that her parents had to look up on a map before properly showing their disdain, "Really, dear?" It had been their favorite phrase for dealing with their difficult daughter. Ambition was frowned upon for old Southern families. Especially the kind of ambition that had led her into the high school auto shop instead of the glee club or the cheerleading squad.

Then, to add insult to injury, instead of going to Clemson (where her sister had married a very eligible heir to a shipping empire) or the University of South Carolina (where her brother the lawyer had just proposed to a very popular US senator's daughter, practically guaranteeing his political career)—or even, God forbid, the University of Virginia (where she'd be at risk of meeting a Yankee stockbroker, but it couldn't be helped)—she'd gone straight to the Aviation Institution of Maintenance in that heathen hellhole of Las Vegas. It hadn't taken a genius to crack their code. Her parents had clearly looked up Southern schools with the highest "Meet Your Spouse Here" rankings.

Her parents had also tried to fire Captain Heath for "corrupting their daughter" with flying lessons in the family helicopter. She'd threatened to call the media rags with photos of both of her parents' flagrant affairs—not that she actually had photos, because...*ick!* But the threat had been sufficient to save Captain Heath's job and even up his salary.

The three years getting her Aviation Maintenance Technician Helicopter and two more working maintenance for Grand Canyon Helicopters had stood her in good stead when enlisting in the USCG. ("Maybe she'll at least marry an officer.") She'd decided to follow in Captain Heath's footsteps...but hadn't counted on that path leading to a dive bar on the Oregon Coast for Christmas Eve.

She'd been trying to explain her family to Harvey, for reasons that thoroughly eluded her. She typically did her best to pretend she was an orphan.

"They were probably blind drunk," was as good an explanation as any to explain her parents. She appreciated Harvey's levity, if not the probable accuracy of the statement. As if that would forgive any of the ways they'd tried to manipulate her.

Cocktails on the verandah at five. Mother would pour. Another one or two before dinner if there were guests, and there were always guests at the Adler's. Whether at the Mt. Pleasant house overlooking the first tee at the Snee Farm Country Club near Charleston, or at the country house out on Lake Marion two hours inland (half an hour by helo), they entertained lavishly—which included wine and after-dinner brandies. Father would pontificate. They were relatively new, banker money, so they put on far more airs than any genuine old-money plantation owner with ten times the holdings. Six generations back they had a Yankee, post-Civil War-profiteer ancestor that they kept far more hidden than their affairs. Father's family had "come into" large tracts of land surrounding Charleston, gambling on the city's recovery and expansion—a bet that had paid off very handsomely.

"They offered to buy a new building for my flight school, only if the president agreed to flunk me out first," was what she'd said that prompted his response about their state of inebriation.

Harvey's easy laugh fit right in at the dive's bar where a group of graybeards at the bar were trying to put together an unharmonious cacophony that would have definitely offended Wenceslas—whether or not he was a good king. They wore matching ball caps with pictures of beer steins on the front and the words "Christmas Cheers" in red-and-green glitter. They'd definitely had their share of Christmas beers.

She tried to read what lay behind Harvey's reaction. She didn't like revealing that she came from money—if her parents had bought the school a building, it would be far from their biggest investment that year. Revealing that wasn't her first choice. Or her hundredth.

Then why did you say it, girl? And to the overconfident Coastie she'd known less than forty-eight hours.

To shock the unflappable rescue swimmer? As if she actually *was* more than she appeared because of her family's wealth? That was her parents' game, not hers. And if that was her goal, it hadn't worked at all. Instead Harvey looked around the bar and nodded to himself before cutting back into his prime rib—which she had had to admit was amazingly good.

"Pop would have liked this place," Harvey gave her a subject change. "I spent a lot of time as a kid in a place like this."

"You grew up in a dive bar?"

"Kinda. My pop sure grew old in one," his frown said she wasn't the only one with parents best left in the past. "But it literally *was* a dive bar down in Coronado, California. I made friends with the old, Vietnam-era Navy swimmer who owned the place. Joel trained me himself off the same beaches the Navy SEALs train from."

"And you aren't a SEAL because…" The graybeards hunched at the bar were onto something that might have been "Jumpin' Jack Flash" to the tune of "Jingle Bells." Or maybe it was "Yellow Submarine." Hard to tell.

He tipped his head as if cracking his neck. As if he was deciding whether or not to tell the truth.

She sipped her decaf coffee and waited to see where the coin was going to drop. Ten bucks would get her a hundred that he'd backpedal and cover the momentary lapse of honesty with another subject change.

Then he sighed and looked her straight in the eyes. "I decided, since I couldn't save Pop's life—even from his own, self-dug hole— that I'd rather save lives than take them."

"THREE MINUTES TO LAST KNOWN POS-*I*-TION," Hammond announced over the Dolphin's intercom from his left-hand command seat. There was a distinct hiccup in his voice when they slammed through an air pocket. Sylvester would be handling the bulk of the flying from the right seat.

The tightness in Harvey's neck wasn't going away. It could be three minutes to action or two hours before they had to return for a refuel if they couldn't find the lost Bayliner. Either way, they were in for a hard ride—the storm was still on the build and was slapping around the helo like a baby bird on its first flight.

"Permission to open doors?" Harvey called forward. It was never a good idea to surprise a pilot.

"Okay to open doors," Hammond acknowledged.

Harvey snapped a monkey line from his vest to a D-ring by the door and gave each end a good tug to make sure he didn't get thrown out the open cargo bay door by some nasty turbulence. Only after that did he unbuckle from the small jump seat at the rear of the cargo bay. Vivian remained belted into her seat, which could slide side-to-side so that she could work from close beside either door of the cargo bay.

What mattered now was eyes on the water. More than half the challenge of a rescue was finding the boat in the first place. The fact that there'd been no updates could mean that the Bayliner's passengers had simply forgotten to keep transmitting updates, that their radio's battery had shorted out, or that all that was left to be found was a couple of bodies kept afloat by their life preservers.

Vivian slid her seat all the way to the port side to watch out the massive window of the emergency exit door.

Harvey moved forward enough to unlatch the heavy starboard door. It edged out three inches, then slid backwards to slam into the end of its track. Before leaning out to look, he gave it a tug to make sure it had latched open and wasn't going to come sliding forward like a renegade guillotine when they hit the next air pocket.

"Gotta whole lot of nothing out this side." The pilots had the landing light shining forward, hoping to spot debris or even a smoothing of the wave surface from leaked diesel fuel. But looking off to the side, there were black clouds so thick that not even moonshine could make them glow. A hundred feet below them was the hungry maw of the Pacific waters that had eaten more than two thousand ships since Robert Gray first crossed the Bar in 1792, though Native traditions spoke of washed-up Asian and European ships all the way back to 1700.

"Oh, it's all bright and so purty out this side," Vivian announced breathlessly, actually getting him to turn and look. "Astoria looks like fairy lights at this time of night." Which was fifty miles behind them—five hundred feet would be a good visibility in this mess.

The woman had made him a sucker for a straight line. Just to rub it in, she wasn't even looking out the window as she said it, instead watching him turn and fall for her line. Yeah, she had him, hook, line, and sinker in more ways than one. He turned back to his own window to hide the smile that would have said just how much he was loving it.

Lives on the line somewhere below them, and still Vivian kept a cheerful and positive attitude. Harvey wasn't nearly as good at that as she was, yet another thing to admire about her. In the two months since she'd arrived in Astoria and they'd started flying together, it never varied. Nobody could be that consistently upbeat—yet it didn't feel like a facade.

When they'd lost that college student to stupidity on New Year's Eve. She'd gone quiet, but not downbeat.

The kid and his buddy had gone out on the beach at Seaside, Oregon to play around on an eighty-foot log at least four feet in diameter. Didn't they get that the ocean had put it there and could toss it around any time it wanted? There were plenty of signs posted to stay off the driftwood—but they'd ignored those. They hadn't even started drinking yet, so they hadn't had that as an excuse either.

The kid washed out to sea had been the lucky one, probably dead from hypothermia inside the first ten minutes. His buddy had almost bled to death before they could dig him out from where a sneaker wave had lifted the twenty-five-ton log long enough for him to fall under it before the water dropped it back down. He'd had to have both of his legs amputated. They finally found first kid's battered body washed up on boulders far out along the South Jetty of the Columbia River, ten miles to the north of Seaside.

No graveyard humor defense mechanism from Vivian. Just a soft curse as Harvey had ascended from the wave-beaten jetty on the winch with a body latched onto his harness.

She'd helped him tuck the kid into a body bag without flinching, then rested a hand on his arm. Just rested it there until he could feel the human connection through the thick neoprene swimmer's suit. Until he could get past the first time he'd ever handled a dead body in three years as a rescue swimmer. He'd lost people. Saving two off a crab boat before it sank with the other four hands already dead. But he'd never had to recover a dead person before.

He hoped there was no repeat tonight because finding that kid had been the New Year's present from hell.

"THIS IS GETTING TO BE A HABIT," Vivian couldn't believe that she was back in Workers Tavern—ever. Being here for both Christmas and now New Years was just flat out unnatural.

Mother was threatening to fly out in the family jet to visit her baby girl. Maybe she'd bring Mother here. The graybeards would go crazy over the perfectly-maintained blonde-and-seriously-built Southern belle... Mother just might like that. Vivian blessed that she had taken the darker coloring and slender build of Father's side, allowing her to blend into the background a little better.

The graybeards' Christmas hats had been changed. Instead of two frothing beer mugs with "Christmas Cheers," their hats now had an empty mug and a full one on them and "New Years = New Beers" in silver glitter. They seemed uncertain about climbing the mountain of "Auld Lang Syne" and were now either doing injustice to ABBA's "Happy New Year" or slaughtering "New Year's Day" by Taylor Swift to the tune of Judy Garland's "Over the Rainbow."

Tonight she and Harvey were off shift. Not even in the wings as the backup crew. They'd spent five hours in the air looking for the second boy before finding his remains out at the jetty. The Senior Chief had taken one look at Harvey and told her to take him out and get him drunk.

Having only been in Astoria for ten days, Vivian had taken him to the only bar she knew.

She'd had the French Dip with French fries. He'd had the French toast with bacon and sausage, but not risen to the bait of her teasing in French—even after he'd confirmed that he spoke a high school's worth.

An hour later they were still on their first beers. So much for getting him drunk.

"Tell me something, anything." It was the first time that he'd actually spoken first since they'd hauled that body aboard. Poor drowned boy. Senior in college which made her about three years and an entire lifetime older, except now his lifetime was done.

How did life get so short?

But that didn't seem like the right opener at the moment. She didn't know what to say, so she answered his question with a question, hoping it would help him get past whatever he was feeling.

"Tell me about that Navy swimmer. Joel, was it?" And apparently, she'd hit exactly the right topic.

It rapidly became clear that the young Harvey had taken all that love that his father hadn't cared about and heaped it on the SEAL sixty years his senior. It sounded so clear in his voice it might have been the ringing of a New Year's bell, though he spoke no louder than enough to be heard across the table in a noisy bar. The aged regulars at the bar had descended to a vague form of karaoke, singing along with whatever Golden Oldies were being performed in the televised Times Square celebration where it was almost midnight already.

"Joel didn't know the meaning of half measures," Harvey actually finished his beer and ordered another. She was driving, so she kept nursing her first one. "He took me out to Catalina Island on the ferry one evening near sunset. All we had was a wetsuit, fins, and a snorkel. As soon as we stepped onto the dock, he pushed me over the side into the water. Figured we'd be doing a little recreational swim or something. I was fourteen and pretty convinced I knew everything I'd ever need to know by that point."

"Instead?"

"Instead he jumped in beside me, just bobbing up and down for a long moment, then he pointed out of Avalon Harbor toward the mainland."

She knew that a final, long-distance night swim was part of Rescue Swimmer training. There was a reason the Coast Guard rescue swimmers were considered to be the absolute elite. Them and the Air Force PJs—no one else was better. Their training course typically had an eighty percent failure rate.

But this didn't sound like he was telling a USCG tale. He was talking about something important. Honest men not just trying to get into her pants were outside her experience, but Harvey kept being that.

"I couldn't wrap my head around what he meant. Despite the busy harbor and all of the crowded waterfront restaurants and shops, all I can remember was the silence down there on the water at the foot of that long stone pier. It was so vast that it echoed. Joel just looked at me and said, 'Well, you just gonna tread water all night?' I thought about telling him to go to hell. Instead, I took one last look at the comfortable ferry that was still unloading, turned the other way, and started swimming. Figured I'd show him just what was what. Seventy if he was a day, he stayed right beside me the whole way. Didn't speak again for thirty-two-point-three kilometers. That's the shortest slice across the channel. We actually swam closer to forty by where we finally fetched up."

"How did you find your way?" He hadn't mentioned having a compass.

"Stars," Harvey waved a fork up toward the bar's ceiling stained black with years of smoke off the kitchen grill. "I navigated back to the mainland using the stars. The ships go every which way through that channel so they gave no clues, though we had to avoid those as well. From the height of a two-meter swell, the horizon lies less than four kilometers away. That's as far as you can see ahead even under ideal conditions—one-tenth of the distance we covered. We finally fetched up on Balboa Peninsula at Newport Beach seventeen hours later."

"*Seventeen?*" She tried to do an hour in the pool a couple times a week. To swim for seventeen straight hours in the ocean was… Vivian didn't know what it was other than amazing.

"He didn't speak once that whole time until we landed on the beach in front of those luxury homes and lay like a pair of dead fish. Our throats were raw with sea salt and dehydration. Our faces and the backs of our hands, the only exposed places, were sunburned lobster red. The hardest part was the last five meters, hauling myself out of the water and up onto that dry beach as a crowd of gawkers gathered around us. They actually called the cops on us like we were an invading force."

"What did he say?" What could Joel have possibly said that could tell a fourteen-year-old boy just how amazing he was, despite his father?

"He said, 'Now you know what *that* feels like.'"

"He *what?*" Her shout was loud enough to get all the graybeards at the bar losing what little rhythm they had as they turned to look over at her. "He didn't tell you how incredible that was or anything?"

"Nope," now Harvey was starting to smile for the first time since they'd been called out on this morning's search for the college kid washed out to sea.

"I don't get it."

"Joel gave everything he had to teach me that limits are only there as long as we believe in them. Sure, what I did was a damned tough swim."

"Duh!"

"What Joel really showed me was that even at seventy he still didn't believe in limits."

It was only after she'd taken him home and they'd made love that night—because if Harvey the boy had been incredible, the man he'd become was amazing—that he returned to the story. As New Year's Eve midnight rolled across the Pacific Time Zone, with her curled up against Harvey and him toying with a single lock of her hair, he whispered so softly as if he was afraid the world would hear.

"He never swam again. Died less than six months later—mercifully fast, a stroke and gone. I always feel as if he passed the best of himself to me during that long night-and-day swim. After that he knew he was done."

She turned her face into his shoulder to breathe him in. He didn't smell of the ocean or even of wet neoprene that always seemed to permeate her skin for days after wearing a wetsuit.

"I keep thinking about that kid today. I'm wondering if someone had passed something on to him and now it was cut off."

"Joel gave you so much," Vivian almost felt envious. "All you can do is do your best to live up to that."

He considered, tugged lightly on the lock of her hair once more, then she could feel his nod.

As he turned to make love to her at the start of the new year as he had at the end of the old one, she knew what he smelled like. It was something she had so little experience with that it had taken her lying in his arms for hours to recognize it.

He smelled like hope.

"AHOY! I'VE GOT A FLARE," Vivian's voice sang out loud and clear over the intercom.

Harvey's eyes actually hurt from the entire hour they'd been quartering back and forth across the violent waves searching for any sign. The silence had been as echoing as that long-ago day by the Catalina Island pier. The whine of the engines, the beat of the rotor, and the howl of the wind did little to penetrate the wall of six people's lives at stake.

Now a flare. Someone had survived. The helo must have finally flown close enough for the blacked-out boat to have spotted them.

In moments, they were hovering above the pitching craft. It was still afloat, but that was about all it had going for it. The waves—now at least the three stories tall of Sea State 7—were washing it end-to-end. All semblance of "pretty" had been ripped away: canvas, seat cushions, even the plastic windshields were now little more than twisted metal frames. The survivors were huddled miserably in the cockpit. At least they were wearing life vests, but how soon before hypothermia started taking them out—if it hadn't already—he couldn't tell from up here.

"What's the nearest cutter or lifeboat?"

"An hour out."

Harvey knew exactly what that meant. That boat didn't have an hour. They'd be lucky if it had fifteen minutes. "How much time do we have left?"

"Bingo fuel in twenty-seven minutes," Hammond called back. "Fighting the storm really is chewing it up."

"Let's get the basket moving! Diver off headset." Harvey didn't wait for the response before peeling off his headset and pulling on his swimmer's hood, googles, and snorkel. Once he had those secure, he began on his fins. He turned to shout at Vivian that they needed to deploy the lift basket *now*, but she already had it unfolded and was just waiting for him to get out of the doorway.

Perching on the edge, with his feet dangling out over the deep, he waited for her.

She slid her chair close behind him and locked it in place.

When her hand rested on his shoulder, the whole situation snapped into sharp focus. For six weeks since she'd first touched his arm after that failed New Year's rescue, the merest contact with her did that to him. Whether it was on a mission, walking down the street holding hands, or curled up in bed together didn't matter.

Right now, he could see the rise and slap of the waves. The way every fifth one slammed through with an extra ferocity. The sluggish wallow of the down-flooded hull. The debris field of canvas and lines dragging off the stern. All that crap served to make a sea anchor that kept the boat's bow pointed mostly into the waves—that's what had saved them. But it would be a death trap to a diver.

"Boat or water drop?" Vivian shouted. She didn't need to ask if he was going in. Any rescue was at the swimmer's discretion, but as long as there was a soul breathing down there, she knew he was going.

He was about to call for her to winch him down onto the boat when a wave slapped sideways across the boat and nearly tumbled it.

"Water."

"Definitely. We'll drop you upwind."

Harvey set his goggles and allowed himself to feel nothing but her hand on his shoulder. Listen to nothing except the quiet words they shared only in the deepest darkness of the night. Those moments together which oddly felt like when he'd been hanging with Joel. Vivian's arms were the place he was *supposed* to be.

The Dolphin had exceptional visibility for the pilots, but the final call was up to the crew chief, because only she could see directly below and even behind.

"Continue at four o'clock." They eased over and finally passed the boat. "Give me a nudge dead astern." She placed him exactly upwind.

He was just about to point out that he didn't want to be swept into the side of the boat by the very first wave that slapped him, but there was no need. Vivian continued her adjustments until she had the helo exactly where she wanted it.

She'd been doing the same to him—or perhaps they'd been doing it to each other. Six years in the Guard and he'd never flown with someone who he could so utterly trust. Not that the other guys had been bad. Nor was it that she was a woman who consumed his waking thoughts as thoroughly as she did his body, though she did. She was simply that exceptionally good.

"Were you top of your class?" Harvey had asked her one night as they lay awake with the dawn.

"Were you?" She shot it back short and sharp. Thankfully, her issues weren't his issues and he'd long since learned to answer those odd parental-reaction buttons of hers by remaining dead calm. It let her catch herself and cool down rather than heating up even more.

" 'A' School doesn't quite work like that," he'd answered her. "To graduate as an Aviation Survival Technician is half a year of learning to survive. If you survive, you're sent to a two-month EMT course and a six-month internship. Yeah, I could outswim the other guys, but that's about ten percent of being a Rescue Swimmer."

"Oh," she sounded deeply chagrined. Then she buried her face against his shoulder and he'd indulged himself in toying with her softly curling hair. She continued, "Getting to crew chief is a little different. Yes, I was top of my class and we were *insanely* competitive with each other." She said it like she was waiting for some judgement of why hadn't she somehow done better. She'd mentioned that the reverse putdown was also really popular in her family: "Oh, I guess the other people in your class aren't very good."

"Thought so," was all he said.

"Why?" she eventually whispered into his pectoral muscle.

"Because you're the best crew chief I've ever flown with."

"The best what?" She'd scooted up enough to take his earlobe in her teeth—hard.

"Flying with you is awesome," he held out.

"*And?*" She growled through clenched teeth.

"Oh yeah. I like your body, too."

"Harvey Whitman! You're—"

He'd never found out what he was, because he'd set about showing her exactly what he thought of her body and the wonderful things it could do to him.

"Swimmer ready?" She shouted over the roar of the rotors, bringing him back to the present.

He gave her a thumbs up.

"Deploying swimmer!" She held his shoulder hard for just a moment, as hard as when the releases shot through her shuddering body, then she slapped his shoulder and he pushed out of the helo.

Her timing was perfect, as always. The helo was hovering two stories above the wave tops, which was five stories above the troughs. A five-story fall into the sea would hurt like hell, ten stories would likely kill him. A two-story drop barely gave him time to grab his goggles with one hand so they weren't ripped off when he hit the water and wrap the other arm across his chest to keep his extra gear pinned in place.

The cold water was a hard slap anyway, but he was too pumped up to notice more than that. He surfaced with his raised thumb breaking the water first. By the time his head broke the surface, he slammed that raised arm into the water and speed-crawled down the wave face toward the boat. It took two minutes swimming flat out to reach it, despite body-surfing down the wave faces.

He hit the side of the boat, literally, but managed to grab the chrome bow rail one-handed. He yelled out against the wrenching pull as the boat lifted its nose high off the wave. If he let go, the bow could crash down on his head and the Coast Guard would need a new rescue swimmer.

Harvey hung on until the bow slammed down over the back of the wave. He let himself float up and executed a back flip over the rail and onto the deck as the boat buried its bow underwater.

On the next climb out of the water, he let the runoff sweep him along the deck until he reached the cockpit. There he slid sideways into the seating area and crashed into one of the people huddled there. Pretty clean entry.

"Hi there. My name is Harvey Whitman and I'll be your Rescue Swimmer today." The rote phrase marked the move to the next phase of the operation even as it consoled the survivors. "How are we doing, folks?"

He answered the question for himself. Three shaking so badly that they'd need a hospital soon if they were going to live. Two alert. One unconscious or close enough.

"We're going to be lifting you out by basket today."

"What about my boat?" Alert Number Two shouted over the wind and the waves, identifying him as both the captain and a man without a clue. Portly was too kind a word to describe the man's massive girth.

"Let's worry about your people first, okay?" *And your boat is going to the bottom of the ocean any minute; you're an idiot if you don't already know that.*

Vivian never tired of watching Harvey work. The world simply moved more smoothly around him. Even as he appeared to be calming someone, he casually raised an arm to signal for her to lower the basket, pointing to the downwind side of the boat.

She already had it hooked to the winch on the pylon just outside the cargo bay door. As the basket lowered, she kept a gloved hand on the wire. Part of it was so that she could feel any frays to the cable. It also let her dampen oscillations of the swinging basket and feel what the world's wind was doing, because it was hard to tell up here under the main rotor's downwash.

A wave slapped the basket, threatening to drive it into the group of survivors despite her lowering it on the downwind side of the boat.

Harvey grabbed it and wrestled it into place. All those miles he did in the pool every morning did far more than give him a magnificent body for her personal pleasure. It made him appear effortless in situations that mere mortals would be lucky to survive.

He'd taught her that so many times since they'd met. Not that he was exceptional—that was a given—but that *she* was. At first she hadn't believed him. But there was only so many times you could hear something and refuse to believe it.

That's what her parents, her family had done. For her entire life up until this last Christmas, she'd always been "less than." Harvey saw her as "more than." And he said it so often, that she'd come to believe it as well—almost.

Vivian could see that there was an argument down on the deck, which Harvey solved by bodily lifting someone into the basket, then spinning his arm over his head. For the moment he was touching the basket, she'd swear she could feel him right up the wire clenched in her hand.

As she reversed the winch to lift the basket and the first rescuee, she called to the pilots for a five-meter climb. The Dolphin had a four-axis autopilot that let the pilots set a hover and then spend their time paying attention to everything from remaining fuel to flying debris and rogue waves rather than fighting the controls. Bumping up the hover altitude during the basket lift added work for them, but it also got the survivor clear of the boat and the next wave faster.

The winch lifted the basket to be even with the door, but the survivor was a dead weight. She timed an air gust that robbed the helicopter of some lift and gave a yank just as the person went partly weightless. They tumbled to the cargo deck like an empty sack. All she could do at the moment was snap a safety line on the person and send the basket back down.

With every cycle of the basket down to the wallowing boat and back, each victim's condition became less acute—Harvey was sending up the worst first, exactly as he should. Frankly it was amazing any of them were alive with how little appropriate gear they wore. The Pacific Northwest winter called for wetsuits and Mustang float jackets, not a sweater and a slicker. The fourth one managed a muttered "Thanks" but was still shaking too hard to even crack her own heat pack. Vivian cracked one for her and tucked it in the front of her jacket. Warming up their extremities was too great a risk. She had to heat their cores first or risk making their maxed-out hearts fail.

On the fifth lift, Harvey nearly had to wrestle the remaining Survivor Number Six to the deck to let the basket rise. Because of the momentary delay, a wave caught the basket—heavily weighted with Survivor Number Five—and smacked it hard into Harvey's back. It sent him sprawling before she could get it aloft.

It took all the training the Coast Guard had ever given her to keep her cry of fear inside.

HARVEY SERIOUSLY CONSIDERED THROWING the boat's owner over the side and let there only be five survivors.

God damn, but his shoulder hurt. And his knee where he'd caught it as he crashed to the deck.

Whatever happened to the old adage of captain being last off? Letting the man go down with his ship sounded pretty good at the moment. Harvey had spent as much time arguing with the guy as watching the waves. Too much time.

It had taken Harvey a while to realize the guy was mostly drunk, just used to hiding it well. He'd certainly seen it on Dad enough times —the "functional" drunk. It should have made Captain Dan far more susceptible to hypothermia, but perhaps his bulk buffered him.

Foolishly, Harvey thought that the self-proclaimed captain made a good distraction from the decaying condition of the boat. The bow wasn't even lifting clear of the waves anymore.

However, being so distracted from his job that he'd let a basket clobber him absolutely wouldn't do. He lay sprawled over what had once been the captain's pride and joy, the pilot's console with twice the number of controls and readouts than the boat really needed. Sound system controls, remotely operated searchlight (which the guy probably used for illegal night fishing), auto-pilot (that definitely should have been set to never let the guy leave the harbor), and more.

He shrugged a shoulder. Big damn mistake!

He dragged his focus back to the crisis; his head swam with a bout of nausea like he hadn't had since drown-proof training back in A School. He wasn't ready for the next wave that plastered him in the face and stole his breath away.

A chance grab at the steering wheel was all that kept him aboard as the biggest wave yet swept the boat. The other hand wasn't cooperating so well.

Something tried to push him aside. Then it thudded into his gut, but the blow was slowed by the water. Still, it drove out what little air he'd managed to catch. He was about to release his hold and hope he could follow the bubbles to the surface in the dark, when he resurfaced into the storm.

Beneath him, trapped against the deck between the console and the captain's chair, was the beefy boat's owner. That's what had hit him in the gut. But the prolonged dunking seemed to have taken most of the fight out of him.

The basket almost caught Harvey again on the next swing, but he managed to grab it, and heave the sputtering captain in. He was about to latch himself onto the basket and ride up with it from the doomed boat when his head cleared enough to ask the crucial body-count question.

"You're the last one, right? There were six of you. Right?"

"Six. Sure. Except for the dead one in the cabin."

Harvey's blood chilled. Something didn't sound right. If the others had survived out here in the elements, why would the one in the cabin be dead? He let his harness drop and waved the basket aloft.

"Harve—" Vivian's voice crackled over the radio. "We're bing…el in thre…utes."

"Roger, just have to check something."

"Repe—" was all he got back. Three minutes to bingo fuel, he didn't waste time repeating his words. Besides his bad arm was coming online now. The blow that had merely hurt, now screamed like a beast each time he tried to use his right hand.

The cabin door had been shut the entire time. The chances were that it was all that was keeping the boat afloat.

Watching the waves, he waited until they were sliding down the back of one. If he was right, once he opened the hatch, he'd have only ten to fifteen seconds before the next wave or two swept the boat under for good.

The boat punched through a wave rather than climbing over it. A chaotic cross wave actually rolled the boat, but he hung on until it righted itself. After it punched through another wave without going under, there was a momentary lull.

Out of the corner of his eye, he saw that Vivian had lowered a lifting ring in place of the basket—far less likely to clobber him in the storm's growing chaos. Though he'd have to be sure to watch for the cable weight just above the hook.

He threw open the cabin door.

A truly nasty curse worthy of a severely pissed off crew chief crackled in over the radio, but it wasn't clear enough to understand so he ignored it. His radio must have taken a hit when the basket had struck him. His headlamp revealed a kitchenette on the left—with granite counters. Open cupboards revealed a pantry, well stocked with expensive alcohols. Couch to the right. Bed straight ahead in the forward point of the cabin. The water floated as high as the mattress —knee deep. No body floating in it.

He turned to exit.

Two doors that he'd rushed past on his way in.

Door Number One led to a closet.

Bank on Door Number Two.

A head—marine toilet. With someone slumped on the floor and hugging the commode, sitting in the water up to her chest.

Out of time, he slapped the woman hard on the cheek.

She coughed, sputtered, cursed. And reeked of whisky.

Alive.

Harvey grabbed her by the collar and fought her back to the deck.

She didn't wear a lifting harness, or even a life preserver.

Out of options, he snagged the lifting collar dangling from the helo's winch and shoved her arms and head through the opening. He slapped her again, brutally hard, even if it was left-handed.

"Huh? Whassup? I'm alive?" A trickle of blood ran from her lips. "Oh, wish I wasn't. My aching head."

"Stay awake and keep your arms down if you want to live. Do you understand?"

She nodded once, then again a little more convincingly.

He signaled Vivian to lift.

Nothing happened.

When his call on the radio went unanswered, he signaled more emphatically.

Vivian knew what came next.

Bingo fuel wasn't something that could be argued with. Helicopters were desperately unforgiving about running out of fuel. If they didn't want to punch a hole in the ocean themselves, they had to turn for shore right now. Any arguments about reserves in the tanks were always shut down—not even up for discussion.

"Is there a cutter closer than the shore?" she begged Hammond even as she continued lifting the seventh victim.

"No. Even if there was, we couldn't land on it in this weather."

"I have six aboard, Number Seven on the line. That's capacity."

"Good. Let's go."

"Swimmer is still in the water."

"He's what? Shit! Time?" Hammond wasn't asking about time until bingo fuel, he'd called that while Harvey was still in the cabin.

"Two full minutes to unload and cycle the winch back down. Have we burned enough fuel to take the extra person?"

"We're bingo now. Average weight?" Hammond asked, his voice betraying his own anxiety through his professional cool.

Vivian surveyed the rescuees piled up like cordwood on the helo's deck. "High. Very high." There wasn't a single person aboard who could clock in at under two hundred pounds and a couple were three-plus. And even as it ripped at her, she knew what she had to do next.

Hammond held the hover for a moment longer.

Vivian kicked out the raft package. "Raft away." The container wouldn't inflate until Harvey reached it. How many rafts had auto-inflated then blown away before the engineers had learned about that one?

Over the last survivor's head, she saw Harvey diving off the boat as it planed under the water. For some reason he was swimming one-armed toward the raft.

The boat never resurfaced.

Harvey sat in the Workers Tavern with his arm in a sling.

"No swimming for a month. How am I supposed to stay in shape with one damned arm?"

"How is it that you're still alive to grouse about it?" Hammond chided him but still sounded relieved.

Sylvester joined in the game, "Couldn't they have kept you in the hospital longer so that we could eat in peace?"

Vivian just looked sad. He'd told her a dozen times that he'd torn up his shoulder trying to heave the captain into the basket, because she already felt too guilty about having to leave him behind. She didn't need to know that getting clobbered by the basket had started the problem, then bodily lifting first the captain and then his wife—who her husband had left for dead—had made it so much worse.

Harvey definitely hadn't told Vivian about the bitter thirty minutes he'd spent trying to get into the raft. Once it had inflated, he could either hang onto it one-handed or get aboard, but it had taken a slow trip through Hell before Charon the mythical boatman gave him a wave that he could ride into the half-flooded raft rather than dragging him across the river Styx into Hell proper.

He did consider telling her about *why* he'd managed to hang on though.

When the captain's wife had sobered enough in the hospital to understand that her husband had abandoned her for dead, all she'd said was, "That's my Dan all over."

After the challenge of getting on the raft, Harvey then had a three-hour wait for another helo to track down the raft's emergency transponder and come fetch him. At least they hadn't had to drop another rescue swimmer into the maelstrom, he'd been able to climb into the basket himself despite the storm continuing to build and his dislocated shoulder.

Riding out a full gale gave a man a lot of time to think.

"I—Shit!" He held a fork in his non-dominant hand and stared at his slab of prime rib. This one-handed lifestyle was gonna suck big time.

"Just jab it up and eat it caveman style," Hammond suggested, then made a show of cutting a neat piece and stuffing it happily into his mouth.

"Face down in it, dog style," was Sylvester's suggestion.

Vivian thumped the butt of her steak knife on the battered table and held it there with the tip pointing straight up. "Either of you want to try sitting on it? Don't think I can't make you."

Both of the guys were officers rather than enlisted and outranked her by at least six inches to boot. But over the last weeks, they'd learned not to argue with Vivian.

Satisfied, she made quick work of cutting her own prime rib into bite size pieces then traded plates with him.

HARVEY STARED at the plate she'd cut up until Vivian wondered what she'd done wrong.

"We both had the *same* dinner."

He nodded but didn't look up.

"Not gonna feed you when you've got a perfectly good hand."

He shook his head, that wasn't it.

She glanced sideways, but Hammond and Sylvester were chatting up a couple of local women who'd sat at the next table over. Vivian might not have much experience at being a woman in addition to being female in a very male world, but even she could see that they were selling it hard: over-bright smiles, teasing giggles, shoulders up and back to display their figures to best advantage. Couldn't the guys see that? Maybe that's what guys *wanted.* Fine, let them fall down that hole and figure their own way back out. Her problem was the rescue swimmer across the table.

"What?" She whispered low enough to not interrupt the pilots' flirtations with doom.

"It's stupid."

"If that ever stopped you, you'd have left that Captain Dan to go down with his boat and gotten on the helo."

That earned her a brief glance and an almost smile.

"Explain yourself, swimmer boy."

He slowly forked up a piece of meat and began eating. "Death is a very strange thing."

"No shit."

"No," he looked at her as directly as he always did when he was talking about something important.

Vivian was worse than a deer in the headlights when he looked at her that way. She couldn't even look down to cut the next piece of her own roast.

"We don't talk about it. Swimmers I mean. It's the enemy. We drag people from its jaws. No matter the cost," he flapped his injured arm then winced as he made his point.

"*So others may live.* That's your motto. You embody that really, really well, Harvey." And it totally scared the shit out of her even if she wouldn't have him be any other way.

The entire flight back, she'd spent every second tending the seven rescues from the Bayliner. Core heat. Dozens of cuts and bruises from the battering they'd taken—blood welling up as they warmed. Not an instant to herself.

She'd finally got the captain to shut up about suing the US Coast Guard for not saving his boat—did it by ramming an empty flare gun up under his chin and threatening to blow his head off if he said another word. She'd heard Hammond's bark of laughter over the headset after Sylvester had turned around enough to see what she was doing and then explained it to his fellow pilot over the intercom.

It was the only laugh on the flight back.

Then off-loading everyone into the line of waiting ambulances. The debriefing, the mission reports, the...madness of not being able to go back after Harvey. Their crew had hit their airborne time limit because they'd done a beach patrol flight through the stormy afternoon. The standby crew had been headed aloft even as her bird had landed. But they'd had a backup hydraulic system failure thirty miles out and had to return before reaching Harvey so that they could change birds.

She'd forced herself to remain calm in the back of the command room.

When they'd finally found Harvey. And recovered him. *And* headed for shore. Only then had she allowed herself to weep. For the first time since childhood—Mother hadn't approved of emotions other than her own—Vivian had wept. Silently, by herself in the darkness of the empty Ready Room, she'd cried herself sick.

That had been this morning. Now they were at Workers again.

Hammond and Sylvester slid over to the next table, thinking it was their charm that was working on the two local girls, not the girls seeing two Coastie officers as their tickets out of whatever their lives were like.

"Swimmers never talk about Death," Harvey continued. Death was definitely a person to him. A personified enemy to be fought to the very limits. "We try never to think about it."

"But you did? Out there in that raft?"

"But I did." Again he looked down at his plate.

"What did you figure out?" Vivian was having trouble breathing. If Harvey gave up, she didn't know what she'd do. He'd made her believe that there was a "best" in people that was worth striving for. Sure, the world had plenty of Captain Dans. But a single Harvey could offset a thousand Dans. Ten thousand.

Harvey shoved around his cut-up meat bits for a moment, studying their patterns. Or maybe studying the depths of the ocean that he'd ridden over for those long hours alone.

"No one ever made a meal for me. Just for me."

"All I did was cut up your prime rib."

"My first memories were microwave dinners and bar food."

"Get a grip, Harvey." And the first thing she was going to do was cook him a real dinner. She'd learned from one of the best private chefs in Charleston, South Carolina. She hadn't learned more than the basics, but hanging with Chef Claude had made a good escape from her parents' pre-dinner social drinking. "You were talking about Death, not quite the same as a cut-up slab of beef."

Again he raised those dark eyes. "I knew that if I gave in for even a second, the ocean would swallow me up as if I'd never been."

Vivian couldn't suppress the cold chill that ran up her spine despite the warmth of the bar.

"I also knew that even if it didn't kill me, I could never face you if I gave in for even a moment."

"Me?" She felt suddenly breathless.

"Top of the class. Best lover a man could ever ask for. And," he stabbed up a piece of meat and held it out as proof, "kindness. A guy has to do a lot to deserve that. Women like you don't exactly grow on trees, Vivian." He nodded over to pilots' table where the flirting was fast moving into far more dangerous waters than they knew.

Vivian hadn't realized that Harvey was aware of what was going on around him. But he was a rescue swimmer. Except for that one brief lapse on the Bayliner, he had intensely trained situational awareness.

"No, we women, ah..." How was she supposed to answer a compliment like that?

We're like hothouse flowers. Except that was her mother—carefully cultivated and very well-tended, perfect as long as she was in her own little world.

We're few and far between? Was she? She'd never thought of herself as special. Not before Harvey anyway.

So...what?

"You're going to pick me from the tree."

"Thought I made that clear."

"Not very. What are you talking about?"

In answer he pointed behind her. She scanned the bar over her shoulder but didn't see anything unusual.

He pointed again, directly at the four aged regulars slouched together over their beers. They were wearing hats with two faces inside a sparkly red heart. They were working their way through Queen's "Crazy Little Thing Called Love" that was almost in the right tune—as if maybe they'd even rehearsed it a couple of times.

That's when she spotted the date on the Budweiser calendar hanging on the wall. The picture was a stout and a pilsner in a red heart. It only took her a moment longer to realize today was the fourteenth, Valentine's Day.

But there was something more going on here.

Vivian felt an odd, floating feeling. There was something familiar about the graybeards' pink hats, though she couldn't imagine what it might be. In a daze, she rose from her seat and moved up to the bar, to where she was close enough to see their hats clearly.

Close enough to see the photos of the boy and girl inside the red heart. One was her. Not some glamor shot or official photo. It was her wearing her full kit, including her helmet and grinning at the camera —grinning at Harvey who had just told her that he loved her moments before a standard patrol flight two weeks ago. It had been one of the best moments of her life.

The other photo was Harvey plunging out of a helicopter: etched against the blue sky in his black fins and International Orange neoprene, going in to battle Death man-to-man. Someone on a sailboat had snapped the photo as Harvey had jumped in to airlift a heart attack victim to shore. The head-on shot was a powerful statement of "Help is on its way."

On the graybeards' hats, there was a small set of wings below the hearts. They spread wide from a circular center which contained crossed swimming fins—the Rescue Swimmer emblem.

The old guys were grinning wildly at her as their harmony swayed and clashed more violently than a storm-tossed sea.

A moment later Harvey's good arm slid around her waist from behind and pulled her tight back against his sling and chest.

"You're having them propose to me—for you?"

"Pretty romantic, huh?" Harvey laughed softly. "That's what I decided out there facing Death."

"What exactly?"

"So that *we* may live," he whispered in her ear as he reached up to tug on that one curl of hair he always toyed with.

He wouldn't be getting any argument from her.

IF YOU ENJOYED THIS, YOU'LL LOVE
THE NIGHT STALKERS CSAR
(COMBAT SEARCH AND RESCUE)
STORIES:

NSDQ (CSAR #1)

(EXCERPT)

US Army Captain Lois Lang circled her Black Hawk helicopter five miles outside the battle zone and ten thousand feet up. Usually height equaled safety in countries like Afghanistan where the Taliban had no air power, especially in the middle of the night. Get above the reach of most of the cheaper weapons—rifles, rocket-propelled grenades, and the like—and you were generally safe.

But the Lataband Pass, visible as a thousand shades of green in her night-vision gear, deep in the heart of the Hindu Kush Mountains, was at eight thousand feet and the surrounding peaks cleared ten easily. Even at night in the mountains, ten thousand was pushing the high-hot limit of the helicopters. The high altitude and mid-summer temperatures gave her helicopter's rotor blades thinner air to push against. To get higher, she'd have to really burn fuel; never a good bet on a long mission.

So, she and her crew circled wide and low, and watched their threat displays closely. Not a soul this far from the pass, not even a goatherd. Nothing to do but wait. Their job was CSAR—she always thought of a seesaw whenever she heard the acronym for Combat Search and Rescue, every time—which meant their night would be quiet and routine, unless something went wrong with the attack the US Army's 160th was about to unleash at the heart of the pass.

A ground team, probably from the 75th Rangers, had been dumped in this barren wasteland a week before to do recon. And for tonight, they'd reported a massive convoy of munitions crossing this disused pass from Jalalabad, Pakistan, to supply the Taliban forces inside Afghanistan. With the drawdown of US troops, the Taliban were gearing up to hit the Afghani government forces and hit them hard. Special Ops Forces' job tonight was to make sure the Talies didn't receive the supplies from the ever-so-innocent Pakistanis.

"Keeping chill?" she asked her crew.

"Chill," Dusty replied from his copilot's seat beside her. He'd been a backender, only recently jumped from a back-seat gunner crew chief to front-seat copilot, and they were rotating him through the different helos for cross-training. He normally flew troop transport but had logged time in the heavy weapons DAP version of the Black Hawk, as well. Now that it was nearing his last flight in CSAR, she'd definitely miss him. It was tradition to scoff at backenders who aspired to be pilots, but Dusty definitely had what it took.

"We be very cool, Superwoman," Chuff and Hi-Gear answered from their crew chief positions right behind the pilots' seats.

Her nickname had been inevitable. Being named for both of Superman's girlfriends, Lois Lane and Lana Lang, had labeled her for life. Her mother had always been a crack up, right to her last comment from her death bed, "Flying out now, honey." The fact that Lois had the same light build, narrow face, and straight dark hair as Margot Kidder—who'd played Lois in the old *Superman* movies— didn't help matters.

The two crew chiefs sat in back-to-back seats facing sideways out either side of the helicopter. Steerable M134 miniguns were mounted right in front of them.

The days of the UH-1 Huey medical helos with the big white square and red cross painted on their unarmed bellies were long gone. Bad guys now thought the red crosses made for good targets. And in the modern world of strike-and-retreat tactics, there was no quiet after-the-battle moment when it would be safe to go in and gather the wounded.

Rescue ops now happened right in the heart of the fray, and a medical helicopter arrived ready to both save lives and deliver death simultaneously. Some of the old-guard guys complained about that but not SOAR. The 160th Special Operations Aviation Regiment had flown into Takur Ghar, bin Laden's compound, and a thousand other hellholes, and CSAR crews like hers had been there to pull the lead crews back out when things went bad.

The two medics, a couple of new guys, checked in with her as well. They were the real crazies: Chuck and Noreen. They went into a hot battle zone armed with a stretcher and a medical bag. Beyond crazy.

"Thirty seconds," she called as the mission clock continued counting down to 0200. The Night Stalkers, as everyone called the 160th SOAR, ruled the night. "Death Waits in the Dark" was their main motto, and they did. They were the most highly trained helicopter pilots in any military, and she'd busted her ass for eight years to fly with them, spent two more years in training, and had now been in the air with them for two more. It was her single finest achievement.

Even five miles out, the flash of the first strike was a clear streak across the infrared night-vision image projected on her helmet's visor. The resulting explosion was small. The night's mission brief had said to stop the convoy, gather intelligence, then destroy the munitions. So, first strike had been merely to stop the gunrunners' forward progress and get their attention.

The latter part definitely worked. Fire raked skyward and not just little stuff. She could see anti-aircraft tracers arcing upward in a white-hot trail of glowing phosphors and hoped that no one was in the way.

"Stay sharp," she warned herself and her crew. The fire show was a distraction for others to worry about. Their worry was—

"CSAR 4. Immediate extract. Grid 37," Archie, the air mission commander called in. He was back at their helibase a hundred miles into Pakistan, watching their world from an MQ-1C Gray Eagle drone circling another fifteen thousand feet above them.

She acknowledged and dove for the roadway. Grid 37 was right in the gut of the pass, so coming in high was just asking for trouble with the on-going battle she could see still in progress. At five feet above Lataband Pass, she unleashed the five thousand horsepower of the twin GE turbine engines. Fifteen thousand pounds of Black Hawk helicopter flung itself toward the battle at two hundred miles an hour. Even with the twists and turns of the narrow gravel road winding between the steep peaks, they were just two minutes out.

These were always the fastest and the slowest two minutes of her life. At her present altitude and the narrow valley she was flying in, even a stray boulder was a life-threatening hazard. Constant adjustments were needed to crest every rise and take advantage of every little dip. This is what SOAR trained for: flying nap-of-the-Earth to come out of nowhere, in the dead of night, exactly on target and on time.

Yet every second that ticked by, someone lay on the battlefield fighting to stay alive long enough to be rescued. She drove the turbines another couple RPMs closer to yellow-line on the engine's tachometers.

This time the faster feeling won out, and they were on the battlefield with a shocking abruptness. And battle was definitely the operative word. Her tactical display showed two Black Hawks and two of the vicious Little Birds dancing across the sky. But there had been three Little Bird helicopters when they left the airbase.

Grid 37.

Pulling back on the cyclic control to right between her knees for a hard flare dumped speed. Pulling up on the collective along the left side of her seat gained just enough altitude to keep her tail rotor out of the dirt as she slowed. She hammered them down less than a hundred feet from the crumpled remains of the Little Bird helicopter.

Everything was happening at once. Chuff and Hi-Gear were already laying down covering fire, their miniguns blazing with a dragon's deep-throated roar. At three thousand rounds a minute, they scorched the earth anywhere they spotted a bad guy. Chuck and Noreen were already out at a dead sprint toward the crumpled helo.

She debated pulling back aloft to offer them better cover, but the intensity of the overhead air battle told her if she went aloft, she'd have to move well out of the area to be of any use. Her people stood a better chance if she stayed on the ground.

So instead, she remained a sitting duck in the heart of Grid 37 and counted the seconds. A hundred-foot sprint, with heavy gear but high adrenaline: ten seconds. If the injured weren't trapped but perhaps delirious enough with pain to fight against rescue: thirty seconds to get them strapped down. A hundred-foot return carrying deadweight on a stretcher or slow-limping someone back to her aircraft: twenty seconds more. If they were bloody lucky, they only had to survive one minute beneath the tracer-lit madness so close above them.

Rather than watch the medics, she watched the tactical displays. She was getting heavy cover from above. A technical appeared from nowhere around an outcrop: a Toyota pickup with a heavy-caliber machine gun mounted on the bed—serious nightmare vehicle. But Hi-Gear was on it, and in moments the truck was adding its own fireball plume to the light and confusion of the night.

"Ten," one of the medics shouted.

Lois shifted from counting up seconds—she'd only reached forty so they were ten full seconds ahead of her best estimate—to counting them down. She eased up on the collective until the helicopter was dancing on the dirt in its eagerness to be aloft.

She ignored the bright sparks of bullets pinging off her forward windscreen, hoping nothing was a big enough caliber to punch through. Her audio-based threat detector filling her ears with muted squeals indicating only small-arms fire; the big stuff was still hunting the SOAR attackers overhead. The directional microphones translated each bullet's trajectory into fire-return data, and her crew chiefs were pounding back on those positions.

At five seconds to go, a crowd came out of the roiling dust kicked up by her rotors.

She glanced over for just an instant and then returned her

attention to tactical while her mind unraveled what she'd just seen. One medic carrying a man over his shoulder, dead-man style. The second medic pulled one end of a stretcher, the other end dragging on the road's gravel surface with a body strapped to it; good, both of her crew accounted for. Two other guys limping in with their arms around each others' shoulders, clearly nothing else keeping them upright.

The last two deserved a second glance. MICH helmets and HK416 rifles rather than the FN SCARs that all of SOAR carried across their chests. Delta Force operators. If Delta were on the ground here, it meant this action was much heavier duty than she'd thought. That explained the unexpected scale of the firefight.

At zero on her countdown, she could feel the shift in her two-inch high hover as the team slammed aboard. She gave the stretcher bearer an extra three seconds to load.

The "GO!" came just as she racked up on the collective getting her off the dirt and airborne without a wasted instant.

Whatever was happening in the cargo bay was no longer her problem. They could do everything that most field hospitals could do. If you were alive when CSAR got you, your life expectancy was very high. And sometimes even if you weren't.

Lois punched through the dust brownout kicked up by her own rotors and headed back the way she'd come. She slewed hard to clear the first turn in the road as the battle behind her moved toward the other end of the pass.

She climbed enough to keep her rotor blades clear of the ground and leaned into the first turn in the ravine.

She barely had time to see the white-hot streak coming in her direction. "RPG!" the warbling tone of the threat detector screeched out. The rocket-propelled grenade impacted her Number One turbine engine with no chance of an evasive maneuver. Dusty pulled the overhead Fire Suppress T-handle as Chuff's minigun announced he was taking care of whoever had gotten them. That was no longer the problem.

The problem was she was in a turn that needed four-thousand

horsepower to recover from, and she now only had twenty-six hundred. She cranked the Number Two engine right into redline and yanked up hard on the collective.

Not enough. The steep rock wall of the pass loomed before them. The night-vision gear gave her a perfect, crystalline view—as well-lit as if it were broad daylight—of the boulder field that was going to kill her Hawk.

And her crew. No! There!

Normally, she'd yank back on the cyclic and let the tail hit first and then belly-flop the bird down—worked well on a flat landing area. The Hawk could take a lot of abuse that way and could often be bounced off its wheels and they'd be on their way.

But not with these boulders. The very worst of the damage path would be right through the center of the cargo bay where she had four injured, two medics, and two crew chiefs.

She slammed over the cyclic and rammed down hard on the right rudder pedal, intentionally driving the pilot's side rotor blade into the cliff wall.

They would tumble in a hard roll, but it offered the best chance of the crew's survival.

Only one problem.

She'd known it even before she'd slammed over the controls but didn't shy away.

US Army Captain Lois Lang's position was the very first point of contact in the developing crash.

Keep reading this completed series at fine retailers everywhere:
NSDQ
Dawn Flight
Night and Day
Guardian of the Heart
Love in a Copper Light
Just Shy of a Dream

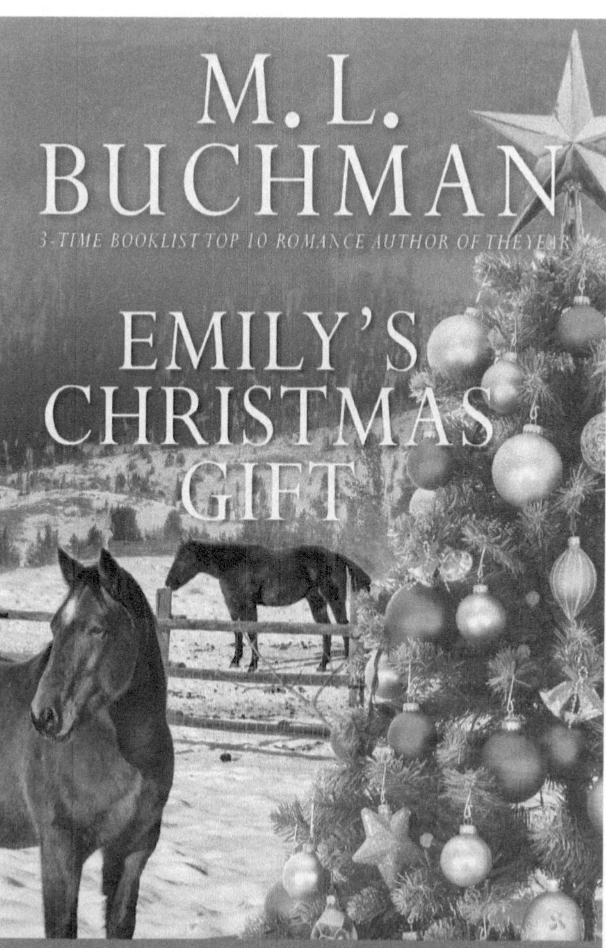

M. L.
BUCHMAN
3-TIME BOOKLIST TOP 10 ROMANCE AUTHOR OF THE YEAR
EMILY'S
CHRISTMAS
GIFT
A HENDERSON'S RANCH BIG SKY STORY

EMILY'S CHRISTMAS GIFT

*ajor **Emily Beale** (retired—mostly) keeps her hand in the Black Ops world remotely from the family horse ranch on Montana's Front Range. Her husband, Major Mark Henderson (fully retired), has settled comfortably into his new role as father and ranch operator.*

But when Emily's childhood friend, the former President of the United States, comes to visit, he raises doubts about the safety of a war orphan Emily helped rescue years before.

No longer so sure of herself, Emily must reach deep into the White House's secret library to find the answers. Little does she know the true location of Emily's Christmas Gift.

This is the last short story in the series that was begun with the earlier *Christmas at Henderson's Ranch.* I wanted to see how my great heroine, Emily Beale, was taking to retirement and being a mom.

Not as well as she'd thought, it turns out.

Again, a little bit of autobiography slipped into this tale. It is ultimately the Christmas tree that provides the answers to her past that points her way toward the future. I definitely know the feeling.

EMILY'S CHRISTMAS GIFT

*E*mily watched Mark being as calm as could be and tried not to resent it. When the heavy Montana snowstorms of December kept them indoors at the main ranch house, he was content to slouch low on the couch and watch a Disney movie with the girls in the cozy family area off the kitchen.

If they wanted to build a fort—Emily always thought of it as a fort, though the girls kept insisting they were tents—Mark would reconfigure the family sitting area off the kitchen no matter what inconvenience it caused the adults.

Between the three of them, they made sure that each construction looked unlike any prior effort. A tropical paradise one time, decorated mostly with one of the ranch hand's awful Hawaiian shirt collection. Another time, a Cheyenne teepee built with Mark's mother's lovely weavings. She'd particularly liked that one. Being in Montana, and especially if Julie was around to help, Western themes were common, often with horse tack or some of her rodeo trophies for decoration.

In the summers Mark lived to fly tourists around in his helicopter and fish, but in the winter his one joy was keeping his girls happy.

That she herself was one of "his girls" always made their daughters giggle with delight. And she *was* happy. All she had to do was watch her daughters and she let their constantly bubbling joy wash over her. They might build their forts—*tents* with their father. But it was never considered complete until she had joined them for the final tour. Mark often left some final task for her to do so that she'd at least feel included. Then they would all lie in it together—Mark at the center with all three of "his girls" clinging happily to him.

Those were the best moments of her life. Perhaps a close second to waking in his arms on the long quiet winter mornings before Tessa and Belle sprang to life like a pair of Jill-in-the-boxes.

She'd known he was a good man and a great commander, but his daughters had never met "The Viper" who used to scare the shit out of everybody, including her. His steel gray eyes had rarely been revealed from behind his mirrored shades. He'd even proposed to her while wearing them—after dark. Which was perhaps the only thing that had kept her from turning into a complete empty-headed mush in that moment.

But his daughters only saw the sky gray that his eyes shone when he was happiest—and the mirrored shades were now worn only in the strong Montana sun. It was impossible for her *not* be happy while she watched the stern, taciturn, demanding Major Mark "The Viper" Henderson (retired) have no compunction about acting as the total goofball with his girls. He was a better father than she was a mother, but she didn't know what to do about that. When they were upset, it was her they came to, so she still had something. But it often meant she got the tears and Mark earned all the cheers.

Emily didn't resent it...much. She mostly just wished it was somehow different.

She turned to the fire and watched what she could see of the flames. They were partially blocked by a great bulge in this week's fort, which was huge by any previous standard.

This room was where the family lived during the day when they weren't out on the ranch. The high-timbered main room and the dining room with its forty-person pine table was for the guests. In the long, bitter, off-season months, it was also where all the locals gathered for the occasional party to break the monotony of winter.

That was for others. The family lived in the kitchen. The kitchen itself was a full commercial setup, decorated like in ranch-house warm timber and cool granite stone. At the near end stood a large plank table of Douglas fir where the family and the ranch hands ate their meals together.

This sitting area to the side had a big stone fireplace, and a scattering of couches and armchairs enough for the entire staff...or there had been until the kids started showing up. Once they graduated from lap-sized, they would have to squeeze in some more furniture. The bookcases that lined the river stone walls already had more shelves added to accommodate the girls' picture books.

Of course more furniture couldn't happen with their latest fort in place—she could only see half the fire from her favorite end of the couch.

It was like a mighty Christmas igloo, its walls built high with pillows raided from all of the guest cabins that were closed for the winter. Mark had waded out into the freezing dawn this morning to cut down and drag home a ten-foot larch to stand at its center. Now, with the tree up and their pillow-wall built, the three of them were madly working away inside. Only the tree's single uppermost branch was visible above the domed roof, like a wide smoke hole escaping the dome of pillows.

Whenever there was a newborn about, either Chelsea's or Julie's boy, their father was instantly abandoned without further thought—which made her feel a little better. Of course, then Emily had to keep a close eye so that the girls didn't smother the two infants with affection. How in the world she'd raised two such...*girls* was a mystery to her. At five, Tessa was an utter extrovert who had all the ranch hands completely wrapped around her tiny pinkie. Belle at three was the steadier one, but only by comparison.

Emily didn't pace when the heavy snow and the biting cold winds forced them to remain indoors, but she wished she'd taken up watching sports on television or something. But after a career of flying helicopters first to war and then to wildfire, watching a bunch of guys chase a football up and down a chunk of AstroTurf in little one- and two-yard spurts couldn't be called exciting.

"I'm absolutely hiring Mark for the next seventeen years," Chelsea plummeted down into the big armchair beside Emily's end of the couch, then had to drag her fingers through her long hair to toss it over her shoulder so she could see. Her cheeks were brilliant red after crossing the snow from where she and her husband, the ranch manager, lived on the other side of the barnyard. Maybe Emily should grow her gold-blonde hair as long, the way Mark kept hinting, but it had been chopped dead straight to her shoulders for her entire life.

Emily saw Mark now sitting on the braided rug with Chelsea's three-month old boy Christopher cradled in his arms—whose hair was already as red as his mother's. Tessa and Belle were leaning on his thighs from either side and reaching over to inspect the infant who watched with such wide, serious eyes. Her own fair hair hadn't been passed on to either daughter, having no chance against Mark's genes from his brown-haired father and Cheyenne mother.

"Or maybe I'll just knock you off and get two husbands, keep Doug for me and have Mark for the kid." Chelsea extended her feet toward the fire.

"I'm notoriously hard to kill." Emily's specialty had been black-in-black missions. Black ops so sensitive that they were talked about with no one, ever. And so dangerous that each one was a curse of its own. Mark accompanied her on or referred vaguely to four—she'd stopped counting as she neared ten.

"Oh, don't worry, Emily," Chelsea slouched lower. "I'd like, uh, get Julie to do it for me. She was raised a cowgirl and knows how to do the icky stuff."

"I'm a horsegirl now. And do what?" Julie settled very slowly on the couch beside Emily, careful not to wake Jared asleep in her arms. Like her own children, Jared had his father's dark hair and eyes rather than Julia's wheat blonde and blue. If he'd slept through the snowy trek down the hill from their cabin, then it would take far more than a small bump to wake him, but Emily knew better than to say such a thing to a new mother. She had to smile at her own worries about Tessa in the beginning.

She did scoop up Jared and hold him while Julie shed her thick coat and tossed it over a maple wood chair. Then she settled back on the plaid sofa and took Jared back, again with infinite care.

Like the toddler-magnets they were, Tessa and Belle appeared on either side of Julie. Tessa sat on Julie's far side, but Belle pushed and squirmed—with plenty of bumps that Jared never noticed—until she was sitting between Emily and Julie. Emily looped an arm around her daughter, not as if there was anywhere else to put it, and kissed her on top of the head.

"I need you to…uh," Chelsea glanced at the two young girls before answering Julie, "…*remove* Emily for me. Kinda permanently so I can have Mark as a full-time babysitter."

"Too late," Julie gently blocked Belle reaching over to wake Jared. Belle was completely enamored of Jared's big eyes and the two of them could stare at each other for hours. "I've already got dibs. Besides, I thought we liked Emily?"

"We do. But where has that gotten us?"

"They grow, you know," Emily decided it was time for a subject change to something other than her demise. "Far too quickly, I might add." She pulled one of Ama's Cheyenne blankets off the back of the couch—this one she'd loved from the first moment, so rich with warm golds and dark reds in a geometric pattern. Spreading it over Julie's and the girls' laps earned her contented smiles.

"See?" Julie looked over at Chelsea. "She knows things. I vote that we keep her."

"Well, she is out there ahead of us," Chelsea finally agreed. "So, what are the good bits waiting for us?"

"We're almost done with diapers."

"Oh God," the two women moaned in unison. "Can't happen too soon."

"Thankfully, Mark is okay trading off on that duty."

"That does it," Chelsea declared. "Sorry, Emily. We really like you, but you're *totally* toast."

"I've still got dibs on Mark." The threat didn't seem too serious as Julie was looking down at her sleeping son with a big smile on her face.

Mark was bent halfway over from placing the now-sleeping Christopher into Chelsea's arms when he finally clued into the last comment. He paused, inspecting all of them carefully.

"Why does this sound like a conversation I want no part of?"

"Because you are a very smart man who loves his wife above any other woman on Earth."

"It's true," Mark shrugged happily before stepping around the back of the couch and leaning down to kiss her from the side.

Emily could feel her internal compass slowly returning to True North. It wasn't often she flew off course, but with Mark's lips on hers, she managed to rediscover her rudder control.

"Oh man," Chelsea groaned in envy.

"Chelsea's right," Julie agreed. "You'd better watch your back, Emily. We're ganging up on you and you're going down. Soon."

"By Christmas."

Emily ignored them both as Mark drew out the kiss to tease them. No complaints from her.

"Where are *your* men?" Mark asked when he finally let her surface for air, leaving her heartrate up about Black Hawk rotor speed. "Two such beautiful women with babies in their arms shouldn't be sitting here unkissed."

"They abandoned us."

"Left us destitute."

"They may have mumbled something about feeding the horses."

"So here we sit."

"In our prime."

"Unkissed," they finished in unison and both aimed ridiculous puckers at Mark and batted their eyelashes. Well, Chelsea did. Julie tried but mostly looked down and blushed for being so forward.

"Feeding the horses, huh? I'd better go check on them." He didn't leave at a run, but he definitely used his best ground-eating stride.

"Ooo," Chelsea cooed loudly. "Looks good from behind too. All mine."

Mark double-timed it out as the three of them shared a laugh.

When he was gone, there was a long silence. Long enough for Belle to slip into a nap against Emily's side and for Tessa to yawn broadly before curling up at the end of the sofa and resting her head on Julie's thigh while Jared wrapped his tiny hand around her pinkie without quite waking.

"What's up with you, Emily?" Julie asked softly.

"There's something up with you?" Chelsea peered at her in surprise.

"Nothing." Emily ignored the slump that Mark had only temporarily lifted. She toyed with the blanket's fringe for a moment before she caught herself at it and tucked her hands out of sight. "Besides, since when can either of you tell what I'm thinking?"

"Since forever. We're your best friends," Julie spoke softly.

"Yeah. Maybe we aren't all experienced and old like you, but we know shit."

They'd both found the love of their life and reproduced in their early twenties. It had taken her until thirty to find love, then more years of service, finally the first kid...and that had been five years ago. Forty wasn't here yet, but it was incoming—fast. She closed her eyes. This was December. She'd been born in... Yep, really fast.

"Is forty bumming you out?"

Emily sat with it for a while. "No, I don't think that's it..."

"Told you something was up with her," Julie whispered to Chelsea.

"Of course, you two youngsters are enough to make a grown woman a little nuts."

"But you love us both anyway, huh?"

Emily looked at Chelsea and couldn't deny that truth.

"Like daughters?" Julie's voice was slightly wistful. Her family life hadn't been real fun. Just the hard life of a cattle ranch with a strict father, a silent mother, and three older brothers, but none of the joy she'd discovered when she'd fallen in love with the man who was now Henderson's Ranch's head chef.

"Daughters?" Emily winced. "Now you're just *trying* to make me feel old. How about younger sisters?"

Julie actually nodded fiercely. As if it was important.

Chelsea too was blinking hard. "If I wasn't afraid of waking this little terror, I'd come over there and give you major kiss."

Curiously, Emily caught herself in mid-sniffle, but managed to take a deep breath to cover it.

"It's just,,," She honestly didn't know.

"Pre-Christmas blues?"

"Year-end blahs?"

"Desperate need for a third child?"

That earned them a bark of laughter that made all four children stir in their sleep.

They all held their breaths until the kids had resettled and the only sounds were the fierce Montana winds struggling vainly to rattle the solid house.

"Not a chance," Emily kept her voice low just in case they weren't fully asleep again. "I don't think Mark would mind, but having your kids late means all sorts of strange things. I'll be sixty before this one graduates from college." She could feel Belle so warm and safe against her side. What would it be like when Belle was a woman grown like Julie or Chelsea and maybe with a child of her own? Out in the world where Emily couldn't protect her?

At Tessa's age, she herself had already had a crush on Peter Matthews—the perfect older boy next door. But he'd married and become President of the United States. She'd gone to West Point and become the first woman of the Night Stalkers. By Julie and Chelsea's age, she'd been flying helicopters on her second tour into war zones with the 101st Airborne.

"Sixty? Shit, you *are* old, sis."

"Go to hell, Chelsea."

"Not gonna happen. I've got you for a big sister, means I've gotta being doing something right."

Emily knew Chelsea had earned a laugh, but she couldn't seem to find it. She lay her head back on the couch and wondered what was wrong with her. Maybe it *was* just the season. Or that Night Stalkers helicopter pilots, unlike most Special Operations Forces, could fly well into their fifties—if they hadn't reproduced. It wasn't some rule that had kept her out. Instead, her own fears for her child's safety had cost her that finely-honed *edge* that made a true Spec Ops pilot. Maybe it was that...

Something was wrong, and she had no idea what.

She heard a soft gasp from Chelsea that made her open her eyes.

And looked up directly into Peter's. Mark and Peter were grinning at her—upside down over the back of the soft, brown-leather couch.

"Surprise, Squirt."

"You're supposed to be in Washington, D.C., Sneaker Boy." Her childhood nickname for the former President of the United States. Except he wasn't anymore. He was the Secretary of State. His nickname was still Sneaker Boy.

She heard a deep, guffaw in the background.

"Hi, Frank."

"Good afternoon, Major Beale," the head of Peter's Secret Service Protection Detail sounded as formal as ever. Yet another reminder of what she'd left behind.

Then she looked over at Mark.

"You seemed kinda down, Emily. So I invited Peter out for Christmas as a surprise. His wife, kid, and maybe a few others will be out next week."

"You're feeling down?" Peter suddenly sounded worried. Just exactly what she didn't need—the Secretary of State and former President flying to Montana in the middle of winter to hover. There'd be no point trying to explain it to Mark; he'd never be convinced he'd overreacted.

"You're what?" "What's wrong?" Apparently done with the horses, Chelsea's and Julie's husbands chimed in from somewhere out of view.

Emily sat up and looked at her younger sisters. "Don't bother killing me, just take Mark for yourselves, please. Now."

"Do you really change diapers?" Chelsea turned to Mark, who shrugged a yes.

"Dibs," Julie said again.

"SERIOUSLY, EM. WHAT'S WRONG?"

She'd led Peter through the bitter cold out to the horse barn, because no matter what Mark thought, the Secretary of State didn't fly to Montana just because a friend was feeling sad. Though she had to give Mark a few points for noticing how she *was* feeling when she'd barely realized it herself.

She stopped at Chesapeake's stall. The barn was warm with the scent of horse and hay. The light was dim beneath the blowing storm, making it feel almost as cozy as the kitchen—as long as you were wearing a jacket or a horse blanket.

She hadn't had the clarity of mind to remember to grab a treat from the house, but Chelsea kept a bag of carrots in her office and Emily had grabbed one as she walked by.

Breaking off a piece, she palmed it to her horse. The big chestnut mare lipped it off her palm and crunched it down. She leaned her cheek against the horse's and felt her chew.

"Mark's right. You are looking down."

"Which isn't why you're here."

"Well, not all of it, but—"

"Why are you here, Sneaker Boy?"

Peter laughed, then startled when Julie's black-and-white painted horse, Clarence, stuck his head out of his stall to see what was going on and almost knocked Peter over.

Emily gave him a chunk of Chesapeake's carrot as a reward.

"I don't know as I'd have come for either reason separately, but when Mark called to invite me out and…" he shrugged. "It's about Dilya."

She spun to face him, but he only looked concerned, not afraid.

"What about her?" Emily barely managed to keep her voice steady.

Dilya was the war-orphan adopted daughter of her best friend Archie and his wife Kee, the first woman to qualify for the Night Stalkers after she herself had. That terrified and starved ten-year-old was now a lovely seventeen-year-old, living in the White House as nanny to the First and Second children.

"She's…" Peter's face showed that he really didn't know as he stumbled to a halt.

"Okay. Not sick. Not in trouble. What?"

Peter finally shrugged. "She reminds me too much of you."

"Of me?" She showed him how to hold some carrot to feed to Clarence before she fed the greens to Chesapeake. Why on earth would that be?

"Remember when we first met?"

"No. I think I was about three days old. My memory is good, but even I have limits."

"I mean when we re-met."

"You mean when I slammed the head of your Protection Detail onto his ass on the White House's main staircase?" She raised her voice enough to make sure Frank Adams could hear her as he returned from checking that there were no four-legged assassins lurking in the horse barn.

"Are we really back to this, Major? You just gotta keep bringing that up, don't you?"

"It *was* memorable."

Frank grumbled as he moved by to check the other end of the barn.

"Yes," Peter waited until Frank was again out of earshot. "I'd been following your career for some time by then. And I was horrified at the dangers you were going into."

"Because I was a woman."

Peter looked down and scuffed one of his perfect leather shoes at the dirty straw. For all his supposed sophistication, he was still a guy —which meant she'd never understand him.

"That," he admitted, "and because you were my friend. You were the little girl next door who was suddenly flying thirty-million-dollar helicopters straight into harm's way."

"What has this got to do with Dilya?"

"You know that girl's nose for trouble?"

"You don't know the half of it." In her first month after they'd rescued her, Dilya had identified two men so intent on revenge that they didn't care if it could start the next World War. Then she'd stowed away on a clandestine insertion deep into Uzbekistan to stop them. A detail that was never included in any action report.

"And I'm guessing I don't want to. But now? I'm getting worried for her, Em."

Emily glanced up at her secure office within the stable. Her Tac Room (short for Tactical) had been built directly over the Tack Room (filled with saddles and bridles). It had been finished with the same, aged wood, so that it didn't stand out at all. Its windows were dark—with special glass that appeared opaque even when lit from within. The only clue from the outside that it was anything special was the very sophisticated lock mounted out of sight from below. From there, at Peter's behest, she'd created the White House Protection Force. The WHPF had proven to be immensely successful, saving the new President's life on three separate occasions and averting any number of other minor disasters.

And despite Emily's best intentions, Dilya had several times ended up far too close to the action for comfort. The last time, nearly being shot down over Canadian soil.

"So, what do you want me to do? Scare her straight?"

She could see Peter's face brighten.

"You know that's not going to happen, don't you?"

And he looked worried again.

"She's an incredibly bright kid. And she's grown up with the elite Night Stalkers company for companions, a sniper mother, a strategic consultant father, and essentially unlimited access to your and now Zachary's White House. You think she was just being cute all those times she 'hung out' in the Oval with you? I guarantee you that Dilya was never an innocent child—at least not since we found her.

Watching both your parents be executed right in front of you will do that to a kid."

Peter leaned sadly against the stall door. His idea of casual was a two-piece suit rather than a three-piece under his heavy black wool coat. Clarence snorted in his ear and made him jump away in alarm. Out of carrot, she made a point of scritching the horse's cheek with her fingers until he huffed out a happy sigh.

"If we can't keep her out of trouble, how do we teach her to judge when she's in too deep or at least to cry for help?"

Emily leaned back against Chesapeake's neck. Her childhood friend had been Peter, who was six years older than she was. Julie had been right, Emily knew things because she was out ahead of them… but Belle was two and Tessa was five. That wasn't seventeen. She knew nothing yet about anything after age five. Her only solution had been to treat Dilya as a small adult…one who wasn't so small anymore.

But it was a crucial question. Peter was right, Dilya's well-being depended on it. And she knew just who to ask.

Convincing Peter that there were some things he didn't want to know had proved just as hard as usual, but Emily had practice at it. With Frank's help, she soon had him shooed back over to the main house.

Mounting the stairs to her Tac Room, she keycoded the door, offered her eye for retinal scan, then locked the door behind her.

The one-way glass gave her a long view of the horse stalls, their occupants lazing through the cold winter day, happily napping and munching on hay. Chelsea came into the barn at the far end of the stalls. She waved up as she always did in case Emily was watching, and headed into her own office. As the ranch's horse manager, she was meticulous in the care of her charges and the recent vet's visit to give all of them a checkup had probably left a pile of paperwork.

Emily liked the company when they were both working out here, even if they were isolated in separate offices. Chelsea didn't have the security clearance to ever be inside this room.

Emily had already done her check of the public world news this morning. Now, in her secure space, she flipped through today's briefing documents from the various agencies. No real surprises—hot spots were still hot, but nothing abnormal. She'd be paged if there was a real crisis calling for her attention, but it wasn't the sort of day where that seemed likely. The First and Second families were having their typical White House workdays without travel. Which also meant Dilya would be rattling around the White House.

She tapped in a coded signal and settled in to wait while she read up on that latest internal status reports from NATO.

Her Tac Room assistant, Lauren, had proved herself immensely capable when dealing with military contacts. But the other side of Emily's information network—the one that reached deep into the White House itself—no one knew about except herself. With Lauren honeymooning at Disneyland over the holidays, Emily didn't have to worry about shooing her out to place this call.

"Hello, my dear." Her central screen lit with the face of one of the White House Protection Force's primary assets. Her gray hair framed an ageless face. Sometimes it seemed she'd aged past old crone and gone straight on to wizened. At other times, her face was clear enough that the gray hair was a shock. Today, she simply appeared what she was—a beautiful woman in her seventies (probably).

Behind her ranged the most unusual library in Washington, DC— which was saying something. Emily knew from her one visit there that it wasn't large. Her office felt even smaller because every inch of wall space from floor to ceiling was packed solid with books. Also on display were some of the more clandestine tools of the spy trade, which the shadows hadn't afforded her a chance to study. It was also perhaps the most accurate library on spies and spy craft ever assembled. There were less than a dozen people who knew where it lay—behind the door of Room 043-Mechanical in the White House Residence's deepest subbasement. And the woman in charge had been one of the greatest spies, including undocumented ones, of them all.

A blurred red-and-green glow stood to one side of the camera's view—too close to be clearly seen. A desktop Christmas tree perhaps? What did a master spy's Christmas tree look like? Probably a cone of stacked red-and-green code books used over the last half-century.

"Hello, Miss Watson. How are you today?"

"Oh, I'm good my dear. Very good. Thank you for asking. Is there something amiss that I'm unaware of?"

"Not likely," Emily sometimes wondered if Miss Watson was helping her keep the White House safe or if she was helping Miss Watson.

Miss Watson offered one of her grandmotherly smiles, "I don't know that you've ever made a social call before."

And at Emily's wince, Miss Watson clearly understood that this one wasn't either.

It wasn't that she didn't want to, it was that she never thought to. Not a single one of those fine skills that her mother, one of DC social queens, had struggled to cultivate in her only offspring had stuck.

"Emily, dear child..."

She almost laughed. She now had two younger "sisters" and all of them had children, yet—

"Tell me the reason you called, then we can talk about why you should have called earlier."

Emily tried looking at the books behind Miss Watson. Was there a guide to mindreading tucked away somewhere on those shelves? Unsure quite what Miss Watson meant, she described Peter's concerns about Dilya.

"That child was never young. Such potential."

Emily suddenly wasn't sure that Miss Watson's influence on Dilya was a good thing. What little she knew of Miss Watson's exploits told of the immense risks a woman could take in the name of the Cold War. It had been inevitable that Dilya's natural inquisitiveness had brought them together. Unfortunately what happened at the White House was outside of her control. Emily could protect, but she couldn't control.

Instead, her skill had always been in locating and cultivating exceptional talent. The President's new driver, one of his dog handlers, and others she'd helped put in place kept the President safer far beyond anything the Secret Service would understand—or ever be told about.

The White House Protection Force did *not* include Dilya, and yet she seemed to end up in the center of every problem—even when those problems became life-threatening.

"The girl is so independent. Perhaps too much so."

"Too much?" Emily had always prided herself on her own independence. It was what had let her succeed in a male world—absolute self-reliance.

"Yes. She knows a great deal more about depending solely on her own judgment than even you, my dear child. Despite your deservedly decorated career. And don't we both know about some of the decorations you can never admit to."

Emily kept her best neutral expression on her face, but Miss Watson merely winked. No one, but *no one* other than the former President and the Joint Chiefs of Staff should know about her medals from black-in-black operations. Even Mark didn't know about those. No more than he'd know that she was technically still on active duty as a consultant.

"Dilya has carefully positioned herself to know more than everyone around her here at the White House," Miss Watson continued blithely. "I even hold a hope that someday she— Well, never mind that now. I believe that you've raised a valid question and I shall give it some thought. It is Christmas soon. Perhaps I shall give her a Christmas gift after all."

Emily considered what that might mean and suddenly wished she hadn't placed this call in the first place. Perhaps she should call Dilya and warn her away from Miss Watson. Actually, she could think of no faster way to drive Dilya directly into the fray. In that, she and Dilya were much alike.

Before Emily could open her mouth to protest or perhaps even try to call Miss Watson off, she continued so smoothly that Emily never managed a word.

"Now, my dear. Let's talk about what's troubling you."

"Nothing's troubling me."

"It isn't age," Miss Watson ignored her fib. "No woman as beautiful as you with two lovely children and such an exceptional husband can doubt that she is in the prime of her life."

She sighed.

"And I must compliment you on the fine job you did helping your husband transition to retired life. You are much better with people than you think you are. You picture yourself so austere and remote, yet people are drawn to you anyway."

Emily opened her mouth to protest, then closed it. She *had* just acquired two younger sisters this morning. Miss Watson couldn't know about them, could she? At least not yet? But she was right, the emotions on their faces had been no lie. Emily had always built team loyalty by being the best—no matter what it cost her. By being the best, she'd attracted the best. Yet it wasn't by outperforming anyone on the team that Julie had asked, *I thought we liked Emily?* And Chelsea had agreed, *We really do.*

"I remember such a time of reflection shortly before I died."

"You...died?"

"Oh yes, dear. Any number of times." She nudged a finger against the Christmas tree that was just a blur on the edge of the screen. It moved, so it wasn't books. Maybe it was better if she didn't know. "It is an easy way to cover your tracks in an on-going operation. But I'm referring to when I let the CIA believe I had died."

"How did they take it?"

"Oh, it was a lovely funeral. I have a star up on their wall, which is quite an honor in my business."

"And they still don't know about you surviving?"

Miss Watson shrugged, "There comes a time in a woman's life where one must move closer to the heart. We aren't men, after all."

Emily felt that was rather obvious.

"You'll want to think about that, child. You are a woman grown. You've fought for the right, and done the duties that a man does. For great achievers like us, struggling within a society not ready for us, we must now come to terms with being...ourselves."

"How did you do it?"

But Miss Watson's ghost of a smile demurred.

How had she done it? From what little Emily knew, Miss Watson might have always been in the White House subbasement. Yet apparently she'd also been a spy in the final years of the Vietnam War and had a Soviet two-star general as a lover. Emily, too, heard things.

She'd first met Miss Watson years before during her brief residence at the White House as the First Lady's personal chef. She'd thought nothing of it at the time—some elderly White House staffer she'd chatted with about the war she was fighting in Afghanistan. In hindsight Emily could see that things had changed for her from that moment. She'd— "Oh, I became *your* weapon."

Miss Watson offered her a slightly surprised expression.

"All those additional black-in-black ops. The toughest missions—"

"—Came to you because of your supreme confidence and exceptional abilities. Don't try to make me the wizard behind the curtain of your career, Emily. You are tactically an exceptional woman. It is the bigger picture that slips by you. Dilya is beginning to see her own bigger picture, which is why you worry about her—we fear what we don't understand."

"But—"

"Oh, my dear child," Miss Watson was gently shaking her head. "In the later years, you are still *yourself*. But the challenges are new. You must learn who you, yourself are. Rediscover or, if that fails, discover for the first time, the amazing woman you are."

"That's your advice?"

"The voice of experience."

Emily couldn't help but remember Julie leaning forward just this morning, *She knows things. I vote that we keep her.*

Man oh man, did she ever have them fooled.

"What did you—"

"Oh no, child. It would be cheating to tell. Besides, Dilya is far more my daughter than you are—at least in how she thinks. You must discover your own woman."

"Why doesn't that feel helpful?"

"Because you're still thinking as if you live in a man's world, challenging the status quo." Then Miss Watson shook herself lightly, glanced at her bookshelves somewhere out of sight, and suddenly appeared much older.

"Miss Watson, are you—"

"It is time I sent for Dilya."

"Miss Watson?" Emily could think of nothing else to say.

"Go see your family, dear." Then she was gone.

Emily sat in her small Tac Room and looked at blank screen, she tried not to feel sadder than before the call. Did the poor woman even have any family? Did she even have someone to spend Christmas with? Not that Emily knew of, and yet here she was dumping her own doubts upon Miss Watson.

She knew she could trust Dilya to Miss Watson's care and she'd hear soon enough what had happened. Emily had forgotten how much she liked Miss Watson and promised herself that her next call would be strictly social. Or when she needed a break from the Montana winter, she'd visit her parents in DC and arrange to drop in on the White House subbasement personally.

As for herself, none of it felt like a solution to anything.

"What are you up to, babe?" Mark slid down on the couch beside her. He flipped up the edge of the big Cheyenne weaving she'd thrown over herself hours before while she'd watched the fire burn. There were only a few embers left, dying from lack of tending.

"What time is it?"

"Way early, but I missed you in bed." He pulled her into his arms and kissed her on the temple.

A week had passed and she was no closer to understanding any of

Miss Watson's life lessons. Now she was out of time and simply had to shake it off.

Later today the ranch house would become much more lively. Vice President Daniel Darlington and his family had decided to fly out for Christmas along with Peter's wife and child. The local ranchers' potluck was going to get a big surprise tonight—for security's sake, no one would be warned ahead of time. Of course surprises were fair on both sides of the coin—she also hadn't forewarned the Secret Service just how many rifles would arrive tonight, hanging in the back windows of Montana pickup trucks.

The girls' pillow igloo fort would have to come down—or it should. Knowing she'd lose that battle, she decided to leave well enough alone. Julie's husband Nathan and Mark's mom Ama would be awake soon and the three of them were planning to cook throughout the day. All week, Peter had practically taken over her secure Tac Room in the barn, doing Secretary of State things, so at least he'd been out from underfoot.

With the ease of long practice, Mark had eased her into his lap with her barely noticing until her head lay on his shoulder and his hand cradled her behind underneath the warm blanket.

"This isn't like you, Emily. Got me worried some." She'd always enjoyed feeling the deep rumble in his chest when he spoke.

"That makes two of us."

"You missing the action?"

She shook her head. At first the adrenaline-junkie withdrawal had been hard, but she'd expected that. Besides, she hadn't gone straight from Spec Ops to civilian—the years flying to wildfire and her occasional calls to consult had eased the transition.

"Sick of the cooking?"

No. She loved that. Mark's mother Ama had run the kitchen for over a decade, but cooked much less now. Nathan, a world-class chef who'd stumbled into love with Julie, had taken over the kitchen with such zeal that Emily could come play whenever the mood struck her, but she didn't have to worry when it didn't.

"Nothing about the kids?"

"I couldn't love Belle and Tessa more if they were part of me."

"They *were* part of you."

"Exactly my point."

As if on cue, the two girls appeared, still rubbing their eyes sleepily. In moments, they were all curled up together under the warm blanket. It was awkward, a little uncomfortable, and amazingly perfect.

"Not…us?" Mark whispered against her ear once the girls were settled. They were huddled under the blanket, mostly on her lap, whispering back and forth.

In answer, she managed to twist around enough to kiss Mark. He made it as thorough and perfect as their very first kiss—and she felt no desire to smash his face into an aircraft carrier's table as she'd done the first time.

"Then what?" Mark asked as she once more lay her head upon his shoulder and tightened her arm around Tessa's waist earning a happy giggle from beneath the big quilt.

For the life of her, she hadn't a clue.

THE MAYHEM HAD STARTED EVEN SOONER than she'd anticipated.

Belle and Tessa, finally coming wide awake under the blanket, had found their father's one ticklish spot and completely undone him. To escape, he'd finally fallen off the couch. Turning it into a roll, he regained his feet and moved over to stoke the fire. The girls knew about not interfering around the flames. By the time she and the girls were dressed, Ama had breakfast on the table. Nathan was eating as he worked, assembling the ingredients for Emily's dry rub on the massive roast they'd planned for the potluck.

Second Lady Alice had arrived with their newborn, and Peter's wife Geneviève brought their little girl. At four, she had all the poise and elegance that her mother embodied and Emily's own daughters completely lacked. Belle and Tessa practically transcended on the spot with the additional playmate. She didn't know if she hoped her girls rubbed off on Adele Gloria—simply to harass Peter—or perhaps the other way round and her own girls might become more comprehensible to her. Either way, kid heaven had taken over much of the floor space in front of the fireplace with Mark often in the fray.

Her mood kept lifting through the day.

She'd never thought of herself as a particularly social or even approachable woman, but there were only so many welcoming hugs and joyous smiles that could be aimed her way before that belief became undeniably foolish.

Thankfully, the storm blew out and all that was left were achingly clear starlit skies and bitter cold. But Montanan ranchers had never yet been stopped by mere cold and soon the house was packed. The local ranchers soon shed their awe of the Washington elite—helped in part by all of the children in their pre-Christmas excitement. As more local children had arrived, they'd strained Tessa's and Belle's "dress up" wardrobe to the limit, but Christmas fairies and elves had abounded.

The big afternoon puppy-pile nap on the kitchen's couch had averted most of the exhaustion meltdowns.

And somehow, through the whole thing, the Christmas igloo fort had survived—no mere "tent" could have made it through the constant stream of children in and out of it. Of all the adults, only Mark had been allowed admittance.

As the evening wound down and the ranchers drifted back home through the chill darkness, the family and Washington guests slowly gathered once more in the kitchen. Chairs and benches were dragged over until everyone was packed in close to the fireplace. Hot cocoa, laced with brandy for the grownups, was served all around.

Emily could only look around the circle in wonder. Julie and Chelsea sat nearby with their husbands and babies. Her childhood friend Peter and his lovely Geneviève sat with her friend Vice President Daniel and his cheery wife. All around the room, there wasn't a person here whose life she hadn't touched, and who hadn't touched hers.

How had she not known this? Why was she just seeing it now?

These were her friends. Her family. Just as surely as the action teams of the Night Stalkers 5th Battalion D Company and the firefighters of Mount Hood Aviation had been her family.

She…belonged.

Is this what Miss Watson had been talking about? That somehow, this was her "woman's" role after having lived in the "man's" world for so many years?

Maybe it was. Maybe—

"I think it's time, girls," Mark called, loudly enough to silence all of the conversations.

With a squeal of delight, they launched to their feet in a mad swirl of excitement and fairy wings. Adele Gloria—Peter's and Geneviève's daughter had devolved only a little under Tessa's influence and Tessa had settled (a little)—was rapidly recruited and the three kids disappeared into the Christmas igloo fort.

"Now it's your turn, honey," Mark rose and held out his hand to her.

Emily was terribly conscious that everyone was watching her as she rose to her feet. She should have gone and locked herself in her Tac Room—nobody would dare to disturb her there. Then she certainly wouldn't be the center of attention.

Once she was on her feet, Mark knelt before her, something he hadn't even done while proposing. What was he—

"Up," he patted his shoulder.

"What?"

He hooked one of her knees and dragged it over his shoulder. "Climb aboard, Emily."

"No. I—" she resisted his attempt to grab her other leg.

"Here, Mommy," Belle came out of the igloo and handed her a package wrapped in Christmas paper before racing back in.

Mark took advantage of her momentary distraction and got her astride his shoulders. Then he stood quickly before she could escape. He faced the Christmas igloo and called out.

"Ready, girls?"

A high chorus of "Yes!" was their answer as she hung onto Mark's forehead with one hand and the wrapped present with the other.

"Go!" Mark roared out like commanding a fleet of weapon-laden helicopters into battle.

The igloo wavered as if hit from the inside. Then it wavered again.

The assembled crowd was absolutely silent in anticipation.

Another impact and one pillow fell off the top of the wall.

Then there was a shout of little girls joining forces in some supreme effort. The three of them, with their arms locked together, burst clean through the side of the pillow igloo, which fell and scattered in every direction.

Emily joined in everyone's gasp of wonder.

The larch tree, that had stood so long in hiding, was revealed. It had been decorated with hand-made ornaments, lights, popcorn-and-cranberry strings, and everything else that little girls and her husband could think of. People were pulling aside the tumbled pillows until a great mound of them had been piled up behind the couch and the tree stood fully revealed.

"It's beautiful," she barely managed a whisper but somehow Mark heard it through all of the applause and general chatter.

"Not finished yet."

"No, it's perfect."

But he stepped up to the tree, giving her the feeling that she was floating along in a helicopter once more. She considered tugging on his ears to see if they acted like rudder controls, or maybe a cyclic to get her down from here. But his big hands were clamped over her thighs, pinning her in place.

"Emily, open your present."

At a loss for what else to do, she unwrapped it as she teetered high in the air. And discovered a golden star.

The bare top of the larch, the only part of the tree that had ever shown above the pillow igloo, was right at eye level. By reaching out as far as she dared, she was just able to slip it onto the top of the tree.

A fresh round of cheers and applause broke out as Mark stepped back and helped her down to the pine floor. The tree was glorious with its wild decorations and brightly colored lights set off by the golden warmth of the fire's flickering glow.

With Mark's arm around her waist, and the girls' hanging on to either side, they all admired the tree.

Or at least Mark and the girls did.

Emily instead heard the joy and the laughter of her friends gathered around her. So many. So true.

"You're my star," Mark whispered—absolutely the romantic one in their relationship.

This right here, this moment was who she *truly* was.

And Emily could feel that gift all the way to her heart.

AND DON'T MISS the companion story: Dilya's Christmas Challenge, a White House Protection Force story.

NATHAN'S BIG SKY (HR #1)

(EXCERPT)

*T*he silence was deafening.

Nathan gripped the crowbar-handle of his car's jack so tightly that it hurt his hand but he couldn't ease up. It was his sole hope of survival.

The only sound for miles on the emptiness of the Montana prairie was the hot-metal pinging of his cooling Miata sports car, lurched awkwardly to the roadside by a flat tire. The chill of the cold April evening almost hurt his lungs. The sun hadn't quite set; instead it illuminated the clouds of his own breath like some horror movie with a fog machine turned on too high.

How was it that he'd come to this place to die?

Chefs were *not* supposed to die alone in the forsaken wilderness; they were supposed to have a butter-induced heart attack in the middle of a meal service. But the safety of his New York kitchen lay an impossible distance behind him. He'd bolted forty-eight hours ago, sleeping only a few fitful hours in Chicago before punching west as if all the hounds of hell were after him.

And they'd caught up with him in the form of a monster.

Two days to cross most of the country and now, like a gunslinger fated to his doom, he was going to be murdered in the emptiness of the Montana wilderness by the largest cow ever born.

It put Paul Bunyan's mythically massive blue ox Babe to shame.

Purest black, it was an inkblot on the continuance of Nathan's life.

Horns the length of a New York cabbie's woes sprang from either side of its head, ending in points that looked sharper than his finest boning knife.

He'd hit Choteau, Montana, in the late afternoon for directions, as his little brother's instructions had turned out to be utterly useless: "Henderson's Ranch, just west of Choteau." There wasn't a single app on his phone that told him where the ranch might be. There'd also been no answer on his brother's phone, but he was used to that. Apparently most of the ranch was beyond the pale of civilization and didn't have reception. His brother had always been useless about answering the phone anyway, unless you were a pretty girl—them he'd always had a sixth sense for, even on a blocked number.

Maybe Patrick's directions sucked because he was messing with his big brother. Or maybe it was because he assumed Nathan would never cross west of the Hudson River—which historically was a reasonable assumption—so it wasn't worth the effort to be more descriptive.

A Choteau (*Cho-toe* that was almost *Sho-toe*) local had known the name, however. In a town only three blocks long, it made sense that he did. "Just go down the highway apiece until you hit Anderson's farm. Can't miss it. He has the last big white cow barn this side of Augusta. Take a right on the main road and go on until you've just about hit the mountains. Out onto the dirt a ways. That'll set you in the right place."

The "highway" was a narrow two-lane called Montana 287.

By the time Choteau was two miles behind him, he'd passed two Andersons, an Andersen, and an Andreassen. This driveway had no mailbox that he could see, but it had a big white barn and a road along one side of the property. The map on his cell phone said that Augusta was fifty miles ahead. Telling him "the last big barn before Augusta" counted as a local having fun chapping his ass. He must have taken one look at Nathan's two-seater Miata and painted a little mental target on Nathan's forehead—just as the monster cow now had one painted on Nathan's life.

The turnoff road was a lane and a half wide. Nathan guessed that in its favor, it was paved and had an actual stop sign where it met the "highway." Sunlight was streaming out the backside of the sign through several bullet holes. He wondered if someone was going to shoot him for being in a sports car instead of a pickup with a gun rack.

Did upstate New York even have roads like this one—not even two lanes wide and with no painted stripes? Or was that only legal west of the Mississippi? Manhattan and Long Island certainly didn't. During his five years in Paris, he'd rarely been farther out than the Metro could carry him.

For thirty miles past the white cow barn, he drove unknowingly toward his doom as the mountains drew closer and closer. He kept assuming he'd reach them in another few miles and they insisted on teasing him just like his brother. After the unremitting flatness of the Great Plains, they had loomed tall and rough to the west as seen from Choteau. Now he was discovering that Australia wasn't the only place that had an Outback.

The peaks kept growing bigger and climbing higher but the land remained flatter than the ocean off Coney Island on a hot summer's day. The peaks' jagged flanks were shrouded in snow despite it being April. He turned on the Miata's heater as the sun settled toward the west, but he left the convertible top down because the view was so amazing. The blue sky arced forever over him until the mountains sliced it off like a kid's construction project: sharp, jagged, unreal.

Each time he'd passed a ranch, he checked the name, but none said Henderson. He even pulled out his phone to check that he'd remembered it right—and almost drove his car into the gaping ditch. Not a good idea. For all he knew, there might not be another person down this road for a week. He'd seen a few tractors—which were far bigger than he thought they would be—far out in the fields, but no one else on the road.

With a crash and thud that made him check his rearview to see if he'd left an axle on the road behind him, the pavement ended.

"Out onto the dirt a ways." Maybe the old-timer in Choteau hadn't been completely chapping his ass.

He slowed down to preserve his suspension. A cloud of brown dust obliterated his past. If he wanted to turn around, he'd have to eat his own dust. That sounded like a properly cowboy-like metaphor for the last decade of his life. Two days ago he'd cut every tie to that past. If only he could figure out how that had led him to the Montanan Outback, he wouldn't feel quite so overwhelmed at the moment. Twenty-eight years old and his life fit in a two-seater sports car—with room to spare. That might not be right, but it didn't make it any less true.

For the last ten miles he'd been hoping to meet someone on the road to ask directions again. Or maybe how to escape, little knowing it would soon be too late.

The dirt road narrowed and then he actually hoped he didn't meet anyone because he'd have to crawl to the side to get by them. Out here he wasn't threatened by ditches anymore, they'd disappeared along with the pavement, but instead by barbed wire running close down either side of the dirt track. Not a chance that his Soul Red Metallic paint job would survive the encounter.

After a few miles of dodging potholes and gritting his teeth over washboard ripples, he started looking for a place to turn around. The road wasn't wide enough to be sure he could turn even his small car without dinging it up.

He'd been climbing slowly since Choteau, and spring had turned back into winter. There was a bitter snap to the evening air that promised what looked like snow and ice up ahead...really *was* snow and ice up ahead. By this point the mountains were so high they looked as if they were going to roll over and land on him.

Manhattan didn't have places like this. Neither did Paris, where he'd done his time at Le Cordon Bleu and three years servitude for Chef Guevarre—may his brutal training and magnificent palate both be in hell by now. There was something wrong about the flatness behind and the impossible mountains ahead.

Then, topping a low rise, facing straight into the setting sun, he was confronted by the beast from hell that was going to kill him.

He'd slammed on the brakes, skidding sideways on the washboard gravel, and barely managed to avoid hitting the cow. A tire caught in a pothole where it had blown with a loud bang that scared him almost as much as the creature of his doom had.

Now he stood in the middle of the road between his crippled car, pinging the last dying notes of its hot-metal song, and the monstrous black cow that was about to charge him. The damn thing didn't so much as blink its malevolent eyes, as if it was trying to hypnotize him.

His only weapon choices were his chef's knives, which would be very useful if the cow was already dead and butchered but not until then, and his car's jack handle. Retreating into his car and pulling up the convertible's roof would be pointless—this monster was so big it could practically step over the Miata. And the tips of its horns were actually wider than the car itself.

His ears rang with the silence, now broken only by a scuffing of one New York metro bus-sized hoof as the cow prepared to charge. Nathan had served a thousand roasts, ten thousand steaks, and this meal-still-on-the-hoof knew it. It had come to exact revenge for all of its spiritual forebears...fore-steaks?

The last thing Nathan was going to smell was the crackling dry grass of the prairie, the biting chill of the fast-approaching night, and the hot breath of the demon cow so big it seemed to block out even the vast expanse of the Montana sky. There had been fourteen hundred miles of flat since Chicago, but here, with his back up against the mountains, the vast horizon seemed far bigger than should be possible. His last-ever vision would be to actually see the curvature of the earth.

Then, impossibly, as if it wasn't bad enough that his epitaph was going to read: *Here a once-decent chef was trampled to death by a cow—* trampled sounded like a marginally more pleasant way to go than gored—he heard a clip-clop sound coming from behind him.

He didn't dare turn, because he knew the beast-cow would charge the moment he looked aside.

Still, the sound behind him grew.

Unable to stand it any longer—the sound was so close—he spun and raised his foot-long jack handle in one last desperate bid for life.

Backed by the sun, a silhouetted cowboy sat up on a horse even taller than the cow and looked down at Nathan from under the brim of his cowboy hat.

"What are you doing out in the road?"

Not cowboy, cowgirl. A soft voice, but no less disgusted for all that. Against the dazzling sun he could see that she wore cowboy boots, a heavy leather jacket, and had a rifle tucked close to hand.

Hope?

Maybe she could shoot the demon cow before it trampled, trompled, gored, or whatever demon cows did.

He tried to speak, but his throat was clogged dry with fear and road dust. The air was so dry it seemed to suck the moisture right out of him.

She rode around him and his car as if he wasn't even there. "Go on now, Lucy. Scoot!"

A hell-beast named Lucy?

Keep reading this completed series at fine retailers everywhere:
Christmas at Henderson's Ranch
Reaching Out at Henderson's Ranch
Nathan's Big Sky
Welcome at Henderson's Ranch
Big Sky, Loyal Heart
Finding Henderson's Ranch
Emily's Christmas Gift
Big Sky Dog Whisperer

M.L. BUCHMAN
3-time Booklist Top 10 Romance Author of the Year
Dilya's
Christmas Challenge
WHITE HOUSE PROTECTION FORCE STORY

DILYA'S CHRISTMAS CHALLENGE

*Teenager **Dilya Stevenson's** life at the White House is like no one else's. As the First Family's nanny and dog walker, her duties are sometimes light and always enjoyable. Which leaves her plenty of time to keep her eyes and ears open behind the scenes. Facing danger and even death as a child, she learned to be a loner—too much so her elders fear.*

***Retired spy Miss Watson** takes pride in trusting no one. But she keeps a weather eye on Dilya from her secret library in the White House's deepest basement. Both she and Major Emily Beale, an old friend, wish to save the girl from following in either of their footsteps. Little knowing that all their lives will be impacted, they set Dilya's Christmas Challenge.*

The last story in this collection was a direct outgrowth of the prior tale. It is set in my active series, the White House Protection Force, about the clandestine agency formed to protect the institution of the White House and the government without anyone else knowing.

But that's the series it was written in, not why it was written.

Dilya crashed onto the scene in the second book of the original Night Stalkers: *I Own the Dawn* ("Top 5 Romance of the Year" – Barnes & Noble). She was another of those characters with a mind of her own who walked onto the scene fully formed. She had a bit part in a single scene, not even any dialogue. But all my subsequent attempts to write the young war orphan out of the story weren't refused, they were simply ignored. Dilya was here and she was here to stay.

That she has become one of my most important and popular on-going characters is, I regret to say, far more her doing than mine.

She introduced herself to the public, on the page six years ago. In that time, she has grown from a strangely wise pre-teen, to a lovely and perceptive young woman. But family and trust and friendship have long been challenges for her.

I set out to write the prior tale, *Emily's Christmas Gift,* with no thought that Dilya would stick her foot in. Not only did she do so, but she highlighted just how alone she was and let me know that she was seriously tired of being that way.

Of course with Dilya being so smart, nothing is easy or straightforward. But I'm glad to say that I found a way, and this is the first adventure of Dilya and her new-found friends. I'm sure we'll be seeing them all again.

DILYA'S CHRISTMAS CHALLENGE

*M*iss Watson had considered painting a giant spider web on her door. If it wouldn't draw undue attention, she well might have. Room 043-Mechanical in the White House Residence's lowest subbasement had nothing mechanical in it, at least nothing that a building engineer would ever care about. Good cover because the best cover was a bland one.

Her small desk had once belonged to Assistant Secretary of the Treasury, Harry Dexter White, who had run the Silvermaster spy ring for the Soviet Union for years. Her walls were packed with every biography or interview transcript from a spy going back to the early days of the American colonies. The rubbish about The Craft that consumed so much of the CIA's libraries—written by analysts and others even less informed—were not to be found within her four walls. She also kept a number of the more gruesome tools of the trade on display to remind her of just what horrors the human psyche was capable.

But even at her age, a woman wasn't supposed to feel like Moriarty —Sherlock Holmes' greatest opponent—curled "motionless, like a spider in the centre of its web, but that web has a thousand radiations, and he knows well every quiver of each of them."

She rarely left her office anymore, instead listening only to the information that flowed into her domain rather than gathering it. She allowed only a few bits, a very precious few, to flow back out. Maybe she'd paint the spider web in blacklight or some other ink that wouldn't show. But she'd know was there.

It always surprised her when a thread was activated that she hadn't anticipated. When the computer beeped she dropped a stitch in her knitting in surprise—a nice bit of double-sided colorwork scarf recalling a long ago sunset along the shore of the Black Sea.

Assumptions are dangerous, she reminded herself.

She forced herself to pick up the stitch and count to make sure that everything was put to rights before she answered.

"Hello, my dear." Her screen lit to reveal one of her favorite people. Major Emily Beale (retired—at least according to most official records) had a mind that worked so differently from her own. For that reason if no other, Emily would have been very useful to her. But as a force of nature in her own right, the immensely skilled and well-connected woman brought far more assets than most could muster.

However, she should have known a call was coming. It wasn't unusual for Emily to call from her Montana ranch, but it was strange that she herself had no inkling of what the topic might be.

"Hello, Miss Watson. How are you today?"

"Oh, I'm good my dear. Very good. Thank you for asking. Is there something amiss that I'm unaware of?"

"Not likely."

Miss Watson couldn't quite resist smiling at the compliment. "I don't know that you've ever made a social call before."

Emily's grimace communicated a great deal. It wasn't social, which was disappointing. But she saw in how Emily's eyes shifted to the side, beyond the breadth of the screen she'd be using, that Emily wished it had been. She was such a sweet woman.

"Emily, dear child..." Miss Watson merely said it to herself, but saw Emily react much more strongly than expected.

A laugh?

A hysterical one?

Major Emily Beale was not the sort given to hysterics.

"Tell me the reason you called, then we can talk about why you should have called earlier."

Emily nodded, "I'm worried about Dilya. She keeps placing herself at risk. I don't want her to create a situation that's over her head when she's too young to know what she's doing."

"That child was never young. Such potential." She regretted the last as soon as she said it aloud. She could see the sudden wariness in Emily's eyes—so protective of the teen, despite the girl being adopted not by her but by one of her teammates. That protectiveness was one of Emily's great strengths. Her own instincts were far more honed to self-preservation.

Dilya, as a seventeen-year-old war orphan, was much the same. She'd been afforded the best training imaginable: her deep involvement with the fighting elements of the Night Stalkers 5th Battalion D Company, who had rescued her originally. Her placement in the White House as a nanny and then the dog minder for the First Dog had placed her in the way of exceptional information. Her skills at passing through a room unremarked were truly exceptional. It definitely reminded Miss Watson of her own, long ago youth.

And most importantly, Dilya possessed the sharp mind to go with it.

That girl's mind… Yet Emily had a point.

"The girl is so independent. Perhaps too much so." How different would her own past be if she had learned to rely upon others? Even occasionally?

"Too much?" And there was Emily's limitation. Her definition of success was the survival of her team and the destruction of her target. She was terribly linear. Independence was a lesson that Emily only thought she had learned. She had been embedded in teams her entire life.

"Yes. She knows a great deal more about depending solely on her own judgment than even you, my dear child. Despite your deservedly decorated career. And don't we both know about some of the decorations you can never admit to."

Emily's bland expression would be a sufficient denial—to anyone who hadn't spent a lifetime surviving by studying human body language. She almost considered pointing out how easy she was to read for a professional, but decided that there were some things Emily would be happier never knowing.

Dilya's strength was in her covert gathering of knowledge. But oh, the price that was paid for such a gift. Miss Watson both envied and pitied the girl.

"Dilya has carefully positioned herself to know more than everyone around her," Miss Watson continued, more to herself than Emily. "I even hold a hope that someday she—"

Not yet. She didn't dare think that far ahead. Hope often hurt as much as it helped.

"Well, never mind that now. I believe that you've raised a valid question and I shall give it some thought. It is Christmas soon. Perhaps I shall give her a Christmas gift."

Emily looked relieved to hand off the problem. Miss Watson found that trust to be the nicest compliment of all, it actually warmed her old heart.

"Now, my dear. Let's talk about what's troubling you."

Through the rest of the conversation, Miss Watson wondered at how curiously innocent Emily was. She was one of the finest warriors Miss Watson had ever met, yet she was curiously unaware of what it meant to be a woman.

One thing Miss Watson envied her was motherhood. She herself had launched a hundred women on their careers in espionage, giving birth to their nascent dreams of adventure, danger, and intrigue. But she'd only given her own heart once—and the price that the Cold War had exacted upon her for that single mistake had been a chilly one indeed.

"No woman as beautiful as you with two lovely children and such an exceptional husband can doubt that she is in the prime of her life," she assured Emily.

There was so much she herself had lost.

Lieutenant General Sergei Kulakov of Soviet Union's KGB First

Directorate had unwittingly taught the United States more about the Soviet intelligence operations than any other man. As his mistress, she had siphoned away his secrets until it destroyed his life. Like a Stalinesque purge, he and his family were erased from history by the Soviet regime—from re-doctored photos to a "training accident" that had leveled his Black Sea dacha with a firebomb. To this day she didn't know where the leak had come that destroyed her best source and the love of her life in a single, vicious stroke. Whereas Emily…

"And I must compliment you on the fine job you did helping your husband transition to retired life. You are much better with people than you think you are. You picture yourself so austere and remote, yet people are drawn to you anyway." The pain swelled in her chest until she feared it really would kill her. As they had never been drawn to her. Except for that one time. There had never been a man for her like Sergei. "I remember such a time of reflection shortly before I died."

"You…died?"

"Oh yes, dear. Any number of times," Miss Watson shook off the memories. She was the reason they had bombed the dacha, to kill Sergei's mistress. Some instinct had sent her racing away across the Black Sea in a tiny open boat that stormy December night. That instinct had saved her life, if not her heart. She nudged her tiny Christmas tree on the desk, so bright and cheery—it didn't fully mask that old memory, but it helped. It was impossible to look at it without smiling.

"It is an easy way to cover your tracks in an on-going CIA operation. But I'm referring to when I let the CIA itself believe I had died." Because she desperately needed to stop thinking about her cherished Sergei.

"How did they take it?"

"Oh, it was a lovely funeral. I have a star up on their wall, which is quite an honor in my business."

"And they still don't know about you surviving?"

Not a chance. She'd die for real before she'd work for the cretins now in charge. The CIA was no longer about national security or even trade security. It was all about political gain, which she had no stomach for.

"There comes a time in a woman's life where one must move closer to the heart. We aren't men, after all. You'll want to think about that, child. You are a woman grown. You've fought for the right, and done the duties that a man does. For great achievers like us, struggling within a society not ready for us, we must now come to terms with being…ourselves."

"How did you do it?"

She'd been babbling. Now, having professed her evolved state, she certainly couldn't admit to lacking such. Instead she offered her best enigmatic smile.

"Oh, I became *your* weapon," Emily had thankfully jumped topics. Perhaps her thoughts were more creative than Miss Watson had previously given her credit for. "All those additional black-in-black ops. The toughest missions—"

"—Came to you because of your supreme confidence and exceptional abilities." Oh how she wished she could take credit for Emily's achievements, they were so very impressive. "Don't try to make me the wizard behind the curtain of your career, Emily. You are tactically an exceptional woman. It is the bigger picture that slips by you. Dilya is beginning to see her own bigger picture, which is why you worry about her—we fear what we don't understand."

Yes. Dilya. She was the important one, because she had the potential to be so much more.

"But—"

"Oh, my dear child. In the later years, you are still *yourself.* But the challenges are new. You must learn who you, yourself are. Rediscover or, if that fails, discover for the first time, the amazing woman you are."

"That's your advice?"

"The voice of experience." And perhaps she'd try to follow it someday.

"What did you—"

"Oh no, my dear. It would be cheating to tell," though she might, if she knew. She had grown to like Emily more than any woman in her past. "Besides, Dilya is far more my daughter than you are—at least in how she thinks. You must discover your own woman."

"Why doesn't that feel helpful?"

"Because you're still thinking as if you live in a man's world, challenging the status quo." And if she didn't help Dilya see that soon, the girl would walk the same horrid path she had. By seventeen, she'd already been recruited and embedded in the depths of the Vietnam War. JFK, such a pretty man, had asked what she could do for her country and she'd joined the CIA. For forty years she'd done the horrific and the unthinkable.

"Miss Watson, are you—"

"It is time I sent for Dilya." She needed to shift the girl's path—immediately. She could only hope she wasn't too late to turn Dilya from the fateful missteps she had made in her own long-ago youth.

"Miss Watson?" Emily sympathy was sweet but misguided.

"Go see your family, dear." She cut the connection and listened.

Not to the noises of the dishwashers flushing water through the pipes that ran along her ceiling. Not the low hum from the massive air conditioning units across the hall. None of her alarms were lit. In fact, at the moment even the laundry and the sub-basement usher's office were unpeopled.

Normally she liked it when she was the only person on this level. At the moment, it left her feeling cold and...old.

DILYA HAD NEVER BEEN CALLED by Miss Watson before. It was a strange experience.

She was in the curator's library on the White House Residence's ground floor. It lay down the hall from the kitchen, between the Secret Service room and the library. When the call came, she'd been poking through the records and trying to find out just how much trouble she was in for letting First Dog Zackie break the small antique table in the hallway outside the First Lady's secretary's office.

Especially because she'd supposedly been over in the Residence that morning and not eavesdropping on the second floor of the East Wing.

She'd hoped it was a reproduction and not a 1789 Thomas Sheraton original, but the photo she'd just found in the curator's library wasn't encouraging. It was late at night, so the curator and his assistant had gone home hours ago, not realizing that Dilya had breezed in one door to wave hello and not breezed out the other on her way to the Chocolate Shop as usual. It was one of the advantages of creating predictable patterns, it made other people have assumptions.

Then the assistant curator's phone range.

She'd frozen in place for the three rings, then it stopped.

She knew that voicemail took over at four rings, so she didn't think anything of it...until the senior curator's phone rang three times.

On the third round of ping-pong between the two phones, she gingerly answered one.

There was nothing but silence...and the sound of dishwashers draining through overhead pipes.

All she said was, "Yes, ma'am." before hanging up the phone. The White House was quiet tonight, but she avoided the stairs by the kitchen. Instead, she slipped out the curator office's back door and down the two flights of steps—perhaps the least used in the entire White House. She circled twice around the elevator machinery space and ducked into the lone bathroom at the east end of the lowest subbasement.

Five minutes later, she stepped out. She'd long since observed that most people grew impatient after two minutes. Even most of the Secret Service agents would start looking around by three minutes. By five, almost everyone was bored out of their skull. They'd start moving about, making noise. When she stepped back into the hall, there were only the noises she'd cataloged in her thoughts as "typical" of this level.

Nothing changed as she found her way to Room 043-Mechanical

and slipped in through the narrow opening before shutting the door behind her.

"Took your time, girl," Miss Watson sounded almost stern.

"You've never called me before. I decided that I'd better be cautious."

Miss Watson harrumphed thoughtfully. She was never the sort of woman who would grunt, but it seemed to carry meaning—but nothing that Dilya could interpret.

"Have a seat, child."

Dilya used to welcome that diminutive—most people discounted and thus ignored children—but at seventeen, she was finding it less than charming. Especially from someone close to her. But one didn't lightly correct Miss Watson.

She slipped onto the chair and idly wished Zackie was here so that she could scratch his head. He loved her without question or judgment and there were times she needed that. Even her parents would ask about school or boys...as if setting a trap without meaning to.

"What's that?" Dilya bit her tongue, but the little Christmas tree on Miss Watson's desk was very peculiar. Tiny rectangular boxes of red-and-green wire had been stacked up to make a foot-high cone. Miniature blinking lights had been woven through them.

"It's a lobster pot Christmas tree. And, yes girl, sometimes it is best to just ask the question."

It was one of the first things that Miss Watson had ever told her that didn't ring true—there was a strain in her voice as she'd said it. Dilya would have to keep an ear out for why. She also made a note to herself to look up more information about lobster pots. She'd seen lobsters arrive in the kitchen for White House state dinners and knew they'd never fit in these. The entire tree wasn't much bigger than a lobster.

"A gift from a friend."

She'd never thought about Miss Watson having friends, but she supposed everyone did. Of course, everything Miss Watson ever said contained a double or even a triple meaning. *Friend.* Did she herself have them? It was hard to tell. Her world was defined by the adults of the military and the White House, and by the President's and Vice President's newborns who she was a nanny for. Super busy when they were here. Time to observe things when they weren't. Though lately she'd come to appreciate that people observed the baby in a room, but not the person carrying her.

High school had garnered her no friends. The stigma of working personally for the First Family had marked her as an outsider from the beginning, even in the most elite school of Washington, DC. It had also taken her too long to understand that there was such a thing as competitive sports. Her life in war zones had taught her that only victory mattered—only survival. Her intensity didn't go over well in harmless games. She'd learned to temper that instinct, but not soon enough. She'd scared her classmates and they didn't forget that easily.

"That's nice," Dilya finally acknowledged that Miss Watson had friends. It would be nice to have one of her own, who was her own age. But she could count the number of seventeen-year-olds who worked in the White House on one finger. And the number of people who actually lived here on one hand: the three members of the First Family, the rotating watch officer with the Nuclear Football (the launch codes and radio that were never more than a hundred meters from the President), and herself when both her parents were out of town. Which was surprisingly often: her father Archie off consulting and Kee on a training mission, or a live one, with the Hostage Rescue Team.

She didn't mind though, not really. When she slept at the White House, she lived in the same small apartment that Emily Beale had occupied when she'd been a chef here a long time ago. Dilya had seen how good a fighter Major Beale was—even Michael from Delta Force had said the major was especially good. She so wanted to be like her: really smart and totally lethal.

Dilya had hated her looks in her early teens because short girls with Uzbekistani dark skin and riffled hair would never be tall and blonde and bright like Major Beale. Once she'd understood that it wasn't the appearance that mattered, she'd forgiven her heritage and focused on what else she could learn.

"You present a fascinating problem, child."

"I don't mean to." For half an instant she wondered if Miss Watson was referring to the broken Thomas Sheraton table in the East Wing, but decided that was silly. Not that she wouldn't know, but that she wouldn't care. Then Dilya was sorry she presented a problem, because it meant she was doing something imperfectly that must have come to Miss Watson's attention.

"What have you learned in your expeditions today?"

Fridays were generally quiet, especially in the weeks before Christmas. The decorators had been through at the beginning of December and turned the White House into a winter wonderland. How could everyone ooh and ahh over it? It reminded her too much of her freezing walk over the Hindu Kush Mountains of Afghanistan when she'd been a child of ten. She tried not to look too closely in case she imagined her parents' blood spattered on the snow as it had been when they'd been murdered shortly afterward.

Still, she thought of a few things to tell Miss Watson that she heard lately. In the beginning, she wasn't sure if she should share things with the old woman. But then she'd managed to eavesdrop on a surprisingly frank conversation between Miss Watson and Emily Beale regarding the risks of a new White House intern—who was dismissed almost immediately afterward. There were now few things she held back. Because if Emily trusted Miss Watson, so would she —mostly.

Miss Watson nodded in surprise at the passing remark between two of the cabinet secretaries about "coal futures." Yet another thing for Dilya to now research the meaning of the next time she was online.

"Let's have some tea," Miss Watson rose to her feet.

DILYA KNEW which hidden trigger to press inside the bookcase's shelving to release it so it swing aside.

Miss Watson let her do it herself. The heavy cases were on silent rollers, but they still required force to move—something Dilya did so easily and that she herself now had to work at.

The bookcase folded aside, opening a doorway into her inner parlor. In sharp contrast to the outer library, this was a warm and cozy space. The rich Oriental rug, white-rose wallpaper covered with photos of history's greatest female spies, and the comfortable armchairs before the marble-mantled fireplace was often all that kept her morale up.

She eased into the armchair as Dilya went about making tea and setting out cookies that she herself had baked last night. It was her one solace, a skill she'd learned years ago. She'd learned to cook to endear herself to the men she was spying on, but she'd always baked for herself.

When everything was set out and served, they drank a while in silence. The Harvey and Sons chamomile from Egypt was very floral, but the taste was incredibly smooth and lulled her nerves after even the first few sips.

She looked across at Dilya and tried to think how to teach this girl the lesson that she needed, the lesson that she'd never learned for herself. Yet Emily had done it. How?

Miss Watson had become caught in a trap of her own making. Emily had appeared to take her advice to heart. So, to ask how Emily had learned what Dilya needed—how to value the team above independent action—would have undercut her own advice. It was crucial knowledge, she knew it by her own lack. She'd always undervalued the importance of people in her life as anything other than targets and potential threats.

When Emily accepted the amazing woman she already was, then she would truly step into her power. She hoped that Emily did it soon so that she'd still be alive to watch.

Yet Dilya needed...

"Tell me about your friends."

Dilya's face revealed no telltale expression as Emily's had. Dilya was almost perfectly unreadable. Not chill, but so self-contained that she didn't reveal anything of who she was. It was startling to realize that though she was so pretty, she wasn't beautiful. It was because the girl kept herself locked away so safe behind her mystical green eyes that her features appeared slightly lifeless.

Oh, she could appear animated at a moment's notice, but this blankness was her normal, silent self.

"You have no friends." Miss Watson didn't make it a question.

Dilya didn't argue.

And there was the difference between herself and Emily. Emily had garnered a team, a family, and a circle of friends so loyal that it might take her years to understand their true depths. The only reason that the wives of the White House's leaders—who were so dependent upon Emily—didn't become jealous, was because Emily Beale had won them over as well with her immense integrity. And as the coming years of friendship mellowed the awe they held her in, their true friendships would grow.

Her own friends? All except for a very select group of fellow librarians thought she had died fifteen years ago. And her closest friends might indeed be Emily—who she'd only met once in person—and this young girl watching her so carefully.

That was the different path Dilya must learn to walk.

"I'm sending you to school."

"I already go to school."

"Tomorrow."

"It's the weekend and my high school is closed, but you know that. Which school?"

"The White House kitchen."

Dilya actually let enough emotion through to blink at her in surprise.

"Saturday at nine a.m. And you aren't allowed to leave early."

Miss Watson was very pleased that she was able to finish her tea before Dilya even thought to take another sip of her own.

DILYA HAD BEEN in the White House kitchen any number of times, though not nearly as often as visiting Chef Clive in the Chocolate Shop.

Chef Klaus was terribly strict, far more likely to explode with German epithets than to deliver praise. She knew he tolerated her presence, but she'd failed to make him smile even once. He was a tall, spare man, far above her own five-foot five. He seemed to look down at her like a stooping vulture. His tall chef's hat often hanging directly overhead when he was scowling down at her.

This morning, he was in "a mood". She'd heard the pastry chef and soup chef making a joke that if Chef Klaus was ever not in "a mood" the kitchen would freeze over. Only when, three months later, she heard a cabinet member saying he would agree with a new policy when hell froze over, did she understand the chefs' joke. She also knew from listening to the others that he was immensely respected. Whether his kitchen created a plated five-course dinner for two hundred guests or a sandwich for the President to eat in the Oval, the kitchen ran with the same clockwork precision.

He was thumping down bags of flour and sugar. Crashing mixing bowls against one another so hard that she was surprised they didn't break, even if they were steel.

"*Es ist verrückt! Warum heute* must my pastry chef be sick? Someone tell me why?"

"He caught it from his son," Dilya ventured. She liked Chef Emile, who still slipped her choice pastries like she was a little girl. "He brought the cold home from his kindergarten class."

"Eh? Oh, Dilya."

"He must be very sick to not be here, chef."

"So. Today *you* are my assistant?"

"It was..." She didn't think that Chef Klaus would know about Miss Watson. "I heard there was school here today. I thought I'd come learn."

"What? Someone who acts as if I have something to teach them instead of just doing my commands? *Gut! Gut!*" He waved a hand at the pantry. "Bring me butter, five pounds. Molasses, cinnamon, nutmeg, allspice, ginger—crystallized, powdered, and fresh. Well don't stand their looking so surprised. *Schnell! Schnell!* And take them with you." He waved a hand over her shoulder. "Oh, *ja*. Eggs, we must have two dozen to start," he stomped into the walk-in refrigerator to fetch those himself.

"Don't forget the butter while you're in there," she called after him.

"Now she thinks she runs kitchen." At least that's what it sounded like. She didn't know enough German to be certain. She committed it to memory to look up later and see if she was right, *"Jetzt glaubt sie, sie leite die Küche."*

She turned.

Four kids were standing in the doorway, frozen in place as if they'd been cast in ice like the rest of the White House's horrid winter wonderland nightmare.

Everybody in the school knew Trevor, he was captain of the soccer team. He was tall, with dark straight hair and very good-looking. He was standing just a little too close behind Kimberlee. She'd seen Major Henderson do it when he thought his wife needed protecting—as if Major Emily Beale ever needed anyone to do that.

Kimberlee made up for average features with a cheery personality —she was an Alabama senator's daughter with medium skin similar in darkness to Dilya's, but a very different hue. She'd dyed her wavy hair with a blonde so bright it was almost gold. It reminded her of the thin stripe of blonde that her adoptive mother Kee wore in own dark hair, to remember a dead friend. The color choice made her like Kimberlee even if she was one of the school's super-popular crowd.

She didn't really recognize the other two, though she thought she'd seen them around. A tall, serious blonde girl and a boy about her own height with messy brown hair that needed a comb. He was the one scanning the kitchen as if he was cataloging everything in the room against some internal image. He'd clearly done some research before coming.

"You run the kitchen?" The tall blonde asked.

Well at least she wasn't going to have to look up the translation of Klaus' comment.

"No, but I guess Chef Klaus needs someone to order around. Let's get moving; he doesn't like delays. *Nicht hier!*" She tried to imitate his gruff tone. It actually earned her a laugh.

She had their names by the time she'd shown them where the spices were, though she had to think to remember that the fresh ginger would be in with the other root vegetables.

Trevor, Mister Soccer, was indeed following Kimberlee around.

Kimberlee didn't seem to notice, though it seemed obvious. She was also head of the Debate Club that had just taken down Georgetown University's freshman debate team.

The quiet blonde was Valentina—"But call her Val," Kimberlee had stuck in. Once Dilya heard her name she remembered all of the details. Val was the daughter of the brigadier general stationed at the French embassy as the Defense Attaché. She was also the valedictorian who was taking every advanced placement class on the planet. Well, not every one, because she wasn't in Dilya's Government Affairs, American History, or Political Science. And if she was taking a language, it wasn't Russian or Mandarin. Val was a science-and-math nerd's science-and-math nerd.

"Trevor's the best cook," Val said in that soft voice of hers. She looked a bit like Emily Beale, but she didn't sound at all like her. Too gentle.

"Mom runs kitchen at the Hay Adams Hotel. If you'd met my mom, you'd know I couldn't help but learn."

"Sound kinda defensive there, Trev," Kimberlee winked at Dilya. "But because Val's French, we made her be the president of the Chef's Club."

"The Chef's Club?" Dilya let her guard down for a moment. Miss Watson wanted her to spend the day going to school with a Chef's Club? She didn't even know that her high school had a such a thing.

"Yeah, the four of us are the whole club, unless you want to join?" Mr. Observant Jimmy made it a little funny. He was the misfit in this group of misfits.

"Ha!" Dilya figured that response would cover a lot of ground. Joining wasn't something she did. Of course she could cook. The chow cooks at the secret Night Stalkers base in Pakistan—where she'd lived after Kee rescued her at age ten—had been her source of food. As soon as she'd figured that out, she'd made friends with them and in turn they'd taught her to cook—and turned a blind eye whenever she secreted away a bit of dinner in case life went wrong again. She'd eventually managed to observe the food locker combinations and had no longer needed to hide food under her cot.

She'd also watched Emily Beale cook. Often, when there was no mission, Emily would make a special meal for her crew. Dilya had never helped, but she'd watched and done her best to memorize each step.

"King of war games," Kimberlee offered another of her asides, nodding toward Jimmy.

"Not war games. They're strategy games."

"Guns, tanks, spaceships with nuclear weapons?"

"Yeah," Jimmy admitted and tipped his face down just enough for a long chunk of wavy brown hair to slip over his eyes.

"King of the war games," Kimberlee summed up.

Kimberlee might not know the difference, but Dilya certainly did. Her mother was a sniper, the ultimate in *tactical* warfare. And her father was a leading geopolitical global *strategy* consultant to the President and the Joint Chiefs of Staff.

"Why do you cook?"

But Chef Klaus returned from where he'd been called away to consult on a soup before Jimmy could answer her question.

"Today we're going to start with learning how to a sharpen a knife," Chef Klaus did his looming vulture thing over them. "Then if you somehow manage to master that task, I will teach you how to peel ginger."

AN HOUR later it seemed they were no closer to satisfying him than when they began. Trevor was the closest with Val as a near second—she finally had graduated to a mere sniff of disdain before he blunted her knife's edge on a steel and told her to try again.

"I never knew there was so much to just sharpening a blade," Kimberlee whispered sadly after her latest effort was blunted and returned with an outright scoff.

Then Chef Klaus focused his ire on her. "That's not a weapon of war you're wielding there, Miss Dilya Stevenson. It's a tool of art." And with a single stroke he wiped out twenty minutes of painstaking work. She'd had about enough of this.

"I'm sorry, sir," Dilya glared at him across the table. "My first knife was a KA-BAR 11-7/8" knife. But I was only ten and the leather-wrapped handle was too big for my hand. So my mother bought me a Cold Steel Recon 11-3/4" Tanto point with a black DLC coating over a VG-1 stainless blade. *That* is what I learned to sharpen."

Klaus stared down his long nose at her.

"Es ist hier?"

"Jawohl." She'd heard Val use that as a strong affirmative.

With a tip of his head, he sent her to fetch it. On her return, she considered doing many things, but common sense had prevailed and she handed it, still in its sheath, across the steel table where they sat lined up on their stools. The members of the Chef's Club didn't even pretend to be sharpening their knives, instead watching her avidly. She tried to ignore it, but wasn't having much luck.

Chef Klaus tugged the knife free—on his third try. It required a strong pull and it was easier if the sheath was strapped to a body part. When he glared at her, she was careful to show nothing.

After inspecting the blade carefully, he stepped to the cutting board and dragged it lightly across one of the overripe tomatoes they'd been trying to slice. It slid through the loose skin without a wrinkle and created a slice so clean that the tomato might have still been fresh and firm.

He wiped it carefully with a cloth, replaced it in the sheath and returned it to her. She made a show of strapping it onto her thigh over her jeans. It wasn't the sort of thing to be left lying about. She had a small combination knife safe in her room. The Secret Service had made her leave her sidearm at her parents' house.

"Do you know how to use that blade?"

"I've been trained by my mother," Dilya offered him her best smile. "But I haven't had a reason to use it…yet."

"I could almost like you, Miss Stevenson," Chef Klaus condescended before waving for them to return to their sharpening.

"Super cool," Jimmy whispered.

Which might be the first compliment she'd ever received from a classmate in the two years she'd been in the States and going to a real school.

"You really know how to use that?" Trevor asked as he once again began working his blade in a swirl of vegetable oil on the slab of black sharpening stone. It didn't sound like he doubted her, more like she'd surprised him.

"Her mom is a sniper on the Hostage Rescue Team," Val answered for her.

Dilya could only blink at her. She'd thought she was invisible at school—as invisible as was possible in such a group of DC's overachiever kids. School hadn't mattered to her, but it had been important to Kee and Archie, so she worked hard to get her A's…and to *not* be noticed.

"Oh, man," Jimmy groaned. "That isn't super cool, that's super wicked extra cool."

"If you think my mom is cool," Dilya couldn't help being pleased. Kee was an awesome mom. "You should have met her commanding officer before she retired. She was the first woman to fly helicopters for the Night Stalkers."

Dilya didn't know if they'd ever let her do that, but if they did, that was her dream. A sniper like Kee or a pilot like Emily. That would indeed be super wicked extra cool.

THEY'D EVENTUALLY GRADUATED from knife sharpening to ginger

peeling—by the end of which Jimmy was wearing a pair of bright blue Band-Aids. The lunch was a rich borscht and corned beef on rye sandwiches, big enough to satisfy even Trevor, served right there at the counter with the other chefs.

That was a welcome respite. All morning they had kept asking her questions—about her and about the White House. While it would be rude not to answer, she wished she'd managed to slip in more questions of her own. Except she wasn't used to speaking. She was used to listening. By the time she'd think up her own question, someone would already be talking again.

At least over lunch they started asking questions of the sous chefs instead.

Finally able to listen, Dilya realized that the Chef's Club had been doing this for a while. They'd ask to meet some elite chef—there were a lot of those in DC—and they'd go get a free class.

"I know the chefs at Pauley's Island. Would that help?"

"We didn't even dare try there." "Wow, really?"

One of the chefs was amused that the group had braved asking the White House for a visit, but not Pauley's.

"One of my mom's closest friend's family owns it." Actually, Tim was also one of her friends. He'd been there at the 5D's base since the very first day—doing his best to make her laugh when everything had been so different and terrifying. "I'm sure Tim Maloney would be glad to set it up. Wait, I don't know where he's stationed. I guess I could call his mom."

"That does it," Kimberlee declared.

"It absolutely does," Trevor agreed.

"Madame President?" Jimmy turned to Val.

Val thumped her soup spoon on the counter like a gavel with a bright ting, "You are hereby inducted as an official member of the Chef's Club. All in favor?"

The others all said, "Aye!"

"The ayes have it. Welcome, Dilya Stevenson."

Dilya didn't know what to do with that. She'd never belonged to anything. But she couldn't figure how to get out of it without hurting their feelings.

That question plagued her through lessons on: measuring flour (by weight, never by volume), grating ginger (never mincing), mincing crystallized ginger (never grating), sampling a dozen different sugars, and tasting butter (salted, unsalted, organic, English Midlands, and finally French butter from Brittany). They spent the whole afternoon on ingredients. There were only thirteen ingredients in gingerbread, including all the spices and everything, but they spent a long time learning about each one.

Did Emily Beale know all this? Dilya made a bet with herself that she did. So she paid extra attention and made sure to ask about anything that was unclear, even if it meant interrupting someone.

"Tomorrow, we will mix and bake," Chef Klaus announced. "If you learn very fast, we will decorate as well. Now go away. Get out of my kitchen, *Kinder*. I have a dinner that must be served to people far more important than you."

"I hate being called a child," Val whispered once they were well clear of the kitchen.

Dilya agreed completely. She also wasn't quite ready to see everyone go. She was unsure why, but she'd learned to trust her instincts—or at least the ones that told her when to hide or run. Maybe she'd listen to this one too.

"You know, just down this hall, the White House has a Chocolate Shop. The chef is my friend." There was that word again. She'd always applied it to friendly adults: the former and current President, the Chief of Staff, chefs, pilots, gunners.

If they were friends, then what was she supposed to call the Chef's Club's members? What was their agenda for "inducting" her? Just to get into Pauley's? No, she'd already made the offer before they did that.

She'd always loved the amazing scents of the Chocolate Shop, almost as much as the treats themselves. Chef Clive Andrews teased her with funny looks about her silence. As if she'd ever known what to say. If the others noticed, they were too excited to comment on it as the chef explained the tempering of chocolate and pulled out a tray of holiday truffles he was developing.

She was no wiser by the time she escorted them back to the East Wing entrance.

"ARE YOU MY FRIEND?"

Emily tried to make sense of the question. Was the problem the question or because it was four in the morning?

"Who is this?"

"It's me, Dilya." Then there was a small gasp. "I'm so sorry. I forgot about the time zones. How far away is Montana?"

"Three thousand…" No. "Two hours. I think." She'd know for sure if she could wake up.

"I'm sorry. I'll go away and—"

"Wait! Just hang on, Dilya." She took her phone into the bathroom and shut the door. She'd accidentally left the ringer on and, thankfully, it seemed as if Mark had slept through it. "Now what was your question?" She sat on the edge of the tub, then stood to throw a towel over it before she sat back down. She pulled another one over her bare legs. It was only a little damp.

"It's stupid."

"Good. Because if it was a smart question, I wouldn't be able to answer it right now."

Dilya remained silent. Emily tried to remember the last time she'd received a call from the girl, and wasn't sure she ever had.

"You asked if I was your friend?"

"Yes," her voice was tiny.

"Well, you aren't my daughter, so I guess that's about the best word for it. Yes, I'm your friend." She had her own issues with that, but this call wasn't about her, so she shut them out. "Don't you want to be?"

"No. Yes. I… Oh pooh!"

Emily had to fight hard not to laugh. Winnie-the-Pooh was the first book Dilya had learned English from and Pooh's typical curse had stuck with Dilya ever since. Emily also remembered that odd negatives still tripped Dilya up sometimes.

"Do you want to be my friend?"

"Yes. I—" Dilya sighed. "I bet I'd make more sense if I'd slept last night. Is a kid supposed to have adults for friends?"

"Sure, why not? Besides, you aren't really a kid anymore." Especially not with the things she'd survived.

"But if adults are my friends, then what do I call people my age?"

"Hasn't this ever come up before?"

"No!" Dilya practically shouted. "My friends are Tim and Big John. They're White House chefs and the heads of Secret Service details. Don't know how to have friends!" Then she seemed to manage a breath. "I guess… Like at school and stuff."

Emily hung her head and tried not to think about the parallels in her own life. Friends were a new concept to her as well.

"I—" she started then stopped again. "I've always just had a team. Or at least for a long time that's all I had. I flew with your mom and dad, Connie, Lola, and all the others."

"But you're *Emily Beale,*" Dilya protested.

Emily sat up and narrowed her eyes, until she saw herself in the bathroom mirror wearing a faded West Point t-shirt and a slightly damp bath towel. She closed her eyes again.

"What do you mean?"

Dilya sputtered in surprise. "You're…you! Everyone wants to be just like you."

"You want to be just like me?"

"Well, not the blonde and tall part, I've kinda given up on that, but the rest of it, absolutely!"

"Dilya," Emily had had many strange conversations, including the one with Miss Watson yesterday, but this was fast outpacing that. "I'm just a woman. I'm not even a pilot anymore."

"But you're Emily Beale!"

"Stop saying that. Please?"

"Well, okay… But you *totally* are!"

"Dilya."

"Okay. I'm sorry I called. I'm sorry I woke you up."

"I'm not."

Again her voice had gone tiny, "You're not?"

"You get to call me anytime you want. Day or night. I mean it."

"Because my mom was on your team?"

"Because I like you. *You* are my friend."

Dilya actually sniffled. "Okay…thanks." Another sniffle. "Emily?"

"Uh-huh."

"Is it okay if I still want to be like you, even though you're my friend?"

"How about you being more like *you?*" That definitely echoed some pieces of what Miss Watson had told her.

"I don't know. It's kind of…I guess…lonely being me."

"You'll find friends your own age, Dilya. It doesn't mean that the grownups are going to be any less your friends."

"Kinda like a team? Everyone always wanted to be on your team."

"Teams are different than friends."

"How?"

"It's four in the morning, Dilya. Give me a break." She'd forgotten about Dilya's insatiable appetite for answers. She always wanted to know.

"Okay," Emily tried to clear her head. "You lead a team. You have responsibilities for their actions, if not their lives. But you get to be yourself with friends."

There was a long pause before Dilya responded, "I like that explanation."

"I do to," she just hoped that she remembered it when she woke up.

"Thanks. I'm…no longer sorry I called."

"Anytime. Seriously," though she had to fight to keep a massive yawn silent.

"Emily?"

"Uh-huh?"

"I love you, Emily."

"Love you too, Dilya." The end-of-call tone came so fast, she wasn't sure Dilya had heard her answer. As far as she knew, Dilya had never told anyone except her new parents that she loved them.

The innocence of a child's love. Except Dilya was no child. She was a young woman who had seen an even worse slice of the world than Emily had. And if Miss Watson was right, she understood exactly what was happening to her in a way that Emily never had.

When she crawled back into bed, she didn't care if Mark was asleep, she just curled up against him. Without questions, he held her as she cried on his shoulder.

When she was done, she whispered to him softly, "I love you, Mark."

In answer, he just kept holding her tight. It was all she needed.

DILYA HAD the kitchen set up, even before Chef Klaus came in. She had each of the ingredients aligned in an arc, including the ones they'd spent so much time preparing yesterday. She even prepared the cookie sheets with parchment paper—better for crispy edges and bottoms than silicone mats he'd told them. She tore off the correct lengths and tacked them in place with quick swipes of butter underneath the corners.

Chef Klaus looked surprised for only an instant when he came in.

He neatened the rows to make everything perfectly linear, orderly and symmetrical. She let him. As soon as he was done and had gone to hang up his coat, she moved everything back to the arc it had been. It would be easier to reach everything, radially from one position, the way she'd arranged it.

He stepped back into the main kitchen and stuttered to a halt just as the others arrived.

Without speaking, she simply reached out her hands to touch each item without moving from where she stood, rather than having them spread neatly down the length of the table.

The chef made a show of buttoning up his white chef's coat and pulling on his towering hat before he offered her a nod. He even made a grimace that just might have been a smile.

Through the morning they made numerous batches of dough. The variations to make hard sheets of gingerbread and soft ginger cookies. The difference between over- and under-beaten. Proper aeration of the mixture. Why different ingredients were added at different times. That was when quiet Val finally stepped into her own. She and the chef discussed baking soda activation, protein molecule deformation in the eggs, ingredient density, different mixing techniques to ensure even distribution of the grated versus the minced ginger...

Even Kimberlee's eyes were crossing by the time they were done with Val's questions. And Dilya suspected that it only stopped because Val finally realized how thoroughly she'd monopolized the chef. She wasn't a team leader the way Emily was—charging to the front and proving who was best, while beckoning others to try to follow. Val was simply one of the Chef's Club with her own interests and specialties.

Maybe these people didn't need a leader.

Maybe they were just friends.

She toyed with that idea through the rest of the day. They'd rolled out the dough perfectly evenly—done by placing thick rubber bands on either end of the rolling pins so that every spot of dough was exactly the same thickness.

"What should we make?"

A gingerbread house was out of the question. They'd all seen the framework of the massive traditional Christmas gingerbread White House taking shape in Clive's kitchen yesterday afternoon.

"Is there a game that the President likes to play? Maybe we could make a gingerbread version of it for the First Family." Jimmy was clearly picturing ray guns and spaceships.

"Yes there is." First Lady Anne Darlington-Thomas stepped into the kitchen. "My husband likes to think he can do *The New York Times* Sunday crossword. Which means every week my Sunday breakfast is about telling him the answers. *Two across. A seven-letter word for a fool.* Easy: *husband.* As in one who thinks he's doing the crossword on his own. I'm so glad that's now done for the week." Though her easy smile said she might enjoy the weekly ritual just as much as the President.

All the kids of the Chef's Club laughed despite their obvious awe at being in the First Lady's presence.

"Good morning, Dilya."

"Hi, Anne." The others looked at her goggle-eyed.

"Are you all having fun?"

There were a lot of mumbled, "Yes ma'am."

"Well, if Chef Klaus gets out of line, just sic Dilya on him. If anyone can keep Herman in line, she's the one. Now I have to go face him about the menu for next week's Residence reception for the Australian Prime Minister." And she breezed off into the back of the kitchen.

"Whoa!" Kimberlee whispered.

"Why did you use her first name?" Even Trevor was whispering.

"She asked me to. Besides, I'm nanny for her kid most days after school."

They all exchanged looks, but it was Jimmy who voiced the group's consensus opinion. "Super wicked uber-cool."

DILYA'S FACE and sides hurt.

She'd didn't get why, until Val made one of her dry French observations or Kimberlee teased Trevor.

Laughing and smiling. She simply wasn't used to doing that for a whole afternoon.

With Kimberlee, as head of Debate Club, leading the way, they'd mapped out a gingerbread crossword puzzle. *Christmas* down the middle; the First Family's names attached crosswise (though they had to use the First Daughter's middle name to make it all work—she actually had two of them, so she got to be in twice). Then they'd toyed with words until it was totally filled.

Chef Klaus had taught them piping and flooding techniques—requiring different mixes of royal icing because one had to stay where it was placed and the other had to flow to fill in the squares that needed to be white. Jimmy tackled the vast expanse of cookie that needed conversion into the puzzle. He was in nerd heaven.

Val had the best handwriting with a piping bag, so she took a large sheet of dark gingerbread and began writing humorous clues on it.

Dilya sat with Kimberlee and Trevor calling out suggestions for Val and making ornate letters on round, softer ginger cookies.

Whenever a cookie was broken or had its icing smeared past recovery, it was shared around, until they were all sick of them—even with tall glasses of milk. Kimberlee scrounged up a brown paper bag and started filling it with the broken bits and pieces.

All through the long afternoon, they sat together and worked on the ginger crossword. And all afternoon, Dilya could only sit in wonder. At school lunchtime, Kimberlee's table was always popular. Trevor sometimes sat with her and sometimes with his teammates. Val sat with a few other equally brilliant friends. She wasn't sure where Jimmy ate lunch.

Dilya ate with no one. Half the time, she didn't even go into the cafeteria, preferring to find a quiet corner. For this one great day though, her afternoon was filled with laughter and ideas.

As the day progressed, it became clearer and clearer where the members of the Chef's Club would end up.

Val was headed straight for the diplomatic corps—that was so obvious. She was too smart and too nice to do anything else. Maybe a science liaison or something.

Kimberlee could well follow in her senator-father's footsteps. Maybe she'd even end up in the White House someday.

Trevor was going to cook—it was clear that he was in the club for a lot more reasons than following around after Kimberlee. Dilya did wonder how long it was going to take him to ask her out. Kimberlee was going to be in for a big surprise, as she really was clueless that Trevor was hot for her.

And even in joking, she could sense Jimmy's clear grasp of how strategy worked. He could teach her some things about that, but he was weak in the real world. They'd have to talk about his strategy skills and what was actually going on globally—instead of inside some online game.

And she…was totally fooling herself. Why would they want her around? To get into Pauley's Island restaurant and the White House Chocolate Shop. To have a story to tell in the cafeteria.

She wouldn't fit in at any of their lunch tables. Everything they'd built this weekend was just about this weekend. Dilya wasn't dumb enough to believe there was a future here. She'd enjoy the day, but that would be the end of it.

They finished the giant crossword, scooting it onto a big silver platter she found in the butler's pantry. A shallow silver bowl with FDR's family crest stamped into the side was filled with the lettered cookies while Val wrote "A First Family Christmas" across the top of the puzzle. In the bottom corner, she wrote "Thanks for having us." Below that they each signed their names with piped royal icing.

Dilya looked at the five names together. For a weekend they'd come together just like one of Emily's teams. She liked that. It gave her ideas for the future. Someday she'd have a team. More importantly, someday she'd have friends. Maybe like these.

It was hard leaving the kitchen. Chef Klaus actually did smile when he saw the finished project. He promised to make sure it was delivered this evening with after-dinner tea. He came around and shook each person's hand and gave them a personalized signed copy of his White House cookbook. Dilya peeked at her own, it simply said, *"Niemals aufhören!"* Thankfully, beneath that he'd written, "Don't stop!" As if.

When they neared the exit, Kimberlee slipped a brown paper bag to her. Dilya peeked inside; it contained all of the failed and broken cookies.

"I'm too nervous to try and smuggle it out through security. But you can do it. Everyone likes you."

Dilya looked down at the bag and back at Kimberlee. "I don't understand."

"They taste awesome. We can't let these go to waste. You smuggle them out of the White House tomorrow and we can share them during lunch."

Then with a wave, they were all gone.

Dilya stood inside the East Wing entrance as she weighed the cookies in her hand. There would be plenty to share at a lunch. It was silly, it was just a place to sit. A place to sit…with people. With *friends!* And she could feel the smile tug at her cheeks once more.

As she walked back through the White House, she looked upon the shining winter wonderland of plastic icicles dripping from high ceilings and fake snow sweeping under brightly lit Christmas trees.

Emily was right. There were teams and there were friends. And she'd make sure that her life was filled with both of them.

BE sure not to miss the companion story: *Emily's Christmas Gift, a Henderson's Ranch story.*

OFF THE LEASH (WHITE HOUSE PROTECTION FORCE #1)

(EXCERPT)

"*Y*ou're joking."

"Nope. That's his name. And he's yours now."

Sergeant Linda Hamlin wondered quite what it would take to wipe that smile off Lieutenant Jurgen's face. A 120mm round from an M1A1 Abrams Main Battle Tank came to mind.

The kennel master of the US Secret Service's Canine Team was clearly a misogynistic jerk from the top of his polished head to the bottoms of his equally polished boots. She wondered if the shoelaces were polished as well.

Then she looked over at the poor dog sitting hopefully on the concrete kennel floor. His stall had a dog bed three times his size and a water bowl deep enough for him to bathe in. No toys, because toys always came from the handler as a reward. He offered her a sad sigh and a liquid doggy gaze. The kennel even smelled wrong, more of sanitizer than dog. The walls seemed to echo with each bark down the long line of kennels housing the candidate hopefuls for the next addition to the Secret Service's team.

Thor—really?—was a brindle-colored mutt, part who-knew and part no-one-cared. He looked like a cross between an oversized, long-haired schnauzer and a dust mop that someone had spilled dark gray paint on. After mixing in streaks of tawny brown, they'd left one white paw just to make him all the more laughable.

And of course Lieutenant Jerk Jurgen would assign Thor to the first woman on the USSS K-9 team.

Unable to resist, she leaned over far enough to scruff the dog's ears. He was the physical opposite of the sleek and powerful Malinois MWDs—military war dogs—that she'd been handling for the 75th Rangers for the last five years. They twitched with eagerness and nerves. A good MWD was seventy pounds of pure drive—every damn second of the day. If the mild-mannered Thor weighed thirty pounds, she'd be surprised. And he looked like a little girl's best friend who should have a pink bow on his collar.

Jurgen was clearly ex-Marine and would have no respect for the Army. Of course, having been in the Army's Special Operations Forces, she knew better than to respect a Marine.

"We won't let any old swabbie bother us, will we?"

Jurgen snarled—definitely Marine Corps. Swabbie was slang for a Navy sailor and a Marine always took offense at being lumped in with them no matter how much they belonged. Of course the swabbies took offense at having the Marines lumped with *them*. Too bad there weren't any Navy around so that she could get two for the price of one. Jurgen wouldn't be her boss, so appeasing him wasn't high on her to-do list.

At least she wouldn't need any of the protective bite gear working with Thor. With his stature, he was an explosives detection dog without also being an attack one.

"Where was he trained?" She stood back up to face the beast.

"Private outfit in Montana—some place called Henderson's Ranch. Didn't make their MWD program," his scoff said exactly what he thought the likelihood of any dog outfit in Montana being worthwhile. "They wanted us to try the little runt out."

She'd never heard of a training program in Montana. MWDs all came out of Lackland Air Force Base training. The Secret Service mostly trained their own and they all came from Vohne Liche Kennels in Indiana. Unless... Special Operations Forces dogs were trained by private contractors. She'd worked beside a Delta Force dog for a single month—he'd been incredible.

"Is he trained in English or German?" Most American MWDs were trained in German so that there was no confusion in case a command word happened to be part of a spoken sentence. It also made it harder for any random person on the battlefield to shout something that would confuse the dog.

"German according to his paperwork, but he won't listen to me much in either language."

Might as well give the diminutive Thor a few basic tests. A snap of her fingers and a slap on her thigh had the dog dropping into a smart "heel" position. No need to call out *Fuss—by my foot.*

"Pass auf!" Guard! She made a pistol with her thumb and forefinger and aimed it at Jurgen as she grabbed her forearm with her other hand—the military hand sign for enemy.

The little dog snarled at Jurgen sharply enough to have him backing out of the kennel. "Goddamn it!"

"Ruhig." Quiet. Thor maintained his fierce posture but dropped the snarl.

"Gute Hund." Good dog, Linda countered the command.

Thor looked up at her and wagged his tail happily. She tossed him a doggie treat, which he caught midair and crunched happily.

She didn't bother looking up at Jurgen as she knelt once more to check over the little dog. His scruffy fur was so soft that it tickled. Good strength in the jaw, enough to show he'd had bite training despite his size—perfect if she ever needed to take down a three-foot-tall terrorist. Legs said he was a jumper.

"Take your time, Hamlin. I've got nothing else to do with the rest of my goddamn day except babysit you and this mutt."

"Is the course set?"

"Sure. Take him out," Jurgen's snarl sounded almost as nasty as Thor's before he stalked off.

She stood and slapped a hand on her opposite shoulder.

Thor sprang aloft as if he was attached to springs and she caught him easily. He'd cleared well over double his own height. Definitely trained…and far easier to catch than seventy pounds of hyperactive Malinois.

She plopped him back down on the ground. On lead or off? She'd give him the benefit of the doubt and try off first to see what happened.

Linda zipped up her brand-new USSS jacket against the cold and led the way out of the kennel into the hard sunlight of the January morning. Snow had brushed the higher hills around the USSS James J. Rowley Training Center—which this close to Washington, DC, wasn't saying much—but was melting quickly. Scents wouldn't carry as well on the cool air, making it more of a challenge for Thor to locate the explosives. She didn't know where they were either. The course was a test for handler as well as dog.

Jurgen would be up in the observer turret looking for any excuse to mark down his newest team. Perhaps teasing him about being just a Marine hadn't been her best tactical choice. She sighed. At least she was consistent—she'd always been good at finding ways to piss people off before she could stop herself and consider the wisdom of doing so.

This test was the culmination of a crazy three months, so she'd forgive herself this time—something she also wasn't very good at.

In October she'd been out of the Army and unsure what to do next. Tucked in the packet with her DD 214 honorable discharge form had been a flyer on career opportunities with the US Secret Service dog team: *Be all your dog can be!* No one else being released from Fort Benning that day had received any kind of a job flyer at all that she'd seen, so she kept quiet about it.

She had to pass through DC on her way back to Vermont—her parent's place. Burlington would work for, honestly, not very long at all, but she lacked anywhere else to go after a decade of service. So, she'd stopped off in DC to see what was up with that job flyer. Five interviews and three months to complete a standard six-month training course later—which was mostly a cakewalk after fighting with the US Rangers—she was on-board and this chill January day was her first chance with a dog. First chance to prove that she still had it. First chance to prove that she hadn't made a mistake in deciding that she'd seen enough bloodshed and war zones for one lifetime and leaving the Army.

The Start Here sign made it obvious where to begin, but she didn't dare hesitate to take in her surroundings past a quick glimpse. Jurgen's score would count a great deal toward where she and Thor were assigned in the future. Mostly likely on some field prep team, clearing the way for presidential visits.

As usual, hindsight informed her that harassing the lieutenant hadn't been an optimal strategy. A hindsight that had served her equally poorly with regular Army commanders before she'd finally hooked up with the Rangers—kowtowing to officers had never been one of her strengths.

Thankfully, the Special Operations Forces hadn't given a damn about anything except performance and *that* she could always deliver, since the day she'd been named the team captain for both soccer and volleyball. She was never popular, but both teams had made all-state her last two years in school.

The canine training course at James J. Rowley was a two-acre lot. A hard-packed path of tramped-down dirt led through the brown grass. It followed a predictable pattern from the gate to a junker car, over to tool shed, then a truck, and so on into a compressed version of an intersection in a small town. Beyond it ran an urban street of gray clapboard two- and three-story buildings and an eight-story office tower, all without windows. Clearly a playground for Secret Service training teams.

Her target was the town, so she blocked the city street out of her mind. Focus on the problem: two roads, twenty storefronts, six houses, vehicles, pedestrians.

It might look normal...normalish with its missing windows and no movement. It would be anything but. Stocked with fake IEDs, a bombmaker's stash, suicide cars, weapons caches, and dozens of other traps, all waiting for her and Thor to find. He had to be sensitive to hundreds of scents and it was her job to guide him so that he didn't miss the opportunity to find and evaluate each one.

There would be easy scents, from fertilizer and diesel fuel used so destructively in the 1995 Oklahoma City bombing, to almost as obvious TNT to the very difficult to detect C-4 plastic explosive.

Mannequins on the street carried grocery bags and briefcases. Some held fresh meat, a powerful smell demanding any dog's attention, but would count as a false lead if they went for it. On the job, an explosives detection dog wasn't supposed to care about anything except explosives. Other mannequins were wrapped in suicide vests loaded with Semtex or wearing knapsacks filled with package bombs made from Russian PVV-5A.

She spotted Jurgen stepping into a glassed-in observer turret atop the corner drugstore. Someone else was already there and watching.

She looked down once more at the ridiculous little dog and could only hope for the best.

"Thor?"

He looked up at her.

She pointed to the left, away from the beaten path.

"*Such!*" *Find.*

Thor sniffed left, then right. Then he headed forward quickly in the direction she pointed.

CLIVE ANDREWS SAT in the second-story window at the corner of Main and First, the only two streets in town. Downstairs was a drugstore all rigged to explode, except there were no triggers and there was barely enough explosive to blow up a candy box.

Not that he'd know, but that's what Lieutenant Jurgen had promised him.

It didn't really matter if it was rigged to blow for real, because when Miss Watson—never Ms. or Mrs.—asked for a "favor," you did it. At least he did. Actually, he had yet to meet anyone else who knew her. Not that he'd asked around. She wasn't the sort of person one talked about with strangers, or even close friends. He'd bet even if they did, it would be in whispers. That's just what she was like.

So he'd traveled across town from the White House and into

Maryland on a cold winter's morning, barely past a sunrise that did nothing to warm the day. Now he sat in an unheated glass icebox and watched a new officer run a test course he didn't begin to understand.

Keep reading this title in the complete White House Protection Force "Dogs"
trilogy at fine retailers everywhere (also in audio):
Off the Leash
On Your Mark
In the Weeds

Thank you for joining me on my Christmas adventures.

There is one other that I feel I should mention. It didn't fit in here because it is a novel, not a short story. But it lives at the center of my first-ever series, which was also my first romance series, Where Dreams.

The Where Dreams series is about three best friends from college whose lives meet up a decade later in Seattle. One of the through-characters, and hero of the second novel, is an Italian chef named Angelo.

I'll just say this about *Where Dreams Are of Christmas,* the third novel: Angelo's lovely mother was never supposed to be in the series. But Maria, with the strength of Dilya and others, simply showed up one day, literally, arriving at her son's restaurant with her suitcase and informing him she was here to stay. She was so vibrant, that she insisted on a novel of her own true love. Suddenly a three-novel series became four...then five when a final walk-on character, Melanie, refused to walk back off.

There are other Christmas tales:

The Night Stalkers White House six-book series includes four

Christmas novels and two July 4th romances set principally at the White House.

The Night Stalkers and the Navy titles are *Christmas at Steel Beach* and *Christmas at Peleliu Cove*—both set on a helicopter carrier ship used by the Night Stalkers.

There are more tales to come…I can't wait until I get to find them. The joys of Christmas are definitely an essential part of who I am now. So, see you soon.

Until then, I wish you a Happy and Merry time the whole year round.

M. L. Buchman

-north shore of Massachusetts, 2019

ABOUT THE AUTHOR

M.L. Buchman started the first of over 60 novels, 75 short stories, and an ever-growing pile of audiobooks while flying from South Korea to ride across the Australian Outback. All part of a solo around-the-world bicycle trip (a mid-life crisis on wheels) that ultimately launched his writing career.

American Library Association's *Booklist* recently named the start of M.L.'s Night Stalkers series in *The Best 20 Romantic Suspense Novels: Modern Masterpieces*. His military and firefighter series(es) have won "Top 10 Romance of the Year" 3 times. NPR and Barnes & Noble have named other titles "Top 5 Romance of the Year."

He has flown and jumped out of airplanes, can single-hand a fifty-foot sailboat, and has designed and built two houses. In between writing, he also quilts. M.L. is constantly amazed at what can be done with a degree in geophysics. He also writes: contemporary romance, thrillers, and SF. Join the conversation at: www.mlbuchman.com.

Other works by M. L. Buchman:

White House Protection Force
Off the Leash
On Your Mark
In the Weeds

The Night Stalkers
MAIN FLIGHT
The Night Is Mine
I Own the Dawn
Wait Until Dark
Take Over at Midnight
Light Up the Night
Bring On the Dusk
By Break of Day
WHITE HOUSE HOLIDAY
Daniel's Christmas
Frank's Independence Day
Peter's Christmas
Zachary's Christmas
Roy's Independence Day
Damien's Christmas
AND THE NAVY
Christmas at Steel Beach
Christmas at Peleliu Cove
5E
Target of the Heart
Target Lock on Love
Target of Mine
Target of One's Own

Firehawks
MAIN FLIGHT
Pure Heat
Full Blaze
Hot Point
Flash of Fire
Wild Fire
SMOKEJUMPERS
Wildfire at Dawn
Wildfire at Larch Creek
Wildfire on the Skagit

Delta Force
Target Engaged
Heart Strike
Wild Justice
Midnight Trust

Where Dreams
Where Dreams are Born
Where Dreams Reside
Where Dreams Are of Christmas
Where Dreams Unfold
Where Dreams Are Written

Eagle Cove
Return to Eagle Cove
Recipe for Eagle Cove
Longing for Eagle Cove
Keepsake for Eagle Cove

Henderson's Ranch
Nathan's Big Sky
Big Sky, Loyal Heart
Big Sky Dog Whisperer

Love Abroad
Heart of the Cotswolds: England
Path of Love: Cinque Terre, Italy

Dead Chef Thrillers
Swap Out!
One Chef!
Two Chef!

Deities Anonymous
Cookbook from Hell: Reheated
Saviors 101

SF/F Titles
The Nara Reaction
Monk's Maze
the Me and Elsie Chronicles

Strategies for Success (NF)
Managing Your Inner Artist/Writer
Estate Planning for Authors

Short Story Series by M. L. Buchman:

The Night Stalkers
The Night Stalkers
The Night Stalkers 5E
The Night Stalkers CSAR
The Night Stalkers Wedding Stories

Firehawks
The Firehawks Lookouts
The Firehawks Hotshots
The Firebirds

Delta Force
Delta Force Short Stories

US Coast Guard
US Coast Guard

White House Protection Force
White House Protection Force Short Stories

Where Dreams
Where Dreams Short Stories

Eagle Cove
Eagle Cove Short Story

Henderson's Ranch
Henderson's Ranch Short Stories

Dead Chef Thrillers
Dead Chef Short Stories

Deities Anonymous
Deities Anonymouse Short Stories

SF/F Titles
The Future Night Stalkers
Single Titles

SIGN UP FOR M. L. BUCHMAN'S NEWSLETTER TODAY

and receive:
Release News
Free Short Stories
a Free Book

Get your free book today. Do it now.
free-book.mlbuchman.com

www.ingramcontent.com/pod-product-compliance
Lightning Source LLC
Chambersburg PA
CBHW032155180726
48284CB00001B/58